THE SURGEON

KARL HILL

BLOODHOUND
BOOKS

First published in 2023 by Bloodhound Books.

www.bloodhoundbooks.com

Print ISBN: 978-1-916978-02-7

CHAPTER ONE

Screaming? Laughter? Something. He could not be sure. A noise, on the periphery of his senses. It woke him. Startled him. Perhaps he had imagined it. Perhaps not. Either way, it scared him. He lay, blanket stretched up to his nose, eyes wide open. The dark was a solid thing. Like black concrete. Like he was at the bottom of a deep hole. Like he was in a tomb, locked away, where the dead slept. He was eight years old. In the depths of the night, his imagination dredged up things monstrous and fearful.

He kept perfectly still. He thought, if he moved, then he would be noticed, and the darkness would stir, and something terrible might morph from the shadows. A sound filled his head – his heartbeat. He strained to listen.

Another sound. From downstairs. The kitchen. A man's voice. Deep and rumbling. Like thunder. Like the worst storm. Shouting something, the words unclear. But the tone behind the words was clear enough. He knew anger when he heard it. This was worse than anger. This was... the noise a monster might make, from the back of a cave, or from the corner of a lightless cellar. A wicked noise, he thought. It scared him more than the darkness. He jerked round, fumbling for the bedside lamp, found the switch. Suddenly, the room was bathed in soft light. Familiar images sprang into being. An armchair, and on it, sitting lopsided, a large stuffed Mickey Mouse, smiling his smile. There, the dressing table, upon which, standing in a neat line, *Star Wars* figures. The tall single wardrobe. In a corner, a big Scalextric box.

He sat up, remained still. He realised he was holding his breath. He exhaled, quiet as a whisper. Listening.

Now, other noises. Normal noises. The faint creak and groan of an old house in the knuckle of winter. A breeze causing the trees outside to sway and leaves to rustle.

And then... A sound he recognised, but out of place. His breath caught. His heart pulsed. With exquisite care, he pulled back the covers, swivelled round, placed his feet on the carpet. The air was freezing cold. He shivered. His dressing gown hung from the wardrobe door. He went over, creeping on his toes, shuffled it on, and stood, motionless, facing the drawn curtains of his bedroom window.

He waited. Two seconds. Then it came again. He gasped. The sound was distinctive. He had heard it a thousand times – the gate at the back garden being pulled open. It was stiff, and sagged on its hinges, the bottom scraping on the flagstones, requiring effort to shift.

He went over. He opened the curtains. The sky was clear, unobscured by cloud, filled with a million stars. The moon shimmered, round and silver-grey. The back gate opened to a narrow lane. A single lamp provided illumination, casting a pale-yellow glow.

He looked down. There! A figure, its back to him. Wearing a long black coat. A sliver of darkness. A shadow in the shadows. Hunched forward, both hands on the latch. Tugging. With every tug, the gate scraped open another few inches. The figure stopped, became still. Another two seconds. It straightened, and with deliberation, turned, and looked up.

A face, bone-white. A man's face. Their eyes met. Eyes black as sockets. The man raised an arm, pointed. His lips quivered into a smile, revealing teeth like tiny pearls. The words he spoke were soft and clear.

"I see you."

The man remained motionless. He stood, in that strange way, pointing. Then, in a swirl of movement, he turned, grasped the gate, wrenched it open, and disappeared out into the lane and away. Like a phantom.

He stood at the window. His breath had steamed the glass up. His mouth was dry. His body trembled. He stepped away. The curtains fell back, hiding the moon and the stars and the frosty trees. He had seen a man in the back garden. Coming from the house, he assumed. Where else? He also assumed it was the man's raised voice he had heard, from the kitchen downstairs.

He made his way to the bedroom door. The fear he felt for himself, suddenly, was eclipsed by the fear he felt for someone else.

His mother.

He opened the door, went out onto the top landing. Silence. He made his slow, careful way down the stairs. One step, two steps. On his tiptoes. The staircase creaked. He knew the creaks by heart. He gripped the banister. He got to the bottom. Before him, a short hall. Beyond, the kitchen. He got to the kitchen door, opened it.

And from that moment, his world changed.

CHAPTER TWO

TWENTY YEARS LATER

Chance. Or something more maybe. He couldn't be sure. He wasn't sure of anything. And yet…

Saturday afternoon. He was sitting outside a coffee shop. It was warm enough for him to do this. Warm enough for a T-shirt. There was no wind, not even a breeze. A stillness seemed to have settled on the world. The coffee was strong. And good. And cheap, which made it better. Which was why he came to this particular place. It was the cheapest place he knew. Today, he decided to hit the high life, and bought a croissant, warmed up, and buttered. Plus, at the side of the plate, there was a miniature pot of strawberry jam. He hadn't asked for it. It was complimentary. He didn't like jam on his croissant. It made it too sweet.

He was reading a book he'd picked up from the library. Some inane crime thriller. Instantly forgettable garbage. He really had no idea why he had chosen it. But he had. And because he had, he felt compelled to read the damn thing, from cover to cover. A flaw of the mind, according to one of the many psychiatrists he had seen. Compulsive behaviour. Undoubtedly a manifest of earlier shocking events.

At the specific moment, at the crucial time, he could have had his head down, eyes glued to the book. Or he could have been looking in the opposite direction. Or he might have been distracted by the people sitting at the next table. Or he might have gone to the loo. A thousand mights or maybes. But he hadn't been doing any of these. Perhaps it was fate. But at that moment, between lifting the coffee cup to his lips, and glancing at the adjacent street, he saw something which made him stop. Made him freeze. And an old memory came surging back.

He stared.

His attention was focused on a man, strolling past in no apparent hurry. In particular, the man's face. The man walked by, oblivious to the attention, disappearing down the street, and was gone.

He placed the coffee carefully back on its saucer, closed the book, stood, and followed.

Thus the next chapter of his life began.

CHAPTER THREE

A letter had arrived.

Jonathan Stark, upon returning to his flat, had picked it up off the doormat, and placed it in the centre of the kitchen table. The postman had been early. On those occasions when Stark received mail, it was usually after work. Perhaps the postman was new. Perhaps the postman had been told to shift up a gear. Perhaps anything. Stark didn't care. He was too excited to ponder the inconsistencies of the Royal Mail.

It was 7am. Stark had been for a three-mile run. He liked to go early. It set him up for the day ahead. If he missed a run, he felt stale. He started work at 8.30, giving him time for a shower and some coffee and toast and perhaps a little fruit. Maybe a banana. His nod to 'five a day'.

But this particular morning, the shower and the breakfast would wait. Not the coffee, however. He would freely admit he was a coffee addict, liking it black and strong, and lots of it. Plus, he had invested in a rather complicated coffee machine. A rare display of extravagance, given the strict confines of his budget. The air in his tiny one-bedroomed flat was now rich with the scent of freshly ground coffee beans. He sat at the kitchen table, dripping sweat, sipping full roast from a mug bearing a colourful picture of Iron Man. He couldn't remember precisely how he got it, but it was the only mug he had, and provided it didn't leak, and it did the job, then it hardly mattered.

The moment was everything, to be savoured. The seconds before elation or profound disappointment. He rarely got letters. And if he did, they were usually bills. Rent demands. Unpleasant reminders from the bank. Other such shit. He knew exactly who had sent this one, because he was expecting it, and wasn't expecting anything from anyone else. A plain, standard white envelope, with a window-box, and in the window-box, his name and address neatly typed. Bearing a first-class stamp. That was a good sign. A minor victory. It meant the sender was prepared to spend a little money on him. Then again, he thought, maybe they sent everything first class. Perhaps second class from a prestigious law firm was poor show. It was easy to overthink such things.

He licked his lips. They were salty. He got up, pulled a dish towel from a hook on the wall, dabbed his face. He sat back down. The coffee tasted particularly fine this morning. It was summer. The day looked like it would turn out warm and bright. His run earlier had been smooth and pain free. He could have run all day. The omens were there. He felt something good was going to happen. Irrational, he knew. But the response had been quick. He'd only sent the application off four days before. And here was the reply, before him on the kitchen table. Neatly packaged in its little white envelope. Either yes or no. That simple.

He took a deep breath, wiped sweat from his eyes, and tore it open, pulled out the letter. It was an A4 sheet, cream-coloured, folded into three precise sections. Looked expensive. Felt expensive. He couldn't keep the tremble from his hand. He took another calming breath, focused, laid the folded letter on the table. Suddenly, he didn't want to read its contents. He had been down this road before, years ago. Five years, to be exact.

Receiving rejection letters. The hope, the disappointment. He was well practised. He would know in a single glance. If it was three lines or less, then it was too damned short. And short meant 'no'. Beginning with *We regret to advise you*, ending in *We wish you all the best for the future.*

He picked the letter up, and with care, unfolded it.

And stared.

First thing. It wasn't typed. It was handwritten. Looked like ink from an old-fashioned nib pen. This shocked him. This was something new.

Second thing. It wasn't the factory-standard three lines. It was a whole goddamned page.

And the best thing of all – it started with the words *We would be very interested...*

He took a gulp of coffee. He'd never tasted better. His heart sang. He couldn't keep the smile off his face.

The omens were true.

Today was the day.

CHAPTER FOUR

"I can't do this on my own."

"Of course you can." She laughed. A light tinkling sound. When his sister laughed, Stark's heart always melted. "But seeing as it's you," she said, "I could make an exception."

"That's very noble of you. I am flattered, truly." He did his best to keep the humour from his voice. "I have to cut the right impression. These guys. Snake-oil salesmen. They could sell me anything. A tartan three-piece suit, for example. Too long in the legs, too short in the arms. I could end up working in the circus, instead of a law firm."

Laughter again. "I rather think you'd look quite fetching in tartan. Like one of those vaudeville comedians. And baggy trousers are absolutely the rage. Hadn't you heard?"

"I hadn't."

"Tush, little brother. You have to keep up with the times. I'll go with you on one condition."

"Which is?"

"You buy the coffees."

"Deal."

"And a pastry."

"You drive a hard bargain. That's two conditions, by the way."

"Typical lawyer. I'm not counting. Lack of pastry is a deal breaker."

"What type?"

"Not sure. Apple Danish. Or maybe carrot cake. Or an empire biscuit."

"Very well. Fashion, it seems, has a price."

"Yup. Like everything, dude. Like everything."

Stark met his sister at one of Glasgow's biggest shopping complexes. A sprawling high-sided structure, shaped – so it was claimed – like a winding river. Stark, who detested such places, saw it merely as one long concrete monstrosity, devoid of any charm or character. Nevertheless, he needed a damned suit. He couldn't turn up for his interview in somewhat faded joggers and sweat top. Nor his work clothes. Stark was working temporary, grinding out a nine-hour shift at a soft-drink bottling plant in the arse end of Glasgow, his primary function to load and unload crates of bottles and cans, and sweep up broken glass from the factory floor. Temporary. It was the latest of a long line of shit-end jobs. He'd being doing it for eight months, and the way things were going, he'd be doing it forever, and "temporary" was blossoming into "permanent".

Until the letter.

It was Saturday morning. The place was packed. The rendezvous was outside a particular menswear shop. He saw Maggie immediately. An artful tangle of dark hair, bright grey eyes alight with inquisitive intelligence. For the occasion, and perhaps with reference to their telephone conversation, she wore bright tartan trousers, and an off-white, twill jacket a size too large. Stark allowed himself a wry smile. The joke was on him.

She hugged him, then held him at arm's length, gave him a reproachful glare.

"The only time I hear from my little brother is when he wants something."

"This is true," he said. "I use you mercilessly."

She inspected him with a critical eye. "You'll need to shave. You can't go to a job interview with a beard."

"I like my beard."

"But it doesn't like you. Maybe even a haircut. We need to lose the unwashed yeti look." She grinned. "Don't worry. We'll get you sorted."

He grinned back. "That's what I'm paying you for."

"Onwards then." She laughed her infectious laugh. "Into the breach."

"*Unto* the breach, I think," said Stark.

"Unto, into," replied Maggie. "It hardly matters. I'll bet Shakespeare didn't have an awful bloody beard like yours."

There was little Stark could add to the comment.

The suit was chosen. Measurements were taken, minor alterations required. It would be ready to be picked up next day. A dark, somewhat sombre look, decided Stark. Bordering on funereal. But Maggie had given it the thumbs up, so he guessed it was okay. The price, in his estimation, was staggering. But what the hell. And as Maggie explained, as if she were addressing a simple instruction to a small child, *good fashion comes at a price.* He didn't quite understand the concept, because he didn't really understand good fashion, but if that was Maggie's view of the matter, he guessed that was okay as well. In a flurry of enthusiasm, he pushed the boat way out, and bought a couple of crisp white shirts and silk ties. And a coat, even though it was summer. Almost a month's wages, and representing another bite into his already extended overdraft. But he reckoned, if he was going to blow money he didn't have, then it might as well be for a good cause. And if it swung him the job, then it was the best possible cause he could think of.

"Plus," reminded Maggie, "this is a one-shot chance." Which it was.

They found a seat at one of the many trendy little coffee shops scattered throughout the complex. Stark got the coffees and cakes.

"We should do this more often," she said. "It's fun to watch you spend money. The range of facial expressions is fascinating. From shock to downright pain. And a whole gamut of drama in between. You should have been an actor. Wonderful stuff."

"I wasn't acting, though I'm glad you find me amusing. It's gratifying to know I have a purpose in life."

"Don't worry, little brother. You'll knock 'em dead."

Stark sipped his coffee. "I wish I shared your confidence."

Maggie tested the edge of her carrot cake, nodded, dabbed her mouth with a paper napkin.

"Nice. So tell me."

"It's a medium-sized firm. Stoddart, Jeffrey, Pritchard and Sloss." He gave her a serious look. "Please. Don't say a thing."

Maggie held his stare, smiling broadly. "You have to be kidding. I mean, really? Where's their office? Trumpton? Next to Postman Pat's house? Beside the Magic Roundabout?"

Stark smiled back. He couldn't help it. "Not quite. Though you're showing your age. A rather posh part in the west end. A leafy suburb sort of place, where perfect people live perfect lives. And yes – it's a mouthful. Strangely, they've got the type of name that's difficult to remember, but once remembered, is difficult to forget."

Maggie scooped another forkful of cake into her mouth, chewed thoughtfully. "Never heard of them. But with a name like that, I love them already. They sound… funky." She stifled a laugh. "Their business cards must be the size of dinner mats."

"They're… how can I describe it. Low-key. Fifteen partners. Ten associates. Probably a small army of assistants and paralegals."

"And soon a brand-new trainee."

Stark smiled. "Of course. How could it be anything else? They specialise in stuff like property, estates and wills, commercial work. Big in litigation. They've got some high-end clients."

"Why them?"

"Why them what?"

"Why choose them?"

Stark laughed out loud. "Choose? There's a word. I should be so lucky. I'll take what I can get."

He had never lied to his sister, not once, but the truth was too bizarre and complicated to handle. Even for himself. His response brought a pang of guilt–

"I've waded my way through every page of the legal directory," he said, "and applied to every firm I could see. Small, middle, big. Anywhere. Any place. Funny names. Boring names. It doesn't matter what they do, or don't do. If they'll have me, then I'm their man."

"You're just a common slut, little brother."

"Indeed I am."

"Who's the guy in charge?"

"Edward Stoddart. Mr Stoddart to plebs like you and me."

"*Master* Edward Stoddart, I would have thought."

"Sounds about right."

"And he's the one taking the interview?"

"Could be. Not sure."

Maggie leaned closer, like a conspirator. "How's your tongue?" she asked.

"Perfectly fine, thank you. Are you asking in your capacity as a doctor? Or just out of general interest."

"Get it into shape. I would recommend rolling and flicking exercises, twice a day. It needs to be strong and supple to fit into the groove of Master Stoddart's arse."

Stark sighed. "Nothing changes."

Again, that light infectious laugh. "I should hope not. And?"

"Another and?"

"The biggest 'and' of all."

"Aha. Money. The golden question. Not anywhere near what I deserve. Obviously. A trainee's wage is equivalent to... let me think... what a monkey might earn dancing to the tune of the organ grinder."

"The Peanut Factor. We've all been there."

"I would earn more sticking with the job I've got and shifting crates of lemonade the rest of my life."

"It would be more fun."

"Possibly true."

Maggie leaned back. She regarded him with a candid expression, eyes sparkling with a playful mischief he loved so dearly.

"I'm proud of you, dude," she said.

"You're only saying that because I bought the coffee. But I'll take it anyway."

"You're buying the coffee? Great. I'll have another one please. Double-shot vanilla latte. And while you're at it, another slice of carrot cake. It's delicious. And if you're going to take anything from this little chat then it has to be one important thing."

"Which is?"

"Get your tongue into gear. And shave the bloody beard."

"That's two things."

CHAPTER FIVE

It was planned. Always. With meticulous care. Spontaneity would, inevitably, lead to disaster, despite how he craved it. The planning took time. Months. Careful research. And patience. Such patience. Details considered, weighed delicately in his mind, thought through. Actions and consequences. Each project treated like a military campaign requiring endurance and restraint. Restraint was the hardest. He was a lord of discipline.

He'd watched them, scrutinised their movements. She was a wife and mother. She worked as a dental hygienist for a practice in Giffnock, an upmarket Glasgow suburb. She lived two miles from her work, in a tidy semi-detached house in a street full of tidy semi-detached houses, where all the gardens were neat, cars were washed at the weekends, bins were put out regular as clockwork, leaves were swept in the autumn, lawns mowed in the summer.

He had been watching for six months.

Her husband – an architect – left the house earlier than she did. Very early: 6.30. He drove a 3 series BMW. Metallic blue. Convertible. Leather upholstery. Business was doing well. He stayed at work until 5.30, usually returning straight home. His behaviour was wonderfully predictable, which was advantageous.

She left the house later. Usually 8am. Made breakfast for the kids first. Two kids. Twins. Eight years old. Cute little girls. Then she drove them to school. She drove a five-year-old Range Rover. Reliable and robust. Sporting a couple of minor bashes. She dropped the kids off, made her way to work.

She didn't work Wednesdays and Sundays. On Wednesdays, after the drop-off, she went back to the house. Which was when the fun started. A car pulled hard up on the pavement, a short distance away. 9.30. Never earlier. Rarely later. The same car every time. A silver Peugeot 508. A man got out. Young. Younger than her. Clean shaven, impeccably dressed. Well groomed. A different suit every week. He spent a lot of money on his clothes. Handsome in a fresh, boyish way. He went to the house, always stopped at the front gate, checking. Establishing the way was clear. He got to the door, which invariably opened before he rang the bell. He slipped in, the door shutting behind him. An hour later, he left.

Delicious.

Now, he was ready. It had come to this. All his painstaking surveillance. His research. His planning. His infinite patience. Diluted down to this moment. His *ecstasy time*. For that's exactly what it was. There was no better way to describe it. *Sheer goddamned ecstasy.*

He checked his watch: 9.45. He had come in a plain white van – a departure from his usual mode of transport, a Ford Mondeo. This was a daytime adventure. White van equated to invisibility. Nothing to distinguish it from a trillion others. It would be disposed of later.

He got out. He wore a heavy blue boiler suit. He held a plain sports bag in his left hand. It was summer, warm, and he was sweating. He made his way to the front garden. So neat, though he noticed the beginnings of weeds peeping sporadically in the spaces between the slabs. *Tut-tut. Untidy.* To be attended to at the weekend. Of course, that would never happen. Not after the events to be enacted.

He took a breath, calmed himself. But his heart thrummed, like it always did at this special time.

He rang the doorbell. He imagined their surprise. A surge of anxiety, perhaps. Maybe the husband's come home early. Maybe he's forgotten something. A thousand maybes. None of them close.

He waited twenty seconds. He saw the outline of a figure approach through the bevelled glass of the front door.

The door opened.

She stood before him. Flustered. And puzzled. She had changed. She'd worn joggers, flat shoes and a loose T-shirt when she'd dropped the kids off. Now, she wore a short red dress, black stockings, black heels.

"Yes?"

He spoke. Strange, but when the dialogue began on these occasions, he felt he was witnessing himself from a distance. One might have described it as an almost *out of body* experience. It was, he thought, a spiritual thing.

"I like your house."

She frowned, her forehead creasing into tiny wrinkles. His excitement escalated, almost spiked, right there, at that moment. She was immensely appealing, with a thousand charms and graces.

"I'm sorry?" she said.

"Don't be. Can I come inside?"

She blinked.

"Who are you?"

"Someone who's taken an interest."

Silence. *Now she's worried. Perhaps she thinks I know about her Wednesday morning hobby. Which I do.*

She shook her head, spoke, an edge to her voice. "I have no

idea what you're talking about. You're frightening me. If you don't leave, I'll call the police."

"And I'll call your husband."

"I'm sorry?"

"You keep saying that. Let me in, Evelyn. We should have a chat."

She kept his stare, straightened. *Defiance. My, there's a beautiful thing. But also puzzlement, that I should know her name.*

"I'm going to call the police. I don't know who you are. I don't know what you're talking about."

She made to close the door. He put his foot forward. Today, he wore metal-toe-capped boots. Black and shiny. The door juddered. He pushed her inside. She gave a small, startled yelp, staggered back. He followed her, shut the door. She stared. Shocked. Unable to understand this new situation. Unable to comprehend. *A special moment, when they're conflicted, grappling with the idea that this cannot possibly be real; that this could not be happening to them.*

The thud of footsteps on the stairs. A man appeared in the hall. Her Wednesday morning visitor. Shirt crumpled, no tie.

The same look – confusion. And anger. The man started towards him, bristling with intent.

The pockets of his boiler suit were wide and deep. Good for holding tools and such. Good for holding a Glock 19 semi-automatic handgun, complete with silencer. He pulled it out, pointed.

The confliction was gone. He had them focused. Now they knew this was real life and as deadly as it was ever going to get.

"If you would both please go upstairs."

The man said nothing. She bit her lip. Her chin wobbled, her face pale and frightened. Her voice was a whisper. She said, "What do you want?"

"Didn't you hear me, Evelyn? I want you to go upstairs. A very simple instruction. You first. Then your handsome toy boy."

She hesitated. "You know my name."

He gave her a small sympathetic smile. "I know everything about you, Evelyn. Now hurry. We don't have much time. Upstairs, and into the bedroom."

The man attempted bluster. "You're crazy. It's not even real."

"No?" He straightened his arm, aimed, shot the man in the eye. Once, twice. Two quick, sharp sounds, morphing almost into one. Like a Christmas cracker. Instant. Over in a heartbeat. The man stood for all of two seconds, the back of his head erupting in a spume of bright colour. His mouth flapped open, shut. *Was he trying to speak? Wonderful.*

The man tottered, fell on his back, as if in slow motion.

The woman – Evelyn – didn't move, didn't scream. *Shock.*

"I think he knows it's real now," he said. "But that's okay. I wasn't here for him. His presence was... a bonus?" He shifted his aim to Evelyn, the tip of the silencer two inches from her forehead. "If you want to join him, then that's fine. If you want to see through this day, then you'll go upstairs, like I asked you. Please, Evelyn. It's for the best."

She swallowed. She was trembling. *Like a horse under the gun. God, this is beautiful.*

She turned, slowly. Walked back the way she had come, to the foot of the stairs, began to climb. He followed her. Her movements were slow, mechanical. On autopilot. He kept close behind her. The scent of her perfume was intoxicating. *The ecstasy moment.* They got to the top landing. She walked to the far door, which was open, entered. They were in the bedroom. The bed was unmade, the covers swept back and in a huddle on the floor.

She kept her back to him.

"Face me, please."

Her chest rose and fell. Little short shuddering gasps. In, out. She turned. Her shoulders trembled. *Trying so hard not to cry. What composure.*

"Lie on the bed." He gestured with the pistol.

She found her voice. "Please..."

"No talking, Evelyn. Don't spoil things. You've done so well up to this point."

She got on the bed. She started to sob. Not loud. *A whimper, not a sob.*

"Thank you, Evelyn."

He placed the sports bag on the floor, unzipped it, removed its contents, and set to work with zeal.

Thirty minutes later.

He left the bedroom, closing the door gently behind him. The emotion never changed. Profound sadness when it was over. Spent. Weary. After such an intoxicating high, the low was inevitable. It would pass, as all things do. And then he would plan for the next project.

He made his way downstairs. He had left his mark, and was proud of his craftmanship. He wished to savour. But, as was always the case, the clock was ticking. He stepped over the dead body of the woman's secret lover, who lay on his back, one eye open wide, as if still registering disbelief at the abrupt ending of his existence. The other eye was a cavity, where both bullets had entered, chewing up the insides, exiting through the back in a profusion of blood and bone.

He got down on one knee, crouched over the dead man's face. Life. Death. Like the flick of a switch. Everything. Then nothing.

This is the power a god wields.

He stood. *Adios, amigo.*

He made his way to the front door, took one last look back.

Easy.

He turned the handle, opened...

And stopped, dead in his tracks.
Suddenly, he'd hit a problem.
And suddenly, for the first time in five years, he panicked.

CHAPTER SIX

The building was old and large, possessing a somewhat sombre elegance. *Gothic,* thought Stark. And fitting, for such a firm as this. He had done his homework. Established over one hundred and fifty years ago, which didn't make it the oldest in the city, but damned close. Founded by William Stoddart. The other named partners had joined subsequently. All of them long dead, but the name stayed. Why change a good thing? The years had drifted by. The firm increased in size. Lawyers came and went. William Stoddart's great grandson was the current senior partner. Edward Stoddart. He was seventy years old. There were now fifteen partners. Small compared to the new-style mega-firms which seemed so trendy, but still big enough and prestigious enough to hold its own.

Two miles from the city centre, set in an acre of mature gardens bordered by a six-foot stone wall and high-growing spruce trees, it was a place easily missed. There were no signs, save a bronze plaque about the size of a dinner tray bolted into the stone, the name of the firm engraved in letters you had to squint to make out.

Stark went through an open gate, approached the front

entrance. He noted a small parking area, large enough for three cars. Stark had parked on the street outside. He drove a ten-year-old oil-leaking Nissan Micra with a sagging exhaust and an embarrassment of bashes. Thankfully there were no meters. He didn't carry any change. In fact, he didn't carry any money at all, the remnants of his overdraft spent on his new attire, and he didn't get paid for two days. But, as his sister had said, this was a "one-shot" chance. And he had to take it.

He entered the building, into a short foyer, then through a double glass door, and emerged into a large, surprisingly modern reception area. Clean white walls, high ceiling, pale-yellow, shot-blasted marble floor tiles, a broad L-shaped reception desk of metal and glass, behind which sat a male and female, studying computer screens. To one side, a wide staircase. On the other, a waiting room. This was no functional dentist's waiting room, thought Stark. No metal-legged hard plastic chairs lined in a row along the walls. No, sir. Long leather sofas, the colour of soft cream. Low coffee tables scattered about with magazines. On a side cabinet, a coffee machine. The smell of freshly filtered coffee beans suffused the air, rich and heady. The place looked clean and bright, morning sunshine streaming through a high window.

It was 9am. The room was empty. This, thought Stark, was a positive sign. His dread was that he would come to this place, and encounter a half dozen suited reflections of himself, sitting in a row, rigid as stone, waiting for their golden chance. But it seemed he was alone. Unless he was merely first in a long line of candidates, stretched throughout the day. Suddenly, he didn't feel so positive.

He went to the front desk. The female receptionist raised her head from the screen. He reckoned they were about the same age. Late twenties, hair scraped back into a tight ponytail. She looked efficient and humourless.

"Hi," he said. "I have an interview at nine."

She nodded, clicked her keyboard, studied the screen.

"Mr Stark?"

"Yes."

She gestured – "If you have a seat, please. Someone will be with you shortly."

Stark hesitated. "Are there others…?"

She looked at him, expressionless. "Excuse me?"

"Nothing. It doesn't matter."

He went across to the waiting area, poured some coffee into a paper cup, got a seat. He took a sip. Strong and bitter. The problem with filter coffee was that it was never hot.

The walls were devoid of ornamentation save a single painting, spanning the length of the room. A random swirl of dark colour, with no apparent structure or form. *Dramatic,* thought Stark. *And bewildering.* He wondered how much they paid for it. Too much, he reckoned. He wondered if he could do better. Perhaps the law was the wrong profession.

"You like it?"

Stark jerked round, almost spilling his coffee. A woman stood next to the couch. He hadn't seen her approach.

"Sorry I startled you." She gave a small sympathetic smile. "We have offices adjacent to the waiting room."

Stark looked round. "I can't see any doors?"

Her smile widened. "It's a magic trick." She flicked her hand, as if she were waving a wand. "A requirement of the job."

"Teleporting. I wish they'd told me. I would have researched."

She laughed. "The door through to the ground-floor offices was created to blend in with the colour and texture of the wall. Like camouflage."

"A hidden door."

"Correct. So we can sneak up on our clients. Catch them unawares."

"The element of surprise. Novel concept."

He placed his cup on the coffee table, stood. They shook hands. Her handshake was strong, assured.

"I'm Jenny Flynn. I'm one of the associates."

"Jonathan Stark."

She gave a polite nod. She was dressed immaculately. Grey skirt with the faintest of pinstripe, white blouse, grey heels. Simple but stylish, bordering on officious. The required uniform of a thousand associates in a thousand legal firms. A hint of expensive perfume. Not unappealing, thought Stark. Copper hair, her face wide of forehead and cheekbone, curving down to a small chin. Dark-blue eyes. The eyes. Bone weary. She'd probably been packing in sixty-hour weeks for the last five years to get the associates badge. She faced the prospect of doing it for the next ten years before she even got a sniff of partnership. But she would do it, because it was all she knew, and because that was what was expected.

Not for the first time, he wondered if the law was the right profession. But like Jenny, it was all he knew. Except heaving crates of lemonade.

"Do you like it?" she asked.

Stark had to think. "The painting? I'm not sure. It's trying to tell me something." He grinned. "I'm just not certain what it is."

Jenny's lips curled into a half smile.

"I'm not convinced anyone does. It's called *Fury*. Apparently. Make of it what you will."

Stark's curiosity was piqued. "Fury?" He attempted a little humour, hoped he wasn't too forward – "Is that when the client gets the bill?"

She reacted with the merest twitch of her shoulders. "I expect so." She laughed. "With a sprinkling of outrage and bewilderment. If you'd like to come with me. We're going to the first floor, to the conference room."

She led him past the reception desk. The phones had started bleeping. They went upstairs. The staircase was a dark crimson carpet, a sleek curving wooden banister, sweeping up in a half circle to the first landing. A vivid contrast to the white tiles and glass structures on the ground floor. *This,* thought Stark, *is more in keeping with a one-hundred-and-fifty-year-old law firm.*

They reached the first floor, corridors either side. The walls were dark oak panelling. On the walls, portraits, underneath which, in little gold inscriptions, names. Former partners, assumed Stark. No smiles. Rather, brooding frowns. *Fun city.*

He passed doors, some closed, some open. The place was busy. People working. The hum of quiet industry. A man appeared, flustered, face flushed, hugging a wad of files to his chest, a black court gown draped over his arm. He gave a fleeting smile, brushed past them in a shambling trot.

"Late again," muttered Jenny. They got to a closed door at the end. Solid wood, an old-style brass handle. She glanced at Stark, her expression unreadable.

"Good luck, Jonathan."

"Thank you."

She knocked the door gently, turned the handle. They went in.

CHAPTER SEVEN

"It's beyond comprehension."

"Perhaps, if we hadn't seen it before. And because we have, it's possible to comprehend. Which makes it worse."

But it could be that the tide was turning, and despite the gruesome discovery, Detective Chief Inspector Harry McGuigan had reason to feel a glimmer of optimism. They had a break. It had only taken five years. Maybe there was a God after all. He doubted it. And if there were, he possessed a devilish streak.

Detective Sergeant Kenny Dawson merely nodded. Dawson had been working with the task force for three years, and as such, had never witnessed the early kills. But even three years was still a long time, given the nature of the murders. And despite having attended ten similar – *identical* – crime scenes, DCI McGuigan knew his colleague was right in his assertion. It was truly beyond comprehension.

But they had a break.

There was a witness. Which was more than they'd ever had.

"Check on Mr Chapel," said McGuigan. "I'll catch up shortly."

Both he and Dawson were head to toe in white papery-plastic forensic overalls, zipped up to the neck, hoods drawn tight.

Dawson acknowledged the command, left the room. McGuigan stepped back, into a corner, and stood, absorbing the carnage. Altogether three bodies. A man downstairs, sprawled in the hallway, shot in the face at close range, his head a mash of blood and hair. According to the driver's licence found in his wallet, his name was William Patrick.

The second body was lying on the garden path outside. Looked like he had been approaching the house when he had been shot. Several times. Nowhere near as clinical and clean as the man in the hallway. Rather a spray of bullets. Leg, groin, stomach, neck, jaw. Peter Stephens.

The third body. In the main bedroom. The room in which he was standing. Lying on the bed before them, positioned in a way he had come to recognise, was Evelyn Stephens, sheets and pillows saturated in blood. Wife of Peter, the man on the garden path.

The room was busy. Men and women, similarly suited in forensic overalls, worked with sombre concentration. Photographs, fingerprints, hairs, fibres. Measurements. One officer was taking video evidence. Another, handwritten notes. Methodical and painstaking collection of data. Each room in the house would be subject, in due course, to the same scrutiny. But for now, attention was levelled on the bedroom, where it seemed the main event had taken place.

The pathologist – Laura Singleton, a woman in her mid-forties, hardened by a thousand crime scenes – worked with quiet efficiency.

McGuigan wondered, not for the first time, what would drive a human being to inflict such outrage on another. He had never been a religious man. He knew little about the Bible, or God, or Jesus Christ. He had never really pondered such concepts as good and evil. People simply did crazy things. End of. Greed, drugs, alcohol, jealousy, passion. A thousand reasons, distilled down to a flaw in the human psyche.

Then the equation changed, and the killings started. Five years ago. Killings of a sort no one had seen before. Things shifted. The murders brought the question into a new and uncharted dimension. McGuigan had started joining his wife to church. Initially, just an occasional thing. Now, pretty damned regular. He still didn't believe there was a God. Not really. Not deep down. But he needed an answer as to why. Maybe the answer wasn't in plain sight. Maybe the answer was hidden, and if there really was a God, maybe that's where the answer lay.

And perhaps God had been listening after all. Because now they had a witness.

The pathologist appraised McGuigan, nodded to the door. They both left the room, and stood in the hall. She spoke in a low, tired voice. *Resigned,* thought McGuigan.

"I don't really need to tell you." She sighed, removed her latex gloves, rubbed her eyes. "The same as the others. You would think, after so long, he would seek a little variety. He must be a crushing bore at dinner parties."

Gallows humour, thought McGuigan. It kept them sane.

"He's predictable. I'll grant him that."

"Predictable. I suppose it makes my job easier." She took a deep breath, assumed a carefully neutral voice. "Death by penetration to the brain. Skilfully performed. First, he rendered her unconscious. A blow to the side of the head. No sign of a struggle."

"Not just any blow," said McGuigan. She reacted with a small shrug. McGuigan continued. "A bolt gun, yes? The type slaughterhouses use to stun animals. Tell me I'm wrong. She was too scared to struggle. And the bolt gun would have been fired quickly, before she understood what was happening."

Her face was tight when she answered. "Too early to say. But if you would like to provide your own pathologist's opinion, it would save me time and effort and a shitload of paperwork, and I would be delighted to hear your conclusions."

McGuigan gave a polite tilt of his head. "I'm all ears."

"Thank you. A blow to the head. Powerful and penetrative. Probably causing brain injury, but in itself, not enough to kill."

"Merely to stun."

"The brain injury came later by way of the insertion of a rod or needle inserted in the initial penetration. The rod probably cut the brain stem and spinal cord tissue. Death, I imagine, would have been instant and painless."

"A pithing rod," said McGuigan. "To kill animals. Which is what you're saying."

The pathologist cleared her throat, continued. "The facial incisions would have been carried out shortly after death. But I can't be entirely certain."

"Of course."

"But they probably were. The cutting of the eyelids, the splitting at the corners of the mouth, the thinning of the nose, all probably performed with a scalpel or similar instrument. Sharp and accurate. Performed with skill."

"He's had plenty of practice. If he hadn't picked it up by now, I'd be disappointed."

"The skin around the chin was peeled away. Carefully, I might add. Again, the use of a scalpel or similar instrument. Then, the skin was replaced, and stapled back in place – using a surgical stapler."

"Unsightly. And I wonder why he did that?"

"Without a post-mortem, it's impossible to know."

"But we do know."

"I wouldn't like to guess."

"Allow me. He removes the skin, to get to the bone. Whereupon he scrapes and moulds it with a chisel or smoothing plane or some such similar tool, to change its shape, ever so slightly. Presumably to suit his requirements. Our friend is versatile, possessing both the qualities of a surgeon and a sculptor. Then he puts the skin back on, tucks it into place, clicks his staple machine, and voila! He has created a new face. He didn't touch the cheeks this time. I suppose he must have been happy with what God had given her."

"I can't say," she replied. "Not until I have conducted a full examination. But I would like to mention that it's been five years. Five long years. And here we are, talking about another woman, murdered and mutilated by the same goddamned psycho. And let's not forget the two men he shot. So while you're telling me all about my job, maybe someone should be telling you how to do yours! Because I don't want to be standing in some hallway in another five years' time, listening to you talk about the shit this fucking freak performs on his victims." She took a deep breath. "Christ, I could murder a cigarette."

"Me too," said McGuigan. "And a large Scotch. Sorry. I spoke out of turn. And if it's any consolation, we'll never last another five years. Not you anyway. Living in the fast lane, with all that smoking and drinking and whatever else you pathologists get up to."

She gave a weary smile. "I wish. There's a rumour going about."

"Yes?"

"That you've started going to church. You've turned to God, Harry? That's something I would like to see."

"I use all the help I can get."

"In which case, tell him please, from me, to get his fucking arse into gear."

"I doubt he'll listen. But one never knows."

CHAPTER EIGHT

The room was dominated by a long table of solid wood, polished and gleaming in the soft illumination of downlighters. It was big enough to accommodate easily twenty people. When Stark entered, there were only four people seated – three next to each other, on one side, and the fourth at the far end, some distance from the others.

The room was carpeted, a vibrant burgundy colour. Along one wall, arranged on shelves polished and gleaming like the table, were rows of law books. There were no windows. The table was bare, save a silver coffee pot, a silver pouring jug of milk, cups and saucers. At the far wall, a wide hearth beneath a sculptured mantelpiece of black marble, above which, a painting similar to the one in the waiting room, only in miniature. A mass of wild dark colour.

Impressive, thought Stark. *If this is designed to intimidate, then it's working.*

He followed Jenny to the opposite side of the table, facing the three seated individuals. Two men and a woman.

Jenny gestured to a chair. Stark sat. She smiled at the three opposite. They smiled back. One of the men spoke.

"Thank you, Jenny."

Jenny gave a polite nod, left the room.

Stark noted that each of the three had a sheet of paper placed before them. He had never perfected the art of reading upside down, but each sheet looked pretty much like a copy of his CV.

"Good morning, Jonathan," said the same man who had initially spoken. "Do you mind if I use your first name? We try not to be overly formal."

"Good morning. And no. I don't mind at all." *Why would I?*

"Coffee? Help yourself."

"Thank you." Stark poured himself a cup. It smelled good.

"I hope you didn't have difficulties finding us. We don't go out of our way to advertise, as you may have guessed."

"No problem," said Stark. The man he was speaking to wore a deep-blue three-piece suit, a crisp white shirt, matching white tie. Slight physique, tanned, hair swept back from a high forehead in an oily silver wave. His posture was one of languid ease.

"I'm Walter Hill," he said, voice smooth as silk. "I'm one of the managing partners. I'm also head partner in Commercial." He raised himself from his chair, stretched over, offered a handshake. Stark did likewise. Hill's handshake was firm and sure. Firmer than Stark would have guessed, given his delicate build.

Hill glanced round. "And this is Winnifred Marshall."

Same routine again. Winnifred Marshall wore a neat tweed jacket, a white blouse. A woman possibly in her late fifties. A sharp chin, harsh cheekbones, blonde hair chopped short with a somewhat severe side fringe, narrow rimless glasses, behind which, shrewd inquisitive eyes.

"Hello," she said. "I'm head of Property and Estates."

"Hello," replied Stark. "It's nice to meet you."

"And this is Paul Hutchison," said Hill. "Paul heads up our litigation team."

Hutchison was overweight. His jacket was possibly a size too small. Maybe two. Moist bland features set in a moon face, bald as a stone. Short arms, plump hands resting on the table. He gazed at Stark with limpid blue eyes. He didn't offer a handshake.

"I don't do that," he said. "Germs. You can't be too careful. I try to avoid contact whenever possible. I suffer from a number of allergies. No disrespect meant."

"Of course not," Stark said. "I understand completely." *Arsehole.*

Hill laughed, a little too loudly. "Paul has been described as *fastidious.*"

Stark said nothing. There was nothing he could think of to say.

Walter Hill continued. "We have your CV. Thank you for sending it through." He made a show of reading it, looked up. "Tell us a little about yourself, Jonathan. Family?"

"I have a sister. She's a doctor. She works at A and E at Hairmyres Hospital."

Hill gave an approving nod.

"Parents?"

Stark shook his head. "Both dead."

Now a sympathetic nod. Hill again made a show of studying Stark's CV.

"Impressive. One might even say *glowing.* First-class honours at Aberdeen University. You were the only one that year. Plus you got distinctions in Contract and Delict."

They've done their diligence, Stark thought. *Thorough.* He expected no less.

"And then you completed a masters at Glasgow. Again, impressive. Why change universities?"

Stark smiled. "Change? To be honest, it was all down to money."

Winnifred Marshall gave an airy laugh. "It always is, Jonathan."

"I had to find the money for the post-grad tuition fees. Which meant something had to give. Rental is a lot cheaper in Glasgow. So I moved. Not through choice."

"Expediency," said Hill. "Understandable. You're originally from Eaglesham? That's a nice part of the world. Quaint. And quiet. I'm sure you have a lot of happy memories."

"Some." *And some not so happy.*

Silence. Then the litigator spoke – Paul Hutchison.

"What then? You got your masters five years ago. Your CV appears to be silent during this period. Please, enlighten us."

His voice had a tinny undertone. No false bonhomie from this guy, thought Jonathan. Rather, a dry subtle aggression. Stark imagined him a ferocious adversary in the courtroom. But still an arsehole.

Stark hesitated, said, "I was… sidetracked."

Silence. Hutchison stared at him with his round eyes, expression unreadable. Stark was reminded of a waiting lizard.

"Sidetracked? That's an interesting phrase. Interesting, but not particularly helpful. Expand, if you will."

Here it comes, Stark thought. *The truth.* But they would know anyway, if they'd done their research, which he knew they had. If he lied, he was doomed.

He took a breath.

"After I got my masters, I applied for traineeships with a number of law firms. I got a job, eventually, with AK Willow, in Edinburgh. Five years ago."

"Yes?" prompted Hutchison.

Stark regarded the three people opposite. He glanced round to the man sitting at the top of the table. The man he had not been introduced to. The man who so far had remained silent.

"I'm sure you know what happened," said Stark, addressing each of them. "I think everyone knows what happened."

"Tell us, Jonathan," said Winnifred gently.

"You understand why we need to have this information," chimed Hutchison, voice far less gentle. "We need to know as much as possible about candidates who want to work with this firm. Otherwise, we can't make an informed decision as to whether they're suitable. You understand this, I'm sure. Five years is a long time."

Jonathan hesitated. "It was a difficult period. As I said, I got… sidetracked."

"It's a five-year gap," responded Hutchison in a brassy voice. "If you want to have any prospect of working here, then we have a right to know what you've been doing." To accentuate his point, he kept jabbing one plump index finger on the tabletop. "Sidetracked doesn't cut it."

Stark felt the familiar tremble in his hands. He kept them on his lap, so they wouldn't see. Sweat dribbled down the nape of his neck, under the collar of his new crisp white shirt. He held Hutchison's round-eyed stare.

"It was a difficult time," he said quietly.

Suddenly, Stark didn't want to be in this room, in this place, with these people. Suddenly, he wanted to be back lifting crates in a shithole warehouse in a shithole part of Glasgow. He swallowed back a wave of nausea, took a long breath, calmed, focused. He was here. He would cope. He couldn't continue being a hostage to his past.

Okay – if these ghouls want to listen to the whole goddamned story, then let it play.

"AK Willow was a commercial firm based in Edinburgh City Centre," he said. "I'm sure you know this already."

The only response came from Winnifred, who gave a slow nod of her head.

Stark continued, his voice flat and hard. "Alfie Willow was the senior partner. He'd started the business from scratch, and within ten years had built it up to one of the most progressive and innovative law firms in the country. Which was why I had applied there, as did every other law graduate. And which was why, when I got the job, I thought I was the luckiest person on the planet. No one knew that Alfie Willow had been embezzling millions from his clients. Except Alfie Willow."

Another deep breath. Memories, always scratching just below the surface of his mind, reared up, monstrous and fearful.

"I had been working two months. Alfie rented the entire ground floor of a building in Princes Street. Altogether, there were twenty staff." He paused, said, "But I'm sure you all know this already."

No response. *They really want to hear this. They want all the details. So be it.*

"Alfie had reached the end. Too many questions were being asked. The police were taking an interest. None of us were aware. None of us had any indication. We went to work every day, innocent and oblivious to the fact that our boss was a thief on the grandest scale. But in those last moments, Alfie didn't run. Alfie was a man who liked to see things finished. Right to the end. It was a Wednesday morning. It was February, and it was cold. Alfie, so I learned, started with his family. Apparently he was a keen gun collector. Kept a whole arsenal in a neat little hidden cellar under his kitchen floor. A wife and three children. Ten, twelve and fifteen. I remember these things."

Another deep breath. He hadn't spoken about this for five years. Not even to his sister. And here he was, vomiting it all out to four strangers at a goddamned job interview. But for some reason, he didn't want to stop.

"He arrived at work at 10am. This was late for him. But I suppose he had been preoccupied with slaughtering his family. We were all there. All twenty staff, plus several clients. The whole place was open-plan cubicles. Modern architecture. Flowing and spacious and all that bullshit. Do you mind if I use that word? Because bullshit sort of sums it up. Everybody could see everybody else. Transparency. I watched him come in the front door. He was carrying a gym bag. Adidas. You know the brand, I'm sure. Strange the inconsequential things you remember. He placed the bag on the reception counter, opened it up. You want to hear this?"

Silence. They'd asked for this. By Christ, he was going to give it to them. Both fucking barrels.

"The receptionist was still smiling when he pulled out a rifle, pointed it at her face, and took the top of her skull off. I saw that. I saw it, and thought I hadn't really seen it, that it was some monstrous joke. The upper half of her head spun away, like a discus. After that, he was methodical. Alfie was a methodical man. He went from cubicle to cubicle, almost like he was *strolling*, casually firing his rifle, and casually killing people. You want to hear this?"

He looked from face to face. They didn't respond. They were getting way more than they had asked for. God, he felt good, getting it all out, like pus from a boil.

"And the screams. I wake up at three in the morning, and I hear these screams. Like nothing you've heard before." He paused again. The next bit was difficult. But this was the bit that counted.

"Then Alfie arrived at my cubicle with his parting gift, and he pointed his rifle, while I sat beside my laptop in a strange dreamlike state, thinking none of it was real, and he aimed, and he fired."

Another deep breath. He felt hollow and weary. He wanted to go home and sleep for a year.

"I was in a coma for two months. The bullet hit the side of my head. I have the scar to prove it, if you're interested. Alfie performed a little more killing after me, so I understand. Then he put the rifle in his mouth and blew his brains out. Poor old Alfie. I've heard it said that when people revive from a coma, they don't remember a thing. Well, that's not true."

Again he swept his gaze across the three faces opposite.

"I remember everything. A curse, I suppose."

He fixed his attention on Paul Hutchison. "When I got out of hospital, I was in no state to do anything. It took me two months to walk properly. I needed therapy. Lots of it. I got blinding headaches. I still do. I get nightmares. Real bad ones. They never go away. I lost my nerve. I lost my confidence. So, as for the five-year gap in my CV, I've been doing nothing except drift from job to job, until I plucked up the courage to apply to this firm. And now I wish I hadn't. Now I don't know why the hell I'm here."

He stood up, tried to rein in his anger, but couldn't help himself.

"Now you have some context. Now you understand what got me *sidetracked.*" He focused on Paul Hutchison. "I'm damaged goods. That's what you want to hear. Well, there you are. You've heard it. So in conclusion – you can take your job, and shove it up your arse. Thank you for your time."

He gave a curt nod, left the room, and wished, not for the first time, that Alfie Willow had aimed better that cold Wednesday morning, and shot him dead.

CHAPTER NINE

Nothing was said, as each pondered Stark's outburst. Paul Hutchison broke the silence.

"Well, that's that. Good riddance, I say." He looked round at the figure sitting at the top of the table, his expression accusatory. "You probably wished you'd never penned that letter. Just goes to show. You give someone a chance, and this is the thanks you get."

The figure did not respond.

"We probably shouldn't have pushed him," said Winnifred. "After all, we already knew he'd worked at Willow's, and we already knew, along with most of the civilised world, what went down there."

"We didn't push him," retorted Hutchison, voice raised, cheeks flushed. "He had a gap in his CV. We had to know. And thank God we did. Loose cannon. We don't want loose cannons in our workplace. So, we put him under a bit of pressure. Big deal. If he can't handle it, which he clearly can't, then he doesn't belong here."

"First-class honours degree," remarked Hill. "A rare commodity. The boy has talent."

"He's hardly a boy," snapped Hutchison. "He's twenty-eight. And that's another thing – he's too old to be a trainee. We need young, fresh-faced men straight from university, eager and enthusiastic, without any emotional baggage."

"Men?" said Winnifred in a nasal voice. "Don't forget, we women exist as well."

"Of course," muttered Hutchison. "A slip of the tongue."

"Emotional baggage," said Hill. "You're being a trifle harsh, Paul. Nevertheless, perhaps we should be looking for less..." he cleared his throat, "...mercurial candidates."

"We're not going to get anyone better qualified," said Winnifred. "Plus, I have no idea what relevance age has." She turned to Hutchison. "If memory serves me correctly, didn't you begin your traineeship in your later years?"

"That's beside the point. I think he's trouble. I get vibes about these things. And Jonathan Stark gives me bad vibes."

Winnifred shook her head, raised her eyes to the ceiling. "Our recruitment policy now hinges on your vibes? Unbelievable. The guy's been through a shitstorm. I wonder how much courage it took for him to come here for an interview?"

"Courage has nothing to do with it," retorted Hutchison. "As he said himself, he's *damaged goods.*"

They fell silent. They each turned their attention to the figure at the far end of the table, who up to this point, had remained silent.

"What do you think, Edward?"

Edward Stoddart, great grandson of one of the founding partners, and the most senior lawyer there, and who, as such, generally had the final say, reacted with a small shrug.

"I'm not sure," he said. "But I liked him."

CHAPTER TEN

The witness, given his importance, was asked to attend Stewart Street police station for a more detailed statement. McGuigan desired to speak to him directly, while events were still fresh in the mind.

McGuigan now sat in an interview room with DS Kenny Dawson at his side. Opposite sat a forty-year-old man, dapper to the point of foppishness – tailored powder-blue wool suit, matching blue silk tie, shoes polished to a sparkle, his hair a cushion of black curls shaped close to his skull, his mouth prim. When McGuigan entered the interview room, his nostrils were assailed by the man's aftershave.

"Thank you for coming," McGuigan said. He scrutinised notes he had been given. "Mr Chapel?"

The man gave a delicate tilt of his head. "Bronson Chapel. Call me Bronson."

Colourful name, thought McGuigan. *The parents should be shot.*

"Thank you, Bronson. My name is Detective Chief Inspector McGuigan, and my colleague is Detective Sergeant Dawson. I would like to go over your statement, if that's okay. For clarity."

Bronson gave a brief nod of assent. "Of course. For clarity." He leaned forward. "It's him, isn't it?" His eyes seemed to shine.

McGuigan raised an eyebrow. "Him?"

"The Surgeon. Isn't that what the media call him?"

Goddamned loose lips, thought McGuigan. *This place leaks worse than a worn-out gasket. Heads will roll.*

"Let's stick to what you saw, Bronson."

Bronson sat back, smiled, showing the tips of his teeth. "How can I help you, DCI McGuigan?"

"You were driving towards the house where the incident took place?"

"On my way to court. I was running a tad late. The particular judge I was due to appear before is a martinet when it comes to timekeeping. A real ballbreaker. That particular road can cut five minutes off my journey."

"You're a lawyer."

He raised his hands, theatrically. "Guilty as charged. Don't hold it against me."

"Who do you work for?"

"I'm a partner. SJPS."

McGuigan's brow furrowed in bemusement. "Pardon me?"

"Stoddart, Jeffrey, Pritchard and Sloss. It doesn't quite roll off the tongue. It's a tad clumsy. We like to abbreviate. Adds a bit more... glitz, don't you think? A bit more shine."

He's a garrulous one, thought McGuigan.

"I hope we're not keeping you back."

Bronson gave a broad grin. "No panic. I got the hearing rescheduled. Under the circumstances, how could they refuse?"

"What did you see, Bronson?"

Again, Bronson leaned forward. He exhibited a nervous energy. His fingers tapped on the desktop as he spoke, his heel tapped on the floor.

"I might have seen nothing if it hadn't been for the cat."

Dawson spoke up. "The cat?"

"Correct. A tabby. Big as a damned fox. Bigger. Ugly as sin. Ugliest cat you will ever see. Ran straight across the road. I jammed on the brakes. It missed being squashed by a whisker." He smiled a pearly white smile. "No pun intended."

McGuigan failed to see the humour. He was not in a humorous mood.

"I had stopped directly adjacent to the house," continued Bronson. "I saw a man going up the front garden path. As he was doing that, another man came out of the house. He was closing the door, and had his back to the first man. I didn't think anything of it. Why would I? I was about to pull off, when all hell broke loose. Like something you see in the movies. Hard to believe it was real."

"It was very real, Bronson. How far were you from the front garden?"

"Yards. I'm no good at distances. Twenty yards maybe. Close enough."

"What happened next?" said McGuigan.

"The man leaving the house pulled out a gun, from one of his pockets. A pistol. Don't ask me what type. I don't know the first thing about firearms. Other than they fire bullets. But the barrel was long. I think it had a silencer. Is that the right word – silencer?"

"You would recognise a silencer?" asked Dawson.

"It might not have been. But it looked the type of thing you see in the movies. You've seen *Day of the Jackal*? It was similar to that."

"You like the movies, Bronson?"

"I do rather, yes. Everybody likes the movies. Don't they? I'm sure you do, Detective Inspector McGuigan."

"Detective Chief Inspector," corrected McGuigan. "Please, continue."

"The guy walking towards the house stopped, and just stood. Presumably in shock. The other one – the one leaving the house

– didn't move, like he was in shock too. Then he marched up to him, the gun in his hand. Arm out straight, like so..." Bronson demonstrated by stretching his own arm out, "...and he started firing. Gunfight at the OK Corral!"

"You could hear the shots?" said Dawson.

"Sounded like the pop of a champagne bottle. But much louder. Which is odd, don't you think?"

"Why odd?"

"I thought the point of a silencer was to mask the sound."

"To a degree," said McGuigan. "It dampens the noise a little, but it's still loud."

"He kept firing. The other man – the one who was being shot – sort of... shook. Shuddered. As if a tremor had rippled through him. I suppose from the impact of the bullets. He stood. He didn't fall. Not immediately. Then he did. The other one – the shooter – was over him, and..." Bronson took a breath, licked his lips.

Not really like the movies, thought McGuigan.

"...shot him when the guy was lying there. Then he remained still. Just staring at the guy on the ground. As if he were... fascinated. Mesmerised, even."

Bronson paused, rubbed his eyes, brushed away a bead of sweat from his forehead.

"Would you like a glass of water, Bronson?" said Dawson.

Bronson gave a tight smile. "You wouldn't have a Glenfiddich? I could handle a single malt. No? Never mind."

"What happened then, Bronson?" asked McGuigan gently.

Bronson cleared his throat, regained his composure. "Apologies. It's not every day you see a man being shot in someone's front garden. Or anywhere, for that matter. Still takes a little getting used to."

"Of course. Take your time."

"I'm sitting in my car, in the middle of the road, and I'm watching this surreal scene unfold. I'm having an 'out of body experience', thinking perhaps the whole thing is in my imagination. And I couldn't move. I just… sat. I suppose I was rather like a bird, hypnotised by a snake."

McGuigan shook his head a fraction. Bronson's need to use flowery language was becoming a monumental pain in the arse.

"A manifestation of shock," he said patiently. "The inability to move. A state of paralysis. And I believe the notion of a snake able to hypnotise is a myth."

"I'm sure," replied Bronson. "The guy snapped out his trance, and walked down the garden path. He walked straight towards me. Not in any hurry, I might add. Almost nonchalant."

"You saw his face?"

"Clear as day. And he saw me. He couldn't miss me."

"And?"

"The spell was broken." Bronson gave a brittle laugh. "I came to my senses, put the foot down, and got the hell away."

"You drove off," said McGuigan. "What happened then?"

"I watched him in my rear-view mirror. I was worried he might try and shoot. But instead he got into a white van. I slowed a little. He did a three-point turn, and drove away in the opposite direction. And then I phoned the police. Quite a morning."

"Quite," said McGuigan. "You can describe this man?"

"I saw his face, clear as day. He had on dark-blue overalls. The type a tradesman might wear. You know the sort. Lots of pockets and zips. But I can remember his face. Something I won't forget. The striking thing was his complexion."

"Yes?"

"Bone white. White as death."

"Thank you, Bronson," said McGuigan. "This is very helpful. If you don't mind, we'll now ask you to give a more detailed description to allow us to complete a photofit. You okay with that?"

"Delighted to help. But you didn't answer my question."

"Which was?"

"Did I see The Surgeon? Was it him? You've got to tell me."

McGuigan regarded him, kept his voice level. "Thank you, Bronson. As I said, you have been most helpful."

Bronson shrugged, sat back in his chair. He spoke, almost sulkily. "My pleasure."

Bronson had been escorted from the interview room. The remnants of his aftershave lingered, suffused with his sweat, creating a raw, unpleasant odour.

"The Surgeon," said Dawson. "Bloody media. Our star witness was more interested in a serial killer than the poor guy shot on his front lawn."

"You can't blame him," mused McGuigan. "Our killer is prolific, he kills his victims with a barbaric but artistic flair, he has an ability to evade detection, and he's been successful over a long period. I suppose it's inevitable that such a person acquires an almost mystical status, despite the heinous nature of his crimes. People love a mystery. They love the grotesque. The wheres, the whys, the whens. Especially the whys. Make no mistake, books will be written, documentaries will be made. Maybe a film or two."

"We have to catch him first."

"We're getting close. I can feel it in my bones."

"I'm afraid my bones don't share your feelings," said Dawson.

"We have a witness. Plus, look at the third victim. Shot in public, and shot in a spray of bullets. Spontaneous. Which means to say, our pilgrim was caught off guard. He committed an unplanned, instinctive act. An impulsive act. Completely contrary to his normal behaviour. Our killer is careful and methodical. Obsessively so. His victims are targeted, his kills timed. He watches. He waits. He is the human equivalent of a spider, weaving his web, targeting his prey, lurking in the shadows. Imagine the patience required. The discipline. But this time, everything changes. The husband arrives home. This was unexpected. This was something he had not foreseen. Which tells us something."

Dawson said nothing.

McGuigan allowed a wintry grin. "He's becoming sloppy. Or complacent. Or maybe both. Which means we have a chance. Do you believe in God, Kenny?"

"I haven't given it much thought."

McGuigan rummaged in his jacket pocket, pulled out a bright-orange packet of bubblegum, carefully unwrapped one, popped it in his mouth, put the packet back in his pocket. He chewed as he spoke.

"My wife is an ardent fan. She is of the belief that all things are ordained, that we go down a path already set in stone. If this were indeed the case, then The Surgeon is merely following God's will. I once put that to her. I asked her – why would God set such a path, allowing all these innocents to die, in such horrific fashion? It's not very hospitable of him."

"And her reply?"

McGuigan gave a small rueful smile. "As we walk the road, we have a constant companion, always present, always close to our side, who whispers in our ear. We choose either to listen, or ignore."

"A companion?"

"The Devil. Who else? And in this case, our friendly neighbourhood serial killer loves to listen."

CHAPTER ELEVEN

Bronson Chapel left the police station an hour later. As requested, he had provided a description to a police officer, who listened attentively as Bronson relayed the details, piecing together a face using photographic imagery. A photofit. A distinctive square jaw, thin lips, clean shaven, broad cheeks, a slender nose. Blue eyes. Ice-cold, Bronson had said, for a little extra effect. Most accurate, according to the officer. Perfect, Bronson had replied. You've captured the guy's face exactly.

But this was far from the truth. The description given was nowhere close to the killer's true likeness. Providing the correct information was not to Bronson's advantage.

Bronson got in his car. A one-month-old BMW X5. It still had the "new car" smell. He took out his mobile phone, swiped through the many pictures in the "gallery" section. He stopped at one, scrutinised it. He had neglected to mention to Detective Chief Inspector McGuigan that he had taken a photograph of the assailant. A photograph, clear and focused. *The wonders of modern technology,* he thought. He tapped on the screen, used his thumb and index finger to enlarge the image. He studied it with care. He could scarcely believe what he was looking at. It seemed luck had landed square on his lap. This was his moment. His time. And he was going to damn well exploit it to the full.

He went to "contacts", scrolled down, found the name he was searching for, pressed the screen. It went to voice message.

"Hi," he said, his tone solemn and portentous. "Bronson here. Think we should have a chat. It's important. Call me back."

He disconnected.

Life, suddenly, seemed a whole lot better. Bronson envisaged a bright new horizon spread before him, with a pot of gold at the end of a splendid rainbow. *How peculiar the twists in life,* he thought. *How, in a matter of one morning, everything can alter radically and wonderfully.*

He drove off and out of the police station car park, and plotted.

CHAPTER TWELVE

They sat in his little living room, she on a faded sagging couch, he on an armchair bedizened with a patchwork of stains. Charity shop furniture. Functional – barely. It was the afternoon of the interview. Stark had got the day off work. It was a Tuesday, but he didn't care. He was set on getting drunk, and if he had to go into work the following day shit-faced, then so be it. He hadn't asked his sister to come round, but she did when he didn't answer his phone. He was glad she did. He was in just such a mood to share his misery.

He had a box of cheap beer, placed on the floor beside him. He had already killed off three bottles. Three more, then back to the corner shop, if he was able.

"Are crate-shifters allowed to smell of alcohol?" Maggie asked.

He took a swig. The beer frothed up over the bottle, to create another stain on the chair, but he hardly cared. "Of course. Alcohol's a fuel. Keeps us 'crate-shifters' going. Shouldn't you be extracting a banana from someone's anus?"

"I'm on late shift tonight. And it's not usually a banana, for your information. It's generally a deodorant stick. Once, a six-inch ruler. Which can be awkward. And delicate."

Stark gave a frosty laugh. "Sounds fun. Perhaps I ought to try it."

"Is this the answer?" she said, gesturing at the beer. "Oblivion?"

"I would think so. In fact, a definite yes. Oblivion sounds perfect."

A silence fell. Then she spoke, her voice soft.

"What happened?"

Stark took a long breath. "You would have loved it. High drama. A tragic scene. Ending in anger, swearing, and a theatrical exit. In essence, a shitstorm. Next time, I should sell tickets. That way, I would make a little money."

She blew through her lips. "Interesting summary. Perhaps you could be more specific?"

"What do you think they asked about? Take a guess."

She nodded. "I don't need to guess. They asked about 'it'."

Another swig. He wiped the top of the bottle with the palm of his hand. "It. What else. They'd have to be mad not to." He gave his sister a level stare. "I've been out the game for too long. I'm too old. Why the hell would anyone want to employ someone like me, when they can get someone eight years younger, and who isn't fucked up. I'm kidding myself. The whole thing is one massive joke, and it's on me." His bottle was finished. He placed it by the side of the chair, where he had placed the others, leaned down, and pulled out another from the box. There was a bottle opener strategically placed on the armrest, which he used to prise off the top. He immediately took another long glug.

Maggie regarded him critically. "I don't think that's the answer, dude."

"I think drinking oneself to a blissful state of unconsciousness is the perfect answer."

"I'll give you the perfect answer," she said. "Fuck them. Fuck them all. What's the issue? There'll be other jobs, other interviews."

No there won't, big sister, he thought. *There was only ever one interview. And now there's nothing.*

"You should be home," he said, voice tainted with the slightest slur. "Don't you have a husband somewhere? You shouldn't be wasting your time on a loser wading through a river of self-pity." He gave a sardonic smile. "Though I love the attention."

"Sure you do." She chuckled. "All the symptoms of a narcissist. My husband? Who's he? I barely remember what he looks like. He's working. He works. I work. Married life is reduced to a series of soundbites and fragments of brief pleasantries. We socialise by schedule. We are like... passing ships in the night. Excuse the cliché. Have you got food in? Or is this a new alcohol-only diet."

"As endorsed by Dr Budweiser."

"The one and only." She looked at him solemnly. Again, she kept her voice soft. "You've got to move on, little brother. Easy to say. It just trips off the tongue. A few glib words. But it's the only way. I'm not saying you should bury it. You can't do that. You were shot. You almost died. A momentous, horrendous life-changing event. But you lived. It will stay with you the rest of your life, because it's something that can't be shifted. And because it can't be shifted, it has to be..." she frowned as she searched for the right word, "*...accepted.* Once it's accepted, then it's lost its hold on you. Don't be a prisoner to the past, dude."

Stark sipped his beer. "You want to hear something funny?"

"That would be a pleasant change."

"I was in a coma for just over eight weeks."

"Strangely, I remember that episode in your life. Did you think I'd forgotten? Was that the funny bit? You really should do stand-up."

"Do you know what goes through a person's mind when they're in a coma?"

She regarded him curiously. "You're being serious? You should know."

He said nothing, held her stare.

She sighed. "Technically nothing, I suppose. If you're in a coma, there's no response. To light, to touch, to sound, to anything. If the heart weren't beating, it would be regarded almost as a state of death. Generally, if a person dreams, they give off certain brain pattern signals. Signs of a sleep-wakefulness cycle. A person in a coma gives off nothing. Generally. I should really charge for these little morsels of advice."

"Technically. Generally. You love your adverbs."

"Sure do."

He put the bottle on the floor beside the others. Suddenly, he didn't want to drink anymore.

"Let me tell you what went on in here…" he tapped the side of his head, "…when I was in a coma. Just to set the record straight."

She said nothing. *This is new territory,* he thought. Something he has never told anyone, including his sister.

"I was in a vast space of darkness. I think it was vast. It *felt* vast. And it pressed in close. Constricting me. Suffocating. And it went on and on. Endless emptiness. Never ending. Here's the thing. I was *aware* of this. I knew I was trapped in this place, wherever this place was. I was *conscious.* And the worst thing was – I thought I might be there forever." He took a deep breath, licked his lips, swallowed back a ball of dread. "Eternal nothingness. It was terrifying. And I felt the terror. Every moment." He lowered his voice, remembering, and wishing he didn't. "Every moment." He hesitated, trying to articulate into words something impossible to describe. "When I… got out – woke up – I felt different." He gazed at his sister, as if the mere act of looking at her would bring sense to what he was saying. "Different. Changed. Perhaps some of that darkness… had infected me." Here, he pressed one hand on his chest. "Seeped into my soul."

He took another deep breath. His head spun. He was feeling uncomfortably queasy. "Or maybe it's the drink talking."

"Whatever it was, whatever happened, there is one certainty," said Maggie.

"Tell me. I need some certainty."

"It's over. It's past."

"I still get the nightmares."

"But not as frequently. And in time, even they will pass. I promise. Time has that effect. It heals, eventually."

Stark's response was only a small sad smile.

"If you say so, Maggie. You're the doctor. You'd better get home. I think I'm going to vomit."

Stark didn't vomit. Instead, he watched the news on television, which depressed him more. He listened to some music through the headphones, then decided to have more beer, thinking "oblivion" didn't sound so bad after all. He fell into a doze in his armchair round about midnight...

...and immediately plummeted down into the same nightmare – always the same since the coma, spanning over five years. An image, powerful and vivid, striking terror to his core. The gaunt shape of a man, standing silhouetted in some cold, dark place. A brooding figure, bristling with malice. And he – Stark – is beneath, deep in the ground with the worms and the slugs, clawing for the surface, unable to breathe, gasping for air, lungs burning. Soil enters his mouth, clogging his throat, filling his chest. Suffocating.

He woke abruptly, in a state of panic and fear, drenched in sweat. He took a minute to focus, find his bearings. He wasn't buried under the ground. He was in his flat, in his living room, sitting in his chair. He took deep breaths, filling his lungs.

He got up. He felt old and weary. And drunk. His head spun. The world whirled. He staggered to the toilet.

And it was then he vomited.

CHAPTER THIRTEEN

Despite a pounding head, waves of nausea, and a burning thirst, Stark dragged himself to work the following day. He missed out his early morning run. The first time he'd missed it for months. He knew that if he tried even a shambling jog, he'd leave puddles of puke every hundred yards.

Somehow, amazingly, he got through the day. He reckoned he consumed a gallon of water, filling up a plastic sports bottle every half hour from the tap in the factory toilet. The pounding lessened, the nausea subsided, the thirst disappeared. He got back to his flat at 6pm, feeling considerably more human than he did when the day had started.

There, on the floor by the door, was a letter.

He ignored it, and went straight to the kitchen to fix a coffee. It was probably another damned bill. Electric. He was always behind on his electric. He had never quite been disconnected, but often teetered on the edge.

He began the process of pouring coffee beans into the grinder, then decided he wasn't in the mood, that the whole thing was too much effort, and coffee always tasted shit after a "day before" drinking session.

He went through to the living room, slumped into his armchair, got his headphones, scrolled through his mobile, found some insipid piano music, and drifted off into a half-doze, letting his mind go blank.

He got up at midnight, and padded through to the kitchen. Suddenly he was ravenous. He checked the freezer, pulled out a twelve-inch pepperoni pizza, shoved it in the oven.

He remembered the letter. It lay as before, on the doormat. He debated. Either do it now, get it over and done with, or wait until morning, and open it when he would doubtless feel a million times better. He watched the pizza bubble and pop through the glass of the oven door.

He came to a decision. He went over, picked the letter up. He glanced at the envelope, then studied it with a little more care. Same neat window-box, his name and address typed in the same neat manner, same first-class stamp.

A next-day rejection, he thought. *This firm likes to send bad news at blistering speed.*

He was tempted to toss it into the bin, unopened. *What the hell.* He tore it open, tugged out the letter inside, unfolded it, gave the contents a cursory glance, expecting maybe a three-line special. Perhaps two, depending on how much he'd pissed them off. Same damned handwriting. Neat and precise.

He glanced again, focused, read what it said, read it again. He took a breath, sat on the kitchen chair, and placed the letter on the table before him.

He ran his hands through his hair, and thought *This can't be right. Something's wrong.* He read the letter again. He allowed himself a grim chuckle. *Funny the tricks life can play.*

He had been offered the job. Trainee solicitor. Starting salary not great, but still better than his current position. Telephone to confirm acceptance. If so, starting on Monday, 9am.

All this in three lines.

He smelled burning. He'd forgotten his pizza. He darted over, grabbed a dish towel to cover his hands, rescued what was left, turned the oven off. He slid something resembling a yellow-and-brown frisbee onto a plate, and sat back on the kitchen chair. He took a bite, and reckoned this was how cardboard tasted, but he couldn't have cared less.

Unbelievably, incredibly, he had been offered the job.

His ambition was not yet crushed. An ambition not to become a lawyer, which was a mere side issue. Rather, an ambition to find the truth. And he believed he was one step closer.

CHAPTER FOURTEEN

FRIDAY

Bronson Chapel was part of the litigation team of SJPS, the team leader being Paul Hutchison. Bronson had an office on the first floor, as indeed had all the partners. It was, by a clear country mile, the most extravagant in the building. He despised the notion of minimalism. The thought of having a clear desk appalled him. He was a collector. He loved *things.* Especially expensive *things.* His office was large, with an oval window, looking onto the grounds behind the building. He sat behind a mahogany desk, complete with brass edging and handles. The chairs, both for himself and his clients, were also mahogany, of Victorian design. On the desk were various ornaments – an abstract bust sculpture fashioned from differing shades of marble; a rough-hewn art deco jaguar made of bronze; other oddments, all of them exquisite and expensive.

On the wall, dotted randomly, was a bright array of framed cinema posters, each original and collectable and bearing signatures. There – *Butch Cassidy and the Sundance Kid.* And there – a rare print of Humphrey Bogart, relaxing on a chaise longue, a secret half-smile on his lips, smoking. A scene from *Casablanca.*

Also autographed, and worth a small fortune. Plus, Bronson was a devotee of post-modern paintings, all vivid colours and startling scenes, and all original. The walls were a contrast to the dark sombre furniture. Bronson loved contrasts. He also loved to spend money. He couldn't help himself. A flaw in his personality, he assumed. A habit he couldn't kick. But for the equation to work, it was important to have the money in the first place, which was where, for Bronson, the equation collapsed.

To compound his problems, Bronson also had another habit, one which he was now feeding on a daily basis, and as such, was consuming his life – to the extent he had become involved with men who were both dangerous and unsympathetic towards those customers who failed to pay promptly.

Bronson had been ignoring the repeated calls on his mobile for most of the day. Calls from the same number. It was 4.45. He could no longer avoid the issue. He was in his office. In the bottom drawer of his desk, which he kept locked, was an envelope. He needed courage. He unlocked the drawer, took out the envelope, carefully tapped out white powder on the desktop, arranging it into a neat line. He crouched over, hoovered the stuff up his right nostril. He never used his left. He didn't get the same suction power, due to a fractionally twisted septum. He sat back, took a full breath, let the buzz suffuse his body, his mind. Lately, the buzz was taking longer, was less sharp. But he still felt damned good. In control.

He phoned the number back, which was answered immediately –

"You been avoiding me, Bronson?"

Bronson sniffed, licked his lips. He felt invincible.

"Been busy all day," he said. "Court, meetings, court, meetings. Never ends. A conveyor belt of constant shit. But here I am. Always ready to return your calls. Always available.Twenty-four/seven."

Silence. Then the voice spoke.

"You been partaking, Bronson? You're speaking awful fast."

Bronson laughed, but even to his own ears, it sounded way too loud, and way too false. He was too wired to care.

"You don't have to worry about a thing. It's under control."

"That's reassuring. But you need to be more specific, Bronson. When you don't pick up my calls, I get anxious for my old friend."

Old friend, thought Bronson. *Hardly that. The friendship bullshit stops when the money stops.*

"Don't be anxious. Everything's fine."

"Everything's fine. It's under control. This is what you're telling me. But I'm concerned it's not, Bronson. You know why I'm concerned, old pal? Specifically?"

"As I said…"

"You've not answered my question. Think that powdery stuff you sniff up your nasal cavities is making you deaf. Do you know why I'm concerned?"

Bronson felt his heart race. It pulsed in his chest as if about to explode. A consequence of drugs and nerves and fear.

"I know why you're concerned. But my point is, you don't have to be…"

Now the other man laughed. A heavy booming sound.

"You lawyers! Incapable of a simple answer. Round and round, making people dizzy with the slick words and the games you play, and the shit which trips off the tongue so easy. You don't make me dizzy, Bronson, because I play the game too. But my game has rules. And you've broken them. Big style. I'll answer the question for you." His voice lowered to a hiss. "You've not been paying for your fucking cocaine, you fucking lawyer fucking sleazebag. It was due this morning. Which means you're late. Again. Which means you have one huge fucking problem."

The sudden vitriolic attack buffeted Bronson's drug-induced confidence. He took a second to regain his composure.

"But the money's coming," he spluttered. "I'll have it together by next week. No problem. You'll get paid in full. This I can guarantee." The words fairly rattled out of Bronson's mouth.

Another barking laugh. "Guarantee? I don't think so. That promise was lost long ago. The thirty grand has now gone up to thirty-five, and will go up by five grand a day. Call it... penalty interest. You understand the concept. Next week, Bronson. Tuesday. Then, we will come to collect. At your house. Let's say 9pm? Is that okay? We're not interrupting any good TV? Any dinner engagements? Good. If you fail to pay, or suddenly discover you have to be elsewhere, or anything at all, and we don't get what we're owed, then the niceties end, and I lose my pleasant disposition. Things become... unsavoury."

Bronson licked his lips. His throat was dry. He always felt thirsty after a score.

"Unsavoury? I'll not be threatened. I don't care who you are. I won't be intimidated."

The man responded, apparently unfazed by Bronson's bluster. He spoke, his voice easy. "Sure you won't. But I'm doing it anyway. Listen carefully. I know you can listen when you put your mind to it. No money, and we'll hammer a nail in your eye, and melt the skin off your face. With acid. Down to the bone. You'll lose your boyish good looks, but hey! Looks aren't everything. Your fancy law firm will have to keep you locked away in a cupboard, so you don't scare the clients. Plus, you'll still owe us the money. Get it together, Bronson. A man like you, with your conniving mind, and ferret-like cunning, should think of something." Another sudden booming laugh. "You could start by selling some of that shit on your desk."

He disconnected.

Bronson took a deep breath. The drugs didn't dispel fear. He felt it, fresh and raw.

But he had an answer. Something which would make his

problem go away, and make life a little easier. Considerably easier. He flicked through the photographs on his phone, stopped at one in particular. He gazed at the figure.

This was his solution. Arrangements were in place. Monday morning, and then his life would change.

CHAPTER FIFTEEN

Billy Watson disconnected. He was phoning from his flat in Glasgow's trendy south side. An apartment on the top floor of a new luxury development. The view was impressive, which was why he bought it. Rooftops, streets, parks, office blocks, stretching on in a muddled maze, and in the far distance, beyond the periphery of buildings, the sweep and rise of the Eaglesham Moors. In summer, on such a day as this, the view was clear and perfect. He sipped red wine. He drank, at most, a bottle of wine a week. Usually less. He maintained a quiet existence. He rarely went out. If he did, it was perhaps to a discreet restaurant, maybe a coffee shop. The cinema. He was divorced, with no kids. No ties. He liked to stay focused. Money focused him. Money was everything. Dealing drugs paid handsomely. Occasionally, there were blips in the process, such as the lawyer Bronson Chapel. But he had a way of dealing with blips. And he had a knack for turning blips to his advantage.

Sitting on a couch opposite was his associate, Frank Fitzsimmons. Frank had acquired a number of "nicknames". *Frankie F, Fitzy, Lemonhead.* Lemonhead, on account of his hair, which some thought was the colour of lemons. Billy called him simply Frank.

Frank now regarded Billy Watson. He sipped from a bottle of beer.

"He'll never find that kind of money," he said.

Watson gave a small shrug, said nothing.

"I say, we cut our loss," Frank continued. "Give him a proper doing, send a message. A few broken bones. Let others know we've not gone soft. Then move on. There are bigger and better fish than Bronson Chapel."

Watson smiled. "Bronson," he said softly. "Who would call their child such a name."

"The parents had a sense of humour," suggested Frank.

"Or a sadistic touch. You're forgetting something important, Frank."

"Which is?"

"Our friend is a lawyer. What's more, he's a partner."

Frank took another small sip, looked puzzled. "Lawyers. Ten a penny. No big deal. I just heard you call him a sleazebag, which sums him up nicely. Broom him fast, and move on. The guy's finished."

"Sometimes, you have to think out the box. The firm he works with is ancient. Over a hundred and fifty years old. It's established. It has prestige. Which means it's rich."

Frank stared at Watson, brow furrowed – "And?"

"And everything. I imagine that in any one day, it will have many millions in its clients account. Clients' money, going in and out, flowing through their bank, and always constant. A river of cash. You said there are bigger and better fish. Well then, let's do some real fishing. Bronson is a partner. He has complete unrestricted access to his clients' money. With a little persuasion..."

"You mean," interrupted Frank, smiling broadly, "a little acid on the face."

"...with a little persuasion," said Watson, ignoring the remark, "our coke-head friend can dip his fishing net, and make us wealthy."

Frank nodded slowly, as if contemplating the situation. "It might work. But he gets only a small window before he's caught. And he *will* be caught. Men like Bronson always get caught. As certain as the fucking sun rising. And then *we're* caught. The cops aren't stupid. There's such a thing as a money trail."

"Six million," said Watson. "That's all we need. Three million each. A bank transfer would take minutes, to any bank, anywhere in the world. Then we disappear."

"It might just work. If we're careful."

"We're always careful. But we have to get him frightened. Terrified. And we have to crank it up. We'll see him next Tuesday, and get him so shit scared, he'd sell his fucking soul."

"He might call the police."

"We make him think otherwise."

Frank gave an appreciative tilt of his head. "That we can do. He might simply refuse."

Watson laughed out loud. "He might."

They both fell silent, each absorbed in their own thoughts. Then Frank spoke.

"Acid? That's a new one. Really?"

"It was the first thing which came to mind. But it sounded good. Perhaps a bit complicated. The nail in the eye however. More practical. Yes?"

Frank raised his bottle. "Definitely."

CHAPTER SIXTEEN

MONDAY

Stark got there at 8.30. He'd left early, making provision for an engine fail which, mercifully, didn't happen. The offices were open. The female receptionist was there, sipping from a plastic coffee cup, engrossed in her mobile phone. She looked up when Stark entered, smiled, her demeanour entirely changed from their last encounter.

"Hi," she said. "Welcome aboard. I'm Sarah. Go on through." She gestured to the waiting room. "I'll let Jenny know you're here. She wants to show you around. Help yourself to coffee. Nice to see a new face."

"Thank you."

He went through to the waiting room. Nothing had changed. He helped himself to coffee. He heard Sarah on the phone. A minute later, the disguised door opened. Jenny entered. Today she wore a dark flared skirt, a dark puffy-sleeved blouse, a silk necktie the colour of pale cream. Her hair fell to her shoulders in an appealing tousled bob.

"You made it," said Jenny.

"Amazingly the car didn't break down."

She reacted with a light careless laugh. He was reminded of his sister.

"That's something," she said. "But I meant, you got the job."

"So it would seem. The trick now is to try and keep it."

"Do you surf?" she asked.

Stark gave a somewhat bemused answer. "I haven't tried it."

"Nor me. But I'm sure staying in a job like ours is like surfing. Impossible at the beginning. But after a while, you learn to keep your feet on the board."

"Unless a really big wave comes along."

"But that's when the fun begins. Follow me. I'll give you the tour."

He followed her, back through the door she had entered from.

"This is where we minions work," she said. "Assistants and associates. You've heard of *The West Wing?* This is *The Sweat Wing*, as it's fondly described by those required to endure it." She glanced archly at him. "Only kidding. It's far worse."

They were in a corridor of bare white walls, illuminated by striplights on the ceiling. Doors on either side, all open, all occupied by people. Talking, on the phone, dictating into hand-held machines, tapping on laptops or computer keyboards, studying screens.

"Altogether, there are twenty of us on the ground floor, including you. We're an assortment of lawyers and paralegals. There are ten offices on this level. We share. Two per office. You can get to know the team as you go along." They got to the end of the corridor, to a closed door, which she opened. She turned on the lights.

"This is the meeting room we use for clients. That is to say – *average, Joe Bloggs-type clients.* For 'specials' – the wealthy and powerful – the partners see them in the conference room upstairs. Where you had your interview."

"I feel honoured," said Stark.

The room was a poor man's substitute to the one on the first floor. The walls were as bare as the corridor, with the exception of a painting of some nameless mountain range. A simple table took centre stage, around which, four blue plastic chairs with metal legs. No frills. No requirement to schmooze clients on this floor, thought Stark. It was all business, without the glitz. A tall window at the far wall, looking out onto some trees. The same striplighting on the ceiling, bright and clinical.

"And your room…" said Jenny, turning to him, "…is right in here." She beckoned him to an office closest to the meeting room, the door of which was open, the lights on.

It contained two desks, chairs, computers. Shelves on one wall lined with books and folders. Three filing cabinets. One desk was laden with files, a pen holder full of coloured pens, an open book, a notepad, discarded elastic bands and paperclips, a framed picture, and a coffee mug, which, judging by the steam rising, was freshly made.

The other desk was bare, with the exception of a closed laptop.

"Someone's not finished their coffee," remarked Stark.

"That would be me," replied Jenny. "Say hello to your brand-new roommate."

"You drew the short straw. My sympathies."

She grinned. "Provided you're clean, have no annoying habits, and don't pick your teeth, then we'll be fine."

"I'll keep that in mind."

"There's also a small kitchen of sorts. A microwave, a fridge, and a cupboard. I suppose that counts as a kitchen. You'll find that coffee and sandwiches form your staple diet in this place. Coffee, especially. If you're not addicted to caffeine yet, you will be. If you want to smoke, go out into the garden, but don't let the partners catch you. There's also rooms for the typists. We share them as well. Ten typists, which means roughly two per typist. Needless to say, the partners each have their own personal secretary. Not us. We're not deemed worthy, but there's no point in complaining, because no one listens. If you need something out urgently," and here she fluttered her fingers, "use these, and type it yourself."

"Sounds daunting. As long as there's a 'spellcheck', I should survive."

"Glad to hear it. Without it, none of us would survive. The first floor consists of the partners' offices, secretaries' rooms, and the main conference room. Plus, there's a library, for everyone's use, and it's well stocked and bang up to date. If you need anything, you'll find it there. If not, then you have the magic of Professor Google. The second floor has only one office. And it's out of bounds."

"Only one office?" said Stark. "For the entire floor?"

"For the exclusive use of our senior partner. Edward Stoddart. Great grandson of the founding partner. And it's not really an office. It's more of a house. He rarely comes down to visit, and when he does, the men doff their caps and bow, and the females – including myself – perform a reverential curtsy."

Stark couldn't help smiling. "As one would expect, when royalty calls."

"Exactly so. Now brace yourself, Jonathan. The next bit's the creepy bit."

"Creepy?"

"I'm going to show you the basement."

The basement was accessed directly from the "Sweat Wing". The door was heavier than the others, and Jenny had to tug it open.

"We got a new door put in, to keep out the draught," she explained. "But the draught keeps coming. There's always a chill in the basement."

She switched on a light. Illumination came from suspended

striplights, which flickered. Open metal stairs reached down to a large room, stretching either side.

They made their way down, shoes clanking with each step. The floor comprised ancient wooden planks, some parts springy underfoot. Looked like it had been laid a thousand years ago, thought Stark. Everywhere, rows of high, free-standing wooden shelving, upon which, cardboard boxes, forming a maze of narrow aisles. Each box had a coloured label with letters and numbers. The room smelled damp and musty. Stark noted cobwebs. Jenny was right. It was summer, but here, in the basement, it felt like winter.

"It stretches the entire width and length of the building," said Jenny. "Which makes it rather large. We're in the process of committing files to a database. But we've got a hundred and fifty years of clients to go through. And it's all here. Everything we've ever done, from the day the firm started. We all take turns, when we get a chance. We come down, look through the files, make a record of the names, subject matter, and pack them in a box. Then they're sent off to be uploaded, and then destroyed."

"Sounds fun," said Stark.

Jenny shivered. "Fun it ain't." She made a show of looking about. "As I said, creepy. I used to come down after work for an hour. But there's too many dark corners." She gave a strained laugh. "And if there's no one about, who would hear me scream?"

"*Murder in the Basement.* Would be a good name for a book."

"As long as it's not me getting murdered. I'm sorry to say, as our brand-new fledgling trainee solicitor, you'll be spending more time than most down here." Another laugh. "Part of your induction."

"Perhaps I should come to work in jeans and a hoodie."

"Good idea. And thermals. I should mention, this place has a name."

"A name?"

"We call it *The Dungeon.*"

CHAPTER SEVENTEEN

As Stark was being given the guided tour of the basement, on the first floor, Bronson Chapel was in a state of anxiety. As anticipated, when he had informed his client they had to meet urgently, he knew she would demand an immediate appointment. Which she did. Only natural. Anyone getting an unexpected and somewhat cryptic call from their lawyer would want to find out what the hell was going on, and pretty damned quickly. He'd spoken to her on Friday. He'd hinted of urgency, and potential trouble. Enough to get her worried. He didn't want to arrange anything over the weekend. That wouldn't look good. It would smack of desperation. But an appointment, in his office, first thing on Monday morning – that, in Bronson's view, was the best approach. Here, in the cloistered confines of Stoddart, Jeffrey, Pritchard and Sloss, he was in secure territory. *His* territory, where he felt emboldened.

And now was the moment to be bold. For extra oomph, he had taken a line of purest cocaine. His supply was running low. He vowed, as soon as he got the money together, he would buy enough for a year. His brain buzzed. His heart pumped hard and fast, pounding like a drum in his ears. Sweat dribbled into his eyes. *Not a good look,* he thought. Like all the partner's offices, there was a small en suite bathroom. Functional. Sink, toilet. He went to the sink, splashed his face with cold water. He was about to embark on a course from which there was no return. There was still time. He could turn back. He could run away. Hide. But there was no hiding place from the men he did business with. Their world was one of brutality and pain. His was the opposite end of the spectrum. Law books and civilised discourse and reasoned arguments before a judge.

He could run to the police. He laughed out loud at the thought. He had nothing to go to them with. He bought drugs from a man called Billy Watson. He wasn't even sure that was his real name. Billy Watson would deny. Deny everything. Deny the threat made on the phone. Deny, deny, deny. And then? Back to brutality and pain, only a hundred times worse.

Plus, at the end of the day, cutting through all the bullshit, Bronson wanted desperately to pay Billy Watson, because if he did that, he would get his supply back again. Because Bronson was an addict.

He gazed at his reflection in the mirror above the sink, and wondered, for a brief second, just who the hell he had become. For a brief second only. He forced himself to dispel such maudlin thoughts. He had to focus on the moment. Focus on what he was about to do. The coke gave him clarity. The coke gave him strength.

He dabbed his face with a towel. He opened a small unit on the wall, where he kept some expensive eau de cologne. He sprayed his neck, cheeks, his hands, which he ran through his hair. It was 9am. His client was exact about punctuality.

On cue, his phone bleeped. He took a breath, collected his thoughts, went back through to his office, answered.

"Mrs Shawbridge is here for her nine o'clock appointment."

He licked his lips with the tip of his tongue. He could taste the cologne.

"Please ask her up."

"Yes, Mr Chapel."

He sat behind his desk. He placed his mobile phone on the desktop. He waited. His heart thrummed, fast as a racehorse, and suddenly he was scared shitless, not because of the terrible thing he was about to do, but rather, if it failed, he would have no money to buy his next fix.

A minute passed. Two. There was a knock on his door.

Mrs Shawbridge entered.

CHAPTER EIGHTEEN

A press conference was held at 11am that morning. In attendance, Chief Constable Robert Blakely – the man in charge of Police Scotland – and Detective Chief Inspector Harry McGuigan. The venue was a function hall forming part of Hampden Stadium, chosen because parking was easy, and congestion could be controlled. This wasn't the first such conference. Over the last five years – the period The Surgeon had so far been active – there had been five. Each similar, to the extent they did not reveal anything new to the public, which only heightened the perception the police were incompetent. It was an embarrassment. Plus, it was political. The previous chief constable and deputy chief constable had both been sacked over it. A *new broom* had been appointed, all guns blazing, a firebrand, promising overhauls and shake-ups and radical changes, and most importantly, results.

Which was three years ago. And so far, zilch results. The new – *not so new,* mused McGuigan – chief constable was staring into oblivion. Now however they had a real lead. Something substantive to show, and as soon as the chief constable was made aware of the development, he called the press conference with a renewed and shining confidence.

McGuigan watched the congregated mass before him. The place was packed. All seats were full. Reporters, cameramen. If they didn't have a seat, they stood, along each side, and at the back. Media from all over the world. Same old faces, thought McGuigan. And some new faces. Five years. The world kept spinning. People had retired, died, changed jobs, moved on, got married, had kids, got divorced. Human life fluctuated, changed, went through a million permutations. But one constant throughout was the psychopath named The Surgeon. Every year, he raised his head, reminding people with a jolly wave and a dreadful deed. *Still here,* he was saying. *See you next time. Love you.*

McGuigan heaved a sigh. He was bone weary. Weary to the core. He was sick of the circus. Sick of the murders. Sick to death. But they had a lead. Which was more than they ever had. He ought to have been positive. Pleased, almost. He glanced at the chief constable at his side, who was most definitely pleased, and who appeared to have forgotten a young woman horrifyingly mutilated, and two men shot to death.

It was all politics. All fucking politics.

Behind them, on the wall, hung a huge photograph of the photofit likeness of the killer, as described by the lawyer called Bronson Chapel. McGuigan craned his head round, and for the hundredth time, gazed at the face staring back out at the press. There it was. The face of a psychopath. And yet… McGuigan experienced a niggle. A flicker of doubt. He'd been a cop all his life, and a damned good one, and somehow, something didn't seem right. He had a feeling. A bad feeling. He felt it deep in his bones, in his gut. Something vague and insubstantial. But persistent. A feeling that wouldn't go away.

Chief Constable Robert Blakely spoke into a microphone. He was a man in his early fifties, lean as a whippet, balding grey hair. Significantly greyer than when he was first given the job. The pallor of his skin was grey too, his eyes dark and brooding. A tired reflection of the man brought in to sort things out. *That's another thing,* reflected McGuigan. *Our neighbourhood psychopath had the ability to age people. Surely this man is magical.*

"Thank you for coming at such short notice," Blakely said. His voice was low and soulful. He waited for the general rumble of activity to quieten to silence. Tension was wire tight. Lenses focused, cameras flashed, tape recorders clicked on, notepads were opened. No one spoke.

"You will all be aware of the dreadful events which took place last week. For the record, three people were killed in a house on Kelvinside Gardens, in Glasgow's west end. We believe, given the circumstances, this was perpetrated by the same individual who has carried out several attacks over the last few years."

Several. Few. McGuigan found the descriptions almost humorous. More like ten, over five years. And more than *attacks.* More like goddamned mutilations both bizarre and grotesque, beyond the imagination of any sane person. The bullshit was flowing, and the chief had only started. McGuigan could hardly blame him.

"However," continued the chief, "thanks to robust and dedicated detective work..." *Jesus.* "...we believe we have a major breakthrough. The picture behind you is an accurate representation of a man we would like to question in connection with the attacks. I'm appealing to the public. To anyone watching this. Please consider the face carefully. If you think you know this person, then it's important you speak to us, any time, day or night. Please come forward. This man, we believe, is dangerous. He is not to be approached."

A pause. Then, "If you have any questions, then please ask. I'll hand you over to Detective Chief Inspector McGuigan, who is in charge of this investigation, and who can provide you with any relevant details."

Gee – thanks a bunch. Talk about arse covering.

McGuigan stood, assumed a solemn face. He was hit with a barrage of sudden noise. A hundred people all talking at once. All talking to him. *At him.* He pointed to a young woman on the front row, who immediately asked the inevitable question.

"Were these murders committed by The Surgeon?"

"This is a name concocted by the tabloid press. I would say the recent killings bear a resemblance to previous incidents."

"What type of resemblance?" came another voice from the front row. *Why ask that?* McGuigan wondered. They already knew the peccadillos of the killer. Hence The Surgeon. The ghoulish nature of the media. Everybody loved the macabre.

"I'm not at liberty to say." *Stock answer.* "But there are definite similarities."

"Are the police sure that's the picture of the killer?" came another voice.

No, we're not.

"As sure as we can be."

"What does that mean, exactly?"

An obtuse question, thought McGuigan. *What the hell did he think it means? Absolutely nothing.*

"With the information we have, this seems a reasonably accurate picture of the killer's face. I would also like to mention, we think the attacker was wearing a blue 'boiler suit'-type garment. The type a tradesman might wear. Also, we believe he was possibly driving a white van."

Another voice – "Do you think the attacker knew his victims?"

"Our investigations are continuing."

Another – "With respect, investigations have been continuing for the last five years. Are the police any closer to catching this person?"

Not really.

"I believe we are."

Another voice piped up, from the back, and asked the question he knew he would be asked, and the one he dreaded.

"There's a strong public perception that the police are out of their depth. That they simply do not have the resources, or the ability, to catch this man. What do you say to that, Chief Inspector?"

What the hell do you want me to say! That it's true? That this guy's running circles round us? That we're incompetent?

McGuigan glanced down at his chief, who sat, rigid, staring stonily ahead, face set.

Thanks again.

"I want to say to the public that we are doing our utmost to catch this individual. And make no mistake, he will be caught. We are focused, and determined. We're getting closer." *Another stock cliché coming up.* "We're leaving no stone unturned." As soon as he said it, he wished he hadn't. It sounded trite and superficial. And pathetic.

"You said that five years ago," shouted a man from somewhere in the middle.

McGuigan offered no response. The man was right. There was little argument to the accusation.

"What do you have to say to the families of the victims? With still no closure after such a lengthy period?"

McGuigan swallowed, tried to think of a reply which was not inane and insulting. The chief constable stood, at last.

"Our liaison officers work closely with the families," he said. "Now, I would again like to thank you for coming. Once more, we would ask you look closely at the picture, and if you think you have seen this person, or know this person, then please contact us. Any information, however small, might be vital in apprehending this man. Thank you."

The conference was over. Blakely left, via a side door, McGuigan following, emerging into a corridor, at the end of which, an exit, where Blakely's car waited. As soon as the door was closed, Blakely turned, leaned in close, his voice low and harsh.

"What is it with you, McGuigan?"

McGuigan frowned. "I'm not sure I follow, sir."

"Follow this. You're out there, speaking to the press like a bloody robot. Unconvincing. Paying lip service. If you're trying to calm the population, then I suggest you up your game, and at least sound like you believe what you're saying. Because if you don't, you can bet your bottom fucking dollar, no one else will. You get the gist of what I'm saying? You follow now?"

"Apologies, sir. I hadn't realised this was about me."

The chief's eyes narrowed. "Your sarcasm stretches so far. Then it hangs you. Make no mistake. We look like bloody fools. I'll not have it. Not on my watch." He leaned in close, an inch away. McGuigan got the faint whiff of aftershave. *Old Spice?* Surely not.

"I'll not go down over this," Blakely hissed. "Shape up. Look the fucking part. Next time we arrange one of these circus sideshows, I'll be expecting to tell the world we've caught this psycho. And get this into your head, McGuigan."

"Yes, sir?"

"This isn't about you. It's about me."

He turned away, marched off.

McGuigan watched him go. And then, suddenly, the flicker sparked into a flame. A brief bright moment of intuition.

He tapped the screen of his mobile, got Kenny Dawson's number.

"It's the photofit," he said. "I know what's wrong."

"Which is?"

"Let's renew our acquaintance with Bronson Chapel."

CHAPTER NINETEEN

He turned the television off. He phoned the number he always phoned. It was picked up immediately, the voice answering hard and flat –

"You've seen it?"

"I'm not understanding," he said. "It makes no sense."

"You were careless. Worse than careless. Complacent." A silence, save the sound of breathing. He said nothing. He waited. He was filled with self-loathing. The voice continued, every word a lash –

"You're shameful. You're an embarrassment. Always you seek to disappoint me. And always you succeed."

He found his voice. "Sorry." He bit his lip. He truly was sorry. He felt like sobbing. He held his tears in, requiring effort. He swallowed, tried to contain his emotion.

"But I'm not understanding," he said. His tone was like a whine, which made him feel worse. "The picture they've got makes no sense. What does it mean?"

The voice did not answer immediately. He waited.

"I don't know."

His heart caught. So strange and terrifying to hear those words.

"What will I do?"

"How can you ask this?" the voice rasped. "Your stupidity offends me. Is that what you're doing? Are you trying to offend me?"

He swallowed again, hard, took a second to answer, though his voice faltered.

"No."

"You still haven't found her. You keep going, until I say. You understand? Next time, no mistakes. You don't want to disappoint me again. You know how much I hate it when you disappoint me."

He felt crushed. "I'm sorry. Please forgive me." Again, a staggering breath, to contain the tears. But the tears came.

The voice suddenly soothed. "You're forgiven."

A surge of joy. Though the fear remained. "But the picture they've got. It makes no sense."

"I know." A pause, then – "A storm is brewing."

"Please say you'll sort it."

"Of course. I sort everything."

"I love you."

"I love you too."

The phone disconnected.

A storm is brewing. For the first time in five years, he felt scared.

CHAPTER TWENTY

TUESDAY

Stark was thrust into the action from the outset. He had been provided with his own email address. He discovered email was the main mode of communication. The art of oral conversation, within the legal fraternity, was dead. As it was with most of Western civilisation.

"Remember," Jenny had said, "the shit flows in a downward direction."

Her words proved accurate. Monday, he was asked to review a commercial lease for new tenants in a shopping complex, provide detailed notes and observations, and submit them to one of the property partners. Over fifty pages. Plus, another partner had emailed him details of a somewhat complex will for an elderly client, and asked him to cobble it together for that afternoon. Then another, requesting a power of attorney. Stark received much needed help from Jenny, who supplied him with files from which he could extract relevant information. Also, he had visited the library. Jenny was right. It was large and well stocked. Easily as good as any university law library. Stark was impressed. He had worked until 7.30pm, had gone home in a state of exhaustion, and was asleep by 8.30. This time, no nightmares of suffocating in a tomb. Rather, a deep and dreamless sleep.

On Tuesday morning, he got an internal call from reception.

"Paul Hutchison would like to see you in his office."

Stark hesitated. "Of course."

Four yards away, Jenny sat at her desk, books piled round her like a fortification, preparing for a court case that afternoon. Acting for a major bank, which was suing another firm of lawyers for negligence. *Complicated and unpleasant,* she had described it. No lawyer wants to sue another lawyer, she'd explained. Except *SJPS,* of course, who would do anything if the money was right.

She was stressed. He discovered, in such moments, her swearing intensified. *Cute,* he thought. She was human. An uncommon quality in most lawyers.

"I've just had a call from reception," he said, "who got a call from Paul Hutchison, who must have asked them to call me, to ask me to go up to his office."

She was scribbling into a notepad. "That's a lot of asks."

"Why couldn't he just phone me? Isn't that the normal course of behaviour?"

"Fuck him," she said simply. "The man's an enigma."

"An enigma?"

She looked up, sat back, clasped her hands behind her head. "There are three managing partners in the firm. They each head their own department. You met them at your interview. There's Winnifred Marshall. Shrewd as a lynx. Got caught up in a messy divorce some years back, and carries a wedge of bitterness in her handbag. Don't be fooled by her soft exterior. She's as hard as nails. Everything is calculated with dear old Winnifred. She has as much empathy as a wasp."

"Then there's Walter Hill. Smooth as silk. Cool and slippery. Knows everything there is about commercial law. It's said he was involved in a scandal twenty years ago. Money went missing.

Fingers were pointed, primarily in his direction. Nothing proved, but the smell lingers. A sadistic little shit. He owns land up in some bleak, shitty part of the Highlands and likes to hunt animals with his big guns, for the sheer thrill of seeing their blood.'

"And then there's Paul Hutchison. A curmudgeon in the courtroom. But an enigma. Most people – normal people that is – have good days and bad. He's on a permanent bad day. If you could get a diploma for acting like a right proper bastard, he'd get a diploma with a fucking gold star and a plastic whistle."

"Plastic whistle. I wasn't aware that was a thing."

She managed a tight smile. "Sorry, Jonathan. I shouldn't speak like that about others in the firm. But you've obviously met him."

"Yes."

"Then you know what I'm talking about. A right proper bastard. Other than being breathtakingly arrogant, rude, ignorant, condescending, and generally unappealing, both to look at and to listen to, he's a perfect gentleman. Oh! Did I mention he was a fucking bully? Good luck."

Stark laughed. "Thanks for that. Excellent pep talk. Next time, please tell it like it is."

She laughed back. "I try not to be judgemental. Now I've got a fucking court case in three hours."

Stark made his way to the reception area, through the clients' waiting room. A half-dozen people were sitting, respectfully silent and solemn, presumably booked in for early morning appointments. He passed the front desk, to make his way up the stairs to the first level. Two men stood, addressing the receptionists. Suited, unsmiling. *Intense,* thought Stark. One older, maybe in his mid-fifties. Pale complexion. Craggy features. Hair cropped short at the sides, a grey bristle on top. He caught a snippet of the conversation. The older man was speaking –

"...Detective Chief Inspector McGuigan. And this is Detective Sergeant Dawson. Do you know when he'll be in..."

The older man's gaze, briefly, hovered past the receptionist, and for a second, he locked eyes with Stark. Stark faltered. A sudden image, unbidden, reared up in his mind. Clear and sharp, present for an instant, then gone –

A house of grey stone, beneath a hill, under a grey sky, in a barren grey landscape.

Stark reached out, grabbed the banister on the stairs, steadied himself. Déjà vu? A trick of the mind? The other man gave a polite tilt of his head. Stark reciprocated, turned, made his way up the stairs, grasping to understand what had happened, but reaching no conclusion, thrust it from his thoughts. He had a meeting with Paul Hutchison – *the perfect gentleman* – to distract him.

CHAPTER TWENTY-ONE

McGuigan, along with Dawson, had gone to the offices of SJPS to speak to Bronson Chapel once again, to be informed that he hadn't arrived.

"When does he usually get in?" McGuigan had enquired.

The receptionist had reacted with a frown. "Nine. He's rarely later."

"Can you phone him?"

"Of course." Bronson's mobile had gone to voicemail.

"Do you mind if we wait for him?"

"Of course not. I'm sure he'll be in shortly. There's fresh coffee, if you'd like."

"Thank you."

They went through to the waiting room. They each got coffee from the machine, sat on plush chairs.

They regarded the painting opposite, taking up almost entirely one wall.

"Impressive…" remarked Dawson, cocking his head to one side as he studied it. "…I think."

"The artist is trying to tell us something."

Dawson looked at McGuigan curiously. "Which is?"

"What every artist tries to tell. The truth, I suspect."

Dawson took a deep breath. "You're becoming very philosophical in your old age."

McGuigan responded with a wry smile. "I'm not that old, despite how I look. The 'truth' is what we're all looking for, don't you think?"

"It would be nice if more people chose to tell it."

"And our friend Bronson Chapel. I wonder how he feels about the notion of truth."

"Which leads us nicely to the subject," said Dawson. "Not only are you turning philosophical, but cryptic. What's so special about Chapel? He's our star witness. And if you don't mind me asking, why exactly are we here? It would be nice if you shared your thoughts occasionally."

McGuigan folded his arms, absorbed in the painting, said, "The photofit. What did you make of it?"

Dawson furrowed his brow, obviously puzzled. "It's just a man's face. What am I supposed to make of it?"

"But have you ever seen a face quite like that?"

Dawson seemed to consider. "I suppose there were no particularly distinguishing features. What am I missing?"

"No distinguishing features," echoed McGuigan. "There you are. But I would go a stage further. The face in the photofit is *perfect.* Hollywood movie-star perfect. Too perfect, for my liking. Too… *artificial.* If that makes sense. It's the face of a model, not a psychopath."

Dawson gave an incredulous laugh. "Can't models be psychopaths?"

"I suppose they can."

Dawson sighed. "You're just jealous."

McGuigan chuckled. "Perhaps."

"And," continued Dawson, "with all due respect, and speaking as a friend, it looks – dare I say it – like you're reaching. People's recollections are often inaccurate. Or just plain wrong. But of course, we're skipping round the elephant in the room."

"Yes?"

"That Bronson Chapel is good at remembering faces, and the description he gave is entirely accurate."

"Perhaps. Possibly. Probably. But I look at that photofit, and then I think back to Bronson, sitting in the interview room, keen as mustard, all charged up, and something's *off.* Something which belongs in my *niggling doubt* category. He doesn't look to me like a man who'll forget a face. He looks like a man who remembers everything. But yet the face doesn't fit."

Now it was Dawson's turn to fold his arms, as he fixed his attention back on the painting on the wall.

"I still don't get it."

"The painting or my niggling doubt."

"Both. The question, ultimately, is why? Why would Bronson want to give us the wrong description?"

"Why indeed."

They sat in silence. Then Dawson spoke.

"I know what this is about."

"Enlighten me, please."

"You just hate lawyers."

Another chuckle. "I'm only human."

A half hour passed, and Bronson Chapel still hadn't appeared. They went back to the reception desk, got Bronson's mobile number. They left their cards, asked the receptionist to pass a message on to Bronson when he arrived, that they would like him to call, then left the law offices of SJPS.

They made their way to their car, parked on the street adjacent to the building, behind an ancient Nissan Micra, bright red, significantly battered, riven with rust, its exhaust, so they noted, held in place by loops of string.

"That must be illegal," remarked Dawson.

"I can think of worse things."

McGuigan unwrapped some pink bubblegum and popped it in his mouth. He chewed on it thoughtfully. "Find out where our friend Bronson lives. Perhaps we ought to pay him a visit."

"I don't think that'll take us very far."

"From where I'm standing," replied McGuigan, "any distance will do."

CHAPTER TWENTY-TWO

Stark got to the first floor. Each of the doors on the corridors had little bronze nameplates. Paul Hutchison's office was not hard to find.

He knocked, entered. The room was spacious. A large desk occupied the far wall, upon which, a general muddle of papers. Behind sat Paul Hutchison. The smell of the place was reminiscent of a Burger King. He appeared to be eating something from a Styrofoam food carton, hooking food into his mouth with a plastic fork, some of which missed, trailing down his chin, falling onto the desk top. Looked like scrambled eggs. He glanced up at Stark, pointed to a chair on the opposite side of the desk, continued eating. Stark said nothing, trying to maintain a degree of dignity, approached, and sat. Hutchison didn't look up, concentrating on the contents of the food carton. He continued this for twenty seconds. Stark counted. He finished, closed the carton, tossed it into a metal bin. He reached for a plastic coffee cup, took a slurp, then brought his attention to Stark.

"You're probably wondering why I asked you up here," he said. Stark tried hard to ignore a sliver of egg on the side of

Hutchison's mouth. Stark had no opportunity to respond. Hutchison answered for him.

"You may have guessed from your interview, I'm not your number one fan." Another slurp of coffee, then, "I'd like you to know, the situation remains the same."

Stark said nothing.

"I have a talent, Stark. A special talent. Call it a gift. Do you want to know what it is?"

Stark said nothing.

"Let me tell you. I can see through people."

He paused, obviously wishing the words to sink in. He stared at Stark with his round, moist unblinking eyes. *Definitely like a lizard.*

"It's a useful ability to have," he continued. "Being a court litigator. Understanding the opposition. Reading the signs. Gauging weaknesses, measuring vulnerabilities. Knowing the buttons to press, and when to press them. You understand how advantageous it is to have such a talent, yes?"

Stark remained silent, wondering where the hell this was going.

Hutchison went on, seemingly unperturbed by Stark's lack of response.

"And here's the thing." He put both elbows on the table, leaned his heavy shoulders forward. The table creaked. "I can see through *you.*"

Stark didn't reply. There was nothing he could think of to say. Hutchison continued, clearly on a roll.

"You're not a right fit for this firm. We don't like people with a past. Because people with a past always drag it into the present. When that happens, things start to go wrong. Work becomes secondary. Suddenly, the issues these people have are paramount, to the exclusion of everything else. In a nutshell, you're damaged goods. Those are your words. *Damaged goods.* And I don't trade with damaged goods. Damaged goods need to be returned, to whatever shithole they came from. You get the drift, Stark. It's not personal. I just don't think I can trust you to do the job I would expect you to do. I think you're going to let the firm down."

Stark sat, motionless.

"In conclusion," said Hutchison, "I don't want you here. And people I don't want here don't tend to last long. Perhaps, to save yourself grief and worry, you might want to think about your future, and what you're going to do with it." He leaned back in his chair, curling his mouth into a wintry smile. "Any comments, Stark?"

Stark nodded slowly. He stood, reached into his trouser pocket, pulled out a paper napkin he'd got with his early morning coffee, tossed it onto the desk, and said, "You've got egg on your chin."

CHAPTER TWENTY-THREE

Billy Watson phoned Bronson, ostensibly to remind him of their meeting that evening, but in reality, to crank up the fear factor. A man terrified was considerably more pliant. And Billy Watson needed Bronson terrified. Watson was adept at such matters, having spent a good portion of his life travelling a path darker than most. Extortion, drug dealing, violence. He was a master. The risks were high, but the profits were exceptional. Plus, it was a thrill.

But Bronson didn't pick up the phone. Answer machine again, which caused Watson irritation.

"Perhaps he's done a runner," remarked Frank, who was never far from Watson's side. They sat in a coffee shop in Glasgow's Victoria Road. Tables had been set outside on the pavement, and the place was busy. It was late Tuesday morning, and the streets were warm. They sat, sipping cappuccinos, at ease in their surroundings, dressed in casual designer gear, enjoying the sun, taking in the view. Men of leisure. At first glance, a couple of tourists, enjoying the day.

"Perhaps," replied Watson. "It's a possibility. Remote, I think. Where would he go? His life is here. Everything he has.

Everything he knows. And let's not forget, we supply him with a product which, for a man like Bronson, is the most important thing in the world. He can never stray far from it. He might think he can, but in the end, it sucks him back."

Frank appeared unconvinced.

"He's scared shitless. If it were me, I'd get the hell out."

"But Bronson isn't you. Bronson isn't even himself." His eyes gleamed as he spoke. "Bronson belongs to me. And everything he has is mine."

Frank laughed: a heavy booming sound. People at adjacent tables looked round.

"Even his soul?"

"Especially his soul."

CHAPTER TWENTY-FOUR

Stark spent the afternoon submerged in work. The conversation with Hutchison had irked him, but little more, and he had dismissed it from his mind. Stark had encountered worse. Five years before, he'd been shot in the head and left for dead. In the great scale of things, a few mildly threatening words from an overweight arsehole were of little consequence.

Jenny was gone for the afternoon. He had the office to himself. He had been asked to look up obscure points of law, and check through a bunch of title deeds. Laborious, but part of the job. Typical stuff for a trainee to wade through. Stuff associates and partners loved to delegate. Stark expected no less. He gave a rueful smile. *Shit flows down,* Jenny had said. And she was bang on target.

At 4.30, someone – he didn't know who – knocked, popped their head round the door. A guy in his mid-thirties, a florid complexion, rough pockmarked cheeks – a legacy of old acne. A shock of red hair.

"Hi," he said. "I'm Des. I'm Edward Stoddart's personal assistant." He paused, perhaps for dramatic effect, as if the information he had imparted should be of great significance to Stark. Stark pretended to be impressed.

"Edward Stoddart. The senior partner. Goodness."

"The very one." He gave a mischievous grin. "I come with good news."

"Really?"

"Not really. Files have to be packed up in the basement. At the far end, on the shelf marked 'C'. Record the names of the client and subject matter in the book on the table. It's alphabetical. Then stick the files in the blue boxes. Try and fill two up. Command from above."

"Roger that," said Stark, with a sigh. Any thoughts of leaving at five were dashed. *Shit flows down.*

"Good to meet you," said Des. He disappeared, then a second later, his head reappeared. "Forgot to say. Mr Stoddart would like you to join him for lunch tomorrow. 1pm."

Stark blinked. This time, the words really did have dramatic effect. "Of course. Where?"

"Where else?" replied Des, as if the answer to the question was so obvious, the question ought not to have been asked. "At his place."

"His place?"

"The top floor. Catch up soon."

The door closed. Stark, somewhat bemused, wondered what it meant. *Asked for lunch by the senior partner on my second day of employment.* Strange times. His mind prickled with concern. It might mean nothing. On the other hand, it might mean everything.

CHAPTER TWENTY-FIVE

THE BEGINNING

The Dungeon.

Stark went down at 5.30. He switched the lights on, but the lighting was poor, and flickered in some sections. He thought, jokingly, it was like descending into a movie set designed exclusively for slasher horror. The joke stopped when he reached the bottom of the stairs.

Jenny was right. It seemed to form the entire length and breadth of the building. Corridors, passages, lanes, all created from shelves lined with boxes. In each box, a minor history of legal matters. Sales, purchases. Commercial transactions. Leases. Divorces. Separations. Disputes. Litigation. Every conceivable legal situation. Including death – wills, estates. A smorgasbord of stuff.

Stark followed the instruction given by Des, as best he could. *At the far end.* He hadn't been any more specific, and Stark hadn't asked for clarification. *Which end?* The place was massive.

There – the table with the record book. The book wasn't a book. Much more. It was a tome. Thick as an outstretched hand. Stark suddenly felt he was in an odd Dickensian world, where computers didn't exist, the handwritten word being the only mode of communication. He picked it up, tucked it under his arm. It was like carrying a small vanity case.

Left or right? He had no idea. He went right. What the hell. He wound his way toward the "far end". Here, the striplighting seemed to fade, as if on the verge of dying, but clinging on. A weak vestigial source of illumination. A glow, rather than a full light. Stark understood the reluctance of Jenny – and no doubt others – to descend to this place, after work, to venture into a labyrinth of shadows and dust.

On the shelf marked "C". Des had been most specific. Stark scanned the shelves on either side. There! A postcard-sized plastic sheet, nailed into the wood, bearing one letter – C. Stark followed the passage to a far wall. There, empty blue plastic boxes piled up, waiting to be filled. Beside it, a metal stool. The glamorous side of the law, he thought ruefully.

Two boxes. It wouldn't take long. An hour tops. As a gesture, he might even do three. After all, what the hell else was he doing? His social calendar was a bleak affair.

He heaved a box off a middle shelf, heavy with files. The box was cardboard, and sagged with mould. He dropped it to the floor beside the stool, and sat, the record book on his lap. He reached down, pulled out the top file. The front bore a general description, written in felt pen –

Rebecca Chatham – sale of 29 Blair Avenue, Glasgow

He flicked through the contents. The file was over forty years old. He wondered, briefly, if Rebecca was alive or dead, where she'd gone, what had happened in her life. He would never know.

He recorded the details in the book, tossed the file in a blue box. Rebecca Chatham, destined for destruction.

Stark, hunched on the stool, ploughed through the files. Their age varied, ranging from ten to sixty years old, each dealing with different matters. Segments of strangers' lives. An hour passed. The second blue box was almost full. He abandoned the idea of doing another. The place was altogether too creepy to linger. One more file, he decided, then home.

He came to another, which puzzled him –

Debora Ferry – executory.

Put in the wrong box, he assumed. A misfile. Somebody didn't know their alphabet. He would leave it to the side. He hesitated. He was curious, for a reason he was unable to explain. It was coloured a deep and vibrant red, its texture embossed, suggesting a more expensive make. A file to catch the eye. He opened it.

The firm had dealt with the winding up of Debora Ferry's estate. She had died ten years ago. She was married. She had no children. She and her husband owned a house. Some small savings. No other assets. She had died relatively young – thirty-six. Her original death certificate was in the file. Stark gazed at it.

Cause of Death – Asphyxia by Hanging.

He touched the words gently with the tip of his finger. He could feel the faint imprint of the typing. His mouth felt dry. He swallowed. A noise, soft as a whisper, from the next aisle. The flutter of wings? He paused, remained still. The noise did not reoccur. Stark closed the file, laid it on the floor. He felt cold. The place had a bad feel. Beside him, two full blue boxes, as required. Time to get the hell out.

CHAPTER TWENTY-SIX

Bronson Chapel lived in a flat in a converted church a mile from the offices of SJPS, in the trendy west end. His address was not difficult to find. It was late afternoon. Before they set off, McGuigan had phoned both the law offices, and Bronson's mobile. The mobile went straight to answer machine. The receptionist at SJPS had put him through to Bronson's secretary, who had informed him that Bronson hadn't shown up for work, nor had he phoned in to say why.

"Perhaps he's working from home?" she'd suggested.

"Does he often do that?" he'd replied.

A pause, then, "Now that you mention it, he's never done it before."

"Was he due to see clients?"

Another pause. "Yes. He had a full day. We had to cancel them."

"Thank you."

From the police station, the journey would take about fifteen minutes. Dawson drove.

"Maybe he's ill," he ventured. "Or maybe he really is working from home. Maybe he decided just to take the day off. He's a partner. He can do what he wants. You don't think you're over-elaborating this situation?"

"That's a lot of maybes. My wife says exactly that. That I over-elaborate. That I think too much. Imagine that. Have you ever heard of anyone being blamed for thinking too much? Often the accusers are those who tend not to think at all. But of course, you're right. He could be in bed with a fever. Though not to call his work? Miss all those appointments without giving any reason? I'm not so sure." He gave his head a weary shake. "I'd like to speak to him again. To satisfy my *over-elaborate* mind."

Dawson blew through his lips. "I was only saying. It's just... I'm not sure of the road we're going down."

"Me neither," said McGuigan. "And to date, all the roads have one thing in common."

"What's that?"

"A dead end."

They got to Bronson's address. 10a Turnberry Avenue. It was 5.15. Despite being converted into flats, the building still resembled a church, complete with a small tower and steeple, and a high-peaked grey slate roof, and built with heavy blond sandstone. *Not inexpensive,* thought McGuigan. *The upkeep of the steeple alone would be a fortune.* The entrance was a mahogany wood door, Gothic, with large black iron brackets and fittings. Probably original, he mused. Required to be kept for tight planning laws. At one side, the door entry system. A metal rectangle of names, twelve in total, and beside each, a buzzer. Dawson pressed the one for *Chapel.*

They waited. No response. Dawson tried again. Nothing.

"No one's in," said Dawson.

"Or he's not answering. Try the rest."

Dawson drew a heavy sigh. It was clear from his demeanour

he thought the whole thing a wild waste of time. McGuigan felt inclined to agree. He had no solid idea why he wanted to talk to Bronson. To satisfy an itch which didn't want to go away. His *niggling doubt.*

Dawson pressed a number of buttons. A man's voice crackled.

"Yes?"

"Hello. Detective Sergeant Kenny Dawson looking for Bronson Chapel. Can you let us in?"

"The police?"

"Yes."

A pause. The door clicked. They entered. Bronson's flat was on the first of two floors. The interior was clean and simple. Smooth white walls, carpeted floor. In a corner, a table, upon which, a vase with fresh flowers.

There were six flats on the first floor. They got to Bronson's door. Dawson knocked. Nothing.

"Try again," said McGuigan.

Dawson knocked louder.

Silence. The place felt empty. The door to the neighbouring flat opened. A man appeared, possibly in his seventies, short and overweight, dressed in a loose pullover, baggy white joggers, slippers.

"You're the police?"

McGuigan was immediately interested.

"Indeed we are."

"You're looking for Bronson?"

"And you are?"

"Bert Biggins. Albert Biggins, if you want my Sunday name. I'm Bronson's neighbour. Lived here for ten years. Bought the place when I retired. Just after my wife died. One of the first to move in. What's he done?"

McGuigan assumed a knowing smile. "You'll be aware of all the comings and goings, I'll bet. You'll keep your ear to the ground, I'm sure."

Bobby sniffed. "It's a quiet place." He lowered his voice. "Except the young couple through the wall." He gave a lascivious wink. "Hammer and tongs. Oh! To have the energy again. Where does the time go!"

"And Bronson?"

The man took a step closer, as if to confide in sensitive information.

"Keeps himself to himself. Nice young man. He's a lawyer. Works for a fancy firm somewhere. You'll not find him. He's gone away."

"Gone away?"

"Yesterday afternoon. I was coming back from walking Parsley. I walk him four times a day. Once round the park across the road. That does him. That's the advantage of having a chihuahua. Short legs. They don't need much exercise." A hoarse chuckle. "Like a lot of women I know."

As if on cue, a dog began to bark from within the confines of Bert's flat – a jarring, high-pitched noise. McGuigan bit back his frustration.

"Bronson has gone away?"

"It sure looked like that. He had a small suitcase with him. Not a briefcase. *A suitcase.* I passed him in the corridor. I tried to strike up a conversation, to be polite you understand. He was rather rude. He barely said hello. Which was unusual. He's a chatty type, normally. The man was in a hurry. What's he done?"

"Did he happen to say where he was going?"

"As I said, the man was in a hurry." Another step closer. "You think the suitcase was full of money? I've heard of that. Lawyers running away with the client's money. Is that what he's done? I'll bet that's what he's done. Lawyers and politicians. Can't trust them."

The dog's barking continued. "Shut up, Parsley!" Bert raised his shoulders in resignation. "He doesn't stop, when he gets going. You might laugh, but chihuahuas make marvellous watch dogs. It's true. It's an established fact. They might be small, but by God, once they start, they never shut up."

Rather like its owner, thought McGuigan. "I'm sure. Did Bronson happen to mention where he was going?"

"As I said, he barely spoke. Couldn't wait to leave. Rude he was. What's happened to common courtesy? In my day, people had both the time and the decency to strike up some friendly chat. The art of conversation. When good neighbours looked out for each other. What's he up to? These lawyers. Crafty, yes?"

McGuigan handed him his card. "Should you see him, ask him to contact me. Better still, give me a phone when you see him next."

Parsley's barking seemed to raise a notch, perhaps irritated at the lack of attention.

"Say no more," said Bert. He stroked the tip of his nose with his index finger in a conspiratorial gesture. "Hush-hush."

"Thank you. You've been very helpful."

Bert nodded, made his way back into his flat. McGuigan and Dawson headed for the stairs.

Bert turned – "Did I mention the boat house?"

McGuigan stopped, looked back. "Pardon me?"

Bert spoke as if he were imparting information they ought to have known about. "Sure. The boat house."

McGuigan made his way back, Dawson following.

"Tell us about the boat house, Bert."

Bert puffed his chest, clearly enjoying the focus of attention.

"He has another place. Where he goes 'to get away from all his troubles'. He calls it the boat house. His 'little sanctuary'. His words. He told me once, he loves the sound of the water. Personally, I hate the sound. Makes me want to pee."

"He goes there often?" It was Dawson who asked the question.

Bert furrowed his brow, as if in deep contemplation. "Good question."

Parsley's barking continued, an incessant yelp.

"It's pretty regular," said Bert, at length. "Two weekends a month, I would say. Yes. Now I think of it, that sounds about right..."

McGuigan cut in. He sensed a long rambling monologue.

"Did he ever give you an address?"

Bert shook his head. "He never did. I never thought to ask." *Surprising,* thought McGuigan.

"Perhaps he mentioned a landmark. A place nearby he liked to visit. A restaurant maybe? Or a pub?"

"Nope. He just gave me the name. The boat house. And I suppose it must be close to the sea. Is that a clue?"

"Thank you, Bert. I think you'd better see to Parsley."

"It's his walkie time. He becomes crotchety if he thinks I've forgotten. Nothing worse than a crotchety chihuahua."

"I can imagine."

They left the building. McGuigan stopped, looked back, gazed at the architecture, those original parts which hadn't been changed – the tower and spire, the entrance. The overall shape remained – the nave, the transepts on either side.

"A hundred years ago, transforming a church into flats for the wealthy would have caused outrage. Now, the church can't wait to sell off their buildings and fill their coffers."

"Change," observed Dawson. "The world moves on."

"I go to church most Sundays," said McGuigan. He gave a rumbling chuckle. "Have I mentioned that? I've learned a lot about churches recently. This building for example. It's in the shape of a cross. The tower is always on the west end. And the north wall, in the old days, had a special door. This one will be bricked up, no doubt."

"A special door?"

"The Devil's door. Kept open during baptisms to let the evil spirits fly away. Do you believe in evil spirits, Dawson?"

Dawson pursed his lips. "I can't say I've given it a great deal of thought."

"I wonder if that was the root of the problem."

Dawson said nothing, waited. McGuigan gave a frosty smile.

"If the Devil's door was shut tight when our friend The Surgeon was baptised it would explain much." He drew a deep breath. "The boat house. Is that where Bronson's gone?"

"Could be. His *little sanctuary.* Maybe he had a tough time at work, and needed space. I can't see anything in it, sir. He escapes for a little while. Can't say I blame him. If that's where he is. But he could be anywhere."

"The sound of the sea. It's soothing, don't you think?" He turned away, started walking back to the car, Dawson at his side. "Find out where this 'boat house' is. Check the land register. Something will turn up."

Dawson shook his head. "I don't understand your interest in this man."

"He intrigues me. Plus, I think he's a liar."

CHAPTER TWENTY-SEVEN

Naked. This was how he presented himself, to those in the next room. *His special room.* And the excitement. Usually a force, hard as iron. Rock hard. But tonight, the excitement was muted. He opened the door. There were no windows. Here, the darkness was complete, like being blind.

He followed the ritual. He switched the light on. Suddenly the blindness was lifted, and there they were, in full view, visions of wonder. Before him, on one wall, framed in glittering silver, photographs, in neat rows and columns. Faces. Staring out. Staring at him. Exactly as it should be. He was their creator. He was their God. He had the power of death, and in death, he brought something new. A changing. A metamorphosis, from the grub to the butterfly. But each butterfly had proved short of the measure.

On another wall, a single portrait of a woman. Not a photograph. A painting. Completed with skill and attention. Unsmiling. Rather, a solemn, almost stern look. Face white as bone, eyes dark as obsidian, making for a startling contrast. Hair a cascade of silver-grey. Cheeks high and harsh, a wide mouth, lips two pink lines, set. Her nose perfectly centred. Her brow unblemished. A face caught in a frozen moment in time. Often he pondered her expression, and often he arrived at the same conclusion –

Accusatory.

In his hand, a framed photograph of his latest attempt. He hung it beside the others, stepped back. At the time, he thought his modifications were as close as they had ever been. Now, on comparison, he saw how the face he had endeavoured to create was a poor imitation.

He saw how he had failed. A tweak around the eyes, a scrape of bone on the chin, a reduction of the cheeks. Next time, perhaps, he would do better.

If there was a next time. The fear returned. It had never really gone away. Someone had seen him. Someone had taken a photo of him with their phone, as he was leaving the house. He had witnessed this with his own eyes. *Careless. Shameful.* And yet the police had not presented the photo at the press meeting, nor did the photofit bear any resemblance. It made no sense. This scared him the most. Not understanding.

A storm is brewing.

The excitement dissipated to nothing. In its place, a great yawning terror. He turned the light out, left the room, stood in his hallway, swaying on his feet. His hands trembled. His lungs burned, his breathing felt tight, constricted. He collapsed to his knees. His chest spasmed. He began to cry. Great racking sobs. He beat the floorboards with his fists. Hard and furious, a constant motion, like firing pistons, up and down, until the skin burst and the knuckles bled. But the pain was nothing, swallowed up by his fear and self-loathing. *Careless. Shameful.*

Time passed. His tears subsided. He got to his feet, gathered himself, regulated his breathing, padded through to his bedroom. His clothes lay spread on the bed, in an orderly fashion. It was then he became aware of the blood. And the pain. He raised his hands. His right hand was bruised and cut, but functioning. His left hand was puffed and bloody, and he realised, as he tried to move his fingers, it was broken.

One hour later.

The pain was too much to endure. He drove, with a little difficulty, to the nearest hospital, to Accident and Emergency at Hairmyres Hospital. A ten-mile drive from his house deep in the Eaglesham Moors. It was 9pm. The place was busy. The waiting room was full. He gave his details to the receptionist – name, address, date of birth. She asked him briefly the gist of the problem. He raised his hand. It was swollen to double the size, like a pink club. She raised an eyebrow. "Looks nasty," she said. "We'll try and get you seen quickly."

He found a seat. The room, despite being busy, was virtually silent. The faint smell of booze tinged the air. People pissed, fallen or slipped or in a fight, now waiting in a hospital. This was a place where no one wanted to be. Conversation was muted and sullen. He ensured he didn't meet anyone's inquisitive gaze. He kept his hand under his jacket. Already his mind was churning, planning. Thoughts tumbled in his head.

His latest project – Evelyn Stephens – was, he had thought, perfect. Now, on hindsight, he had been way off the mark. Six months wasted. But wasn't it always so? He thought, with a sudden tingle of dread, he might never find the right person. That no matter how many times he employed his skills, he might never produce an acceptable result.

He thrust such thoughts from his mind. He had disappointed. He had to show he was capable. That he was not incompetent. The next one would be much quicker. He would recreate an image so perfect, he would be showered with praise.

An hour passed. His hand was numb. His name was called.

Quicker than he had expected. Other patients watched him askance, vexed that he'd got the green light before them.

He made his way through double doors, to a passage, then another set, into a second reception area, open plan, beyond which, a long corridor with cubicles on either side, each cubicle curtained off. A young nurse met him, directed him to the reception desk. His name was taken again. The nurse escorted him to cubicle '6'. She whisked open the blue plastic curtain. There – a bed, with a machine on one side, and a chair.

The nurse beckoned him to the bed.

"The doctor will be with you soon. Can you take your jacket off?"

"Of course."

The process was awkward. The nurse helped him. She tugged the sleeve gently over his hand.

"That looks a sore one," she commented. "What happened?"

"Slipped. I was... careless."

Her lips twitched into a small smile.

"Accidents happen. No reason to blame yourself." *Ah, but I do.*

The nurse left. She kept the curtains open. He got up, and pulled them shut.

Ten minutes later.

The curtain swept open.

She entered.

He saw her, and his heart soared. Suddenly, the past was forgotten. Everything was forgotten. His existence was diluted down to this one moment, and nothing else in the world mattered.

Her hair, her face, her neck. Her posture. Everything was exactly as it should be. And her smile. She smiled when she saw him, and her smile was perfect. Her gaze immediately focused on his hand.

"Wow," she said. "That's a beauty."

You're a beauty.

He raised his swollen hand, smiled back, apologetically. He felt tongue-tied. The excitement he thought he had lost returned, threefold. He could barely think. He tried to speak, but his throat was dry, his breath short.

She came closer, touched his hand with a tenderness no one had ever shown him. Her body was only inches from his. The scent of her perfume suffused the air, intoxicating. She studied his hand, and he studied her.

Maybe just the tiniest of changes, he thought. *Maybe a tweak round the corners of her eyes. Maybe a tiny fraction off her nose.*

"Can you move your fingers?" she asked.

He found his voice. More of a low whisper.

"No… it's too painful."

She stepped back, still smiling, and met his eyes. His excitement heightened.

"What happened?"

"Slipped," he said. "In the garden. On some slabs. Silly me."

"Are you right or left-handed?"

"Right-handed."

"Just as well. I have a strong suspicion your left hand is going to be out of action for a while."

He said nothing. *Yes – a sliver of bone off her nose, and perhaps a shade off her cheeks. But not much. A skim, no more.* His thoughts drifted to the type of blade he might use.

"You okay?" she asked.

He blinked. "Sorry. I never heard you."

Her smile never left. "I asked you what you did for a living. Your occupation?"

"I'm… between jobs. So to speak."

"Sure. I'm going to get you a wheelchair, and someone's going to take you to get that hand X-rayed. Then we'll see what we do next. Good?"

He nodded. "All good. I'd like to say, Dr…?"

"Doctor Sinclair."

"I'd like to say, Doctor Sinclair, you've been very kind."

"Don't mention it. Let's concentrate on getting you fixed up."

She left the cubicle.

Sinclair.

He had a name. A name was all he needed.

CHAPTER TWENTY-EIGHT

Deborah Ferry – Asphyxia by Hanging

Stark got back to his flat at around 7 that evening. He had picked up a Chinese takeaway on his way home, emptied the contents into a bowl, stuck it in the microwave, then realised he wasn't hungry. He pushed it to one side, decided to phone his sister. It went to voicemail. She would be working. A junior doctor on the A and E ward worked a million hours a week. The ability to function without sleep with nerves shredded to the bare wire were prerequisites of the job.

She was a goddamned warrior, and he loved her for it.

He slung his jacket over the kitchen chair, slipped his shoes off, tossed them into a corner, and slumped on his ancient settee. He looked about for the TV remote. It was nowhere in view. He realised dismally it had doubtless slipped down the side of the couch somewhere, but he couldn't be bothered either searching for it, or shifting off his backside to press the "on" switch. He sat, in a weary daze, on the verge of drifting into a doze. His exhaustion was not physical. It was purely mental. He had been working for the last few months in a bottling warehouse, from eight until six, and as such, was hard as nails. It had been years since he had exercised his mind, and now, suddenly, it was being asked to work full overdrive.

He knew he should summon the energy to get up, get changed, hit the streets in his running shoes. But the thought held little appeal.

He lay on his side, put his feet up on the couch, and fell asleep...

...Night-time. A room. A bedroom. A single bed. The furniture around it was white. Girly. Wardrobe, dressing table, bedside cabinet, with pink edging and handles fashioned in the shape of butterflies. A doll's house in one corner. On the cabinet, a lamp, the shade a bright selection of rainbow colours. Posters on the walls. All sorts – Harry Potter; flying unicorns; princess fairies; an orange fox with a multicoloured tail. From the ceiling, a hanging lamp – a hand-crocheted hot-air balloon, Peter Rabbit peeping out its tiny basket. All popcorn and candy sweet. Illumination was faint – a revolving glow globe on the dressing table, creating soft stars on the walls. Stark stood to one side, quiet as a shadow, and watched the events unfold, consumed with a dread the likes of which he never knew existed.

The door to the bedroom opened, allowing in a fracture of light. There! – he discerned a shape under the covers of the bed, huddled tight, a bob of blonde hair. A figure slipped into the room, quick and sly. Stark's dread blossomed into throat-constricting horror.

The door closed. The dark returned. But Stark, transfixed where he stood, saw. The figure crept to the bed, pulled the covers back. A voice whispered, dripping sweet as honey. The bed creaked as the figure entered, and Stark, suddenly able to move, screamed for the obscenity to stop. His screams went unheeded. He felt every particle of her terror, her revulsion, her pain as if it was he who was being brutalised.

But there was nothing he could do.

In the instant it takes for a single second to pass, Stark was in a different place. Different surroundings. The dread remained, possessing a different texture. Latent, slow burning. A dread bubbling deep in the bones over many years…

...A wood. Night-time, the sky caught in sharp relief, the moon pale and clear, unobscured, encircled by a million stars.

The trees were tinged silver-grey, touched, so it seemed, by a dark magic. The air was chilled. Stark walked a snaking path. He thought he heard a stream somewhere. His steps felt sluggish. This was a journey he had no desire to take, but yet, he was compelled. He came to a clearing. In the clearing was a single tree. A cherry-blossom tree. In that strange moonlight, the leaves seemed to glow. Beside it, standing solemn and still, was a woman. Slender, a mere wisp. She gazed upwards, at the night sky. She was crying softly. Stark had never felt such sadness. Time passed. Stark could not tell how long, in that timeless place. The crying stopped. The woman nodded pensively, as if she had reached a clarity of thought. She touched the trunk of the tree, the tips of the leaves, and in the silver glow of the moon, she hung herself.

Tears coursed down his cheeks. Stark sank to his knees, dug his fingers into the cold earth. Something floated down, to land on the grass beside him. A local newspaper. The date was clear. The front page was emblazoned with the marriage of Prince William and Kate Middleton. Stark opened it, to page eighteen – a variety of happenings. A factory gone bust; a footballer pictured drunk at a nightclub; and tucked in a corner, a single paragraph, the sad story of a young woman who, tragically, had taken her own life in Chatelherault Woods.

Stark woke with a start. The dream remained vivid in his mind. The details were clear, the images fresh. He sat up, ran a fretful hand through his hair. He felt cold. His heart thumped, like he'd sprinted two hundred yards. He waited, expecting the events to drift to nothing, as dreams do, dissipating like mist under a morning sun. They didn't. He looked at his watch. It was 2am. He could hardly believe he had slept that long. He got up, made himself a coffee, sat at the kitchen table.

The dream had shaken him. He sipped his coffee with a trembling hand. The scenes tumbled over and over in his mind. He knew he wouldn't sleep. He toyed with the idea of eating the takeaway, but the thought made him nauseous. He checked his watch again: 2.10am.

Since the shooting massacre at the hands of Alfie Willow, Stark had suffered episodes. *Panic attacks,* his psychiatrist had explained. Also, nightmares. That he was locked below the ground, unable to breathe. Manifestations of post-traumatic stress disorder. A natural consequence of dramatic events. As time wore on, the panic attacks diminished, though the nightmares persisted. When it got bad, his first reaction was to phone his sister. He hated himself for doing it. But she was all he had, and she was always there, with her smile, and her grit.

He made a decision, and pressed her number on speed dial. It was answered almost immediately.

"After 2," she said. "Just as well I don't sleep." She sounded breathless.

"Where are you?" he asked.

"Just finished. Walking to my car as we speak. Another shift over at the zoo. What's up?"

He faltered. He was embarrassed. There was really nothing up. But the dream wouldn't go away. He saw the shadow crawl under the little girl's covers. He saw the woman crying by the cherry-blossom tree.

"I... nothing. I'm sorry. I shouldn't have..."

Her voice was stern. "Don't bullshit me, little brother. I'll be over in half an hour."

She disconnected. *God, he loved her more than anything in the world.*

She was there twenty-five minutes later. Dressed still in her blue scrubs, under a worn beige leather jacket. Hair tied back, somewhat severely, for functional purposes. Slung over her shoulder, a rather shapeless satchel, passing barely as a handbag. She looked tired. She *was* tired, he knew. He felt guilty and selfish. All this, over a stupid dream. But its impact was profound, and despite everything, he was glad she had come. As indeed he knew she would.

They sat on opposite sides of the kitchen table.

"Are you going to eat that?" she asked, nodding at the untouched bowl of chow mein.

"All yours."

She got a fork from drawer, returned, started to eat.

"Aren't you going to heat it up?" he said.

"Nope. Haven't eaten anything since lunchtime yesterday. Starving. Taste is irrelevant. As long as it fills my gut. Now, Jonathan. Tell me what compelled you to phone me at two in the morning. Despite the chewing and swallowing noises, I'm listening."

Stark had to smile. "I know." He relayed the dream. He found he remembered everything, from beginning to end. No vagueness. No gaps. The details were crisp in his mind, which in itself was unnerving.

"I was there," he said. "I mean, that's how it felt. That *I was actually there.* But more than that. I could feel the emotion. Of the child, of the woman. Their terrible suffering. I knew their thoughts. I knew everything about them. And I shared the dreadful burden they carried." He faltered, as he pondered their plight. "I've never experienced anything like it. I can't shake it off."

"I don't know much about dreams," Maggie said. "But I do know a bit about reality. Or at least as much as the next person. And the reality in your case is that five years ago, you were left for dead. But you didn't die. You survived. And like any survivor from something deeply traumatic, you suffer consequences. You had headaches for months. You suffered depression. You had anxiety attacks. You lost confidence. And no fucking wonder. And you had nightmares. Time passes. Things improve. Bit by tiny bit. But they do improve. And they have improved. Every so often, there's going to be a... relapse. And you know why? Because we're not machines. We're flesh and blood. You had a nightmare. It was going to happen. And it has happened. And no doubt it will happen again. But we see it for what it is. And we do our best to move on. That's all anyone can do. Move on."

"The newspaper," countered Stark. "I can remember every detail. Page eighteen. I could write the contents of each article on that page. It's like..." He raised his hands in frustration. "... branded into my mind!"

Maggie frowned and pursed her lips. "Fair enough. Pen and paper please."

Stark looked at his sister, held her stare. "Seriously?"

"We're going to see this through. Humour me, please."

Stark took out a pen from his inside jacket pocket, opened a kitchen drawer, got a pad of notepaper. He placed both items on the kitchen table.

She picked the pen up.

"An experiment. You're suggesting your dream was more than a dream. That you experienced something almost... what? Mystical? Supernatural? In which case, let's put it to the test. Tell me the name of the newspaper?"

Stark shook his head. "It was just a dream."

Maggie continued as if she hadn't heard. "Name please."

Stark released a sigh. "The *Hamilton Bugle*."

"Never heard of it." She scribbled it down.

"I can write it," said Stark. "There's no need."

"There's every need. I can't read your writing. No one can. The date?"

"April 29th, 2011."

"Okay. Page eighteen?"

"Yup."

"Give me the headline of each article on the page."

Stark did as requested. He saw the words clear in his mind's eye. Maggie kept writing.

"Now, tell me, exactly, the specific item about the young woman's suicide." Stark closed his eyes, allowed the image to appear in his head, slowly read it out, word for word. The process scared him. It was unnatural. Maggie finished writing it down. Her face had paled.

"That was damned specific," she said.

"Sure was."

She straightened, folded the paper, tucked it into her satchel.

"I have a day off tomorrow. Instead of spending it with my darling husband who I rarely see, and whose face is a distant memory, and whose first name I can barely remember, I will take these scribblings to the Mitchell Library. In particular, the archives, which has every copy of every Scottish newspaper ever printed. And then, little brother, once I have proved that you had a dream and not a visitation from God – or the Devil, for that matter – then perhaps we can 'move on'. What do you think?"

Stark couldn't help smiling. He raised his hands. "I concede. It was only a stupid dream, and I'm a needy brother. Spend the day with your husband. I've moved on already."

Maggie sniffed. "I can assure you, a day in the library is considerably more exciting."

Stark laughed. Maggie laughed with him.

"You're the boss," he said.

"Sure am. And don't forget it."

CHAPTER TWENTY-NINE

Maggie left Stark's flat, drove off.

He followed her, keeping well back, one hand bandaged. His car was an automatic, and as such, his injury did not impede him. But that was forgotten. He had one thing on his mind, rendering all else inconsequential. He would wait. He possessed the patience of a God. But not too long. Not long at all.

He pictured her face, envisioned the required subtle changes, as a sculptor might consider when using his chisel, or a surgeon his scalpel, and knew at last, he had found the one.

CHAPTER THIRTY

WEDNESDAY

9.30am. A meeting had been arranged in the upstairs conference room. One which, depending on its outcome, could have serious repercussions for the firm of Stoddart, Jeffrey, Pritchard and Sloss. In attendance were the three solicitors who had interviewed Stark – Walter Hill, Winnifred Marshall and Paul Hutchison – the respective heads of the main departments.

Mrs Patricia Shawbridge was elderly, widowed, and obscenely rich. She was, by a stretch, the firm's wealthiest client. When she needed something done, it was done promptly and with a minimum of fuss. Fees were rendered quickly, and paid quickly. She owned a wide portfolio of properties, in Scotland, in England, throughout the world, inherited from her late husband, who owned a pharmaceutical company. After he died she sold the business for over two hundred million. Never would a week go by, when she didn't issue instructions to her lawyers – buy this, sell that, sue them, defend this. It kept her occupied. It was almost a hobby. It kept the firm smiling. Money, money, money. Mrs Shawbridge was the dripping roast, and her lawyers supped on the gravy with a golden spoon.

Until now, this moment. Mrs Shawbridge was unhappy. She

had arranged a courier to deliver a handwritten intimation of complaint on Monday afternoon, and had demanded a meeting on Wednesday morning. At 9.30. The partners were perplexed, and deeply concerned. The letter hadn't specified the nature of her grievance, which worried them the most. Lawyers hated the unexpected.

Mrs Shawbridge arrived exactly on time, and was immediately shown up to the conference room. The three lawyers sat at the end of the table nearest the door, one on one side, two on the other allowing a space at the top, to give her the impression she was in control, which, essentially, she was.

She entered the room, accompanied by her perfume. She wore a simple navy-blue dress, a matching double-breasted woollen blazer, blue stockings, blue shoes, the picture of austere elegance. She kept trim, a good proportion of her time spent at an exclusive gym. Her face was stern and set, dark flashing eyes under a roiling mass of dark curls. She was in her mid-seventies, and looked fifteen years younger. She worked hard at looking good.

She sat at the table. Fresh coffee was ready to be served.

Hill stood, and displayed his warmest avuncular smile. "Good to see you again, Patricia. I hope you're keeping well. May I offer you some coffee?" He began the process of lifting a silver coffee jug.

"No thanks."

"Of course." Somewhat crestfallen, he put the jug back, and sat down.

A silence fell. She appeared unperturbed by the awkwardness of the situation.

It was Winnifred Marshall who spoke, her voice soft. "You look well, Patricia. How have you been keeping?"

"Poorly," she replied, her tone clipped. "Since Monday morning, in particular. Very poorly. To be candid, I was left in a state of shock. I'm still in shock. I cannot begin to express my feelings on the matter. What occurred was both outrageous and insulting." She took care to meet the stare of each of the lawyers. "And a disgrace."

Hutchison cleared his throat, gave an easy laugh, though it had a tinny undertone. "Perhaps you could elaborate? You have a problem, and we're keen to help. First, however, we have to understand what precisely the problem is? You agree that would be helpful?"

She gave Hutchison a heavy-lidded stare. "I'm not a fool. Don't think I can't detect sarcasm when I hear it."

Hutchison's jowls wobbled like a slobbery dog. His eyes widened in apparent innocence. He was not a subtle man. Subtlety was not a useful requirement for court litigators. Both Hill and Winnifred fixed him meaningful stares – *Shut the hell up. Let us do the talking.*

"Please, Patricia," said Hill, raising two appeasing hands. "We want to help. I promise. Tell us what happened. Please."

She straightened in her chair, pursed her lips, as if considering her response.

"I received a telephone call from Bronson Chapel last Friday afternoon. He asked me to attend his offices on the following Monday, at 9am. The matter, so he told me, was urgent, and delicate. I asked him to expand, but he told me it was something which could not be discussed over the phone."

Winnifred raised an eyebrow. "Really?"

"Really," replied Mrs Shawbridge in a flat voice. "Needless to say, I spent the weekend wondering – and worrying – about this somewhat odd, cryptic message." She darted an acid glance at Hutchison. "If he'd told me what it was about, that would have been helpful, yes?"

Hutchison chose not to respond.

"But he didn't tell me," she continued. "And no wonder." She paused, recollecting the events. The three lawyers waited.

"I arrived as requested. Nine sharp. I went up to his office." She took a breath. "He was sitting behind his desk. He appeared agitated. Twitchy. I said nothing. The first thing he asked was how my son was keeping. The question took me by surprise. Before I had the chance to answer, he explained that he had met my son several months ago at some dinner engagement, and that they had got on well. He was talking rapidly. The words were almost tripping over each other. Then, he placed his mobile phone on the desk, and asked me to look at a photograph he had taken. I did. I saw a picture of a man leaving a house. Dressed in what appeared to be a blue tradesman's overall. He asked me if I recognised this person. I said I emphatically did not. I asked him to explain." She took another long smouldering breath, struggling to contain her fury.

"Can you imagine what he did next?" She looked at each of them, daring them to speak. "Take a wild guess. No? Let me tell you. He laughed. He told me…" she bit her lip, keeping her voice neutral, "…I was a liar. He told me to admit that I knew the man in the photo. I was shocked. And speechless. But he kept going. He said that he would take it to the police, unless…" and here, tears welled up. Her shoulders trembled. She had a blue leather Gucci handbag placed on her lap. She opened it, pulled out a handkerchief, dabbed her eyes, replaced it back into her handbag, clicked it shut.

"…unless I paid him £200,000." Another deep breath, as she composed herself. "I asked him to explain his conduct. He said, 'Isn't it obvious?'. He told me to take a closer look at the picture. He told me the photo was of the man leaving the house where these horrible murders had taken place. He told me the photo was of the man the tabloid press had given the name The Surgeon." Another pause, as she tried to articulate the thoughts in her head.

"He told me the picture in his phone was my son. He was, in effect, attempting to blackmail me."

The three lawyers said nothing. Hutchison shook his head. "Bronson? You must be mistaken..."

"Do I look as if I'm mistaken!" she snapped. Hutchison blinked, licked his lips, fell silent.

"He said that because of my unwillingness to accept the position, his price had gone up to £250,000. I informed him that his price could escalate to any figure he wished, it would have no bearing. Whilst the man in the photo bore a strong resemblance to my son, I explained that it could not possibly be him. My son is currently in hospital." She gave the three a level stare. "He was diagnosed with lung cancer, and is lying in a hospital bed, attached to a breathing apparatus, and has been for the last two months. Soon, he will be transferred to a hospice. He has weeks to live, if he's lucky."

She paused, gathering her thoughts. The three lawyers waited. The seconds passed, each stretched tight with tension. "I intend to take this matter to the police," she said. "I thought, probably as a misplaced act of courtesy, I would inform you of the situation first. If Bronson Chapel has a photograph of the killer, then it has to be brought to their attention. Plus, I will be speaking to them about the blackmail threat. And I will be seeking Bronson Chapel's disbarment."

She paused again, maintaining her composure, then continued.

"I am, forthwith, withdrawing all my business from this firm. Furthermore, I will be seeking legal advice, with a view to claiming damages for the considerable distress this affair has caused me. I hope you have deep pockets."

She stood, gave each a withering stare.

"I hope never to set foot in this building again. All future communication will be through my new lawyers." She gave a curt nod. "Good day."

She left the room. The door swung shut behind her. The silence which followed was palpable, broken eventually by Hill.

"Jesus Christ," he muttered.

"Where is Bronson?" said Winnifred, her voice brittle.

"He's not been in," said Hutchison. "No one can get a hold of him."

"Jesus Christ," repeated Hill. "If the media get a sniff of this."

Hutchison folded his arms, a posture adopted by an entrenched litigator. "Get a sniff of what! We deny. It's her word against Bronson's."

"You're missing the point," snapped Winnifred. "It doesn't matter what we say or what we do. At this moment, *The Surgeon* is the most talked about individual in the country. And not because of his sparkling personality. To be associated with such an individual would be catastrophic, and the more legal obstacles we put up to distance ourselves makes us look worse. We need to talk to Bronson."

"We should go to the police," said Hill. "Tell them what's happened. Minimise the fallout. Makes us look better."

"Go to the police with what, exactly!" chided Hutchison. "Someone claims to have been shown a photo of a man who might be a serial killer. We don't have the phone, we don't have the picture, and we don't even have Bronson to explain what the hell is going on. We would look like fools. Plus, we'd be inviting trouble."

"Maybe we should get armed up with outside lawyers," said Winnifred.

"Maybe we should sit tight and ride this out," retorted Hutchison. "The less people know, the more we can contain the situation. And meantime find out where the hell Bronson is. He's got some explaining to do. He's not answering his goddamned phone. There's a fucking swarm of angry clients wondering where the hell he is."

"Contain?" said Winnifred. "Really? Patricia Shawbridge is about to tell the world. There's really not much we can contain about that."

"We need to hear Bronson's take," said Hill. "I agree with Paul. Let's talk to Bronson first. Then we can rationalise the situation. I can arrange for someone to go round to his house."

"He lives in one of those church conversions," said Hutchison.

"I think he also has a holiday home," said Hill. "He talks about it. He calls it his *boat house.* We can try there as well. Admin have the address I think."

Winnifred, usually so stoic, seemed to slump. "This can't be happening."

"We have to let Edward know," said Hutchison. There was reluctance in his voice.

"Not in his condition," said Winnifred. "He doesn't need this."

Hutchison gave an abrasive laugh. "None of us need this. But we've fucking got it. If Bronson were here, I swear I would kill him with my two bare fucking hands."

Hill released a long sigh.

"A storm is brewing," he whispered.

No one disagreed.

CHAPTER THIRTY-ONE

Stark was oblivious to the meeting going on above his head in the upstairs conference room, as indeed were most of the staff. He was exhausted. He had slept, eventually, drifting off at five in the morning, to be woken two hours later by the alarm on his phone. The dream was still rich in his mind. It hadn't dissipated to half-forgotten wisps and fragments, as dreams do. It remained clear, and its persistence frightened him.

Jenny was at her desk. It was 9am. She looked tired. The column of files on her desk seemed taller. He wondered if it had ever reached the ceiling. *Such was the life before him,* he thought ruefully.

"Bad night," she said. "Couldn't get a wink of sleep. Things go round and round."

"I know the feeling."

The conversation was sparse. Stark had no desire to talk. He was too tired. It seemed Jenny was of the same disposition. The work kept coming. The emails didn't stop. Stark cursed their invention. They epitomised the "instant" culture, when light-speed responses were expected – demanded – and human beings were expected to behave like machines. Patience, thought, deliberation, consideration; such notions were prehistoric. Joe Public expected everything now. If they didn't get it, then it was easy to complain, because, thought Stark, complaint was now instinctive. *We have become a bunch of wheedling cowards. We need a fucking war.*

But then, who phones their sister at 2am because of a bad dream? He gave a grim smile, as he mooned over his laptop. He was just like everybody else. Christ, he felt resentful. Lack of sleep, he knew. But that didn't change his mood. Again, for the hundredth time, images popped into his head, unbidden. The child assaulted in her bed. The woman touching the branch from which she would hang herself.

Someone had sent him a twenty-page attachment. An impossibly obscure employment contract to review.

"Christ," he said aloud, "I wish I smoked."

Jenny turned, face pale and set. She pushed her chair back. "Well I fucking do. Let's go."

Stark offered no complaint. Jenny grabbed her jacket. He followed her out of the room, along the corridor to the back door. The fire exit. She pushed the crossbar down, shouldered the door open. They emerged into a shaded paved section of the garden, hidden away from prying eyes. Jenny got a packet of Marlboro Red's from an inside pocket, a plastic lighter, and lit up.

She offered him one. For the first time in his life, he was tempted. He shook his head.

She shrugged, leant on the wall, took a deep drag.

"Two things I never did until I started this fucking job. Smoking and swearing."

"At least you're not drinking," he remarked.

"Ah. I forgot. Three things."

Stark gave her a thoughtful gaze. Perhaps it was the effects of the dream, the lack of sleep, his general frame of mind, or maybe a hundred other things, but he asked the question.

"Is it worth it?"

Her lips curled into a sceptical smile – "You're the brand-new trainee. I'd better be careful what I say. After all, we don't want to dispirit our fresh recruits." She inhaled another lungful of nicotine, blew up into the air, attempting a smoke ring. "I can never get the hang of that." She focused her attention back on Stark. "I would say this. And this is an opinion only, so please don't quote. If you want to see the shitty side of human nature, enjoy getting rich bastards richer, bow and grovel to the whims of greedy grasping people, then, my son, this is the job for you. If that's what floats your boat, yes – well worth it."

Stark gave a sardonic grin. "I'm glad I asked."

"You'll learn." A silence fell. The sun dipped, hidden behind rolling clouds. Looked like rain was coming. Stark shivered. Summer was clinging on. Barely.

"You don't need to tell me if you don't want to," Jenny said.

Stark was baffled. "I would tell you if I knew what you were asking. Maybe."

"There's rumours. Law firms love rumours. And gossip. Lawyers need gossip to survive. It gives us... sustenance."

"Sustenance." Stark had a good idea where this was going. "What would you like to know?"

She took another puff, scrutinised Stark. "You don't need to tell me if you don't want to. And I can understand perfectly why you wouldn't."

"Try me."

"Alfie Willow? The chat is that maybe you were caught up in all that? I was wondering..."

Stark leant on the wall beside her. He felt he could sleep for a year. *Run as fast and as hard as you want, the past is always at your shoulder.*

"Yes, is the short answer. He left me in a coma for eight weeks. After that, convalescence. It took me several years before I plucked up the courage to apply for a job in a lawyer's office. And here I am."

Jenny seemed to consider what he said. “It was unbelievable. Unimaginable. I wonder what would drive a man to do what he did.”

“Push the right buttons – or the wrong buttons, for that matter – then anyone can do anything, I suppose.” Memories resurfaced, ones he would never forget. “Alfie Willow had come to the end. He was not the type of man to run. Prison was unthinkable. His ego demanded that if he had to go, that those he thought important should go with him. He was not one who believed in half measures. The two most important things in his life were his family, and his work. It was therefore only logical, at least to Alfie, that if the end had come, then the end should also come for his wife and family, and his staff. If he could have burned the world down, then he would have done that too.”

She studied him, a curious expression on her face. “You’re trying to find sense in the mind of a psychopath.”

Stark gave a wintry grin. “Not me. These were the observations by the doctors trying to help me through my… recovery. For me, there’s little point in trying to rationalise a psychopath’s mind, basically, because they’re mad. They’re sick.”

She gave a small sad smile. “Or misunderstood.”

“Not from the victim’s perspective.”

She finished off her cigarette, stubbed it against the wall, pinged the stub into some bushes.

“Gotta hide the evidence.”

Stark, suddenly, acted on an impulse he could never have predicted. He essayed a somewhat lame smile. “Maybe, if your diary isn’t too full, we could have a drink, sometime? Cheap beer only, until I get paid.”

“I don’t drink.”

Stark blew through his lips, started to flounder. “Well…”

“I’m lying. I drink. All forms of alcohol, without exception. Especially cheap beer. Are you asking me on a date, Jonathan?”

“I believe so.”

"Your third day. You're a fast worker."

"I would have done it on my first day, but that would have seemed presumptuous."

She laughed. He laughed with her. Then her phone buzzed. She glanced at the screen, scowled.

"It never ends. Back to the shit. Don't you have a lunch appointment today?"

"Edward Stoddart requests my presence on the top floor."

They made their way back into the building.

"I've never been to the top floor," she said, as they entered the office. "I don't believe Stoddart even knows I exist. You must be the special one."

"I don't feel particularly special. In fact, as of this moment, I feel particularly ordinary."

They sat at their respective desks. To Stark's dismay, his inbox had three fresh emails. More little mouths to feed.

"You're right," he muttered. "It never ends."

Jenny studied her computer screen, started clicking the keyboard.

"Yes," she said.

Stark looked at her. "Yes?"

"Cheap beer. How could I possibly resist?"

CHAPTER THIRTY-TWO

Billy Watson, accompanied by Frank, had gone to visit Bronson at his flat the previous evening. Unlike McGuigan and Dawson, they did not try the buzzers of his neighbours, essentially because they had no desire to attract attention to themselves.

They were, however, undeterred. On the instruction of Billy, Frank waited in his car adjacent to the church building, all through the night. There was no sign of Bronson. He neither entered nor left. The flat looked out onto the main street. The curtains were open, the lights weren't switched on, there appeared to be no indication of movement. The flat was unoccupied.

"Unless he's dead," said Frank.

"He might be," replied Billy. "Which would be unfortunate."

Billy had arrived to meet him at seven that morning. They were both sitting in the car, Frank in the driver's seat.

"I need to sleep," said Frank. "He's gone. If he's got any sense, he won't come back."

Billy shrugged. "Perhaps. I don't think so. His life is here. I think he's scared. He needs time to think. To plan. The one thing you need to understand with people like Bronson Chapel – they're educated. And they live educated lives. Which is their flaw. They underestimate people. People like us. He won't fully comprehend the situation he is in, nor the measures we will go to."

"You threatened him with an acid facelift, if I recall."

Billy nodded, smiling. "But he doesn't believe such a thing will ever happen, because in his world, such a thing doesn't compute. I reckon he'll lie low, maybe for a week, maybe two, then reappear, and attempt to bluster his way back into his normal existence. He's a lawyer after all, working in a fancy law firm."

"So we wait?"

"Not at all. He has another place. He's mentioned it to me, though he may have forgotten. He called it his 'boat house'."

"You think he's there."

"Possibly."

"You know where it is?"

"I make it my business to know everything about everybody. Go home, Frankie. Sleep. Eat. Then get yourself ready. Pack some tools. We're going on a trip."

CHAPTER THIRTY-THREE

McGuigan and Dawson were in the main incident room. The bleep of the phones was constant, like a drone of insects. The place was busy. Both civilian staff and police officers working round the clock. Since the presentation of the photofit likeness, the calls had been relentless. The influx was a drain on resources. More people had been drafted in. The task force initially created to find the killer had grown exponentially. Everybody, everywhere, wanted the madman caught, and everybody everywhere thought they had seen sight of him. An entire floor of the building was now dedicated to the apprehension of The Surgeon.

The only person who seemed unflustered was Harry McGuigan. He was in an office appended to the main room. He was talking to a number of seasoned police officers, including Kenny Dawson. His "inner circle" as he liked to describe them. People who were dedicated and competent. And who, like McGuigan, required closure.

He was reiterating old ground. But it was a necessary part of the ritual. Something missed. Something remembered. Details reconsidered. A different slant. Points raised, discussed, dismissed. Anything at all. McGuigan would take it, and run with it, as far as he damned well could. All part of the anatomy of desperation.

"Unconnected," he said. "As far as we can gather, Evelyn Stephens was chosen simply because of her age, and facial features."

A young man, red hair, fresh complexion, spoke up. "We've checked everywhere. Doctors, dentists, schools, employment, yoga classes, gym membership, beauty salons, every club, every group. Evelyn was a dental hygienist. We've checked her list of patients. No matches. Absolutely nothing linking her to any of the others. Same old story. Each victim has nothing to connect them with any of the others."

"Except their looks," said Dawson. "They all possess similar facial features."

"Lawyers," said McGuigan. He had their attention. "Has that been checked?"

Silence. "Then check," he said. "Who were the lawyers who bought their houses? Were any involved in litigation? Any injury claims? If any of them used the same lawyer for anything at all, then we follow up."

The silence continued. He was grasping, and they knew it. But he didn't care. Suddenly, lawyers were on his radar.

Dawson cleared his throat. "Okay. Evelyn was having an affair with William Patrick. We believe the killer would have known this. He was killed in the hallway. The weapon was a Glock. His wound was accurate. Fired at close distance. Inches away. Shot twice through the eye. The husband came back to the house early. We believe he did this to confront his wife, and her boyfriend. *In flagrante delicto.* This was an unexpected event. The killer, we believe, did not foresee this, judging by the bullet entry points on the husband's body, which were erratic, and lacked the killer's trademark precision. Panic firing. Also, because the killing took place in broad daylight. Again, a complete break from the pattern."

A female detective continued. "We've done extensive door-to-door. No one saw anything. We don't have CCTV, so we're not sure about passing motorists. Except for..."

"...Bronson Chapel," finished McGuigan. "Our main man. Our *only* man. The man of the moment. The only living person who claims to have seen our friendly neighbourhood psychopath."

"The photofit's sparked a fire," said another. "The calls are avalanching in. We're stretched to hell."

"'Avalanching'," repeated McGuigan. "'Sparked a fire'. 'Hell'. I like those expressions. Biblical, almost. You been going to church recently, Smith? Maybe reading a little of Dante's *Inferno*."

The man who had spoken – Smith – wrinkled his nose. "Haven't been for years. I'm a non-believer, I'm afraid, sir. And to be honest, I've never heard of Dante. I'm not into crime thrillers."

"I'm sure you're not," said McGuigan, shaking his head in mild exasperation. "Nevertheless, it sums up the situation, when the world's gone insane." He focused on Dawson. "Anywhere with the 'boat house'?"

Dawson gave a twitch of his head. "Nothing. Bronson has no immediate family. His parents are dead. No kids, no wife, no siblings. No one knows much about him. I've checked the land register, but if he owns another property, it's not showing. Which means he probably rents. And he hasn't returned to his flat, or his work."

"He's gone AWOL," said McGuigan. "An odd coincidence."

Another voice – "Do you think he's in danger?"

"Could be," said McGuigan. "It's not an unreasonable hypothesis. The killer saw him, we assume. Maybe the killer's tracked him down. Maybe Bronson's got scared, and fled. According to his place of employment, there's a queue of clients waiting to see him."

"Or maybe," said Dawson, "he's decided he wants to get away

for a few days, and maybe he's sitting in the sun somewhere, sipping a cocktail by a pool."

"Maybe," agreed McGuigan. "We'll never know until we find him." His tone altered, had an iron ring. "But I want him found. You've tried his work? They may have an address on record."

Dawson gave a weary hang-dog response. It was clear he was still of the impression they were wasting their time. "I spoke to their HR person. They said they were unable to assist, unless they received the written consent of Bronson himself. Or a warrant. Data protection, and all that. No doubt the request raised a few eyebrows."

McGuigan blew through his lips. "The simplest thing."

There was a knock on the door – a uniformed officer leaned in.

"Sorry, boss. Not sure if you'd be interested. But I thought you might."

"Yes?"

"A woman phoned in ten minutes ago. It's unusual. She specifically wanted to speak to the man in charge."

"You've come to the right place. And?"

"Very posh lady. It could be a crank call. God knows we've had a fair few."

"I'm not convinced God knows as much as we give him credit for. Keep going."

"She claims to have been shown a picture of the killer leaving Evelyn Stephens' house."

The young police officer had McGuigan's full attention.

"That's interesting. You got the woman's name and number?"

"Yes, sir. And her address. She said she would prefer a face-to-face meeting. At her house. She was quite… demanding. Also, she claimed someone had tried to blackmail her. To be honest, it sounded all a bit weird."

The burst of interest McGuigan felt was suddenly punctured. The blackmail element reduced the woman's credibility to zero.

The officer's conclusion was right. Crank caller. He clicked his teeth in frustration.

"Phone her back. Tell her someone will be out to see her. As long as it's not me."

The police officer wavered. "And the man she complained about? The man she claimed tried to blackmail her?" He flicked through a notepad he was holding. "Weird name," he muttered.

"Weird name?"

He got to the page, nodded. "Yes, sir. Bronson Chapel. That's the name she gave me. The name of the man who she said tried to blackmail her."

McGuigan said nothing. He blinked, took a breath. Then he spoke.

"Repeat that name, please."

"Bronson Chapel, sir. I'll pass it on..."

McGuigan gave Dawson a knowing glance, said, "We'll go out and see her now. You have her address?"

"Yes, sir."

"And her name?"

"Mrs Patricia Shawbridge."

CHAPTER THIRTY-FOUR

The top floor. 1pm. Stark's nerves jangled. Possibly down to a mixture of things. Lack of proper sleep, the profound impact of his dream, the general nervousness any employee would experience when meeting the senior partner of a prestigious law firm.

There was another reason. Perhaps the most compelling, and one which he chose not to divulge, not even to his sister.

He got to the foyer. There, a single door. He knocked, entered. A corridor, the walls bare, at the end of which, another door. He did the same again – knocked, entered.

Before him, a large room, the focal point a real fire, crackling under a glossy black-marble fire surround. The walls were dark oak cladding, the floor underfoot a thick carpet the colour of red wine. There – a grandfather clock. Beside it, a polished writing bureau. On one side, an elegant black leather couch, black leather chairs. An impressive cabinet, tall and wide, constructed of the same dark oak as the cladding, containing books, crystal ornaments, other oddments. Lighting was supplied by three antique copper chandeliers, casting a soft amber hue.

At the far end, an oval desk, with a green leather top, brass handles on the drawers, decorated with crossbanding, strapwork borders, intricate pendant garlands on the oak panelling. Stark had never seen a desk quite like it.

Behind it sat Edward Stoddart. He stood when Stark entered. He was smiling. Stark took him for a man who looked older than he was, face gaunt and parchment pale, stooped shoulders. Wire-thin, hair unnaturally black, slicked back from his forehead, lying close to his head like a patch of oil. A sharp beak of a nose. Stark was reminded of a predatory bird. He inspected Stark with eyes like flint.

"Punctual," he said. "I like punctuality."

"Thank you."

Stoddart made his way round the desk, met Stark, shook his hand. He reckoned they were about the same height. Six one, though his stoop made him appear smaller.

"Our brand-new trainee," he said. "Jonathan Stark." He continued his stare with an intensity Stark found unnerving.

Stark reacted with a modest shrug of his shoulders. "That's me."

Stoddart's handshake was firm and assured. "Good to have you on board. It's refreshing to meet young blood. It uplifts the spirit."

Stark was unsure how to respond. He said nothing.

Stoddart beckoned him to one of the leather chairs. "Sit, please."

Stark sat. Stoddart sat on a chair opposite. Between them, a coffee table. On it, a single spherical piece of quartz stone, the size of a fist.

"My great grandfather – William Stoddart – used it as a paperweight. I could never bring myself to get rid of it."

Stark nodded. "Sentimental value."

Stoddart leaned in closer. "Imagine stone could talk." He

picked the object up. "The things it's seen, the secrets locked away in its stony mind. That would be interesting, yes?"

Stark gave a lame smile. He couldn't think of anything to say in response to such an observation.

Stoddart placed the stone back on the coffee table.

"How are you finding things here, at the wondrous firm of Stoddart, Jeffrey, Pritchard and Sloss? Or should I say SJPS, which sounds much more slick and trendy."

"I think I'm doing okay," replied Stark. "At least no one has shouted at me yet. Or threatened me with expulsion." *Except Paul Hutchison*. He kept that particular meeting to himself.

Stoddart gave a rattling laugh. "You *will* get shouted at. That's a given. And usually by clients, or sour-faced judges. Or irritable partners. My advice? Embrace it. All part of the learning curve. Toughens you up. Because that's what this game is about. And not just the law. Everything. Having the strength to tough it out. Have you got that strength, Jonathan?"

"I'm not entirely sure. I hope so."

"I hope so too, Jonathan."

Stoddart kept his gaze. More of an inspection, thought Stark. A silence followed, which Stark tried to fill. He made a show of looking about.

"You have a beautiful office. A real fire. You don't see that too often."

"I find it therapeutic," said Stoddart. "And I'm cold, even in the summer. A consequence of age. And other things. You come from Eaglesham?"

Stark hesitated at the abrupt change in conversation.

"Yes."

"You were born there."

Stark wasn't entirely sure whether this was a statement or a question.

"Yes."

"It's a quiet little place."

"It has its moments."

"I'm sure," said Stoddart. "And its secrets, I dare say." His eyes glittered.

"Like everywhere," said Stark.

"And you said at the interview you have a sister?"

"Maggie. She's a doctor. A and E. I think she's in permanent stress mode."

"You're close to your sister. That's a good thing, Jonathan. There's nothing more important than blood. Blood binds."

"Do you have family, Mr Stoddart?"

Stoddart's lips curled upwards into something approaching a smile, showing the tips of his teeth.

"Please. Edward. I gave up on formality when I realised it was such a waste of time. My wife died five years ago. I have…" he swallowed, licked his lips as he spoke, "…one son. As I get older, I realise how precious a child is. Blood binds, Jonathan. You hungry?"

Stark realised he was. He'd skipped breakfast, and so far had survived on a gallon of coffee and chocolate biscuits taken from a tin in the ground-floor kitchen.

"Follow me," said Stoddart. He got up, went to the far wall, opened a concealed door, similar to the door in the waiting room.

"Agatha Christie would love this place," he said.

"I dare say she would."

They entered a room, as large as the conference chamber on the first floor. Same dark panelling, same thick carpet, chandelier lighting. Two arched windows, allowing in the dreary afternoon sun. A long wooden dining table, shining to a sparkle. Two places had been set. Also, a buffet of heated silver trays containing a variety of food, and a silver canister of water.

"I had caterers prepare. I didn't know what you liked, so I told them to make a mixture."

"Thank you."

They sat. Stark began to dish food onto his plate. Stoddart watched him.

"I have to be careful what I eat," he said. "I have cancer, Jonathan."

Stark put his knife and fork down. "I'm sorry…"

Stoddart raised a hand. "Please. I only mention this as an explanation as to why I'm not joining you. It's a particularly aggressive sort. My diet, I fear, is restricted to pills and drugs and tasteless liquids. Which is why I asked you here." Again, that glittering gaze.

"This firm needs new energy," he continued. "I heard what you had to say at your interview. You've been through a great deal. More than most. Much more. And here you are. You're a strong young man, Jonathan. You have spirit. And courage. And I think this firm, and the world generally, needs a little more of these qualities. Please, eat."

Stark's appetite had diminished. Having Edward Stoddart inspect him as a vulture might inspect a carcass, was unsettling. He picked at his food. Stoddart asked him a few further questions, of a mundane sort. Stark got the impression his sheer presence was more important than any conversation. At 1.45, Stoddart stated he felt unwell. The lunch was over. Stoddart saw him out, shaking his hand.

"New blood," he said. "You're the future of this firm, Jonathan. I can feel it."

Stark could think of no adequate response. He merely nodded, thanked him for lunch, and made his way down the stairs.

His phone beeped. He checked the number. It was Maggie. He answered.

She skipped the niceties.

"Are you bullshitting me?"

"Not that I'm aware of."

"When do you finish?"

"Sixish?"

"I'll come round to the flat. Your dream. It all happened. It's all true. And I'm scared, little brother."

CHAPTER THIRTY-FIVE

Patricia Shawbridge lived in a mansion in Colinton, a suburb of Edinburgh. Million-pound houses in an area less than five miles from the city centre. Her house was the biggest in the street, an example of symmetrical Georgian architecture, complete with side-wings and a grand pillared doorway. Set back from the main road, accessed by a gated entrance, sitting on four acres of manicured gardens, it was an impressive package, thought McGuigan, as he announced their arrival into a metal box fixed on a stone column. The gates clicked, swung ponderously open. McGuigan, accompanied by Dawson, parked up on a white cobbled forecourt.

"I should have worn my best tie," remarked Dawson.

They had left the police station immediately upon receiving the message. The journey, under normal circumstances, would have taken an hour and a half. Dawson had pressed his foot on the pedal, and got there in under an hour.

McGuigan rapped a brass door knocker. They waited. He rapped again. The door was eventually answered by a young woman, face smudged, wearing black plastic gloves and blue overalls covered in dark stains. She appeared flustered.

"Sorry," she said, breathless. "Police?"

"Yes."

"Patricia's in the conservatory. Come in, please."

"Is everything okay?" asked McGuigan.

She gave her head an exasperated shake.

"Raven."

McGuigan and Dawson exchanged puzzled glances. They followed her through a wide, high-ceilinged hallway.

"I don't understand," said McGuigan.

She cast a grinning sidelong glance.

"They always come down the drawing-room chimney. Bloody ravens. Or crows. Sometimes you can't tell the difference. They fly in, down, then out through the hearth, all mad flapping and hopping, bringing with them a bucketload of soot. The mess of the walls. They do it on purpose, just to test me, I swear."

"Must be difficult to catch," said McGuigan.

She gave them a sly smile. "I have my ways."

"I'm sure you do."

They were led to the rear of the house, through a living room, to an expansive conservatory, connected by a series of bi-folding glass doors, the glass imbued with gold and silver motifs. The garden beyond was a display of vivid colour.

A woman sat on a woven rattan chair, her back to them, facing the garden, sipping coffee from a porcelain cup.

She turned her head a slight angle, acknowledging their presence. "Please," she said, without looking at them. "Come, and take a seat."

They sat opposite on similar-style chairs. Soft piano music played, just on the periphery of the senses.

"Tea or coffee, gentlemen."

"We're fine," replied McGuigan.

"As you wish. Thank you, Vivien. I'll let you get back to your tussle with your crow. Or raven. Or whatever it is."

The other woman – Vivien – responded somewhat

sarcastically: "You're very kind." She gave a curt nod, retreated back into the interior of the house.

Patricia gave a dry chuckle. "She'll spend all afternoon trying to catch the damned thing." It seemed to McGuigan she was talking more to herself, than to them. He introduced himself and Dawson.

"I suspect my phone call brought a spark to the fire," she said.

"It was intriguing," replied McGuigan. "We're keen to know what happened, Mrs Shawbridge."

She took a careful sip of her coffee.

"Do you like gardening, Chief Inspector?"

McGuigan pondered at the change of subject, deciding to go with the flow. This, he thought, was a woman who did things in her own time, in her own way.

"I potter, now and again." He looked out at the scenery beyond the glass of the conservatory. "My garden isn't quite in the same league."

Patricia nodded at the comment, as if it carried great weight.

"I like order and precision. Two qualities I believe the modern world lacks. I've spent many years creating the garden you see this afternoon. It's taken time and care and patience. Everything must be just so. My point is this – I am not someone who takes to idle flights of fancy, or who imagines things that never happened. Without order we have chaos."

"Of course."

"Do you read the scriptures?"

"I'm a novice."

Patricia sighed. "Lately, I've taken an interest – *Those that be planted in the house of the Lord shall flourish in the courts of our God.* Psalms. It seems to fit the picture."

"And what picture is that, Mrs Shawbridge?"

Another sip. "My husband died several years ago." She made a vague sweep of her arm. "He left me money, and property. But it counts for little when tragedy enters your life. Which is why, suddenly, the Bible becomes important. My son is dying, Chief Inspector. He's in a private hospice, barely able to move because of a particularly aggressive type of bone cancer. He cannot eat food, because the act of swallowing gives him an agony he cannot endure. He has perhaps weeks. Maybe less. I should be with him. I should be at his side. But instead, I'm here, talking to two policemen, which makes this situation all the more abhorrent."

McGuigan waited. Dawson, next to him, had his notebook on his lap, tapping a biro on the paper. A gesture indicating mild impatience. McGuigan, however, was content to hear her story. She was a woman with everything, and nothing. He felt the sadness in her voice, the ache in her heart, and understood she deserved to be listened to.

She told them what had happened, her speech punctuated with pauses, as she held back tears. McGuigan admired her composure. She told them about the urgent call from her lawyer, Bronson Chapel. She told them about the meeting in his office, that he had presented her with a photograph of a man leaving a house, this man apparently shooting another, then the man approaching the camera. She told them about Bronson's accusation, that the man in the picture was the serial killer known as The Surgeon, that clearly the man was her son, and that he would turn a blind eye, provided she pay him a large amount of money. Essentially, he was attempting blackmail.

"The man in the picture bore a striking resemblance to my son. I can see how he may have made that mistake. I explained that it could not be him, for obvious reasons. He did not take this well. I told him I was first going to report his conduct to his partners, next go to the police, and finally, when I have the strength, seek redress for his disgusting conduct through litigation."

"And did you?" asked Dawson.

"Did I what?"

"Report him to the partners."

She nodded. "I did. I told them exactly what I have just told you. Perhaps with a little more passion. They needed to know that such an individual works under their roof."

"And their reaction?"

"Shock, sympathy, and some resistance. I sensed a 'closing of the ranks'. That's what lawyers do, isn't it?" She allowed a wintry smile. "Rather like the police?"

McGuigan pursed his lips. "I would ask you don't tell anyone else, Mrs Shawbridge. This is sensitive information. For now, the fewer people who know, the better, until we can make some sense of the situation."

Her mood changed. She sat rigid. She spoke in a brittle voice. "There's nothing here that's complicated. The equation is simple. Ask Bronson Chapel. He holds all the answers."

"Your son's name?" said Dawson.

She blinked back tears. She seemed to slump. Her frosty demeanour disappeared. "Wallace Ramsay Shawbridge." She gave a sad, wistful smile. "He used to say he had the type of name a murder-mystery writer might use. His father's idea."

A shuddering breath as she contained her anguish.

"Which hospice, Mrs Shawbridge? I have to ask."

"St Columba's, here in Edinburgh."

McGuigan shifted in his chair, uncomfortable at his next request: "You say that your son – Wallace – looked very similar to the man in the picture. Would you have any..."

He didn't need to finish.

"Yes," she said. "I anticipated this." She stretched over, to a neat little side table, upon which stood a lamp with a delicate shell lightshade, and beside it, a black leather-bound photo album. She opened it, leafed the pages, stopped at one, pulled out a photograph from a clear plastic sleeve.

"My son, six months ago. There's little point in giving you a recent one. He is now..." again the staggered breath, "... completely changed."

McGuigan took the picture. There, a man in his early forties, smiling, sitting at an outdoor table, a glass of red before him. Lean face, hawkish nose, heavy, dark eyebrows, blue eyes sparkling with humour and intelligence. McGuigan scrutinised the face before him, fascinated. Perhaps, for the first time, he was looking at a face resembling one of the most prolific killers in Scottish history. An ice-cold flutter brushed the nape of his neck.

"Can we keep this?"

She tilted her head in acquiescence.

She gave both policemen a candid regard – "What I have said is all true. Do you believe me, Chief Inspector?"

"I do."

"And what of Bronson Chapel? I assume he has denied everything?"

"We have to find him. Bronson seems to have gone off-radar."

"Not surprising," she said. "Given the circumstances. If what he is saying is the truth, and if The Surgeon really does look like my son, then I believe the photofit you showed the public is a million miles off the mark."

"I believe you might be right."

"A tough one, Chief Inspector. I wish you well."

The meeting was over. They stood. Suddenly, for a reason he could not explain, he took her hand, this lady with a perfect garden and a dying son.

"I'll pray for you," he said quietly.

She clasped her other hand in his. Tears welled up. "Why does God allow this?"

He gave a small sad smile. "It's a question that has no answer."

Vivien escorted them out. By the front door was a bucket. In the bucket was the raven, on its side, eyes black and dead as stone, wings twisted.

"You caught it," remarked McGuigan.

She responded in a hard, flat voice – "It got what it deserved."

McGuigan and Dawson remained silent.

During the car journey back to Glasgow, Dawson made the necessary call to the Crown office. They had enough now to seek search warrants and production orders. They would require to speak directly to the Crown's lawyers, face to face, framing their reasons. But the facts were compelling. A reliable witness; a possible picture of the serial killer; alleged blackmail. Strange, thought McGuigan, how only two hours earlier, they were drifting, like flotsam in a fog, and now, amazingly, they had found a direction, and a little daylight to help guide them. But to where? McGuigan wasn't entirely sure.

The parameters had changed. Before, Bronson was merely a hunch in the back of McGuigan's mind. Now he was a clear and unequivocal person of interest. The firm of SJPS would have little choice. They would be compelled to provide details of the 'boat house'. That, of course, was on the presumption they possessed such information. Plus, Bronson's office would be searched, and his flat.

"We'll have to check Mrs Shawbridge's story," said Dawson. "About her son being ill."

"Peculiar, isn't it," replied McGuigan. "How one seems to look to God in times of dread and sadness. But yet, when the sun's out and there's laughter and wine, he tends to be forgotten about."

"Human nature, I suppose. Why look for help when you don't need it? Perhaps all this churchgoing is paying off."

"Perhaps," mused McGuigan.

"But why would Bronson want to go out of his way to come to the police station, give a statement, and describe a completely different face?"

McGuigan looked out through the car window, at the passing trees and hedges and houses. The day was overcast, the sunlight splintered and random. *Life goes on,* he thought, *despite the unfairness of the world.* He was bone weary.

"To make sure."

Dawson cast a quizzical glance.

"To make sure we got it wrong," he continued. "To use a cliché, keep us off the scent. In his mind, if the killer got caught – who he believed was Mrs Shawbridge's son – he wouldn't get his money. Ergo, he tried to sabotage the system. But his plot seems to have backfired magnificently. He got it as wrong as it was possible to get."

Dawson nodded. He was about to speak, but chose to say nothing.

"What is it, Kenny? Speak up."

"Okay. It looks like Bronson's been a bad boy. But…"

"But?"

"…but it doesn't really bring us any closer to capturing the main man."

"The main man. The leading actor in a slasher horror flick. Who knows? We follow the path, and see where it leads. Perhaps, if we find the boat house, we might find Bronson. Maybe Bronson holds the key."

Dawson didn't look convinced, and McGuigan couldn't blame him. An image popped into his mind. The dead raven, its great dark wings broken and mangled, and he wondered, as did Mrs Shawbridge, why God played such evil games.

CHAPTER THIRTY-SIX

Stark left his office at 5pm. He'd had the room to himself for most of the day. After Jenny's clandestine cigarette break, she'd got a call, and left in a fluster – *urgent fucking court hearing,* she'd explained, and she hadn't returned.

To his surprise, Maggie was sitting in the waiting room, in jeans, an old rugby top, a pair of unbranded trainers. Across her shoulder her somewhat frayed and drooping satchel.

"It wouldn't wait," she said. "Is there a coffee shop we can go to?"

"There's one not far. We can walk. The prices are wondrously expensive."

"Excellent. You're buying."

The place was ten minutes away, in a narrow cobbled lane away from the main traffic, pedestrian only, where the shops were quaint and colourful, where people browsed on a sunny day. The coffee shop was called The Yellowbird Coffee House. A wooden structure of irregular dimensions painted blue and yellow in an almost haphazard fashion; an undulating, red-tiled roof; porthole windows with white frames.

Maggie looked at it askance – "Is it falling down? Or falling in? I can't tell which."

"Either way, let's hope not."

They sat at a table. The interior was brushed sandalwood, the air tinged with the aroma of coffee and soft spice. Candles fluttered. The atmosphere was intimate. Not unappealing, thought Stark. They ordered two coffees. Stark was mildly surprised his sister hadn't ordered something more elaborate. Her mood was taut.

She looked at him square in the eyes. She wasn't smiling.

"You promise me this is not some huge bullshit joke."

"I'm not joking."

She held his stare. "Say it!"

He raised his hands – "Hey. I promise."

"Right." She leaned forward. "If I discover there is bullshit even the size of a rat's testicle in all this… thing, whatever this fucking thing is, then I swear, little brother, I will dissect your duodenum with a dessert spoon."

"A rat's testicle? That sounds very small."

She had placed her satchel on the table. She opened it, pulled out a sheaf of photocopied pages, and a pad with handwritten notes.

"Where the hell do I start?" There was no humour in her voice. Stark sat back. In her phone call, she had said she was scared. This, coming from his unflappable sister. She looked pale and tired. Suddenly, he was scared as well.

"I went to the Mitchell Library. The archive section. It has copies of every Scottish newspaper printed. I used to go there when I was studying. The hot chocolate is still amazing."

Stark couldn't help smiling.

"You said the newspaper was the *Hamilton Bugle*, and the date was 29th April 2011. Correct?"

She picked up the topmost photocopy, handed it to him. It was the front page of the newspaper, bearing the same date.

"The *Hamilton Bugle,* as the name would suggest, was a local newspaper for Hamilton and the surrounding area. It had an office in Campbell Street. The company which produced it went bust, and the paper went out of circulation in 2012."

Stark stared at the black-and-white copy. The headlines comprised a half page of a picture of Prince William and Kate Middleton, embracing, on the balcony of Buckingham Palace. Also, other smaller sections, of more mundane matters.

"You said you saw page eighteen in your dream, yes?"

"Yes." His mouth was dry. "I'm frightened, Maggie."

A girl arrived with the coffees, put them on the table.

"Enjoy," she said breezily.

Maggie continued, her face set. She handed him another sheet of paper. "These are the notes I made last night, when I copied down what you remembered."

Stark said nothing.

"And here is a copy of page eighteen of the *Hamilton Bugle.*"

She handed him the third sheet.

There it was. His dream, laid bare before him, morphed somehow into reality, comprising letters, words, paragraphs. He felt dizzy. Everything was exactly as he remembered it. The format, the layout, the spaces between each article. *Jesus,* he thought, *even the misprints.*

"It's identical," she said. "Bottom right-hand. The suicide of a young woman."

She fell silent. Stark read, but he didn't need to read, because he knew what it said already.

He put the copy to one side. "How can this be?"

Maggie sipped her coffee, placed the cup carefully back on its saucer. The cup was the extra-wide type, making her hands look small.

She pursed her lips, as if deliberating her next sentence.

"It seems to me, there are three explanations."

She scratched the end of her nose with the tip of her index

finger – a reflex he knew well enough, usually occurring when she was weighing thoughts in her mind.

"Number one. The whole thing is an elaborate prank. For reasons unknown, you memorised an obscure piece of news, and you're pretending you dreamt it. Weird, bordering on creepy, but nevertheless, an explanation." She eyed him again. "We will however discount this. You've promised it's not bullshit, and I'll stick to that. One thing I do know about my brother is that he's not a liar."

"That's very kind."

"Don't mention it. Explanation number two. Somehow, maybe years ago, you read this article. It's dated 2011. Or perhaps someone showed it to you at a later date. Perhaps it was kicking around the house. Maybe it was used to wrap fish and chips. Who knows? But maybe you read it, and then, as one would expect, you forgot all about it. And then, maybe years later, something triggers your subconscious to bring it back into life. An event. Perhaps you heard about a suicide on TV." She looked at Stark. "Perhaps…"

"Perhaps," interrupted Stark, "…the Alfie Willow massacre spewed up stuff buried deep in my mind. That's what you're saying."

Maggie gave a lame smile. "It's entirely possible. It's *a thing.* The boffins call it Semantic Memory. But this theory has a flaw."

"Yes?"

"If it really was an old memory, you would remember it. I mean, you would remember the moment, when you read the article, and the circumstances surrounding you reading it – the context. But that's not the case. Not here."

Stark shook his head. "No. It came from a dream."

She took a deep breath. She lifted the huge cup, sipped, placed it back.

"Then there's number three."

"Number three," repeated Stark in a heavy voice.

"We look beyond the explainable. We look at psychic phenomenon. We look at factors beyond our understanding."

"Witchcraft and black magic."

"The supernatural. Something outwith the laws of nature."

Stark took a glug of his coffee. It was tepid. He hated tepid coffee.

"I picked up a file in the basement of the building where I work. A place affectionately coined 'the dungeon'. An eerie place. The file shouldn't have been there. It had been put on the wrong shelf. By accident? By design? God only knows. It hardly matters. I looked through it. I don't know why. But I did. It was a file concerning the estate of a dead woman. The firm acted in finalising matters. It didn't consist of much – a collection of assets and general correspondence. And her death certificate, which stated the cause of death as 'asphyxiation'." Suddenly Stark had a thought. "The article in the newspaper didn't give her name."

"Oho!" Maggie lifted her arm, pointed up into the air, as a person might do answering a question in a classroom. "But I found that out!"

"Really?"

"I checked ahead. Three days later – 2nd May – the newspaper produced the name of the woman." She glanced at her notepad. "I have it here..."

"Deborah Ferry," said Stark, in a dull monotone.

Maggie looked up. She blinked. She did that when her mind required to compute complex information.

"Yes."

"Yes."

Maggie did not respond. She was waiting.

"I know all about her," he said. "My dream – if that's what it was – wasn't simply me observing a series of scenes. I *lived* those scenes. *I was that person.* I knew everything she knew. Her past, her present. I felt her fear." He shivered. "Her disgust."

Maggie spoke, almost in a whisper. Her face was a pale orb in the soft glimmer of the candlelight.

"What happened to her, Jonathan?"

Stark stared into his coffee cup. The events of the dream tumbled over and over, like a beast squirming in his mind, all claws and teeth.

"I watched her being abused. I was in her bedroom. I saw him enter her room, and violate her as she lay in bed. Only I *was* her, and I felt every hellish second of that violation." He swallowed, blew through his lips, as he recollected the terror. He felt sick. "She was ten years old. The rapes had been a constant thing since she was eight. Every night she lived in dread."

He took a breath, composed his thoughts as best he could.

"Then, I was in a wood. I watched as this little girl, who was now a woman, tied a rope around her neck, and hanged herself on the branch of a cherry-blossom tree. And you know what she felt, right up to the very last second of her life?"

"Tell me."

"Guilt. She felt she was to blame. That it was all her fault. That she deserved to die. Her heart was consumed with self-loathing. She felt she had no other choice but to rid the stain of her existence from the earth." He ran his hands through his hair. "Jesus, this is fucked up."

Maggie reached over, took his hand. He welcomed her soft touch.

"I don't know what to say, Jonathan. It's all so weird."

He gave a tremulous smile. "I know what you're thinking."

She raised a dubious eyebrow. "Mind-reading as well?"

"You're analysing this with your doctor's mind. That I need to go back to a shrink, who will doubtless provide some obscure and incomprehensible reason for the whole thing."

She wrinkled her nose. "I might, if it weren't for the overwhelming evidence. But there is explanation number four."

"I thought there were only three."

Again, the scratching of the tip of the nose. Then she said, "You were in a coma for eight weeks. Your mind was encased in itself, devoid of any external stimulation. Almost like a form of hibernation." She hesitated, made a small gesture with her shoulders, suggesting she wasn't entirely sure how to articulate her next words. "Maybe... maybe it became hyper-sensitive. Maybe, during this time, it developed a capacity to become... how can I put it... receptive."

Stark's lips twitched into the semblance of a half-smile. "Receptive? To what, I wonder."

"Maybe," she continued, "it developed a form of extra-sensory perception. There's been studies on the subject. Telepathy. Telekinesis. The mind can be a powerful thing."

"You know what I think?"

"Tell me."

"You've been reading way too many Stephen King novels."

She sighed. "Gave up on him years ago." She sat back, folded her arms in that entrenched way, displaying a defiant courage. "I'm worried, Jonathan. I don't understand what's going on. And I don't like things I don't understand. But we'll get through it."

The smile left Jonathan's face. He had never been more serious.

"Can I give you my take on things?"

Maggie nodded.

"How about this scenario. What if, while I was in a coma, down in the darkness, a monster slipped into my head, to become entangled in my mind. What if, this monster tore a hole open, and now whispers to the dead. And what if, the dead whisper back."

It was Maggie's turn to smile. "Wow. That's a lot of 'what ifs'. A monster? Very Gothic, little brother. If I'm reading Stephen King, you're reading *Dracula*."

Stark also sat back, gazed at Maggie. "It's a very scary book."

"It is."

"What am I supposed to do, Maggie?"

"Wait and see," she said. "Maybe it'll pass. Maybe it's a 'one-off' thing." She blinked, looked briefly away, then focused back.

"Can I ask you something?"

"Of course."

"In your dream, the little girl was the subject of prolonged abuse. You said you knew everything about her – her past, her present. And her future. If that's so, then you would know who he was."

"He?"

"The abuser."

"Yes," he responded somewhat bluntly. "I know who he is." He didn't expand.

Maggie knew when to let something go.

CHAPTER THIRTY-SEVEN

It had been a busy day. A long day. Eventful. He had been asked – *told* – to sort out the mess that morning. The mess, he had to admit, created by his own sloppiness. But he had done it, because he had no choice. He was exhausted. It had been a long drive, undertaken at short notice. Now, he hoped matters were back on track. He could concentrate on a much more important matter.

Wearing a bandage and a sling, he had to remain discreet. Doctor Sinclair would recognise him instantly. He therefore had to keep well back. He had followed her to the lawyers' office, and had waited in his car in the adjacent street. She had parked her car only a short distance from his, and had entered the building. He had watched her, the way she moved. So confident, he thought. So poised. Fifteen minutes later she had left, accompanied by a man. He was big. Maybe six-two. Good-looking guy. Wearing a suit. Presumably a lawyer. They looked roughly the same age. She wore a wedding ring. Her husband? Perhaps. He had experienced a prickle of jealousy. He had watched as they walked off together, in the opposite direction of her parked car. He had decided to follow.

And now, here he was, lingering in an antique shop opposite while she had coffee. It was closing time, but he made the pretence of being interested in some expensive stuff, giving the owner hope that there might be a last-minute sale. He cast surreptitious glances towards the coffee shop – quaintly called The Yellowbird Coffee House – and wondered what they were discussing, she and this man.

Already, he had a route map planned in his head. Where and how. The where was easy. She worked night shift at the hospital. She parked her car in the hospital car park. She had her own private parking bay. A relatively secluded spot, at the farthest point from the hospital entrance, shrouded in shadow, on the periphery of the lights. The how was easy too. There was CCTV, which was an irrelevance. He would be suited up – gloves, hood. A shadow amongst shadows. He would act while she was opening her car door, rendering her unconscious, bundle her in his car, and drive her to his special place on the moors.

And the when. He was, by nature, a meticulous planner. His projects demanded discipline and patience. Which had failed him. The last had ended in debacle. As such, his modus operandi had altered dramatically. Now, he would act. Swiftly and efficiently. The change released him, made him feel marvellously free. No more months of reconnaissance and painstaking research and studying patterns of behaviour.

He would take the doctor at the end of the week.

He saw them leave. He thanked the owner of the antique shop, assured him his antiques were very nice, but he would have to pass. The owner nodded, responded with a disappointed smile.

He left, keeping fifty yards behind. They didn't seem to display any outward signs of affection. No holding hands, no arms around shoulders or waists. Perhaps he was merely a friend. Or a brother. Or anything at all. He was slotting back to his old habits. Analysing, assessing. He pushed the thoughts from his mind. The guy was an irrelevance.

The end of the week. He would take her, and make her perfect.

CHAPTER THIRTY-EIGHT

THE BOAT HOUSE

The meeting with Mrs Shawbridge had been a disaster. Even Bronson, his mind slanted by drugs, could see this. But he had to keep going, keep moving, which was possible only through the sustaining power of cocaine. And his stash was running low. He hadn't slept properly for weeks. Concentration was tough. His thoughts were jumbled. He found it impossible to focus. His mind jumped from situation to situation, unable to fix on one thing. Like dancing across hot sand.

One thing he did know. He had fucked up. Big time. He wondered, briefly, how he could have been so stupid. His plan had been infantile and ill-conceived. The consequences were grim. Plus, he had Billy Watson at his heels.

Patricia Shawbridge had left. He gave it five minutes, put his jacket on, then he too had left the building, muttering to the receptionist he had an urgent "home visit", that he would return shortly. He went to his car, drove to his flat. There, he packed a few belongings. On his way out, he met his neighbour. An irritating little busybody with an irritating little dog. Bronson dispensed with pleasantries, choosing to studiously ignore him.

The man was clearly affronted, which, despite the circumstances, Bronson found amusing.

He got back into his car. He checked his mobile. Another missed call from Billy Watson. Billy was keen to get his money. Bronson was keen to replenish his supply. A solution would be worked out, he was sure. But not now. Bronson had to run. Bronson had to clear his head. There was only one place he could think of. His sanctuary.

He drove north.

Strangely, the farther away he got from Glasgow, the more the load lifted. It seemed perhaps it wasn't all as bad as he first thought. The scenery drifted by. The traffic was quiet at this time. Rush hour was over. Most people were working, as indeed he should have been. He played some music – soft classical piano. He wound the window down, felt the breeze on his face. Sure, the old witch had left in a storm. Who could blame her? How the hell was he supposed to know her son was dying. His mind switched instantly to the flip side. Maybe she was lying. Maybe her son was fine, and just maybe he *was* The Surgeon. Maybe she was playing hardball, hoping to face the situation down. She was a tough cookie, for sure.

Then his mind flipped back again, as was often the case when his brain was suffused with cocaine. He saw the look on her face, the downward curl of her lips, the raised eyebrows. The look of disbelief. Then the look of sheer, undiluted anger. There were no theatrics there, he thought. No acting. Her reaction was spontaneous and real.

And then his mind flitted to another scenario. So what if she makes a complaint? So what if she reports him to the police? It was her word against his. He would simply deny. He would claim vigorously the whole thing was a fabrication. That she was insane. That she had always hated him and that she wished to ruin his career.

Yes, he thought, that might work.

He glanced at his mobile phone on the passenger seat. The picture he had taken of the man called The Surgeon was still there. He had chosen not to remove it. Another thought popped into his head. Maybe he could still use it. Sell it to a newspaper. The only pictures in the world of Britain's most horrific serial killer. They'd pay a fortune. A goddamned king's ransom.

He got to Perth, and continued north. He had left his flat at 9.50. It was now 11.15. He thought of his clients, waiting patiently for updates – emails, phone calls, texts, whatever. They'd have a long wait. Tough shit. He had bigger things to think of. An image morphed into his mind. The policeman who had interviewed him. Detective Chief Inspector McGuigan. Bronson had disliked him from the off. Too damned clever for his own good. The type of man, he thought, who was both tenacious and stubborn. Suddenly, the man scared him.

He took a deep breath. The sun was bright. The clouds in Glasgow had dissipated to blue skies in the north. He kept his speed to a relaxed sixty mph. Comical if he were caught speeding. And then got tested for drugs. A spectacular ending to a spectacular day. He laughed out loud at the thought.

He kept north. The mobile thrummed on the seat. It hadn't really stopped since he'd left the office. He was tempted to toss the damn thing out the window. He tried to focus on the music.

Ninety miles later, and he took the Aviemore turn-off. He got to the roundabout at the edge of the town, took the route for Coylumbridge. A place comprising little more than a section of road. Blink and it was missed. He turned off at a road barely wide enough for a single car. A road with no name. He was entering the forests of the Rothiemurchus estate. In the distance, vast and sombre, loomed the Cairngorm mountains, dappled purple in the sunshine.

He drove two miles in, the road winding through trees packed tight. He arrived at his destination. A one-bedroomed house on the banks of Loch an Eilein, built of black timber with a pitched roof of red corrugated metal. It wasn't much, but it was enough.

The boat house. His mother had owned it. A little holiday home. She died, and he never got round to changing it into his name. Maybe, in a strange way, to keep her memory alive. Also, it provided an extra layer of privacy. He experienced a sudden flutter of fear. His recollection was vague, but he may have mentioned its existence to others. Which was the fundamental problem with cocaine. The brain got so wired, so frazzled, you talked about anything and everything, and after a while, it was difficult to keep track. But the place looked as empty as it always did.

He parked the car, then made his way to the loch side. The water was flat calm. It shimmered in the sun. Like a crest of jewels. White and blue and grey. He sat on the strip of sand, leaned back, felt the sun on his face, listened to the sounds of the world. He wished he could absorb himself into the ground. His mind felt sluggish. The craving came on. Something he could not ignore. He got up, went back to his car, opened the glove compartment, retrieved a polythene bag. With great care, he teased the powder onto the bonnet, arranged it into a fine line using one of his business cards, and hoovered the stuff up through his nose. The rush was instant. The loch held a deeper sparkle, the sounds of the forest more intense, the air clearer.

He got his travelling bag, his mobile phone, and went into the house.

Monday afternoon and evening passed without incident. He had no supplies, but there was some tinned food in a cupboard, and coffee. He had switched his mobile phone off.

Tuesday morning. He got up late. The sun was hidden behind a blanket of clouds the colour of old bruising. Looked like rain was coming. His bag was running worryingly low. He reckoned he might get another half dozen hits, if he were careful.

He drove into Aviemore on Tuesday afternoon, three miles distant, bought some milk and some processed food he could stick in the microwave. He bought a packet of cigarettes and a cheap plastic lighter. He hadn't smoked for twenty years, but thought, randomly, he would resurrect the habit. He bought some wine. He browsed the shops, bought a coffee, sat at an outdoor table. Aviemore had always bored him. Shops selling either outdoor gear, or overpriced tourist tat, possessing as much charm as a cheap fun park.

The rain stayed away.

He got back to the house, late afternoon. His nerves jangled. As ever, his mind was in overdrive. He wondered, not without a degree of dread, what mysteries his mobile phone held. Who was wanting what. He guessed Billy Watson was top of the list. Certainly his firm. Perhaps Mrs Shawbridge had stirred things up. If so, the partners would want a little tête-à-tête, for sure. And if things had escalated, perhaps the police were now interested.

But he chose to ignore it. Instead, he took another line. The evening wore on. He went for a walk at 8pm, around the loch, a distance of about four miles. Darkness was falling, but he knew the way. When he was much younger, he cycled the path. He and his mother. She was fit then, well, before the cancer. He felt a swell of profound sadness. If he could turn the clock back...

He got back to the house. He watched some mindless crap on TV. He went to bed at midnight.

On Wednesday, he got up at 8am in a deep state of depression. He took another line of cocaine. His heart and mind buzzed. He was awake once again. He still didn't turn his mobile on. He wanted to toss the damn thing in the loch. He chose not to. Like most people in the civilised world, the phone was like an appendage to the human body. Losing a phone was like losing a limb.

The sun was out again, but in brief slants, finding the spaces between the clouds.

2pm. Just as Stark was finishing his lunch appointment with Edward Stoddart one hundred and eighty miles away, there came a knock on Bronson's front door.

Bronson was sitting in the lounge. The view was directly of the loch. He had the television on, and therefore would not have heard a car approach and park at the side of the building. He did however hear the knock. He jumped at the sound. He remained still. Maybe he'd imagined it? It came again. His mind sparked into a hundred scenarios. He tried to focus. No point in ignoring it. Whoever they were, they knew very well he was here. His car was outside, and the television was blaring. And if they really wanted him, they could simply break the door down. Better then to confront. If it was Billy Watson, he could maybe reason, come to an arrangement. The threat Watson had made reared up – *face burnt with acid.*

The knock came again. More forceful. He heard a voice, shouting his name. He frowned, trying to understand. He went to the front door, opened it. He stared. It took a second before he found his voice. Standing before him was the last person he expected to see.

"Good God Almighty," he said. "What the hell are *you* doing here?"

CHAPTER THIRTY-NINE

Stark went straight back to his flat. He checked his messages, half-hoping Jenny might have contacted him about drinks. But she hadn't, and he wondered if maybe he should message her, then decided against it. Too much, too soon. Last thing he wanted was to be regarded as "pushy". Last thing he wanted was to be rejected.

He experienced a range of emotions. The conclusions of Maggie's research was mind-boggling and weird and terrifying. Yet, not surprising. He knew the truth in his dreams. He had known, all along, deep down, they were real. Maggie had merely "rubber-stamped" his own instinct.

He changed, put on his old, ragged running trousers, a T-shirt, his ancient running shoes, and hit the streets. He hadn't run for days. The first mile was tough. The one thing he knew about running – about any exercise – was how quickly fitness and endurance dissipated through lack of routine. He felt stiff, his lungs tight. After a mile, once the blood started pumping, things got easier. The stiffness disappeared, the lungs were less laboured. He ran five miles, and felt good. Running made him forget, for a little while.

He got back, showered, changed. He had brought some work back with him, files packed into a small rucksack. Perhaps, he mused, he might buy a proper briefcase with his pay cheque. Probably not.

He laid the papers on the kitchen table. He tried to concentrate. But always, his thoughts steered back to the dream, the little girl, her terror and pain. The woman, her sadness and desolation.

He soldiered on, focused on the work. He gave up at 9pm, watched TV, and drifted asleep on the couch…

…and was in the girl's bedroom.

Again watching from the corner. Everything was as before. The room was exactly the same. Dread filled his heart and squeezed his throat. He made out the shape under the covers. The shape moved. The girl sat up, looked at him. She pulled her blanket back. She was wearing pyjamas – bright with pink elephants. She made her way to him, stopped, and looked up. She was so tiny and frail.

"Make him pay," she whispered.

She returned to her bed. Seconds passed. Maybe minutes. Maybe hours. Time meant nothing. Stark knew the sequence of events, and it terrified him. The bedroom door opened, the shadow slithered in…

…and then he was in the wood, in the place where the cherry-blossom tree stood. The woman stood before him. So pale. So tired. She turned, and spoke to him.

"I hid it there." She pointed to the base of the tree. "Make him pay," she whispered, and she touched his cheek. Her fingers were ice cold.

"Make him pay."

CHAPTER FORTY

Stark woke. It was 5am. The TV was still on. He switched it off, let the silence calm him. He got up, went to the kitchen, got a glass of water, sat at his kitchen table. Strewn across it, the papers he had brought home. Also, his unopened laptop. In that quiet moment, he understood what he had to do.

He got a piece of scrap paper, wrote down what he intended to say. He crossed it out. It had to be simple. It had to be compelling. He at last found the words. Not perfect, but this was new territory. He opened his laptop. He typed the message, touched the "send" button, using his own private email address. It went.

What now? he wondered, and not for the first time thought that either he was dreaming, or he was insane, or maybe both.

Stark left his flat at 5.45am. He had a journey to make, to the woods beyond the town of Hamilton. Specifically, to Chatelherault Woods, to a cherry-blossom tree standing solitary in the centre of a clearing. He knew the path to get there, because he had walked it in his dreams. His destination was not far. He would be back in ample time to start another day with the firm of Stoddart, Jeffrey, Pritchard and Sloss.

The journey took him forty-five minutes. It was too early for rush hour, and traffic was light. He found the woods without difficulty. The main entrance was well signposted, comprising an asphalt car park, adjacent to a kids' play area. Stark parked his car. There were no others. A hundred yards from the car park, a garden centre – a large building constructed of glass and bleached timber. Pale sunlight filtered through heavy clouds. At this time, a dreary, cheerless place.

He closed his eyes, focused, allowing his mind to open. The scene in his dream reared up. The way before him was clear. A path led from the car park, into the interior of the wood. He had dreamt this path, and the path was there, exactly as it should be. For a second, his resolve wavered. The sheer weirdness of the situation made his head spin. A new emotion bloomed in his chest – fear. He stood, took deep breaths, dug deep for the courage to continue. He made his way into the gloom.

He followed the main path for a mile. Trees on either side pressed in close, preventing daylight. Here, the world was still and quiet, the air close, almost stifling. A place where secrets were made, and kept. A lone jogger startled him, appearing suddenly from a bend. Stark stepped to one side. The jogger gave a curt nod, passed him, and a second later was gone. Stark stayed motionless, took several heartbeats to compose himself, moved on.

He reached a section where a barely discernible trail branched off from the main path, cutting a twisting swathe through the trees – exactly as he had dreamt. His pulse raced. He was close now.

He followed the trail, downhill, watching his footing. Easy to twist an ankle, to stumble, break a bone. In the near distance, the sound of a river flowing. He brushed back branches, kept moving. Twenty minutes later, the trees thinned a little, the ground flattened. He reached the clearing – a rough circle – the cherry-blossom tree in its centre. The image, vivid and beautiful, again tested his resolve. It was an exact reproduction of the image in his dream. He stopped, stared in fascination. There! The low branch on which she had hanged herself. Nothing had changed. Perhaps nothing would ever change, he thought, until the scales were balanced. Perhaps the tree was frozen in time, fixed forever, until matters were finally resolved.

Sunlight slanted down, finding a way between the clouds. Stark stepped up to the tree. He touched the rough bark with the tips of his fingers. Such tragedy had taken place, the tree a solemn silent witness. There was no wind, no movement. To Stark, the place possessed a perfect stillness.

The evening before, he had purchased a gardening hand trowel from a late-night DIY warehouse, which he'd brought with him, tucked in his coat pocket. He remembered what she had said, where she had pointed. The ground was layered with leaves and twigs, the soil soft. He squatted, began to dig, exactly where he knew he should dig. Less than a minute passed. He found what he was looking for. She hadn't buried it far. He stood, held the object, cocooned in heavy plastic.

His dream was real, and he knew what he had to do.

CHAPTER FORTY-ONE

Much to McGuigan's intense frustration, he didn't get the search warrant until that morning. He had spent over two hours the previous afternoon discussing things with the Crown lawyers. Minutiae. Details. But understandable. Details formed the building blocks, and cases were either won or lost based on the strength of those building blocks. A judge needed compelling evidence before signing off. All they had was a statement from a witness, lacking corroboration. But she was credible. And the significance was massive. A possible photograph of The Surgeon. Sheer gold dust. A real and tangible chance of a breakthrough.

It came at 10am that morning. A warrant faxed from the Crown office. The original wet copy was couriered, granting the requisite power to enter the office of Bronson Chapel, and also his flat. Plus, the authority to seize any papers relevant to Bronson held by the firm of SJPS.

He organised a team of four men and women to attend the flat. He headed a further team of six officers to attend Bronson's place of work. They got there at 11am. The receptionist listened, Kenny Dawson explaining in his slow methodical way what was happening, their faces a mixture of shock and bewilderment. Those people in the waiting room – clients, he assumed – sat and stared, wide-eyed, blank-faced, doubtless bemused at the turn of events.

The receptionist said she would need to contact a partner. A natural reaction, he thought, and one which he had no particular problem with. They waited in the foyer. She spoke into the phone, waited ten seconds, nodded, turned her attention back to Dawson.

"Someone will be down right away," she said.

"Thank you."

They waited. Dawson gave McGuigan a meaningful look, the significance of which, McGuigan understood. *Somewhere in the building, much worry and consternation.*

Ten minutes later, three people came down the stairs behind the reception desk. Two men, a woman.

They noticed the police straight off. They approached them. McGuigan stepped forward, introduced himself.

The woman did likewise. "I'm Winnifred Marshall." She glanced at the two men beside her. "This is Walter Hill, and Paul Hutchison. We're the managing partners."

The lawyer called Walter Hill gave a small courteous nod. The other – Paul Hutchison – gave no acknowledgement.

"Is Bronson Chapel in the building?" McGuigan asked. A long shot, but still.

Winnifred Marshall responded with the slightest shake of her head. "He isn't in." She licked her lips. She looked uncomfortable. A reasonable reaction, thought McGuigan.

She kept her voice low. "Can we go somewhere a little more private, Chief Inspector? Please? This is very… public."

"Of course. If that's what you want."

He indicated to the others to remain where they were. Then he and Dawson followed the three lawyers through the waiting room, to a door at the far end, built to blend in with the surrounding décor. She opened it. They filed through to a corridor far less lavish, with offices on either side, busy with people hunched over computer screens. A young man, maybe in his late twenties, appeared from a room, carrying a file. McGuigan remembered him. The same young man he had seen during his last visit, walking up the stairs behind the reception desk. They exchanged brief looks. McGuigan experienced a tingle of something he could only describe as déjà vu. A flicker of lost memory; a trick, perhaps, of the mind.

He nodded. The young man nodded back, continuing on his way.

They were taken to a somewhat austere meeting room, furnished with some chairs, a table and a side table containing silver canisters of tea and coffee. There were only four chairs. Dawson stood at the door. McGuigan and the three sat. Neither coffee nor tea was offered.

"I have a warrant to search Bronson Chapel's office…" he began.

"We know this," snapped the man called Paul Hutchison. He held his hand out. "Let me see it." His voice was indignant, verging on aggressive.

McGuigan assumed a professional neutrality, handed him the warrant.

"You have to understand," said Winnifred, "as a firm of solicitors, the last thing we want is any trouble."

"I can imagine."

"Our reputation is… well, it's all we have." It was the other man who spoke – Walter Hill.

"It's important, for sure."

"Having a half-dozen police officers arrive at our front door," continued Winnifred, "it's not an ideal situation. It gets tongues wagging. Before you know it, all sorts of rumours are flying about."

Hutchison tossed the warrant on the table. "It's all bullshit."

He glared at McGuigan. "I know what this is about. You cops. Gloating at the prospect of pulling down a fancy law firm. We won't be intimidated. Not by the likes of you."

McGuigan placed the warrant in his inside jacket pocket. He appraised Hutchison. The man looked uncomfortable. He was sweating. He fidgeted. His eyes darted. Nerves? Perhaps.

"We're not here to intimidate," he replied. "We're here to implement a warrant."

"Of course," said Winnifred, smiling. She cast Hutchison a venomous glance. "Paul doesn't mean any offence."

"Don't condescend to me," said Hutchison. "I meant every goddamned word."

McGuigan inspected the man closer. Something was off. Hutchison was sweating, but it wasn't warm. In fact, the room they were occupying was cold. There was a chill in the air. Hutchison was perturbed. Unreasonably so.

"You can't believe a word she says," said Hutchison.

"I beg your pardon?"

"Patricia Shawbridge," he said, voice thick and harsh. "She's the one who started this. My opinion? She's got nothing better to do with her time. She's rich and thinks she can just coast in and make foul accusations about one of our partners, and expect everyone..." and here he jabbed a finger at McGuigan, "... including you, to jump up and dance to every jig she plays. Let me tell you, Chief Inspector McGuigan, I'm not fucking dancing!"

McGuigan said nothing. A silence fell. The other two lawyers kept their focus on McGuigan, ashen-faced. Clearly, the outburst had shocked them.

Hutchison wasn't finished. "To think, a lawyer from this firm would blackmail someone over a fucking photo on a mobile phone."

McGuigan raised an eyebrow. "A photo?"

Hutchison blinked. Hesitation crept into his voice. "Yes."

"Tell me about this photo."

Hutchison began to bluster. "I assume you knew. After all, that's why you're here."

"Please," said McGuigan softly. "Tell me."

"The photo." Hutchison took a breath. "She told us Bronson had shown her a photo of the killer. The Surgeon."

McGuigan assumed an expression of sudden interest. Hutchison had started it, and McGuigan would make damned well sure he would finish it. Nothing like a bit of sport, he thought, especially with an individual as obnoxious as Paul Hutchison. He appraised all three.

"You're telling me Patricia Shawbridge told you that she'd been shown a photograph of one of the most prolific serial killers in British history?" He focused on Hutchison. "That's what you're telling me?"

Hutchison licked his lips. He was about to speak, then thought better of it.

"She told all three of you?"

They gave him blank stares.

"When was this?"

Walter Hill spoke up, a tremor in his voice. "Yesterday."

McGuigan leaned forward. "Someone gave you this information yesterday." He looked specifically at Hutchison, and he said, his voice still soft – "And you didn't think to report this to the police?"

Hutchison's face reddened. He stood up. "This is bullshit," he muttered.

He left the room, raking the others with a look of withering scorn.

Winnifred gave a small hopeless grimace. "What can I say?" she said. "I'm sorry for Paul's outburst. He's clearly not himself. And as for us not reporting the matter to the police, you must understand, we weren't in full possession of the facts. We still aren't. We thought it prudent to hear Bronson's side of the story. I can only apologise..."

"I assume you haven't seen or heard from Bronson since his meeting with Mrs Shawbridge."

"Correct," said Hill. "He's gone off radar. No contact. We have a small army of angry clients to manage. I accept it doesn't look good."

McGuigan gestured with a conciliatory hand. He had no desire to fight these people. He needed them on his side. Paul Hutchison was simply an arrogant man with a temper. An irrelevance. He'd encountered far worse.

"You need us to be discreet," he said. "I understand completely. But we'll need your help. We need to find Bronson. And we certainly need to establish if what Mrs Shawbridge said is true. If so, we'd like to know if he still has the photograph, which could be vital information. The truth is, if Bronson really has taken a picture of this particular killer, then his life might be in danger. Hence, we have to find him. Hence, the warrant."

"I understand," replied Winnifred, her voice tight and brittle.

"We'll commence our search." He searched her face. "Bronson isn't at his house." Again, he spoke gently. "Do you know where he might have gone?"

"He sometimes talked about a small holiday home. His retreat."

"Yes?"

"I think our admin department might have the details."

McGuigan waited.

"He called it the 'boat house'."

CHAPTER FORTY-TWO

The arrival of the police, the flustered meeting, the worried faces – perfect ingredients for rumour and speculation. Stark, whilst intrigued, had other matters on his mind. Jenny sat at her desk. She appeared pale and listless. She stared at her screen, her expression blank.

Stark attempted conversation.

"Bad day at court yesterday?"

She turned, gave him a weary smile.

"The worst. Hopefully never to be repeated."

"Wow. That good. Can I get you a coffee? Or perhaps a vodka?"

She sighed. "I never slept. Again. It's a fucking killer."

"Yes," he agreed. "It can be." Stark was a veteran of sleepless nights. He understood exactly her predicament.

"Plus," she said, "I have a shitstorm of work to get through. And the shitstorm seems to get thicker by the second."

"Anything I can do to lighten the load?"

She reacted with a broad grin. "You could shoot some of my clients."

Stark nodded, said nothing. Jenny frowned, clicked her tongue in annoyance.

"Jesus, Jonathan – I am so sorry. How crass. It was just a slip of the tongue. I didn't..."

Jonathan returned the grin. "I think it should be part of legal training. Learning to shoot clients. It would be both therapeutic and gratifying."

She gave a tired laugh. "Not from the clients' perspective."

"Perhaps not."

The lawyer Stark met briefly during his first day entered the room. Des. His round pimply face seemed to glow with excitement.

"You heard what's happening?" He spoke in a rush, the words fairly tripping over each other.

"I saw some partners going into the meeting room," replied Stark. "With a couple of serious-looking guys. They didn't look like they were out collecting for the Red Cross."

Des closed the door, lowered his voice.

"It's only the police," he said. "There's half a dozen of them going through Bronson's office. They've taken his laptop. Looks like he's in some serious shit. The fucking partners are going ballistic. Even old Stoddart wandered down from his mausoleum to see what the commotion was about. And Paul Hutchison is acting weird. He's hardly spoken. Got his door closed. Whatever Bronson's been up to, it's spooked them."

The news seemed to spark Jenny's interest. Her eyes displayed the bright inquisitiveness Stark had come to recognise.

"What's the word on the street?" she said.

"Not sure. But Bronson's always been a maverick. Doing things his way. And he's got some dodgy clients."

"Everyone's got dodgy clients. Otherwise lawyers wouldn't make any money. Otherwise no one would make any money."

Stark couldn't help laughing. Jenny had the ability of articulating amazing truths.

"Perhaps it's a money-laundering thing?" he suggested, half-jokingly. "Isn't that the new bear trap for unsuspecting lawyers?" He had never met Bronson Chapel, and was only vaguely aware he was part of Paul Hutchison's litigation team.

"Could be," said Des.

"They've taken his laptop," reminded Jenny.

"Exactly," said Des. "I'm thinking paedo. Big time. A regular trawler of the dark web."

Jenny clapped her hands. "There you have it, Jonathan. Now you have witnessed first-hand how rumours are conceived and ripened in a lawyer's office. Before the sun has set, Bronson Chapel will be a money-laundering, dark-web-trawling paedophile, which will stick with him until the day he dies." Her shoulders sagged. She suddenly lost her sparkle. "Until the day he dies," she repeated.

"Gotta go. But I'll keep my ear to the ground." Des disappeared, no doubt to visit other offices to spread the news, if in fact he hadn't already done so.

"God, I'm tired," said Jenny. "I'm not sure I can keep going." There was no flippancy in her voice. She seemed dead serious.

"Maybe you should stop," Stark said.

She regarded him curiously. "Maybe I should. Maybe I could run off to some warm country, and do a little painting, and earn just enough to live on cheese and wine. Maybe not the cheese."

Stark was intrigued. "You paint? Seriously?"

She pursed her lips, exhaled, causing them to ripple. "Sort of. I used to. But then I stopped. I might start again, if I find the right…" She paused, distracted.

"The right…?"

"The right subject material. Did I hear you mention something about coffee?"

Stark nodded. End of conversation. She looked exhausted, and they both had work to do. He got up.

"Jonathan?"

"Yes."

"Didn't you mention something about buying me cheap beer? Just wondering if the offer was still on the table. Or was it just an empty gesture?"

"It is. And no, it wasn't."

"I'm free after work."

He hesitated. "I could meet you later in the evening."

She raised an eyebrow. "You're meeting your other woman?"

"Not quite. But I have to be somewhere important. It's unavoidable, I'm afraid."

Which was the truth. It *was* unavoidable. And he *was* afraid. If he told her where and why, she would think him mad. Perhaps he was. It seemed to Stark, from day one working with the firm of SJPS, he had entered a world of madness.

And soon, maybe, a world of danger.

CHAPTER FORTY-THREE

She had no children. She had a dog. A cocker spaniel she walked in the fields beyond her house. She lived with her partner. Possibly her husband, but he wasn't certain. *Uncertainty.* A new and invigorating sensation. Before, he would have known exactly her situation. Now, he was working virtually on instinct. As a true predator should. The freedom emboldened him.

The man she met at the lawyers' office was, presumably, a friend, or a relative. Or a secret lover? He didn't know and didn't care. She lived in a quaint little house in the village of Jackton, only two miles from the hospital where she worked, and, by a strange quirk of fate, only three miles from the moors. Everything clicked. The signs were there. It was as if God himself had intervened, weaving together the threads of his life, to form a final glorious pattern – the disaster at Evelyn Stephens' house, the wrong photofit the police had shown, his hand breaking, the chance encounter at the hospital. *The signs were there.* God was smiling. He was saying – *you can do any fucking thing you want.*

He didn't need much. A hammer, to reduce the initial struggle, a rag soaked in chloroform to keep her subdued. A pair of handcuffs. A travelling rug. He had one hand in bandages, but it was a minor disadvantage. He had strength and cunning. And most importantly, surprise.

So simple. No need to carry the required tools. All that stuff would be in his house, to be used at his leisure. No time restraints. No pressure. He could spend days, if he so wished, fussing, adjusting, perfecting. The prospect made his heart beat fast. Never had he experienced such thrill.

He watched, through binoculars, from a lay-by three hundred yards away. Watched, as she threw a stick, and her dog bounded across the grass. Watched her movements – so lithe, so supple.

He was tempted to start his car up, drive to her house, go to the fields, and take her. He drew a deep calming breath. There was spontaneity, and then there was sheer carelessness. But still... it was tempting. With supreme effort, he dismissed the notion.

He could wait, barely. His nerves tingled with excitement.

Friday night. His hands trembled so much, he had to put the binoculars down. He closed his eyes and pictured the work ahead in creating his final masterpiece, and thought, *With God on my side, nothing can ever stop me.*

He took another deep breath, composed himself, lifted the binoculars back to his eyes, calmed the tremble in his hands. She had stopped. The dog was running in frantic circles round her, stick clenched in its jaws. She had her mobile pressed to her ear. He wondered who she was talking to, and again felt that prickle of envy.

Her calls would soon stop. He would see to that. Her world would end. His would begin. Such was the power he held.

Stark got a call at 1pm from his sister. He had to admire her. She knew his lunch hour was between one and two. She wouldn't phone during normal working hours. Her work ethic was such, she would think such a call as obtrusive, bordering on damned rude. Work hours were sacrosanct, designed only for working.

"You sound breathless," he said.

"As you would too, if you had an overactive and highly stupid spaniel to walk."

"You could always hire a dog walker."

"Are you offering?"

"Keep the position vacant. Who knows how long I'll last in my current employment."

She gave a rattling chuckle. "It's only a job," she said.

"It's maybe a little more than that."

"Maybe you're right. How you doing?"

"Honestly? Shell-shocked. Reeling. All over the place. Trying to come to terms with what happened. Otherwise, marvellous."

"Completely natural reaction." She stopped talking, the sound over the phone now one of rustling and gasping. Then her voice came back. "Trying to get the bloody stick. His mouth's like a slavering steel trap, I swear." Another sound, the swish of movement. *Throwing the bloody stick,* he assumed.

"Any thoughts?" she asked.

"On what?"

"The way forward. Did you have the same dream last night?"

"When the dead want to chat, they're persistent. Yes, same dream." *But different.* "What's the diagnosis, Dr Sinclair?"

Another pause in the conversation. But there was no background noise. He imagined her, standing in the middle of the field next to her house, staring at the blue yonder, trying desperately to think of something positive to say.

"That's okay," he said quickly. "I don't think this problem has a cure. Not in the conventional sense." He laughed, but he knew it rang false. "I'll just try and not sleep."

"It's overrated, dude." Her voice was soft and serious. "I'm sorry, Jonathan. I wish I had an answer to give you."

"Maybe I have an answer."

She didn't speak. She was waiting for him to explain.

"Maybe they're asking for help. Maybe I should listen to what they're trying to tell me."

"Seriously?" she retorted. "Maybe you should do nothing of the sort. We're back to those Stephen King novels. We're not conversing with the dead. Okay – the dreams are creepy, they're scary, there's obviously something inexplicable going on. But they're dreams. That's all they are. If you start acting on them, then you give them substance, you lend them a credibility they don't need – you don't need – and then it becomes a real mindfuck. They're dreams. My advice – accept them, and in time, they'll dissolve to nothing, like dreams do. Promise me you'll do that."

"But they are credible," he argued, with no real conviction.

"They're dreams. Don't make them real. Please. We'll get through this shit, whatever this shit is."

"I know we will."

"I love you, little brother."

"I love you too, Mags."

He disconnected.

The dead were whispering in the night. And Stark knew, deep down, that for any conclusion to be reached, he had no choice but to listen.

His sister had warned not to give his dreams substance. He had done exactly the opposite. He had sent the email. And more.

It was lunchtime. He had a place to go to, and something to get. A place on the periphery of the city centre, not far from the office, which sold a specific item few others sold. He could get there and back in under an hour. It was a gamble. But he needed to be sure. He had embarked on a strange and twisted journey, and had no earthly idea what lay before him, or the repercussions of his actions. Perhaps nothing at all. Perhaps everything. He checked his watch. He would find out in roughly five hours.

CHAPTER FORTY-FOUR

They had an address. The boat house. On the banks of a pretty loch called An Eilein, deep in the Cairngorms. McGuigan and Dawson left immediately. McGuigan guessed there was little prospect of finding anything useful in Bronson's office, unless he had transferred the picture to the hard drive of his computer, which was unlikely, but not impossible. The prospect of Bronson having left his mobile phone in his office, or indeed his flat, was remote.

But they had an address.

"He's probably not there," said Dawson, as they were driving north. As ever, the voice of scepticism, thought McGuigan, which was why he was such an excellent sounding board. McGuigan offered no immediate response.

"Why should he be?" continued Dawson. "He's been accused of blackmailing a client, withholding material evidence, misleading us. If it's true, he's looking at jail time. So he's done a runner. Who can blame him? Why would he go somewhere obvious? If I were him, a fugitive from the law, I would not be hightailing it to my holiday home in the Highlands. That wouldn't be a clever move."

McGuigan watched the world outside pass by. "Where would you go, Kenny? If you were in Bronson's shoes?"

Dawson considered. "Abroad? Lose myself in Spain or France or somewhere far away with a bit of sun."

"That takes money. And planning. And confidence. And more money."

Dawson, both hands on the steering wheel, shrugged his shoulders. "He's a partner in a fancy law firm. These guys charge serious money. He'll have the dosh, no doubt about it."

"Maybe. I'm not so sure." McGuigan shifted to one side, pulled out a packet of bubblegum from his trouser pocket. He carefully unwrapped it, placed the paper in the little storage compartment in the centre console, popped a piece of marble-sized pink gum in his mouth, and chewed thoughtfully.

"If Mrs Shawbridge is to be believed, Bronson tried to extort a lot of money from her. Therefore, the notion he has enough funds to live in another country is flawed. In fact, it would appear Bronson may be in substantial debt. The way I see it, I don't actually think Bronson wants to run away. Not in the fugitive sense. I think Bronson knows he's done wrong. He's overstepped the boundaries. But not to any huge extent. I genuinely believe he thinks we wouldn't be interested enough to be looking for him. But he still needs time to think things through. Clear his head. Sort his story out. He's a lawyer. He'll rationalise the situation. And at the end of the day, all he needs to do is to deny. It's one word against the other. And as for the supposed photograph, all he has to do is delete it. And even if he gave us the wrong description of The Surgeon, so what? He got mixed up. Shock. No, Dawson. Bronson hasn't flown off to sunnier climes. He isn't far away. The boat house has potential."

Dawson sighed. "If you say so, boss. Still, it's a long way to go on a hunch."

"I'm enjoying the scenery. And the air is far fresher. Don't you think?"

"I'm thinking the local constabulary could check if he's at the address. It would make life much simpler. And save a lot of time. If he's there, he's there. If he's not, he's not. A phone call is all it takes."

McGuigan blew a small bubble, which burst almost immediately. "I need to practise that," he muttered. He started chewing again. "Enjoy the moment, Kenny. The Cairngorm mountains are a wonder to behold. I used to climb them during my days of youthful exuberance. Not now sadly."

"We're going up for the views?"

"Not quite. If Bronson is at his 'boat house', then I want to speak to him first. He's not a suspect. Not yet. I need to hear his version, and, hopefully, entice him to give over the photo on his phone, if indeed he still has it. If uniform pay him a visit, he'll clam up, and then have time to make up a story. I need him fresh, Kenny. I need him… surprised."

Dawson nodded, acknowledging the wisdom of his boss's thought process.

"I didn't know you climbed."

McGuigan relaxed back on the passenger seat. "It's said, if you reach the top of a Scottish Munro, and the sky is clear and the sun is out, then you get a glimpse of heaven."

"Did you glimpse heaven, sir?"

"I never seemed to find it."

CHAPTER FORTY-FIVE

Stark was busy in the afternoon. Work continued, regardless of the situation. Nevertheless, his mind was preoccupied. He had much to consider. The police left at 2.30. No one was the wiser for their visit, and rumours raged. But the partners remained tight-lipped, which only intensified the speculation. Stark couldn't have cared less.

One of the rooms off the hall contained two photocopiers, and a fax machine. The fax machine was rarely used, considered almost as an antique. Stark was in the process of copying a fifty-page commercial lease. He was aware of a presence behind him. He turned. Edward Stoddart stood in the doorway. Stark was caught off guard.

"Make sure you've got it on the black-and-white setting." Stoddart winked and smiled. "Colour copies are twice as expensive."

Stark nodded. "Thank you for lunch…" he began.

Stoddart waved a hand. "Don't mention it. I thought I'd come down, to see how you were doing."

"All good. As you can see…" and he gestured at the photocopier, "…doing all the amazing jobs no one wants to do."

Stoddart leant against the frame of the doorway. He wore a dark suit, white shirt, dark tie. His complexion was deathly pale. Under the bright striplighting, his cheekbones seemed sharp and harsh, his eyes two glossy black pebbles. Skull-like. He looked frail, insubstantial. A wraith, rather than a man. Much frailer than he looked in his rooms on the top floor, where the lighting was muted.

"I should venture to the depths more often," he said, grinning. "To remind myself who the real workers are."

Stark said nothing.

"You will be aware we had a visit from the police," said Stoddart.

"I'd heard something of the sort."

"I dare say you have. Lawyers and fishwives have that particular trait in common – they each wallow in scurrilous rumour. But you must understand, Jonathan, it's the first time anything like this has happened. I hope…" he blinked, seemed suddenly uneasy, "…I hope that it hasn't put you off. I mean working here. As I said before, this firm desperately needs new blood. New blood like yours."

Stark again was taken off guard, not expecting such a comment. "Not at all. I'm pleased to be given this chance."

"That's good, Jonathan. It gives me hope when I hear you say that."

Stark had no response to give. He found the conversation bizarre. But then, the man had cancer. Possibly, he looked at the world from a different perspective.

"You've been down to the basement?" Stoddart asked suddenly.

Stark blinked, adjusting his thoughts to the abrupt change of conversation.

"Yes. A lovely place."

Stoddart gave a sympathetic shake of his head. "A trial to be endured. You know, it holds every file ever opened by this firm.

Or at least it did, until the destruction process started. Now everything's to be 'uploaded' or 'downloaded' or whatever the terminology is. Everything is to disappear, retrieved at the push of a button."

"So it would seem."

Stoddart made a half-step forward, still clutching the doorframe. His eyes gleamed. "But it's not the same," he said. "It's important to have something physical in your hands, to feel and touch these old documents. Documents which make up part of the history of a person's life. The issues and dilemmas and situations they experienced at the time. You look through a file, and you have a window to the past. They capture a moment, preserving it perfectly. Whether good or bad. Don't you think, Jonathan? If I had my way – which, in this regard, I don't – I would keep the files forever, as a shrine to those lives we have touched, and to those who have touched us. Once they're destroyed, something's lost. Something that can't be reproduced by pressing a button on a keyboard."

Stark swallowed. *What was the old man trying to say?*

He uttered a bland response. "I haven't honestly given it much thought."

"Of course not. Why would you? And have you noticed the other feature of our wonderful basement?"

Stark cocked his head, waited.

"It's always cold," said Stoddart. "The chill never leaves."

CHAPTER FORTY-SIX

Satnav was truly a magical thing, thought McGuigan. To find a house in the middle of a forest, where the only road in or out was a single lane barely wide enough for a small car, in his opinion, defied logic. They got there just after midday. They came to a small building, constructed of timber, built in a flat, grassed area with a driveway of uneven slabs. It overlooked the loch. On a nice day, the view would be extraordinary. A place beautiful and yet tinged with melancholy. McGuigan could understand perfectly why Bronson would regard this as a retreat. His 'boat house'.

Parked to one side were two cars. A black BMW, and a silver Jaguar F-Pace.

"Interesting," remarked Dawson. He parked the car on the side of the road adjacent to the house. "The BMW is Bronson's. Looks like you were right. And it seems he has company."

"Yes."

"Perhaps we should call backup."

"Perhaps we should," said McGuigan. "But then again, perhaps we shouldn't. We've driven all this way. A shame for uniform to spoil the surprise. And the tranquillity. And how dangerous can a middle-aged lawyer be?"

"It's not him I'm worried about," replied Dawson. "Rather the company he keeps."

"Let us see."

They got out of the car. The day was overcast. Here, the world was still. No sound, the water flat calm and undisturbed. On the far side, the trees, tightly packed, formed a shimmering green wall. They got to the front door – the only door.

It was open. McGuigan and Dawson exchanged glances. Dawson rapped it with the back of his hand.

"Hello? Anyone in?"

Silence. A particular silence, thought McGuigan. Intense. The type of silence to make the hairs on the nape of the neck tingle.

"Mind if we come in?" Dawson stepped forward, into a short hall. Hanging on pegs, outdoor gear – a ski jacket, a Barbour walking jacket, a light cagoule. In an umbrella stand fashioned in the shape of a flamingo, several walking sticks. On a rack beneath the jackets, a line of shoes – trainers, office brogues, casual shoes, a pair of hiking boots, encrusted with mud.

They emerged into an open-plan kitchen and living area. The kitchen was uncluttered, the units decorated in strange bright-red dots and sprays. As if someone had flicked a wet paint brush here and there, in a careless manner. On the floor lay a man, torso soaked red, lower jaw gone. Odd shapes of bone and gristle sat stuck in the congealed blood around him.

The living room had a suite comprising a beige leather couch and two matching chairs. In the corner, a television. On the walls, some paintings. In another corner, a tall cabinet with glass doors, containing a cluster of bottles – whisky, vodka, gin. One wall was almost entirely glass, and on any other day, would provide a clear and unrestricted view of the loch, and the trees and mountains beyond. But not today. Today, the glass was speckled and streaked, like the scribblings of a small child.

Sitting upright in a chair was Bronson Chapel, his pose such, one might have mistaken him languid and absorbing the view. His throat, however, was torn open, exposing the bone. The top of his head, from just above the eyebrows, was a messy tangle of veins and skull. Otherwise, his expression was almost serene. The kill, so McGuigan surmised, was quick and unexpected.

The third man was sprawled half on the couch, half on the floor, his face, if he had one, staring at the ceiling. But the face had imploded, folded in on itself. As if someone had spiked a hoover though the back of the brain, and sucked in eyes, nose, mouth, rendering it into something alien.

Red was the predominant colour. Red floor, red furniture, red walls.

The place was not dissimilar to an abattoir.

"Now you can call it in," said McGuigan softly. Dawson nodded. He tapped on his mobile, spoke in a low, tight voice.

If this is God's plan, thought McGuigan, *then he's got to be stopped.*

Movement caught his attention. He saw, through a clear patch on the glass, a bird flap down onto the side of the loch. A raven, all dark and glossy. McGuigan was reminded of the raven lying stiff and dead in a bucket in Mrs. Shawbridge's house.

Perhaps we've already been judged, he thought, *and none of us know it. Perhaps this is our penance. Perhaps this is hell.*

CHAPTER FORTY-SEVEN

Stark left early, at 4.30. He slinked out. To leave at such a time for a "new start" was regarded as an act of blasphemy. Jenny was upstairs, in the library. No one noticed his departure, save the receptionists. He gave them a meaningful wave as he was leaving, as if to say *Only popping out for a mo... be back shortly, so don't panic. The world won't end.*

The email he had sent the previous evening was too cryptic for anyone to understand, other than the intended recipient, and if he should appear, then it would add further legitimacy to the situation, not that further legitimacy was needed. He experienced a variety of emotions – dread, excitement, bemusement. Bemused that he was doing what he was doing. A week ago, he would have scoffed at the notion. But here he was, starting up the car, heading out of Glasgow, again towards Chatelherault Woods.

Stark reached the car park at the entrance to the woods, again in a relatively short time. Rush hour hadn't started. The car park was fuller, which was advantageous, as it meant he drew less attention. He had with him the object he had purchased during his lunch hour, wrapped in a white plastic bag. Also, in the bag, the other item – the one he had found early that morning, buried in the dirt. Some kids were playing on the swings, adults watching from red and yellow wooden benches. The sun had disappeared. The wood was a jumble of shadows. So easy to take the wrong path, and end up hopelessly lost. He felt a whisper of rain. Clouds loomed, like bundles of grey gauze. The air carried the faintest nip. Summer was dying.

He followed the same route as he had done that morning. He reached the clearing, and the cherry-blossom tree.

Suddenly, sunlight slanted down, finding a way between the clouds. Stark stepped back into the deeper shadow, hunkered in, and waited. He was sure the sound of his heart would give him away. The urge to get up, run back to the car, was strong. He swallowed back his terror, waited.

At 6.30 came the sound of someone treading the path towards the clearing. Stark hunched low where he sat, tried to make himself invisible, to merge with the dark. The noise grew louder, then stopped. Stark saw a figure, standing still, on the verge of the clearing, half-hidden in the trees. He wondered what the figure was thinking. A million questions. Maybe sharing the same fear Stark felt.

The figure moved again, towards the tree, now in plain sight, then stopped, as if listening, then looked about. Stark remained undetected. The figure stirred, walked forward, reached the tree, and touched its trunk.

It was time. Stark got to his feet with care, trying not to make a sound. The figure had its back to him. Stark stepped into the clearing.

"You got my email."

The figure didn't move. Stark waited. He heard a distinct sound in his ears – the *boom boom* of his heart. Time seemed captured in this one moment. The world held its breath.

The figure turned, and faced him, face pale as death, eyes black pinholes.

"You."

Stark nodded. His fear evaporated. In its place, a weariness to the bone. It had come to this.

"Me," he said.

The man before him said nothing.

The man before him was Paul Hutchison.

CHAPTER FORTY-EIGHT

The boat house was cordoned off within a half hour of the discovery. The pathologist – Laura Singleton – drove from Glasgow, and after an inspection of the bodies, provided McGuigan with her preliminary observations. She didn't give much more information than McGuigan had already guessed.

"Where's this God of yours?" was her parting question, half in humour, half in earnest, as he and Dawson made ready to return to Glasgow, a question to which he had no adequate response to give.

They arrived back at HQ just after 6pm. The chief constable had specifically requested his presence. Such a request was not to be ignored.

His office was large, furnished in a strictly utilitarian fashion. No clutter. No inessential items. He always kept his desk clear. In fact, McGuigan could not remember ever having seen any paperwork on it. He wondered if the chief constable did anything other than cover his own arse, for which he had a special talent.

Blakely was not in a humorous mood. Neither for that matter was McGuigan. They sat across the desk from each other. Pleasantries were ignored. Blakely cut straight to the chase.

"Our witness is dead. Our *only* witness, I might add. This should have been better handled."

McGuigan could only agree. "I dare say, from Bronson Chapel's perspective, you're absolutely right, sir."

"I don't need your sarcastic comments. Don't test me, McGuigan. Not today. What are we assuming here?"

McGuigan sighed. "It's very early to assume anything. Bronson was murdered. Shot in the neck and head. The other two men were also shot. Probably by the same weapon. We should know soon enough."

"What was their connection?"

"I don't know. We have their names. The killer didn't take their wallets – which rules out robbery, I think."

"And?"

"Billy Watson and Frank Fitsimmons. It's bizarre. We've run checks on both names. Fitzsimmons has a varied and sparkling history of previous, ranging from extortion to drug dealing to you name it. Watson has two convictions, for drug-related offences. Both serious criminals. What Bronson was doing with such men is for now, beyond conjecture. Unless..."

"What!" snapped Blakely. With his wide dark eyes and thin face, he resembled a disgruntled lurcher.

"...unless, Bronson had brought them in on the blackmail he was attempting against Mrs Shawbridge. Which is possible, but unlikely."

Blakely blinked. "What blackmail scheme?"

McGuigan pursed his lips. He'd started. Now he had to finish. "Bronson was accused of blackmailing one of his clients. He claimed to have a photograph of The Surgeon. He showed it to a client, Mrs Shawbridge. He thought it was her son. He wanted money from her to keep it quiet."

"Blackmail?"

"Yes, sir."

Blakely ran a fretful hand through the remains of his hair.

"And I'm hearing about this now."

McGuigan said nothing.

"But you don't think that's why they were there."

"It's possible," said McGuigan. "But unlikely. More likely, Bronson owed them."

"For what?"

McGuigan shrugged. "Drugs?"

Blakely gave a dismissive shake of his head. "He was a lawyer, for Christ's sake. A partner in a city firm."

"And he was human. And like most humans, if not all, he had his flaws. I interviewed him. He was nervy. Wired tight. Hyper, one could say."

"So what are you telling me – a deal gone wrong? A fight between drug dealers?"

Mcguigan thought back to the carnage in the little wooden house by the loch, the intricate blood patterns on the walls and units, the final postures of the corpses. Such a scene would remain with him all his days.

"At this stage, anyone's guess, I suppose..."

"I don't need fucking guesswork," interrupted Blakely, his voice harsh. "I don't need suppositions." He glared at McGuigan. "I need fucking answers!"

McGuigan stared at his superior officer. The tension between them was a palpable thing.

"Of course, sir," he said softly. "We have three bodies. One in the kitchen, two in the living room. Bronson was in the living room, sitting upright, his position almost... relaxed. The other man – Billy Watson, was half on the chair, half stretched across the floor. As if killed in motion. As if he were in the process of getting up. Maybe lunging or leaping? The third, Fitzsimmons, was in the kitchen, arms and legs sprawled. Again, caught in mid-motion. The difference in body postures between Bronson and the other two is marked."

"And?"

McGuigan released another sigh. His hypothesis was stretching things. But then, maybe not. Blakely demanded an answer, despite being aware McGuigan could not possibly know.

"Bronson might have known his killer. Maybe chatting. God knows, they might have been discussing the scenery. The killer takes him by surprise. Bronson is dead, without ever being aware his life was in jeopardy. The other two knew exactly what was happening, which suggests the killer took care of Bronson first, and then was surprised. Billy Watson and Fitzsimmons enter the house. They are met by the killer. Fitzsimmons tries to run, is killed in the kitchen. Billy Watson is ushered over to the chair. Maybe the killer wants to obtain information from him. Who he is, why he's there. Watson, seeing his situation not improving any, tries to fight or escape, and is shot."

Blakely seemed to digest this information. He turned, stared out the only window of the office, the view being the wall of another building.

"If this is the case, then Watson and Fitzsimmons were unlucky. Wrong place, wrong time."

"That would be a logical conclusion, sir."

"Which would mean…"

"That Bronson was always the intended target."

Blakely turned back to McGuigan. "And who would want to kill Bronson Chapel?" This was a rhetorical question. McGuigan chose to answer, regardless.

"I don't think it was an angry client aggrieved at his legal bill, sir."

This time, Blakely chose to ignore the sarcasm.

"If it was The Surgeon – and that's still a big if – then how in God's creation would he have known about Bronson being a witness?"

"If it wasn't The Surgeon," countered McGuigan, "then we have the biggest coincidence in the history of coincidences. As for knowing about Bronson, our psychopathic friend is cunning and intelligent and remarkably resourceful. He may have seen Bronson at the scene of the initial crime. Tracked him down. Or, someone may have talked, quite innocently. Bronson was at the police station. Lots of people would be aware of who he was and his importance to the investigation. Loose lips, careless conversation. Maybe Bronson himself talked. Hard not to. Witnessing a prolific serial killer murder someone before his eyes. Maybe word got round. But in all this mess, some good has come out of it."

Blakely cocked his head to one side, like an inquisitive bird, his expression one of exaggerated bemusement.

"Enlighten me please, McGuigan."

"We have a photo of someone who looks identical to the killer. Mrs Shawbridge admitted the photo Bronson showed her bore a strong resemblance to her son. She gave us a picture of him. It looks nothing like the photofit we've shown the public."

Blakely's face suddenly brightened. "And we've interviewed Mrs Shawbridge's son?"

"His name's Wallace. Two constables have visited him. He's in a hospice. He can't talk. He can't move. He can't breathe without the aid of a machine. He's living on morphine. He's dying, sir. For all I know, he may already be dead. He's not The Surgeon. But I have the photo."

Blakely narrowed his eyes. "And what the hell good does that do us?"

McGuigan was confused. "Sir?"

"We've already got a description of the killer. One we've revealed to the entire country."

"Which is the wrong one. I don't understand..."

Blakely slammed his hand on the desktop.

"Don't be so fucking obtuse! How can we possibly tell everybody we got it wrong. Tell me how, McGuigan?"

McGuigan's mind swirled. He swallowed, held back the tremble in his voice.

"But we did get it wrong, sir," he said.

"Who knows about this photograph?"

McGuigan hesitated. He licked his lips. The conversation was surreal.

"Myself. Kenny Dawson."

"No one else?"

McGuigan gave a small shake of his head.

"Then you and Dawson keep a lid on it. You do not breathe one fucking word of this. You understand?"

McGuigan said nothing.

"If word gets out we gave the wrong description, then it's on us. On you. On me. Not only will we look incompetent, we'll look like fucking amateurs. And I won't have that. You hear me, McGuigan? We keep this to ourselves. I cannot – will not – have my reputation tarnished over this. You understand? Nod your head, and tell me you understand what I have just said. Because if you don't, I will whisk you off this case, and have you pounding the fucking streets quicker than shit off a shoe."

McGuigan took a long slow breath. And nodded. And knew then that his soul would burn in hell.

As soon as he left Blakely's office, McGuigan got the call he was waiting for, from Kenny Dawson.

"Nothing," said Dawson. "No mobile phone. Either Bronson ditched it somewhere, or it was taken."

"Thank you."

The chances of it being found had always been remote. Still, he had hoped, because hope was all he had. He was in the dark, the place he had always been since the very first act of savagery. With Bronson, there had been a brief and tenuous slant of light. Now the light was gone.

He made his way out to the car park. He had given up

smoking three years back, hence the bubblegum. But at that moment, in that car park, under a grey and heavy sky, he could have murdered for a cigarette. Instead, he unwrapped a square of gum, and began the chewing process, looked up, and asked for a little help.

He could never have imagined from where that help would come.

CHAPTER FORTY-NINE

A breeze stirred, the delicate branches of the cherry-blossom rippled, the leaves whispered. The two men faced each other.

Hutchison spoke, his voice a growl, his face a contortion of anger. *More beast than man,* thought Stark.

"What the hell is this about? Explain yourself, Stark."

"You came."

"I got an email. From you, I assume. Pack your stuff, Stark. As of now, you no longer work for..."

Stark cut him off. He was tired of the bluster and bullshit and all the fucking stupid threats.

"How did you know to come here?"

Hutchison frowned. "What?"

"The message I sent." Stark knew the words by heart. *6.30 this evening at the cherry-blossom tree. I know what you did. I have proof. And she wants payback.*

"I don't need to take this shit," said Hutchison. He raised a hand, pointed at Stark. His hand trembled. Anger or fear? "Your days of being a lawyer are over. Mark my words. I don't know what this charade is about, but this is it. You're finished. You hear me. You're finished!"

"She was your sister," Stark said. Tears filled his eyes when he spoke. His heart ached for the little girl in his dreams. "She was eight years old when it started. You were nineteen. For six years. Secret, furtive rape. And she never told a soul, not even her parents – *your parents* – because she was terrified and guilt-ridden and consumed with self-hatred." Stark gazed at the tree, his voice gentle. "And even when it was over, she relived it, every day, every hour of her life, until one day she came here, to this place, and chose a way out, because she had no choice."

"You're mad," said Hutchison.

"She told me many things." He dredged the images up into his mind's eye. "Her room, when the abuse began. A pink mermaid lampshade. Butterfly handles. Maybe you don't remember. I think you do."

Hutchison's voice rose. "My sister suffered from depression. How could she tell you anything? She died over ten years ago. You didn't know her. How dare you..."

Stark was weary to the core. "You got her pregnant."

Hutchison stood, his face slack, anger gone. He said nothing.

"She was fourteen. She was here, at this beautiful place, alone and scared and helpless and in great pain, where she suffered a miscarriage."

Hutchison stared, glassy-eyed.

"And she kept a diary."

Hutchison blinked. Still nothing.

"Her writing improves as she gets older," said Stark. "She doesn't hold back. She buried it under the tree the day she lost your child." Stark took a pink spiral-bound book wrapped in polythene from his plastic bag – the item he had gone to find early that morning, where he knew it would be.

He tossed it at Hutchison's feet. Hutchison stared at it.

"Aren't you going to look at it?" said Stark.

Hutchison licked his lips, glanced at Stark. He bent down,

picked it up, held it in his hands as if it were something precious. He carefully peeled off the thick polythene, opened it.

"It's quite explicit, in its childish way," said Stark. "Which makes it all the more harrowing. By the way, it's a copy."

Hutchison leafed through the pages, looked up, appraised Stark with a glittering gaze. "This proves nothing. A kid's scribbles. You're sick in the head, Stark. Your brain got scrambled when you got shot. Pity Alfie Willow didn't finish the job. If you even try..."

"And she left this as well." Stark reached into his bag, pulled out an old VHS video tape, also wrapped in heavy polythene.

"Your parents bought her a video camera when she was eleven. Do you remember? No? I'm sure you do if you think hard enough. She put it to good use. She hid it on her dressing table. Cosied up with some fluffy toys. You're the star of the piece. It's a three-hour tape. The quality is very good. You'll have no trouble recognising yourself. And it has all the sounds. You grunting like an animal. She quietly sobbing and pleading. A little girl begging for you to stop raping her."

He stepped forward, approached Hutchison. He held the package out. "Take it."

Close-up, Stark saw the sweat glisten on Hutchison's face, saw the movement of his Adam's apple as he swallowed. Hutchison took the video tape.

Stark stood close. He could smell the man's aftershave. Mingled with the sweat, a faintly rancid odour. Hutchison was maybe five ten, a clear four inches smaller than Stark. Stark leaned down, whispered in his ear.

"And that's a copy, too."

Hutchison gasped, lurched back, lost his footing, fell on his side. He scrambled to his feet, his office suit smeared with dirt. He backed away.

"What do you want? Money? Is it about money? I can do that. I can get you money."

"It's about justice," said Stark softly.

"Justice!" hissed Hutchison. "She's dead. Why rake up old stories? It happened. It's past." His face contorted into a twisted leer. "She had it coming. Little slut. She wanted it. She just didn't know she wanted it. No one cares about her sad, pathetic little life."

Stark regarded the man before him. Any doubts he had disappeared. The truth was clear. The dead had spoken, and the dead didn't lie. Strangely, knowing this gave him new purpose.

"I care," said Stark. "And I'm pretty sure the police will care as well. And if they don't, it won't matter. I'll make sure the world knows what you did."

"Really?" Hutchison gave him a sly look. Possibly a look he had practised many times in the litigation courts. "What have you got? A kid's notebook, full of fantasy. An old VHS tape showing something over thirty years ago. And you! You couldn't have spoken to my sister. You never knew her." He flung the diary and tape to the side. "You'll get laughed at. I'll make sure of it. The way it looks, the whole thing's a concoction of lies. Everybody knows I dislike you. I'll spin it so well, you'll end up looking like a sad, twisted, vindictive loser, unhinged and dangerous, out to get his boss. You'll lose everything. You'll never work again."

Stark reacted with a cold smile. "You've misjudged this situation, Paul. I have nothing to lose. It seems to me, you're the one who has everything to lose. Big-time lawyer. Prestige. Wealth. Family? So why don't we toss the dice, and let Lady Luck decide how they fall. I'll go to the police, tell them you're a paedophile who raped his sister, and show them what I have. Let's see how that plays out."

Hutchison's demeanour changed. His round face crumpled, his chin wobbled, his shoulders sagged. His breath came in a rattling wheeze. He bowed his head, stared at the ground. "Please," he said. "We can work this out. Tell me what you want? Tell me what you need me to do!"

"Go to the police. Admit your crime."

Hutchison looked up. His eyes glistened.

"I can't do that."

Stark had sudden insight. The repercussions crushed him. He took a breath. "There are others," he whispered. "Your sister was the first." He hesitated. Dread yawned up. "You have a family?"

Hutchison opened his mouth, as if to speak, uttered only a despairing wail. He turned, and ran.

Stark shouted after him. Hutchison glanced round, his expression wild and stricken. He tripped on an exposed root, fell forward, slammed his head on the trunk of the cherry-blossom tree, rolled awkwardly, momentum forcing his torso one way, his head the other. He lay still.

Stark, startled by the turn of events, waited. Hutchison didn't stir. Stark made his way over, tentatively. Hutchison was on his side, neck twisted at an ugly angle, blood flowing from a great gash in his skull. The eyes were open, but the spark was gone. Life had fled. Stark crouched, touched the side of Hutchison's throat, seeking a pulse. Nothing. The neck was broken. His life blood was draining into the soil, into the roots.

Stark took a deep breath, looked up at the sky. Darkness was falling. Clouds loomed heavy. From above, a flicker of movement. A raven flew down, to land on a branch close to where Stark stood. It manoeuvred its body in small jerky movements, to watch sidelong, scrutinising with its button-black eye.

Redress had been achieved. He felt empty. The bizarre events of his life had squeezed him dry, and now here he stood, at the foot of the tree – *her tree* – a husk, energy sapped, weary to the bone.

There was nothing further to do, other than make an anonymous call to the police. He retrieved the diary, and the video tape, and put them in his plastic bag. The video tape had been a gamble. It was blank – purchased that afternoon. He had to be certain. He needed a tipping point, to get Hutchison to panic and admit his crime. It seemed the gamble had paid off. The video camera also had been a bluff. He hoped the mere act of presenting the tape would trigger a false memory, and Hutchison would believe. It seemed that gamble had paid off as well.

He left the clearing, and the cherry-blossom tree, back along the path he had come, to his car. *Whatever this is, it's over,* he thought.

But the journey was far from over. For Jonathan Stark, the journey was just beginning.

CHAPTER FIFTY

He had taken a photograph of her as she was leaving a convenience store. He had parked his car on the opposite side of the road. She had only been in for a minute, and had come out with a plastic litre bottle of milk. She had driven off, back in the direction of her house.

He forwarded the photograph, and waited. He didn't wait long. The text came back within fifteen seconds.

Perfect. When?

Saturday, in the early hours.

So quick?

It needs to be. Simple.

It had better be. Look what happened last time.
And then?

I take her back to mine. No chance of being interrupted. I can spend as long as I want.

He waited. Nothing came back. He got nervous.

Do I have permission?

Another wait. He knew not to push. A full minute passed. He fidgeted in the car seat, took a swig of mineral water. His mobile chimed. The answer came.

Yes.

He took a long breath.

Thank you.

Don't fuck this up.

Do you love me?

Yes. Always.

CHAPTER FIFTY-ONE

Stark got back to his car. The play park was empty. The place was deserted. He left, made his way to his flat. On the way, he stopped at a shopping centre, on the outskirts of Glasgow, and made a call to the police – *dead body in Chatelherault Woods.* He kept it brief. A fitting epitaph for a monster.

He arrived back at his flat at 8.30. The first thing he did was flop onto the couch. The events of the day seemed surreal, stretching reality to the point of disbelief. Did they happen? Perhaps he had hallucinated. Perhaps he was insane, and this thought frightened him more than anything. After the massacre at Alfie Willow's offices, after the coma, insanity was more than an abstract notion. His mind, fragile at best, never strayed far from the abyss.

Beside him, the polythene bag. He took out the pink diary, held it in his hands. This was his anchor. His grounding. The raw, heart-breaking commentary of a little girl. He wasn't mad. The world around him was mad. He had helped, just a little.

His phone beeped. He expected it to be Maggie. Checking up and checking in. He read the number. It wasn't one he recognised instantly. He answered.

"Are you still with the other woman?"

He gave a tired laugh.

"Which one? I have so many."

"I'm still waiting for this offer of cheap beer."

He decided against caution. "I can do better."

"Really?"

"I can offer you totally free beer, by way of bottles in the fridge. But it will mean you'll have to tolerate the most hideously decorated flat in all of Christendom."

There was a pause, then, "I would love that."

He gave Jenny his address. He realised he didn't have much in to eat, but he was past caring. If she was hungry, then toasted cheese would have to do. He adjusted his thoughts. Just toast.

She arrived a half hour later. Stark was still in his suit. He had forgotten to change. He thought briefly he should have showered, but he was past caring about that too.

She sat at his kitchen table. Stark detected the subtle fragrance of amber and musk, which was not unappealing. She wore a simple summer dress of white cotton, a red shawl to keep her shoulders warm. Her hair was loose, to her shoulders, a casual tangle of auburn locks. Like burnished copper, he thought.

"I see what you mean about the décor," she said, inspecting the room.

"I'll sack my interior designer." He reached into the fridge, retrieved two bottles of beer.

"Glass?"

She responded with mock disdain. "Beer gets drunk from the bottle."

"Of course it does. Where's my manners."

He got a bottle opener from the kitchen drawer, popped the bottles open, handed her one. He sat opposite.

She raised it up. "Here's to the endless joy of working for SJPS."

They clinked bottles. "Endless joy," repeated Stark. They drank. The beer tasted good. After the day he'd had, any alcohol would have tasted good. Jenny grimaced. "Jesus. You weren't kidding."

"The wonderful thing about cheap beer, is that it's cheap. Whether it's disgusting or not becomes an irrelevance."

She acknowledged the comment with a smile. "I think there's logic in there somewhere."

He raised his bottle again, in salute, took another swig.

"You look tired," she said.

"I thought exhaustion was expected. Otherwise, the partners might want their money back."

She gave a frosty chuckle. "Slavery was abolished, with the exception of lawyers' offices."

"Now she tells me. And you?"

She regarded him curiously.

"If I recall," he said, "this morning you were almost snoring on your keyboard."

She sighed, seemed to give the matter some thought. "I have trouble sleeping. Bad dreams. I wake at three in the morning. Most mornings. Then I worry about how I'll function in the day ahead if I can't get back to sleep. And before you know it, the whole thing becomes a self-fulfilling prophecy. I don't sleep, because I worry about it too much, and the next day becomes a waking nightmare."

"Waking nightmare," repeated Stark, more to himself than Jenny.

"Don't you ever get bad dreams, Jonathan?"

He looked at her. Strange to ask such a question, in the circumstances.

"I do, yes. Doesn't everybody? Maybe it's your guilty conscience. What are your bad dreams about?"

"Things most people would laugh at. A missed deadline. A court appearance, and I can't get the damned car started."

Stark laughed out loud. The first time he had laughed for as long as he could remember. "You weren't driving my car, perchance? If it's any consolation, your nightmare is my reality. I suffer the same dread every day. I put the key in the ignition, and I never quite know what's going to happen."

"Ignition?"

"Quite."

Her lips twitched into a small pensive smile. "Last night was the worst. I dreamt I had died."

Stark sipped his beer, placed the bottle on the table. "Thankfully, it didn't come true." *Unlike my dreams,* he thought.

She placed the cold bottle against her cheek, closed her eyes. "It was so real. I doubt I shall ever forget it."

"Drink more of the cheap beer. Guaranteed to make you forget everything and anything."

She took another drink, then removed her shawl, and folded it round the back of the chair.

She looked at him archly. "I hope you don't mind a strange woman taking her clothes off in your house."

"I have absolutely no objection."

"Then again," she said, "maybe it's a regular thing."

"Irregular, I can assure you."

She wrinkled her nose. "I'm not quite sure I believe you. Tell me about yourself, Jonathan."

Jonathan sat back. He was tired, he was perhaps still in shock after the dramatic events earlier, and he was profoundly confused by those events. And yet, he felt he could talk to Jenny for a lifetime. His troubles seemed to drift away.

"There's not much to tell. I'm probably the most boring human being on the planet. I have a sister. She's a doctor, and doing extremely well. My parents are dead, so I suppose that makes me an orphan. I was brought up in Eaglesham, which is like one massive retirement home, where the highlight of the year is a missing cat. I like to go for early morning runs. And I'm an expert in packing crates of lemonade." He blew through his lips. "My God. I really am a boring human being."

Jenny leaned forward. She gazed at him. Her eyes shone. "Hardly that. You forgot to mention Archie Willow. What you went through. And to survive. That really is something. But I get you don't want to talk about it."

He finished his bottle. "Would you like something stronger?" he said. "I'm in the mood."

"Absolutely."

He opened a kitchen cupboard, and got out an unopened bottle of ten-year-old Glenmorangie – a birthday gift from his sister, which had remained dormant in his kitchen for months. He had one mug – Iron Man – and one tall lemonade glass. He thought it polite to give Jenny the glass. He poured out healthy measures.

"Straight?" he asked. "And before you answer, there's only water."

"Straight's good."

He handed her the glass, resumed his seat.

"You don't do much entertaining," she said.

"I'm the reclusive type." He put the mug to his lips, allowed his nose to hover over the whisky. Perhaps not as glamorous as drinking from crystal, but the effect was the same. He had never enjoyed its taste. But right now, at this moment, it smelled good. He sipped. It tasted good, too.

"I was lucky," he said. "That morning, he killed fifteen of his staff. Lawyers, paralegals, secretaries, receptionists. He even shot a delivery guy, who'd come in to drop a parcel off. He wasn't choosy. Everyone he shot, he killed. Except me. I used to agonise over it. I wondered *why*. Why would Willow do such a thing? Why did I survive?"

He fell silent. The details would always remain. The terror, the blood, the madness.

"Did you find an answer?"

Another sip.

"I did, in a way. The answer is that there is no answer. Life is random. There is no pattern. There is no reason. We exist. We die. As soon as I came to understand that, I began to heal."

She spoke softly. "You don't believe in God?"

Stark wasn't sure what he believed in. In the last few days, his views on such matters had been blown to hell.

"Do you?"

She gave a sardonic grin. "How can there be? A real God would never allow people like Paul Hutchison to roam the earth."

Stark nodded, said nothing, topped up the whisky, swallowed it back. It tasted thick in his mouth. An image formed in his mind. Hutchison, wide-eyed and staring, neck broken, skull bashed. He moved on quickly.

"What about you, Jenny?"

"Very dull. Left school, and tried art college, much to my parents' vast disapproval. I think I went, just to spite them. It didn't work out. Put simply, I was rubbish. I woke up, and realised if you want to make any sort of decent money, you have to fit in and go with the flow. Rebels are destined to be poor. And when poverty enters through the door, glamour flies out the window. So I chucked it, went to law school, and got my degree. Got a few jobs, until ending up at SJPS. I've been there five years. I think, at least once a week, I feel tempted to tell them to shove it up their arse. But I never quite find the courage. I suppose stress and worry is better than unemployment and worry."

Stark felt light-headed. The whisky hit the spot.

"No boyfriend?" he asked suddenly, not quite knowing why.

"Not yet."

He smiled. She didn't smile. She gave him a level intense gaze, and said, "It's getting late. If I'm staying the night, I'm not sleeping on the couch."

"The couch is uncomfortable."

"In which case, it looks like we're both sleeping in your bed."

He held her gaze. "That sounds like a plan."

"A good plan."

He got up, went over, bent his face to hers; they kissed again and again. He held her hand. They went to his bedroom, silently, then sinking to the bed, lay locked in each other's arms, and lost themselves in ardour.

Stark woke at 6.45am. The sun slanted through the bedroom window. His mouth felt dry, then he remembered the whisky. Then he remembered something else. He turned his head. She lay next to him, her arm draped across his chest, breathing softly. He stroked her hair, her cheek, her neck. She moaned, brought her body closer, stretched her leg over.

"Don't stop," she mumbled.

He said nothing. Another thing he remembered – he had slept the night without dreaming. Or, if he had dreamt, he was blissfully unaware. *Maybe now the dead are at peace,* he thought.

But Stark was unsettled. The spectre of Hutchison's stricken expression floated in his mind. *Make him pay* – words whispered in his ear. Hutchison had paid, for sure. He had made the ultimate payment. It seemed the victims in his dream had high demands.

He wondered, not without a little dread, if the dead expected more.

CHAPTER FIFTY-TWO

FRIDAY, 10.30AM

McGuigan addressed the group of men and women sitting round the table in the briefing room. All competent police officers. All taking notes, listening attentively, all confident enough to voice opinions, if required. Ten in all. The same number as the victims The Surgeon had dispatched over his five-year murder frenzy. The thought made McGuigan more despondent. Behind him, on a large white display, photographs of the same ten victims. Each fresh-faced and pretty, oblivious to the tragedy to befall them. Each vaguely similar; similar jawline, similar cheek structure; perhaps, at a push, same sparkle in the eyes. Beside each, various names. People they knew – friends, children, boyfriends, husbands. Nothing to connect them. They each could have lived on different planets.

Other photographs had been placed on the board. A man, smiling broadly, tanned, perfect teeth, looking damned pleased with himself. Bronson Chapel. Under him, pyramid fashion, two more photos. The other dead men in the house. Each had a label – "Billy Watson" and "Frank Fitzsimmons".

McGuigan hadn't slept. His mind was in overdrive. Doubtless

he would stall midday, but he had his coffee and his bubblegum and sheer undiluted adrenaline to keep him afloat.

He addressed Kenny Dawson, sitting nearest him.

"Give me some wonderful news."

Dawson shook his head, assumed a doleful expression. "No CCTV. Not just the single lane going to the crime scene. No CCTV near the turning point from the main road. In fact, no CCTV on the main road at all. There is one camera in the centre of Aviemore." He looked at his boss, looked at the others. "But it wasn't working. Total loss."

McGuigan reacted with a resigned shrug. The fates, as ever, were against them.

He turned to another – DC Primrose. An astute and dedicated young woman, keen for promotion. Graduate, on a fast-track programme. She responded with analytical detachment. "Forensics, so far, have found nine bullets. It's early days. Ballistics are testing them. We should know by the end of the day if they were fired from the same weapon used at that scene and also at Evelyn Stephens' crime scene."

McGuigan moved on. "And door-to-door?"

A middle-aged man wearing heavy black-framed spectacles cleared his throat, answered. "'Door-to-door' is reaching a bit here, sir. There's not that many doors. Bronson's house was in the middle of a forest. There are houses on the main road, two miles from the scene, though not a lot. There's also a fairly large hotel. We're asking guests and staff if anyone saw anything. A lot of the people visiting are the 'great outdoors' type – dog walkers, hikers, cyclists, joggers, climbers, skiers, and such."

McGuigan nodded like a wise owl. "Keep at it."

Primrose spoke up. "A lot of the ground around the house is grass. We're checking tyre tracks."

"Right." He chewed on his gum. The taste had gone an hour ago. It was like chewing on elastic. "And our two visiting pilgrims?"

A voice came from the end of the table. "This is interesting, sir. We knew both men had previous. Fitzsimmons – affectionally known by his peers as 'Lemonhead' – was a driven career criminal. Violent and sociopathic and highly motivated, and with a record both long and varied. Billy Watson, however, was altogether different. He had a couple of convictions years back, but for the most part, kept himself under the radar. I've spoken to some contacts. The word is, he was running a highly lucrative business in supplying Class A drugs to the rich and famous. He chose his clients carefully. Doctors, accountants, politicians…"

"…and lawyers," finished McGuigan.

"Correct. Everybody paid Billy Watson, because they knew if they didn't, they'd end up having an intimate chat with Lemonhead, which, I dare say, would end badly. A two-man outfit."

McGuigan stroked his eyebrow with the tip of his index finger, an unconscious habit when thoughtful.

"What about Mrs Shawbridge and her son?"

Another: "A wealthy widow. Her husband died, left her a business which she sold for a fortune."

"And her son?"

"We've had access to his medical records. He was diagnosed with cancer six months ago. He's in a chronic state. He'll be lucky to be alive by the end of the week."

"And Bronson's mobile phone?"

The meeting had gone full circle, back to Kenny Dawson, who gave the same doleful shake of his head. "No sign."

"Of course not," responded McGuigan. "Why would there be?"

He drew a breath, gazed at the flat ceiling as he arranged his thoughts.

"Bronson disappeared from his office on Monday. Presumably he high-tailed it to his boat house. Why? If Mrs Shawbridge is to be believed – and we have absolutely no reason to doubt her – Bronson attempted to blackmail her, by claiming he had taken a picture on his phone of The Surgeon at the scene of Evelyn Stephens' murder, and suggesting it was Mrs Shawbridge's son. The idea that such a scheme would work is ridiculous. But my belief is that Bronson's head was scrambled by drugs, and that he was desperate for cash."

He paused, considered, carried on. "He needed the cash because our 'Good Samaritan' Billy Watson was supplying him with white fairy dust, and Billy Watson was looking for his money." He flicked a look at Primrose. "Have forensics discovered any traces of drugs, either in the house or his car?"

She gave a curt shake of her head – "Nothing yet, sir."

"Make sure they know to look. Even the faintest spec. They'll find something for sure."

She scribbled it down on her notepad.

"Bronson and his two Comancheros were shot at the boat house," continued McGuigan. "My guess – they knew where Bronson was, and had gone up north to pay him a visit. Not the friendly type of visit, I might add. And then?"

Another spoke – "If we assume Bronson really did have a picture of The Surgeon, and The Surgeon knew this, then it would be only logical for him to want to retrieve the picture and wipe Bronson out of the equation."

"Which would mean," said Primrose, "that The Surgeon would have to know about Bronson's boat house, and that he would be there."

"Or at least hope he would be there," said Kenny Dawson. "As we did."

"And so," said McGuigan, "The Surgeon toddles up to the Highlands, to the boat house. But disaster! He not only has to deal with Bronson, but Billy and Lemonhead, which he does in his usual and decisive manner."

Primrose raised a hand, as if she were at school, which McGuigan found quite fetching.

"Two prerequisites – The Surgeon would not only need to have known that Bronson had the photo, but that Bronson owned the boat house."

"Indeed. Very specific knowledge. To know one is good fortune. To know two? Damned good fortune."

The man with the black-framed spectacles spoke – "We have to find the connection."

"Bronson could have told any number of people about being a witness to the murder. He certainly told Mrs Shawbridge. He showed her a picture. People talk. And whoever knew, also knew about the boat house." He fell silent, turned to the board behind him, gazed at the photos. He turned back, appraised those sitting.

"Bronson Chapel was a partner in the firm of SJPS. Mrs Shawbridge was a client of Bronson, and, as such, a client of SJPS. Mrs Shawbridge told us she had threatened SJPS with litigation over Bronson's conduct. The admin department of SJPS knew about Bronson's boat house. As I said, people talk. People love gossip. Wouldn't surprise me if half, if not all, of the prestigious and respected firm of SJPS knew all about Bronson and his photo and his boat house. Am I seeing a connection?"

Silence.

"Ladies and gentlemen, it's a start. And it's more of a start than we've ever had. We need to wait for ballistics to confirm that the bullets came from the same gun. Then we have something tangible. Then we work from there." He focused on Primrose again.

"Get ballistics to shift their arse on this one."

"Yes, sir." She hesitated. "Wouldn't it be a good idea to get a picture of Mrs Shawbridge's son? If he's supposed to look like the killer?"

"Never thought you'd ask," replied McGuigan.

At his feet was a frayed and battered satchel. He had been using the same one for the last twenty-five years, sometimes for files, mostly to hold his packed lunch. This time, it was holding something a little different. He put it on the table, unclipped the flap, produced an A4-sized manilla envelope, opened it, and took out a sheaf of photographs, which he distributed to each of the officers.

"This is Wallace Shawbridge. Taken before his illness. If his mother is to be believed, that Bronson showed her a picture of someone he claimed was The Surgeon, and that person bore a strong resemblance to her son, then effectively..."

"...we're looking at him," breathed a detective sergeant, his freckled face crumpled in mild wonder. A hush fell; each gazed at the photo they held. McGuigan debated as to who would be the one to raise the obvious issue.

Primrose looked up, uncertain.

"But, with all due respect, sir, it looks nothing like the photofit."

McGuigan took a long breath. He had been warned by the chief constable. More than warned. Threatened. And here he was, disobeying his superior officer. Two words leapt into his mind – *fuck him.*

"You're absolutely right. There is zilch resemblance. Which goes a long way to legitimising our theory that Bronson really was blackmailing, and really did have a photo of The Surgeon. My view is that Bronson purposefully sent us in the complete wrong direction, so we wouldn't interfere with his ploy, and catch the bad guy before he collected his money."

Another silence, as they pondered this latest revelation.

"Was he mad?" It was the freckled sergeant who ventured this question.

"Possibly. Certainly desperate."

"Which means," said Dawson, "that the world and their brother are looking for a figment of Bronson's imagination."

"We let it play," said McGuigan. "For now. At least until we have ballistics, and we have some certainty the murders are connected." He swept his gaze round the table, ensuring eye contact with each person there. "Meanwhile, let's take another look at the form of Stoddart, Jeffrey, Pritchard and Sloss."

McGuigan went to his office, sat, and pondered. His desk was cluttered with files and memos and random notes and a silver goblet full of biros, some of which he knew didn't work. Also, a photograph of two girls. His daughters, giving impish smiles for the camera, taken... he had to think back, when and where... five years ago, he remembered, at a pizza restaurant in the trendy west end of Glasgow. The occasion – Merryn's eighteenth. He couldn't recall what they had ordered, but he had a good idea. Merryn – meat-feast pizza. Katie – hot and spicy pizza. Their choices never changed. In the photograph, Merryn was clutching a rather complicated cocktail, as if to say, *hey ho, dude, I'm eighteen and there's not a damn thing you can do about it.* The memory brought a small smile to his lips, as it always did. His therapy, when things went to shit. Merryn, the younger, was now twenty-three. Katie, the elder, thirty-two, their ages qualifying them as possible targets of The Surgeon, he thought sombrely, as indeed were most young women in the country.

He emptied his gum into a paper tissue, folded it over, dropped it in the bin, and immediately replaced it with another, his mouth suddenly bursting with the sweet sugary taste of something mildly disgusting. He glanced at the wrapper. *Wild Strawberry Flavour.*

His mind retraced the recent events, the patterns, the links. The connection between SJPS and the killer was tenuous. There was nothing concrete, nothing to join the dots. His theory was exactly that. A theory. Based upon a foundation of supposition and assumption and leaps of faith.

Faith. He had none. God wasn't listening. His wife had said that God worked in mysterious ways. Cliché, he had thought at the time, and still did. God, he had said, was an absent landlord, and his house was burning, to which his wife had replied – *God never started the fire, but he empowers good men to rise and put it out.*

The taste of the gum was disappearing. He chewed, and would have preferred the sweet bite of nicotine filling his lungs.

Soon, he would have an enraged chief constable on his back. Possibly – probably – he would be flung off the case for revealing to his staff the photofit given to the masses was all to shit.

And none of it would make a blind bit of difference. The Surgeon would keep going, like some unstoppable, remorseless machine.

He needed a miracle. The problem was, they didn't exist. But then… he gazed at the photograph of his two sweethearts, and the smile came back, and he realised that of course miracles existed.

The problem was that he needed one with immediate effect, and God, being God, was never in a hurry.

Perhaps for once, he thought, he could jump the queue?

There was a knock on the door.

The dependable, solid figure of Kenny Dawson entered. McGuigan relied on his scepticism, his somewhat dour disposition. It anchored him.

"You're not going to believe this, sir."

McGuigan regarded him, chewed the last of the sugar away. *What now?*

"Enlighten me. What is it I'm not going to believe?"

"A body's been found in Chatelherault Woods."

"Yes?"

"It's one of the lawyers from SJPS. The one that stormed out the room. Paul Hutchison."

McGuigan stood. He couldn't think of any instant response.

The baffled look on Dawson's face was almost humorous. "What does it mean?"

McGuigan suspected the bafflement on his own face was equally as humorous.

"I have no earthly idea," he heard himself say. "I really don't."

CHAPTER FIFTY-THREE

Stark and Jenny had made separate journeys to work that morning. Stark was glad. She drove a rather plush yellow Audi TT convertible, which she'd parked outside his flat the evening before. The thought of driving her in his ancient Nissan Micra was simply beyond contemplation.

The morning passed without incident. Regardless of circumstances, the work continued to flow. There was no awkwardness. Work, as ever, dominated the day. They spoke, they laughed, they joked. The previous evening wasn't mentioned. Life went on.

Word soon filtered through – Paul Hutchison had missed a big court hearing that morning. Simply hadn't turned up. Stark kept his head down, immersed himself in files.

At lunch, he went on his own to the coffee shop he and his sister had visited, and got the cheapest coffee on the menu, and a sandwich. He sat at a table, and decided to text her.

Hey sis.

As always, the response was near instantaneous. He wondered

if she possessed some magical talent allowing her to sense his texts before receiving them.

Hey dude. How you?

All cool.

Seriously?

He never got the chance to type out his response. His phone buzzed.

"All cool?" she said. "Why suddenly all cool?"

"I think *it* – whatever *it* was – is over. I didn't dream last night. It's like my body is telling me that it's done. It's over. Does that make sense?"

"Jesus, little bro, nothing in all this makes any sense. At least not to a simple gal like me. But if you're feeling good about things, then I guess I am too. What now?"

"Now I move on. Hopefully. Get my head down, and start doing some real work."

"I'm finished at midnight. Why don't I drop round just after, just for a chat. I want to make sure that when my brother says he's cool, he really is cool."

There was absolutely no point in trying to dissuade her.

"Okay."

"Okay – it's a date. I might even bring a pizza. If you're lucky."

Stark got back to his office at 1.45. Jenny was with a partner upstairs, discussing a case. In the forty-five minutes he had been out, twenty-two emails had arrived in his in-box. He'd counted them, just for the hell of it. Everyone a miniature bomb which, when opened, released its payload of more work. It seemed Friday afternoons were as frenetic as any other afternoon.

Des entered the room. "Bad news, Johnny boy," he said. Stark sat, nerves tingling. *Perhaps Hutchison had been found.* He said nothing, waited.

"It's Friday afternoon," continued Des.

Stark looked at him, not knowing quite how to respond, waited for him to clarify.

"It's the shift from hell."

"What?"

"Friday afternoon means the newbie gets to go…" and he pointed downwards, pulling an extravagantly glum face, "…you know where."

It took a second for the meaning to register.

Stark raised an indignant hand – "I did the damned thing on Tuesday."

"Yup. Tuesdays and Fridays. Or any other day. Orders from above. Someone's got to do it. That someone's you, old chap. The files need to get shifted. You're still on the 'C' section. You're the man of the moment."

Stark gave a resigned nod. "Of course I am."

Stark went down to the basement at 3.45. As ever, it was cold. Or perhaps it was the cold feeling he felt in his stomach. Maybe both. The place made him afraid. Here, without doubt, lay the root of the darkness. Or perhaps the darkness lay in him already.

He went through the motions. He turned the lights on. They flickered and flashed, stubbornly resisting, as if resentful of the intrusion. Stark waited until they were fully on, although the room looked dimmer than he remembered.

There, the wooden table, and there, upon it, the heavy record book from another time. He picked it up, made the same journey to the far end, though this time, his feet dragged, his skin prickled. The striplights flickered again. He reached the stool, and there, the blue boxes, ready to be filled with files to be carted off for destruction.

Beside the stool, the file he had discarded on his last trip. The one which had been apparently misplaced, and which, at the time, he had opened out of mild curiosity. *Deborah Ferry – Deceased.* He gazed at it. It didn't look as if anyone had moved it. It lay, perfectly innocent, just another folder full of old papers belonging to a dead person.

He took a breath, kept the tremble from his hands, chose to ignore it.

He pulled off a cardboard box from the 'C' shelf, as he had been instructed, dropped it onto the table beside the stool, sat, opened the book, and began the process of recording the relevant details. This time, he had no interest in the contents, other than the basic information he needed to extract. Get the job done, he thought, and get the hell out.

Time passed. He filled up one of the blue boxes. Halfway there. He got another box from the shelf, plonked it on the floor beside him. He reached in. The topmost file was a different colour from the rest. A vibrant red. It seemed untouched by the cold and the dust and the damp. It looked new, like a file still being worked on, having no business being in a box in the basement. It wasn't thick, particularly. In fact, thin for a legal file. Whoever this person was, not a lot of work had been carried out.

He removed it, gently. The texture of the file was marbled and expensive. A file designed to be found. Stark held his breath. He knew it wasn't right. On the cover, a white label, and in thick black felt pen, in block capitals, 'Marie Thomson'.

Another misplaced file. If Stark wasn't so damned scared, he would have laughed.

"Really?" he said aloud. "Can't you be more original?"

He balanced the file in his hands, ran his thumbs along the

edges. His mouth felt dry. He touched the label, the name, and thought *Who the hell is Marie Thomson?* To open this file would mean… what exactly? Perhaps nothing. Perhaps everything. Perhaps another strange and terrifying journey, and one which he had no inclination to take.

"No," he said, keeping his voice firm and level. "I won't do this."

He placed it on the floor to his side, beside Deborah Ferry's file. He took a breath, composed himself, and with fixed concentration, focused on the job in hand – recording information, depositing the files in the blue box. Always, lurking in his mind, Marie Thomson, refusing to leave, casting a shadow on his thoughts.

Who the hell is Marie Thomson? The name bounced around in his head. It triggered something. A memory, a recollection, elusive and just out of reach.

He kept going, until the second blue box was full. He stood, the record book tucked under one arm, made his way back along the passage, towards the table, and then the exit. The flickering of the striplights intensified – or perhaps it was Stark's imagination. He got to the table, placed the book down, turned to the stairs, and then he remembered. *Marie Thomson.* The memory crystallised. He knew the name. *A coincidence?* Possibly. Probably. *Surely!*

But if not, if it was the same person, then maybe he didn't have a choice. Maybe he had an obligation.

He took a long calming breath and decided the whole world was fucked up. That he was fucked up. He walked back to the stool. He sat, once again, and regarded the red file on the floor.

"You win."

He stooped, picked it up, and with delicate fingers, opened it.

The papers inside were held together by an old-fashioned treasury tag. Correspondence relating to the estate of Marie Thomson, deceased. There wasn't much. A couple of savings accounts; a small life policy. Date of death, five years ago. Letters going back and forth, to banks, to relatives, to the funeral directors. He turned the pages, and eventually came to her death certificate.

She was twenty-nine when she died. Hence the relatively small estate. She was unmarried. She lived in a nice area in the south of Glasgow. She was a student. He read the cause of death – *blunt force trauma; crushed spinal cord.*

He blinked, absorbed the information, mind racing. His heart thrummed. He closed the file. Despite the cold, he was sweating. He placed the file back on the floor.

He sat, motionless, dread blooming deep in his chest as he considered the ramifications of his actions. *What now?* He had no real idea. But a bad feeling squirmed in his gut. He stood, and for the second time, made his way to the stairs, and left the basement with heavy steps…

…and met Jenny in the corridor outside, in conversation with another lawyer, whose name he couldn't remember. The talk was muted, low tones. She looked round at Stark, face pinched and pale.

Stark stopped, said nothing, allowing her to speak, though he had a strong suspicion he knew what the serious look meant.

Her voice faltered – "Jonathan. It's so unreal."

He held her gaze, waited. He knew this moment would come. It could never be otherwise. Yet strangely, it still came as a shock, when she said – "It's Paul Hutchison. He's dead. He's fucking dead."

CHAPTER FIFTY-FOUR

McGuigan and Dawson had driven to Chatelherault Woods earlier that afternoon. Police had cordoned off the entrance at the car park. They were escorted to the scene by uniform. There was little conversation. A screen had been erected at the foot of a cherry-blossom tree, shielding the body from casual observers. Given the area, the chance of a casual observer was slim. Three policemen stood on watchful guard. Tape also cordoned off the immediate area – the perimeter of a clearing, roughly the shape of a circle. They changed into protective coveralls, and approached. The pathologist was already there, all suited up, hunched over the body.

"I know what you're going to say," said McGuigan.

Laura Singleton looked up at him quizzically.

"We should stop meeting like this," he said. He gave a sardonic grin. "At least that's what I would say, if I were you."

She responded in a neutral tone. "You're not me. But we *really* should stop meeting like this. Though the locations seem to be improving lately."

Indeed, thought McGuigan. Only yesterday, the tranquil and stunning banks of Loch an Eilein. Today, beneath the boughs of a splendid cherry-blossom tree in the middle of an ancient wood. Where next, he wondered.

He looked down at the body, who was undoubtedly the same man they had met at the law practice of SJPS. Paul Hutchison. Hard to forget. Rude and restless. The accusing finger he had pointed at McGuigan in the austere meeting room not more than forty-eight hours ago, would never point again. The face, once set in an angry snarl, was still and white.

"He died probably yesterday evening," said the pathologist. "You see there," and she pointed at bruising on the neck, "the bone's been broken. And there, a crack to the head."

"He was struck?"

She gave an inconclusive shrug.

"Not sure." She motioned to an exposed root, coated dull red. It resembled a coil of old rope. "Looks like he may have bashed his head, maybe fallen heavily and awkwardly, breaking his neck in the process. Not impossible. Or, he may have been struck. I'll know more as soon as I carry out a full post-mortem. Until then, your guess, Detective Chief Inspector, is as good as mine."

"Never as good as yours." He pursed his lips. "He's still wearing his suit. The same suit he had on when he met us. Looks like he came straight from the office."

"Why here, of all places?" said Dawson.

"Perhaps he was a nature lover," said the pathologist, as she packed away items of her trade in a robust metal carrier case – sealed swabs, dusting brushes, evidence bags, other items.

McGuigan ignored the sarcasm. "To meet someone? This to me would be a nice place to meet."

"Not easy to find," said Dawson.

"Perhaps that was exactly the point. A place far away from prying eyes. A secret place, where secret things happen."

The pathologist had her little case packed up, and appraised the two men, in particular McGuigan.

"It's Friday. It's almost the end of the week. I implore you, no more dead bodies. Can you manage? At least until Monday. It would be pleasant to have the weekend to myself. Just for the novelty value."

McGuigan responded with a formal nod of his head. "Of course. I'll make arrangements."

She replied in a dry voice. "That's very accommodating."

She left the scene. Other forensic officers had arrived. Also, paramedics were getting ready to zip the lifeless form of Paul Hutchison into a large, thick plastic bag. Then the process would begin – lifting him onto a stretcher, carrying him back along the country paths to a waiting ambulance. Then, to the mortuary, where his body would be opened, organs displayed, probed, dissected, analysed, then his flesh sewn back up again, nice and packaged. Paul Hutchison – once swaggering lawyer. Now a lump of dead meat. All in a flash. McGuigan thought of the song – "What a Diff'rence a Day Makes".

He stood, surveying the area. He cocked his head, stepped towards the base of the tree-trunk, careful of his step. The ground was soft soil, presumably kept damp by the nearby river, even in the heart of summer.

"There," he said.

"Looks like something's dug a hole," said Dawson. "An animal? Maybe a fox, or a mole?"

McGuigan squatted down.

"It's shallow. It's fresh. Maybe an animal. Maybe an animal of the two-legged variety. Looking for something. Something buried?" He gestured to one of the forensic officers, who took a photograph of the area.

They made their way back through the woods. McGuigan noted how tightly packed the trees were, how thick and quiet.

"A strange place to die," he said. He ruminated. "Why would a city centre lawyer come out to this place? It's not as if he was set for a hike in the country. Otherwise he would have changed – boots, jeans, old clothes. Yes? He came here, because he had to.

There was urgency." He pursed his lips. He was convinced if he had a cigarette in his mouth, his brain would work faster. Any excuse. "He was *told* to come here. I believe he didn't have a choice. I think he came to meet someone. This was not a random visit."

"Could be," agreed Dawson. "A dog walker found the body. But the police already had a tip-off. Maybe the guy he was meeting called it in. Didn't leave a name. He used a public phone. Untraceable."

"Does he have family?"

"Wife. Two kids. She's been informed. Also, we contacted SJPS. They confirmed he left work yesterday at around six..."

"...and came straight here. Whoever it was who phoned wanted the body to be found, but wished to remain anonymous. Which indicates a lack of culpability."

Dawson frowned. "Meaning?"

"Meaning whatever happened to Hutchison wasn't intended. That he suffered a genuine accident. God knows, Dawson. I'm making this up as I'm going along. But there's a shift in the air, don't you think?"

"A shift?"

"Suddenly, a lot's happening. And I have a sense, whatever this is, it's only the beginning."

CHAPTER FIFTY-FIVE

Drinks had been hastily arranged at a pub a quarter mile from the office building. Never had there been such a week in the history of the firm. Head of litigation was apparently dead in circumstances shrouded in mystery. The police had descended and taken items from Bronson Chapel's room, and Bronson himself appeared still to be missing. Perhaps he was dead too? The gossip engine had cranked up to hyper-drive, burning like a white-hot comet. Most of the staff were flocking to the bar, to discuss, speculate, hypothesise, and get drunk.

Stark had no desire to join them. He went straight home. Jenny had joined the others. Fine. He was in no mood for socialising. The image of Hutchison lying dead in the dirt, face still and white, little pig eyes devoid of spark, was something not easily shifted. The death had been unintended. A balance had been struck. Nevertheless, the event weighed on his conscience. Now a new dread was rising – *Marie Thomson.* Blunt force trauma. The name held vague meaning. He couldn't quite fix it down.

He got in, changed into running trousers, trainers, top, then decided he was in no mood for a run. Much more appealing was the act of finishing off the whisky left over from the previous evening. He toyed with the idea of phoning his sister, for no other reason than to hear her voice. She would be working. He dismissed the notion. Instead, he unscrewed the whisky bottle, poured himself a healthy amount into his Iron Man mug, took a swallow, topped it up. He was definitely acquiring a taste. He opened his laptop, and googled the name, "Marie Thomson".

And found it, in uncompromising detail. And now knew where he had remembered it from. The nature of her death was the stuff of gold for the tabloids, and gruesome enough to reach national news.

Marie Thomson. The first victim of the serial killer christened The Surgeon. Her date of death matched precisely the date mentioned in the death certificate. Twenty-nine years old. Student. On the screen, a picture – reddish dark hair brushing her shoulders, a somewhat mischievous curl on her lips, her eyes clear and candid. Studying veterinary science at Glasgow University. A life cut short. Unimaginably disfigured and left for dead by a madman. The first of many.

He snapped his laptop shut, swallowed back a quiet surge of panic. Was this then to be his nightmare? No. He refused to believe it. He would simply not allow it. It was Friday night. Regardless of his mood, he would set off on a long run, come back in a state of exhaustion, get blind drunk, sink into oblivion, and sleep a deep dreamless sleep. And the next night? He would take it one at a time.

"No more," he said aloud, and not for the first time, wondered if he was going insane.

He remembered his sister had said she would come round after her shift. That, he decided, would not be a good idea. A morose drunk was not ideal company. Plus, he didn't want to worry her. He had done enough of that over the last five years. He phoned to cancel, leaving a message on her answer machine, keeping his voice light and flippant. "Out on a date, unbelievably. Will catch up tomorrow. Later, dude."

He left the flat, hit the streets at a pace, and tried to think of nothing, save keeping to a rhythm, putting one foot in front of the other, and allowing the world to drift by. But a shadow lurked in his mind, and the terror didn't leave.

CHAPTER FIFTY-SIX

He pulled into the hospital car park. There were two entrances. One direct from the main road, the other much less used, reached via a side road through a cluster of houses. No CCTV. Perhaps a watchful neighbour at best, but at this late hour, unlikely. Even if he were seen, it was irrelevant. Just another car. A Ford Mondeo. He had put on false licence plates. The journey from the hospital to his house on the moors was a twenty-minute drive, most of which was along unlit narrow roads, usually devoid of traffic. The chances of being stopped by police were remote. A chance he was willing to take. He was a new man. Risk-taking, spontaneity, impulsiveness – they gave him vitality. Never had he felt so alive. His skin tingled; his senses felt sharp, heightened to a new level of awareness.

Her car was exactly where he knew it would be. The place was quiet where she parked. Closer to the hospital building, the place was busier. He parked his car up level with hers. She would be finishing shortly. He thought about what she might be wearing. The thought excited him. On the seat beside him, the simple tools of his trade. Hammer, chloroform, handcuffs, a strip of cloth. A travelling rug on the back seat. Also, a fixed-blade hunting knife. To be used only as a last resort. A backup, in case things went to shit.

He watched the main entrance to A and E through binoculars which could fold nicely to fit in a pocket. It was Friday night. Busy time. People got drunk, people fought, people fell. Broken bones and split heads and runny noses.

He waited. He felt curiously disjointed from time. Seconds, minutes meant nothing. He was a constant, in a continually moving universe. At 12.15, a figure emerged. He straightened in his seat, attention fully focused. There she was! Blue leather jacket, faded T-shirt, jeans, Nike training shoes. Handbag hanging loose from her shoulder. She stopped. She turned. Someone approached her from the entrance. Another female. They talked. He clenched his jaw in frustration. *How dare she.* The frustration turned to fascination. She seemed deep in conversation. He scrutinised her movements, her demeanour. The nod of her head, the gesticulation of her hands, the twitch of her shoulders as she adjusted the strap of her handbag. She flicked a strand of hair back from her forehead. An unconscious habit, which he found endearing.

In the glimmer of the hospital lights, the profile of her face was a clear outline. He studied it. The cheekbones almost perfect. The tilt of the chin. A few adjustments, of a minor nature. A shift in the structure. Perhaps just a tiny enhancement of the nose.

The conversation ended. She made her way towards the car, a distance of just over 110 yards. He knew, because he had measured it. He was ready. His left forearm and hand were still bandaged. It didn't matter. He had a strong right hand. Plus, he had a system. Engage in friendly conversation. Then the hammer to render disorientation. Chloroform to render unconsciousness. Bundle her in the back. Handcuff her. Cover her. Job done. Easy-peasy lemon-squeezy.

She was near. Fifty yards. He wore a climbing jacket with deep pockets, in which he placed the hammer and knife. He doused the rag with the chloroform. He took a calming breath, prepared himself.

Twenty yards. She was slowing down. She twisted round, as she fished through her handbag. Presumably for car keys. She stopped, engrossed in rummaging through the contents. Success! She increased her pace.

Ten yards.

He got out the car. He had parked facing the hospital. She had parked the opposite way. As such, when he got out, he was effectively blocking her access to the driver's seat. As he had intended. She slowed again. He raised a friendly arm – the one with the bandage.

"Hi," he said.

She was at her car. It bleeped. She'd unlocked it. She was close to him. Within striking distance. His right hand was in his pocket, fingers clenched round the rubber grip of the hammer.

"Hi," she said, hesitant. She frowned. Puzzlement. Then her expression changed. She remembered – "Your hand." Her face broke into a smile. "How's it doing?"

He motioned forward. Suddenly, a shout. A female voice.

"Mags! I didn't give you the name of the place!"

A woman half trotted towards them. The same woman she had been talking to.

She – Mags – was caught, half turned to her friend, but trying to be polite at the same time.

"Sure. Thanks."

He halted, mid-stride. Indecision. The hammer was halfway out his pocket. He remained still. Foolish to attack her. The other one would simply run for help. He knew what to do. He kept smiling. Let things flow. Let this other one come. See what she gets for trying to spoil the show. His show.

He stood, remained where he was, as if he wished to initiate a conversation. Both women were now close. Close enough.

"I didn't give you the name," repeated the other, laughing, glancing at him.

"I'll get a pen," she – Mags – said, again making to open her handbag.

Enough. He strode forward, raised the hammer high, brought a thunderous blow down on the head of the other woman. Her skull cracked open. A great arc of blood shot up into the air, showering the bonnet of his car. She dropped. No sound. He couldn't ask for better. He swivelled. The woman he knew as Mags stood, riveted, unable to articulate, shocked to the core. As he would have expected. He brought the hammer down again, a less ferocious blow. To stun. He had experience in such matters. She staggered back, crumpled.

Now, speed was everything. He turned his attention to the other woman. She lay on the car park tarmacadam, perfectly still. Blood pumped out the hole in her head, like water from a hosepipe. She might be dead already. He couldn't take the chance. He knelt beside her, blood soaking the knees of his trousers. He put the hammer down, and with his right hand, pulled out the knife. The blade was a solid eight-inch wedge of sharp steel, the tip honed to a needle point. He thrust it up under her chin. He felt the resistance of bone, thrust harder, ensuring full insertion. He tugged it out, slit her throat. Better too much than too little. He placed both knife and hammer in his pocket, now got out the cloth. Mags was groaning, feebly shifting to her side. He placed the cloth over her nose and mouth, held it there until he sensed her body relax. He manoeuvred his hands under her body, lifted her. She was light. The bandage on his left arm did not restrict his movement, nor his strength. She hung in his arms, limbs limp. So easy. The back door of the car was already ajar. He prised it open with his foot, placed her on the back seat. Deftly, he handcuffed her wrists behind her back, then covered her with the travelling rug.

He went to the driver's seat, drove off, at a sedate speed. The affair, from the first hammer blow, to leaving the scene, had taken less than a minute.

So wonderfully simple. He was all-powerful. He was a god. And as a god, he would wield his power accordingly, and make her into something new and beautiful.

CHAPTER FIFTY-SEVEN

His mission was almost accomplished. With the exception of the dreamless sleep, he had executed the rest of his plan faithfully. Stark had gone for a long run. Eleven miles, roughly, at a good pace. He had come back, taken a long hot shower, ordered a carry-out pizza and side orders of fries and garlic bread. Perfect food for inducing sleepiness. Then, he finished off the whisky – half a bottle. As a top-up, for a neat package, he consumed five bottles of beer. It was 11.30pm. He was pissed. He checked his phone. A missed call from Jenny. He was too drunk, too tired to respond. Also, despite his condition, the dread festering in the pit of his stomach persisted.

He was sitting on the couch, watching a mindless movie on television. On the coffee table, the empty pizza box, and empty bottles. The sounds blurred into a vague echo, his head was fuzzy, his eyelids drooped. He fell asleep…

…and was in a busy pub, standing in the corner, in the shadows, his view unrestricted. The people he observed were unaware of his presence. The place had a student feel. At one side, two men playing guitars, singing softly. A song he didn't recognise. On a wall, a blackboard advertising cheap beer. Laughter, shouting, talking. Young people

enjoying themselves, a great release of nervous tension. Exam time had finished. It was the cusp of the summer break. He knew this. Sensed it.

There! His attention focused on a group of six, huddled round a table cluttered with empty pint glasses. Four men, two women. Lots of raucous talk and loud laughter. It was still early. An old-fashioned clock on the wall said 10pm. One of the women he recognised. Marie Thomson. She was with her friends and fellow students. All from the same class. Finals. The end of a big year. The biggest. They all agreed, when the pub closed, they would splash the cash, head into town, go clubbing. Which one? They debated, argued, came up with a name. One that was open until six in the morning. A night to remember. To endorse the agreement, they ordered shorts, downed them in a oner. Marie was laughing, and drunk, without a care.

A man, sitting on a high stool at the bar. On his own. Sipping a tall glass of lemonade. He glanced round every so often at the group. He seemed to be interested in them. Stark watched, dread escalating. The man glanced directly at him. Terror rose up in Stark's throat. The man's intentions ran deep. They leapt out at Stark, such dark, horrifying plans, stifling him. Stark couldn't move. He could only watch.

The scene before him melted into new shapes and forms – he was in a large building. Music pounded. People danced. Too loud to maintain any real conversation. He was in a place of darkness. It was late. The group were no longer. Split up. He walked across the dance floor. Those dancing were unaware of his passing. He walked to the bar. To Marie. She was on her own. He knew her thoughts. She was getting ready to go home. She had lost her friends, but she would catch up the next day. There, beside her, a figure, coiled in shadow. Waiting, as a serpent waits.

She had a drink on the bar. She turned away, briefly. A couple of seconds. A couple of seconds was all it took. The figure motioned, slid a hand over her drink, retreated.

She finished the drink. She leaned against the bar. Stark watched. She straightened, was suddenly focused, stepped forward, gazed at Stark in earnest, reached up to whisper in his ear –

"Make him pay."

She went back to the bar, resumed her place. She wobbled. Her face was slack, her eyes glazed, her head drooped. The drug was effective. She never really stood a chance.

She staggered. The shadow moved, propped her up, lips close to her ear, soothing, helpful. Caring. A perfidious presence.

"I'll get a taxi. I'll make sure you're safe. Trust me."

He held her up, one arm around her waist. She had an arm flopped over his shoulders. They were ignored. No one gave a damn. They were invisible. He took her out, onto the street. Stark followed, stood next to them on the pavement, almost brushing shoulders. Now, she was semi-conscious, legs limp, slumped over.

"I'll look after you, my angel," came the soft whisper.

He got her to a car, parked close by, manoeuvred her into the passenger seat. She groaned, tried to speak, managed only an inarticulate mumble. She tried feebly to resist, push him away.

She knows what's happening. She knows she's in jeopardy. But the drug is too strong.

The car was moving. Stark was in the back seat. Buildings floated by. Places he recognised. They were driving from the city centre.

The scene changed. They were pulling into a driveway of a semi-detached house. There were no lights. The car stopped, the garage internal, the door electric. It swung open. Slowly, with care, he drove the car inside. The door swung shut. The house was sealed tight, as was her fate.

Stark followed them, as they shuffled upstairs, she leaning on him, he supporting her. They got to the top, to a hall.

Lit candles in little candle holders on the carpet on each side. A Gothic horror show. The terror, intense, sharpened further. She stumbled, fell. He picked her up, cradled her in his arms. They got to the far end. To a door. He opened it, entered, closed the door behind him.

Stark stood.

Please – enough. But no. The scene dripped away to form a new canvas. He was in the room. A bedroom. She had been placed on the bed. She was naked. Hands and feet tied to the bed posts. She was moving her head. Regaining awareness. A shadow crouched beside her. On the wall above her hung a portrait of a woman. Spread on a trestle, implements. He whispered in his soft tongue. She whimpered. He stroked her brow, kissed her hair, turned his attention to a weird-looking gun-thing. Like a prop from a science-fiction film.

He lifted it, slid his finger over the trigger, rested the nuzzle on her neck. "Hush now," he said.

She opened her eyes wide, fixed Stark a level, steady stare.

Make him pay.

He watched what the man did to her next. He had no choice. He cried, he shrieked, he pleaded for him to stop. But he continued, undeterred, engrossed in his work.

Again, the scene changed, the landscape blurring into another. Woodland. A lay-by adjacent to a narrow country road. It was early morning. It was dark and quiet. Stark watched from the trees as the driver's door closed, and the car drove off. Sitting propped against a fence post, both hands resting on her lap, was Marie Thomson, disfigured and dead.

A section of a newspaper drifted down, to land at his feet. He picked it up. The front page was devoted to the murder. It took him only a second to read, but he caught a name – the police officer in charge of the case.

Detective Chief Inspector Harry McGuigan.

CHAPTER FIFTY-EIGHT

EARLY SATURDAY MORNING

"You promised me a quiet weekend," said Laura Singleton, the pathologist.

A forensic tent had been erected over the immediate crime scene. A section of the hospital car park had been cordoned off. It didn't stop the A and E ward of Hairmyres Hospital being any less busy, reflected McGuigan. Illness and injury never ceased. Not even for murder.

"How can I make it up to you?" he responded in a dry voice.

She gave a dismissive shake of her head. Her mood, he realised, was more sour than usual. Who could possibly blame her? But then, his mood was equally as black.

The young woman on the ground looked no older than thirty, still in hospital scrubs. Once blue, now an altogether different colour.

"This was an attack both controlled and profoundly vicious," she said. "Whoever did it wanted to make damned sure."

McGuigan said nothing. He was beyond words.

"I think she was struck by a heavy instrument on the top of her head," she continued. "See the wound? Used with great force. Probably killed her stone dead. Another wound under her chin.

Very deep. Deep enough to pierce the brain. Maybe a knife. Possibly a survival type, like a weapon used for hunting. The wound to the throat is obvious. A straight slit, again deep. Maybe time of death early hours, maybe midnight, maybe a little after. I'll know more..."

"...when you do a post-mortem," finished McGuigan.

She appraised him, her face solemn. "This attack was carried out with... efficiency. He wanted her dead. Each wound taken on its own was enough to kill. The perpetrator wanted to be triple certain."

"But she wasn't the main target," replied McGuigan absently. "Collateral. Wrong place, wrong time, wrong everything."

"That's your job, Chief Inspector. I look at the how. You look at the why and the who."

One murder. And a probable kidnapping. The handbag left discarded held a glut of information – driver's licence, credit card, house keys, mobile phone. Dr Margaret Sinclair. Residing in the village of Jackton, not far from the hospital. Adjacent to the murder scene, her car, abandoned. Married, no children. Her husband had already been contacted. A building surveyor who had an office in town. Plus, apparently, she had a brother, who they were trying to locate.

Dawson was somewhere in the main building, interviewing staff. Stark sighed, made his way in. He was now beginning to forget when he had last slept properly. He realised he might need a shower. His heart was too heavy to care. Press had already gathered. They stood, congregated to one side, herded there by uniform. They shouted a barrage of questions as he passed, which he ignored.

The waiting room was quiet. He nodded at a woman at reception, went through double doors, to the interior. Three rooms were being used for interviews. He came to an open-plan reception area. Staff sat, or stood, faces expressing a variety of emotion – shock, disbelief, anguish. Police presence was heavy.

How like vultures we are, he thought. *Flocking round the dead.* An image flashed in his mind. The raven, on the shores of Loch an Eilein.

He met Dawson leaving one of the interview rooms.

"No one saw anything," he said simply. "We're contacting every patient who attended last night. It was busy. Friday evening and all."

"He's emboldened."

Dawson regarded him. "He?"

"Who else? So quick after the last murder. The photofit description completely wrong. The lack of planning. He thinks he's invincible. Actually, he's always thought that. Now he's risen to a different level."

Dawson blew through his lips, responded in a sceptical voice.

"Really, sir? This isn't The Surgeon's MO. This is like... spontaneous. A bystander killed in a car park. Right outside a hospital. It doesn't feel right."

"It feels exactly right, Dawson. He was careless last time – he shot a man dead in his front garden, was seen by a witness. And yet, no repercussions. Our serial killer, the consummate planner, has transcended. He believes he's untouchable. He no longer requires to plan to the nth degree. He now simply *acts,* as the mood takes him, to do as he will. Rather like a god. Does this make sense?"

Dawson gestured with a slight shrug of his shoulders. "We won't have any conclusive evidence until..."

"...until we have a body. Until he performs his artistic skills." He lowered his voice, talking more to himself. "I will not allow this to happen. Not again. Enough death, already." He raised his eyes to the flat ceiling above. "Enough, please."

"We might get a break," said Dawson. "Someone might have seen something." He didn't sound convinced. His brow furrowed. He licked his lips, as if processing his next sentence. "Also, Blakely's in a rage. He's looking for you, sir. He's been trying to call you. He's phoned me, to speak to you. He wants to see you. Like, now."

"Like, now," repeated McGuigan. He had been ignoring Blakely's calls. He knew the reason for the rage. The photofit cock-up was supposed to have been kept a cosy secret. The mood of his superior officer was way down McGuigan's pecking order.

"I'm heading back," he said. "Should anything develop, let me know."

McGuigan got back to the incident room a half hour later. He was too tired to deal with the looming tussle with the chief constable. He thought ruefully it might be more than a mere tussle. More of a massacre. He got out, made his way to the front entrance. Something caught his eye. There, parked close by, was an ancient Nissan Micra, battered, rusting, its exhaust clinging to the undercarriage by loops of string. He had seen this car before. His interest was suddenly aroused.

He went in. The duty sergeant caught his attention. He gestured to a man sitting in the reception area. The man stood, approached.

The duty sergeant spoke. "Sir. This gentleman came in an hour ago. He asked for you specifically. Wouldn't give his name. He said it was urgent. I told him you were busy, but he was insistent..."

McGuigan turned, appraised the man. He was tall, possibly six two. Maybe taller. Lean. Thick dark hair cropped short. Handsome in a hard-bitten way. He had seen him before. In the offices of SJPS. Weariness dissolved. McGuigan was fully attentive.

"Chief Inspector McGuigan?"

"Yes?"

"My name is Jonathan Stark. We need to talk."

CHAPTER FIFTY-NINE

He had tied her wrists to the bed post. She was wakening. He was sitting on a chair at the far side of the room. He considered her face, transitioning from sleep to wakefulness, how the lamplight caught the angle of her cheekbones, the movement of her lips, the furrow of her forehead as realisation dawned.

Never had he chosen one so perfect. He raised his phone, took a photograph, sent it. He sat back, waited. Wrapped in cellophane, draped over a coat hanger on the handle of a wardrobe, was a dark, puffy-sleeved blouse, a dark tweed skirt. Beneath, black heels.

He watched as her eyes focused, adjusted to her new surroundings. She blinked. Her expression changed, from sleepy bewilderment to startled terror. She didn't scream. She focused on him, took deep breaths, doubtless trying to gain perspective. He admired her composure. This was new.

She tried to move her arms. The bonds were tight. She took another breath, looked about. There was little to see. The walls were bare, the curtains drawn shut. The only item of furniture, save the bed, was the wardrobe. She focused back on him. Her bottom lip trembled. Her breath came in little ragged gasps. But yet, no tears. No pleading. No sobbing. He was doubly impressed.

She found her voice.

"What is this?"

He sat up straight, attentive.

"Are you thirsty?" he asked.

She gave a weak nod.

"Of course you are. Sparkling or still?"

"What?"

"That's okay. I'll get you both." He got up, went through to the kitchen, pulled out a bottle each of still and sparkling water from the fridge. He'd made sure to buy the expensive type. The type in glass bottles.

He unscrewed the tops, tossed the tops in a plastic bin. His hands were trembling. He was in a state of near rapture. He placed the bottles on a silver tray, went back to the bedroom.

"Which one?"

"Still."

"Of course." He came forward, untied one of her wrists, handed her the bottle. He went back to his seat.

"I always think drinking out the bottle feels better. What do you think, Margaret?"

She took several gulps. She gave him a level stare.

"It depends on what you're drinking. What are you doing?"

He raised his shoulders, smiled. "Enjoying a civilised conversation with a beautiful woman."

"Why am I here?"

"Please. Indulge me. I miss adult interaction. This place can be lonely."

Her eyes never left him. "Is that why you brought me here and tied me to a bed? So we could have a chat?"

He laughed. A merry laugh. He was happy. She was a million times better than he had expected. He knew she was terrified, but the containment of her emotion was exceptional, and something to be appreciated. His heart soared.

"Are you hungry?"

"No."

"I'll fix you something later."

"Why am I here?"

"If you weren't here, then we wouldn't be having this fun."

"I would have more fun if you untied me."

"In time."

Again, her lip trembled. Her chin wobbled. But still no tears. She took another gulp of water.

"If you're not going to tell me why I'm here, tell me where I am? That would only be polite."

"Deep in the Eaglesham moors. The wind never stops blowing. You can hear it now. In the summer, it dies a little. But in the winter, it whips up, like a frenzy."

She nodded, as if considering what he had said.

"I live close by. My husband will be looking for me. A lot of people will be looking for me. Let me go. I'll not say a word. You can carry on, as if nothing had happened."

The smile never left his face. "Let me give that some thought. Do you enjoy being a doctor?"

She didn't answer immediately. Her self-possession was cracking.

"Yes." Her eyes never left his. "I enjoy healing the sick."

"Is that what you think, Margaret? That I'm sick?" He kept his tone light. He found her conversation engaging.

"I can get you help," she said. "The right help. I'll see to it personally. Let me go. Let me speak to people."

"Speak to people? But we're speaking right now. No need to involve anyone else. Not yet." He paused, then said quietly, "We aren't so very different, in our own way. You heal people. I heal people, too. In a manner of speaking."

Her forehead wrinkled in puzzlement. "You're a doctor?"

"I allow people to transcend. Those I deem worthy, I... modify. Make them better. Upgrade? Is that a good word? I oversee the change from the grub to the butterfly. I hope I'm not talking in clichés. But I'm not a doctor. My work is more specialised. Others – people who are beneath the likes of you and I – have given me a name. Which, despite their ignorance, their propensity to rut in the dirt like brute animals, is a name I am happy to accept."

She said nothing. Not once did she take her eyes from his. She was waiting. Did she know? Perhaps. Perhaps she knew all the time. Such courage, he thought.

He kept his voice soft. "Shall I tell you what they call me?"

She remained silent, the cheekbones of her face harsh and sharp.

"They call me The Surgeon."

Now, the tears came, the lips quivered, and she began to cry.

He got a message on his phone. A response to the photo he had sent. The message was one word, simple, and gave him joy.

The message said – *perfect.*

CHAPTER SIXTY

McGuigan took Stark to a vacant interview room on the ground floor of the building. They sat on opposite sides of a bare table, on hard plastic seats with metal legs. Not designed for comfort.

"Tea, coffee?" ventured McGuigan.

"Nothing, thanks. I recognise you from your visits to SJPS. I work there, by the way. I'm their new trainee lawyer."

"I remember you," replied McGuigan. He took out a piece of bubblegum from his jacket pocket, unwrapped it, put the small pink brick shape into his mouth.

"I hope you don't mind," he said. "It's not very professional. But it helps the craving."

"Bazooka bubblegum. I used to chew it when I was a kid. I had no idea you could still get it."

"You're still a kid." He leant back. "I suppose, when you're my age, most people look like kids. What can I do for you, Jonathan?"

Stark's lips twitched into a tremulous smile. He fidgeted on his seat. *He looks damned uncomfortable,* thought McGuigan.

"This isn't easy to explain. I'm not really sure where to start."

McGuigan waited, said nothing. Strangely, for a reason he could not fully understand, he believed this moment was important. That something was happening. That this was the cusp of something much bigger. He waited. His heart raced.

"I've seen the man called The Surgeon."

Quite an opener. McGuigan kept his voice level.

"Really?"

"Really. And he looks nothing like the photofit you've given to the public. I would like to get that straight from the beginning."

McGuigan nodded slowly. "This is very interesting, Jonathan. You've seen him?"

Stark hesitated. He felt like getting up, getting out. But he had started. He doubted, given he had just admitted to having seen the most wanted man in the country, he would be allowed to leave.

"I've seen him, in a manner of speaking."

McGuigan frowned. He chewed on the gum. Raspberry flavour, he decided.

He said, "Perhaps I should ask a colleague in, to take notes, you understand. Procedure, and all that stuff." He gave a wintry grin. "As a lawyer, you'll understand all about procedure."

Stark became more agitated. "No. Just you. Please, Mr McGuigan."

"My name's Harry," replied McGuigan gently. "Of course. Just me. If that's what you want."

Stark considered the man before him. Mid- to late-fifties. Weathered skin, sad wrinkles cobwebbing the sides of each eye. But the eyes were bright. McGuigan chewed his gum. Stark could smell the sugary sweet scent from his breath. This was the man he knew he had to speak to. He hoped, he prayed, for good reason. But where the hell to begin.

"Do you believe in God?"

McGuigan sat back, folded his arms, scrutinised Stark.

"It's funny, but I've been asked this a few times recently. I ask it myself, and I'm not entirely certain of the answer. Do you?"

"I don't know what to believe." He licked his lips with the tip of his tongue. He was hungover. His mouth was dry. His throat was raw. "Can I have that cup of tea?"

McGuigan nodded politely. "Indeed you can. It's from a machine." He gave a warm smile. "The taste ranges from 'insipid', to 'foul', depending on its mood. You have been duly warned."

Stark couldn't help smiling back. He liked this man.

"As long as it's wet."

"Wet, I can do. What do you take with it?"

"Does it matter?"

"No."

He got up, left the room. Stark wondered if he made a bolt out the door, would he be chased by a posse of coppers across the car park. The scene conjured in his mind made him smile. Something from the *Keystone Cops*. At this moment, smiling felt good. The dream was still fresh in his mind. It filled him with fear. He hoped to Jesus Christ above, Harry McGuigan had an open mind.

McGuigan reappeared, holding two white plastic cups, placed them on the table.

He gave a sardonic smile. "Enjoy."

"Thank you." He sipped.

"You were asking me if I believed in God," resumed McGuigan. "My wife and I go to church every Sunday. This causes mild amusement amongst my fellow workers, because they think, given the horrific scenes we witness in this job, God cannot possibly exist. But I go, I listen, I sing the hymns – though I use the term 'singing' very loosely – I pray, like everyone else there. I suppose I'm looking for something. But do I believe? Really? That's a leap." He gave a tired sigh. The kid had asked a question, and here he was, baring his soul. "If he – *God*, that is –

were to give me a sign, a nod, even a wink, then maybe I might take that leap."

"Maybe I can help with that sign," muttered Stark. "I read somewhere that on death, our souls leave our body, to travel to the next... phase."

"Perhaps they do. Someday, each and every one of us will find out."

Stark leaned forward. "I'm going to tell you something, Harry. I'm going to ask you to take that leap. I'm not mad. I'm not on drugs. I'm not on anything. I just need you to take what I say seriously. And that won't be easy."

"Madness is a subjective thing, don't you think? Please. Try me."

Stark took another sip, collected his thoughts. But they swarmed in his head like angry bees.

"I... I seem to have very specific and detailed dreams. In these dreams, I witness events. More than witness. I share the suffering."

McGuigan took a drink from the plastic cup. The bubblegum helped to soften the taste. He said nothing.

"Last night, I dreamt about Marie Thomson."

McGuigan raised an eyebrow. He knew each of their names, branded deep in his mind. "His first victim. Five years ago."

Stark recollected the sequence of events. He shuddered. He continued, because he had to.

"I dreamt how she died. I dreamt where she died. The details were vivid. I felt her pain. Her despair. Every inch of her terror."

McGuigan pursed his lips. The young man before him spoke with an earnestness he found disarming. The sceptical portion of his brain reared up and burst out laughing. A much smaller portion took a reflective view, and paused in its judgement.

"You had a dream," said McGuigan. "Despite its vividness, that's all it was." He fell silent, then said, "Surely?"

"A dream can be much more," said Stark quietly. His voice changed. Became robotic. "Her body was found by the side of a country road. He sat her up, against a fence post. He had rearranged her hair. He had changed her face to suit his requirements."

McGuigan nodded slowly. He knew each case intimately. Unlike Stark, he hadn't dreamt it. The fence post was interesting, but not enough.

"This is true," he said. "But these are details anyone could get from the internet. The country knows that he – for want of a better word – *mutilates* their faces. Hence his nickname."

"Details," repeated Stark. "All right. When she was found, she was wearing a dark blouse, a dark skirt, black heels. He not only mutilates. He changes their clothing. I'm not sure, but if I were to hazard a guess, when found, each victim was dressed in exactly the same manner."

That is interesting, thought McGuigan. He responded with a tilt of his head, suggesting he would like to hear more.

"Marie Thomson was a final year vet student. She was celebrating with friends in a pub called the Fox and Hound." His voice didn't change tone as he recounted the event of that particular evening. "It's a spit-and-sawdust pub for students in the west end. You probably know it. She was wearing jeans, suede boots, a university sweat top, a red leather jacket. She had a necklace of a little golden crucifix, though she wasn't religious. A present from her mum. She had a tattoo on the nape of her neck. Mandarin symbols, denoting 'harmony'. She was a happy girl. She'd just sat her last exam. There were six of them altogether, that night. Six friends. Letting off a little steam. They sat at a table in the corner, and drank pints of lager, then shots. There was live music. He was there, already. Watching. Waiting for his moment. He had targeted her months before. He could hardly contain his excitement. They left the pub, and went to a club called Ringo's in the city centre. It had just opened. It was late.

They got split up. She was drunk." He took a shuddering breath, held back his anger. "All she wanted was to get home. Shall I go on?"

"Please."

"He spiked her drink, rendered her almost unconscious. He put her in a car. A dark Mondeo. He took her back to a house." A scene formed in his mind, one he would never forget. "He killed her, then drove her body to the lay-by." He fell silent. He bowed his head. He had summed up the last shocking moments of a young woman's life in less than a minute of conversation. Somehow, he felt ashamed. She deserved much more. He met McGuigan's eyes once again. "Well? Did I get it right?"

McGuigan pondered. "He took her to a house? You saw this in your dream? You would recognise this house?"

"Of course." A sudden thought struck Stark. He looked at McGuigan, his hangover forgotten – "You didn't know this."

McGuigan held Stark's stare. *Intriguing.* "You dreamt all this?"

"There's more. I think I know why he does it. Why he chooses certain types. Why he feels the need to recreate their faces."

McGuigan waited. He had stopped chewing. He realised he was holding his breath. Now, this was more than intriguing. This was gripping.

"He had handcuffed her to a bed. Above the bed, on the wall, was a portrait of a woman. This woman is important in his life. He models his victims on this woman." He looked away, as he recalled the face, pale and unsmiling. Haunted eyes. Skin so deathly white. "Here's the thing, Harry. I've seen this woman before. Somewhere in the past. I just can't remember where."

McGuigan considered the man sitting on the other side of the table. Jonathan Stark. Trainee lawyer, so claimed. The obvious link, once again – the firm of SJPS. Always, the path seemed to wind back to them. And how the path wound and twisted.

"You understand, of course, that by providing me with this abundance of information, there are two possible conclusions I can draw."

Stark shrugged. He was weary. He had given as much as he could. He hoped he had done enough, that whatever force was driving this situation, was satisfied. Somehow, he thought not. Somehow, he thought the shit had only just begun.

"You're right," he said. He took another swig of tea, which was cold. "It truly is disgusting. Two conclusions? May I?"

Again, McGuigan responded with a polite tilt of his head.

"One – I'm mad," said Stark. "Or two – I'm the killer."

McGuigan allowed a crooked grin. "If you were the killer, it would seem odd that you would come to me, a policeman, and admit your crimes by the weirdest of implications – by way of a dream. And as for the first conclusion – you don't appear to me to be mad."

It was Stark's turn to grin. "'Madness is a subjective thing'. Your words."

McGuigan took a long breath. If only he had the bite of nicotine to sharpen his thoughts. Bazooka bubblegum just didn't crack it. He decided to play along.

He took his phone out, found a photograph he had taken of Mrs Shawbridge's son, and showed it to Stark, an action he scarcely believed he was doing.

"Is this the man you saw in your dream?"

"Very similar."

McGuigan put the phone back in his pocket. The affirmation meant nothing. The man opposite could simply be lying, but McGuigan had gut feelings about things.

"My wife truly believes God works in mysterious ways," he said. "Perhaps he does. Or perhaps he doesn't work at all, and everything is a smorgasbord of random events and situations, without pattern or meaning. Or maybe it's a bit of both. I don't know the answer. But I do know I need help. And suddenly here you are. Look for the signs, I say. Right now, I need all the signs I can get. You might be mad, Jonathan. We might both be mad. But you're here. And you know stuff that you shouldn't know. I'll take that leap, because I have no choice, and I have no other place to go. And the clock's ticking. You said you knew the house he took her to?"

"In my dream, I saw the address. Clock's ticking? What do you mean?"

McGuigan clicked his teeth, looked askance at Stark. Where was the harm?

"I need to move quickly. I believe he – The Surgeon – has taken another. Last night. A doctor, as she was leaving A and E. I have a very limited window of opportunity. If you have this address, then give it to me now. Please."

"A doctor? A and E?" Stark stared, heart pounding in his throat. Conclusions swirled in his mind, too horrific to consider. "Which hospital?"

McGuigan read the sudden concern in his voice. "Why is this important to you, Jonathan?"

"Which hospital?"

"Hairmyres."

"And this was last night? You said 'she'?"

"Yes."

Stark could hardly speak. He dreaded his next words, because they would come as a question he had no desire to ask. But he had no choice. He spoke, his voice leaden.

"Do you know her name?"

"What is it, Jonathan?"

"Do you know her name?"

"Margaret Sinclair. Doctor Margaret Sinclair."

Stark's world imploded. He felt dizzy. He bent over, retched.

Nothing came up. He felt short of breath. He focused on the floor. The floor moved; his vision swam.

He sensed movement – McGuigan standing up, coming round, hovering beside him.

Stark took some deep breaths. His straightened, swallowed back a surge of nausea.

"You know her," said McGuigan.

"She's my sister."

Stark shook his head, tried to gain clarity to his thoughts. "Sinclair's her married name," he mumbled. "None of this makes any goddamned sense."

"Or maybe it does," countered McGuigan. "I really don't know if I believe you, Jonathan, or whether you're deluding yourself, but if this dream really is…" he groped for the right word, "…*something,* then maybe you had the dream precisely because of what's happened to your sister. Tell me! What's the address? I can have it checked out now."

Stark stood, fought the shakiness in his legs, faced McGuigan.

"No. You might have it checked out. You might not. I really don't know if I believe *you,* Harry. But one thing is for certain. *I'm* going to check it. This is my sister. Not yours. You have a choice, Chief Inspector. You can come with me now. Or not. But I'm leaving. And I'd welcome your presence. I think, going with an officer of the law would make life a lot easier. But I'm leaving, with or without you."

McGuigan nodded. Fruitless to remonstrate. Stark would remain undeterred. He was on a mission – who could blame him? Plus, McGuigan needed the address, to follow this line of enquiry through, regardless of whether it was a figment of Stark's imagination. Procedure be damned.

"Fair enough. But we take my car."

As they were leaving the building, the desk sergeant raised his hand, caught McGuigan's attention for the second time that morning.

"Sir! The chief wants a chat. Says it's urgent."

McGuigan stopped in mid-stride, turned.

"Pass this message. Tell him…" and here he mouthed rest of his sentence, "…to fuck right off."

CHAPTER SIXTY-ONE

Edward Stoddart, great grandson of one of the founding partners, never left the offices of SJPS. There was no need. Since his cancer diagnosis, the top floor had been converted. He had everything he needed. Bedroom, en suite, dining room, kitchen. And an office. There was a spare room, for a nurse, if required, if things got bad. All the essentials.

His cancer was aggressive. He knew that the doctors were optimistic when they predicted a year. The ache in his bones, the wheeze in his chest, all said otherwise.

He sat on the couch, in his office. Where Stark had sat, only days before. He was tired. It was sometimes painful to sleep, and when the pain got bad, it was easier to read a book, or watch television, or peruse a legal point he had been asked to consider. On the coffee table was the lump of rock – the paperweight ornament. Beside it, a letter, addressed to Jonathan Stark. He picked it up, and read it for the hundredth time.

He pressed it to his chest, and began to cry.

CHAPTER SIXTY-TWO

McGuigan drove. Stark knew the address. He had seen it in his dream. The street, the house number, the hedge, the trees. Such details were embedded in his mind, and doubtless would remain there, forever.

21 Elm Road. McGuigan keyed it into the satnav. North side of Glasgow. Quiet, respectable, residential, comprising row upon row of semi-detached houses with neat front gardens and nice cars parked in the driveways. Nothing to distinguish it from a thousand other slices of suburbia. Light years from death and torture.

The journey from the police station took twenty-two minutes. Stark counted. They arrived at the address. From the outside, as innocuous and unremarkable as every other house.

McGuigan opened his mouth, about to suggest calm and discretion. Too late. Stark was out of the car, marching towards the front gate. McGuigan cursed, followed.

"Hold up!"

Stark stopped, turned.

"I get it, Jonathan," said McGuigan. "You believe your sister might be in the house. And I've gone along with this, even though every other copper would either have arrested you, or laughed you out of the police station. But I can't call backup, because I can't justify it. So it's just you and me. I'm asking you – let me do this. Please. Right now, the best thing for your sister is for us to keep a calm head. Whatever we confront. You understand this, Jonathan?"

Stark took a long breath. His heart beat heavy and hard; thoughts raced in his mind. He understood nothing anymore.

"Calm head. I get it..."

Their shoes scrunched over clean white pebbles forming the front path. McGuigan had no real idea what he was doing, here, at this place, following the absurd conviction of a man he barely knew. But he had agreed to come, he was part of the show, and he knew if he didn't follow it through, he would wonder for the rest of his days.

He rang the doorbell. The front door was thick bevelled glass. There was no movement or sound from inside. They waited. McGuigan rang again, stepped back. This time, a noise. A shape floated towards them, distorted by the glass, grew bigger. A key turned. A bolt slid. The door opened.

Before them stood an elderly woman, round shouldered, a round placid face, hair white and short.

She regarded them with open curiosity, but without any apparent animosity.

"Yes?"

McGuigan cleared his throat, smiled, assumed a gentle tone.

"Sorry to trouble you. My name is Chief Inspector McGuigan..." and he reached into his inside jacket pocket, pulled out a black leather wallet, opened it to reveal his warrant card, "... and this is my... assistant."

Attached to a cord round her neck was a pair of glasses, which she raised to her eyes to study the card.

"How can I help you?"

"We're trying to trace someone who might be important in

assisting us in our enquiries. A young woman has gone missing. This person, if we found him, could be of significant help."

She frowned.

"I can't see what good I can do."

"This person, perhaps in the past, was linked to this address."

"You're in luck," she said.

"Really?"

"I've just put the kettle on."

They entered the hallway – the wallpaper busy and garish; intertwined red and yellow flowers with bright green leaves. She took them to an open-plan room, a living room merging into a small dining room with patio doors, and beyond, a neat garden.

She asked them to sit at the dining table. She left the room, presumably to the kitchen, and returned with three white porcelain cups on white saucers with spoons, a silver pot of tea, a silver jug of milk, a dainty silver bowl of sugar. She placed the tray on the table, and began to pour tea into the three cups. Her hand trembled as she did so. A sure sign of early Parkinson's.

Stark ground his teeth in frustration. He held his tongue.

"Milk?" she asked.

"You're very kind," replied McGuigan. Stark merely nodded. She poured in the milk. She took a sip, placed the cup back on its saucer.

"Now," she said. "How can I help you boys?"

"Can I ask what your name is?" said McGuigan.

"Mrs Karen Fleming. Full name – Karen Isabel Fleming. Isabel was my mother's name. She died when I was young. Pneumonia."

"I'm sorry to hear that." McGuigan showed his best reassuring smile. "How long have you lived here, Mrs Fleming?"

"Now that's a question. We bought this place forty years ago.

We never felt the need to move. Look at the young folks nowadays. Don't stay in a place for longer than a minute. Then they see something bigger and better and want that instead. Contentment. That's what they lack. And by the time they realise, it's too late."

McGuigan nodded sagely. "That's the modern world. Everybody wants everything yesterday. You said 'we'?"

She took another sip of her tea. She licked her lips. She was clearly warming to the conversation.

"My husband. Donald. He was a retired civil engineer. He worked for the council all his days. Took retirement at sixty-five. He loved his work. It gave him a purpose. Work's important, don't you think? Keeps the mind active, gives a person a reason to get up in the morning. Makes a person feel they're still part of the human race."

"Very true, Mrs Fleming."

She sighed. "That's the thing about being old. You become invisible." She seemed to reflect, then said, "Donald died last year. So sudden." She gestured to the back garden. "He just dropped. Massive heart attack. He loved his flowers and plants. I try to keep it going, but as you might have guessed..." and she gave a joking grin, "...I get the shakes. Old age comes with a lot of baggage."

"Shame we don't have baggage handlers. Life would be a bit easier."

"But this Zoom thing is amazing," she continued. "I can press some buttons on the computer, and I can see my daughter and the grandkids. They grow up so fast."

"You have a daughter?"

"Helen. She married a commercial airline pilot, and they live in Boston. They tell me Boston's colder than Scotland in the winter. But the summers are beautiful."

"Any other children?"

"Just the one. But I go out to see her every year." She leaned forward in a conspiratorial manner, as if about to impart a great secret. "Because he's a pilot, I get the flights for nothing. And I go business class. Have you ever been business class? All the drinks are free."

"Never been so lucky," said McGuigan. "Maybe one day." He gave a meaningful glance to Stark, who understood – it meant *this is getting us nowhere.* Stark's despair escalated by the second. He was sick with worry. The premonition of his dream was proving worthless. And yet, the address existed, the exterior of the house was the same, the picture McGuigan had shown him was close to the man in his dream.

"We're searching for a particular individual, Mrs Fleming. We have reason to believe he may have stayed in this house at some point in the past. Maybe five years ago." He got out his phone, showed her the photo. "Do you recognise him?"

She looked puzzled. "Only Donald and I have ever lived here. I haven't seen this man. I'm so sorry."

"Of course," said McGuigan. "No need to be sorry."

Something is wrong, thought Stark. *We're missing something.* He had a sudden thought, a spark of intuition.

"You visit your daughter in Boston?" he said.

"Every summer. From the beginning of June up to mid-September. If I had my way, I would stay over there." The edges of her mouth curled in a sad droop. "There's nothing much here for me now."

"And the house," continued Stark. "You leave it vacant?"

She nodded. "My neighbours are good people. They watch out for anything strange." She frowned. "Although we did rent it out one year. A short-term let, as it was described."

McGuigan cottoned on. "That's interesting. Can you recall when?"

She looked thoughtful. "Now that I think about it, it was maybe five years back." Her eyes widened with sudden enlightenment. "We rented the house out the same summer I got my hip replacement. I had to wait a year. But what a difference. It's like having a constant toothache, and then suddenly the pain's gone."

"Five years ago," murmured Stark.

"You rented the house out?" said McGuigan. Stark detected the tiniest hint of excitement in his voice.

"We did. We used an agency to do it. They organised the whole thing. They found the tenant, paid the rental straight into our account. When we got back, the place was spotless. Very professional."

"An agency? Can you remember their name? That would be very helpful, Mrs Fleming."

She blinked, forehead creasing as she struggled to remember. Stark stared at her, willing her to spout forth the information.

Again, her expression changed – "I have a file," she said. "Somewhere. I'll get it." But instead, she topped up McGuigan's cup. She noted Stark hadn't touched his tea. "Would you prefer coffee?" she asked.

I would prefer you find the goddamned file.

"I'm fine, thanks."

"You mentioned the file?" prompted McGuigan.

"Of course. One minute, please. I think it's in the bureau."

Stiffly, she got to her feet, and went across to the other side of the room, to a varnished, Victorian-style writing bureau, complete with two drawers and cabriole legs with gilt metal mounts.

"This is French rosewood," she said. "Donald's pride and joy. He inherited it, when his father died."

"It's a beautiful piece," said McGuigan.

She opened a drawer, started to file through papers and files. She tutted, closed the drawer, pulled out the next one. Again, more rifling. "Aha!" She took out a pink folder. Written on the front, in bold thick felt pen – *House Lease.*

She made her way back to the table, sat. She opened the file. Inside, a bundle of papers.

"Will this help?"

She slid across a set of documents, stapled together. McGuigan and Stark looked at the first page. It was a lease document. The preamble was clear –

Lease by Donald Fleming and Karen Fleming in favour of Apollo Letting Company Ltd

Stark picked it up. "It's an agreement between you and the letting company. It allows them to place suitable candidates as tenants, without the need to keep changing the lease should the tenants change."

Karen Fleming chuckled. "It's a lot of jargon to me. Donald did all that sort of stuff. But now that I think of it, the tenant who was here left some personal items. I contacted the company, but they didn't seem to bother. I kept them, in case whoever was here should want them back. I've always hoarded. That's what Donald said. That I was such a hoarder."

McGuigan, with some effort, kept his voice level.

"Can you show me, Karen?"

She took out more papers from the file, and handed him a photograph of a young woman, and segments of newspaper clippings.

"Could I keep these, please?" said McGuigan. "For a little while. I promise I'll get them back to you."

"You said there was a missing woman. Will this help?"

"Very much."

"Keep them. I have no use for them. Would you like some cake, Chief Inspector?"

Karen Fleming stood at the front door, waving goodbye, as they got into the car.

"The portrait the killer had on the bedroom wall," said Stark, "is the same woman in the photo. And the news clippings. All about the same story."

McGuigan nodded. "I remember well. Alfie Willow. He went to work one morning and shot most of his staff."

"I remember well, too. I was there."

McGuigan looked at him, said nothing.

Stark tapped the photo of the woman with the tip of his finger. "I knew I had seen her somewhere before. If I recall, she had just started. Like me. A legal trainee." Stark thought back, as he often did, to that terrible moment in time, when his world turned to blood. "She went to work one morning, and ended up dead."

"In which case," said McGuigan, "if we find who she is, we might establish a connection. I can check records. We'll have details of all the shooting victims in our archives."

"There's more," said Stark. "Apollo Letting. I know this name."

McGuigan waited.

"It's the trading name used by a firm of lawyers for their residential lets. A rather respectable and prestigious firm you've had the pleasure of visiting recently."

"It always comes back to SJPS," breathed McGuigan.

Clock's ticking. "I can check the records," said Stark. He spoke quickly. His mind was in overdrive. Panic, though he tried to contain the swell, threatened to submerge him. With effort, he kept his voice flat and hard. Now, if ever there was a time, he had to keep it together. For his sister's sake.

"There will be something, somewhere. Records of who the particular tenant was. There would have been checks done. References. Bank account details. Proof of ID. Due diligence. Everything's copied. Usually in duplicate. It's a thing lawyers like to do."

"Like Mrs Fleming," replied McGuigan. "You hoard. Which we all do, in our way." He took a deep breath. He was venturing into strange and alien territory, a billion miles from conventional police work. But then, he reflected, he had never been the conventional sort.

"Okay," he said. "We keep going."

Suddenly, Stark gripped him by the arm. "What is this, Harry? What's this about? I don't understand what the hell is going on." His voice broke. His breath was a shudder. He bit back tears.

McGuigan gave him a small sad smile. It was all he had to offer.

"Nor me. I don't have any answers. But a door's been opened. Maybe just enough for us to see a little sunlight. And sunlight is all we need, to see a path."

"A path to what, I wonder."

"Let's find out."

A flicker of movement distracted them. They both looked round – there, standing perched on Karen Fleming's front gate, a raven. Glossy black, beak and talons razor sharp, eyes tiny dark pools. It regarded them with inscrutable detachment.

It flapped its wings, soared up and away.

CHAPTER SIXTY-THREE

He released Margaret, to allow her to use the bathroom. She locked the door. He waited outside. He held a pistol in his right hand. He had given her a simple warning. If she chose not to come out the bathroom, and keep the door locked, then he would shoot it open, and shoot her in the head. The warning worked. There was no fuss. The imminence of death ensured her compliance. When she was done, he tied her back to the bed.

It was 11am.

"Are you hungry?" he asked. "You must be famished."

She kept a steady stare. He knew she was terrified. It was, if he were honest, part of the enjoyment of his task. To see the fear in their faces. This one, however, kept it cool, which gave him more delight.

"I'm not hungry," she said.

He shrugged. "It's up to you." He turned his attention to the clothes on the coat hanger – the blouse, skirt and the shoes beneath.

"You'll look good in them," he said. "More than good. Beautiful."

"You want me to dress up?"

"Those were the identical clothes she wore the day she died." He went over, touched them delicately.

"She?"

He faced her. "Would you care to see her?"

She issued no response. Her eyes were what...? He struggled for a word. Indignant? Arrogant? *Wilful,* he decided. Soon, that would change.

"Let me show you. Yes?"

He didn't wait for her to answer. If there was one, it was an irrelevance. He went through, to his special room, where photographs of dead women decorated his walls. In the corner was a shoulder-high cupboard. He opened it, and with care, lifted out the objects within, and brought them back to the bedroom. She watched him impassively.

The two items were an easel and a portrait. He opened the curtains, to allow the sunlight in. He erected the easel in a corner which attracted the most light. He secured the portrait on it. He stood back, admired it.

"She's beautiful." He turned his head round. "Like you. Don't you think? What's your opinion, Margaret?"

"Who is she?"

With the tip of his finger, with tenderness, he traced a line over her brow, the side of her face, the curve of her jaw, the flow of her lips.

"She was my sister."

CHAPTER SIXTY-FOUR

Agreement had been reached. McGuigan would drop Stark back to his car. Stark would head straight to the offices of SJPS, to find information on Apollo Letting. McGuigan would search the police database for the victims of the Willow massacre, in the hope it would possibly yield a name, and family members. They swapped mobile numbers.

McGuigan headed in and upstairs to the first floor, to the hub of the investigation. It was busy as ever. Busier. Murder and kidnapping. The very worst combination. A frenzy of activity had descended. He searched for the reliable figure of Dawson, but couldn't find him. Presumably still at the hospital. He cornered another of the team – DC Primrose. The young graduate fast-tracker.

"Search what we've got on the Archie Willow case. Everything on every victim. Names, addresses, photographs, next of kin, shoe size."

"Shoe size?"

"I'm being facetious. Dealing with serious matters in an inappropriate comical manner. But it's urgent. Like *now* urgent."

She looked baffled. He could hardly blame her. "The Archie Willow case?"

"Please." His manner became terse. "Just get it fucking done. And I'm not being facetious."

"Of course, sir. And the ballistics report came back."

"The what?"

"It was a match. The pistol used in the Evelyn Stephens case was the same in the Bronson Chapel killing."

Big deal. The development was inconsequential. Matters had moved on. Considerably. "Very good," he muttered. "Now – get me stuff on the Willow case. Priority. Chop-chop."

She darted away, to her workstation. McGuigan was on edge. He pulled out a piece of bubblegum from his pocket, glanced at the clock on the wall. It was after eleven. His thoughts dwelled on Jonathan Stark. A man he had known for approximately two hours. And yet, in that short space, it seemed more had been accomplished than in the last five years. Unless the entire thing was bullshit. But McGuigan didn't think so. He felt an almost forgotten tingle in his heart. The chase was on. The scent of the hunt tweaked the nostrils, fired the blood, got the heart pumping at last.

A man entered the room. A man he had no desire to see. Chief Constable Blakely.

Their eyes met, almost immediately. Blakely pointed to McGuigan's office, at the far end of the room. McGuigan nodded. There was little else he could do. Damned bad timing, he thought. He passed Primrose, who was glued to her computer screen. He leaned down, spoke into her ear.

"Chop-chop."

She gave a fractional twitch of her head, studied the screen harder.

Goddamned graduate fast-trackers, he thought. *Bloody marvellous.*

He entered his office, Blakely at his heels, who slammed the door behind him. Pleasantries were ignored.

"I told you," he said, his voice low, and all the more sinister for it, "we were to keep it confidential."

"What was that, sir?"

"You think you're smart, McGuigan." His voice was a sneer. "The old-school detective, like a condescending Sherlock fucking Holmes, who thinks he knows more than anyone else. You strut about, with an air of moral superiority. Aloof, thinking you're special, in some misguided, misconceived way. Here's the situation as it stands, McGuigan. I warned you. The warning was clear. You were not to tell a soul about the photofit. That was an order. Do you know what an order is, McGuigan? Or is your head so far up your pompous ass that you've forgotten that thing called *chain of command?* But it seems you did, because I discover you've informed the whole fucking unit that the photofit was wrong. Do you know what that's called – what you did? *Insubordination.* I warned you, McGuigan. I truly did..."

McGuigan raised a hand. "You win, sir. You wanted to cover your arse with a lie, and it made me uneasy. Nauseous, actually. In fact, when I think of it, *you* make me nauseous. Now that we've got that covered, I'll let you rant on in your usual self-obsessed way, while I try and rescue a young woman who's been kidnapped by a serial killer. And if you want my badge, you're welcome to it. Because, sir, with people like you at the helm, where honour and dignity and truth play second fiddle to political ambition and success and kudos, then I really don't have much of a stomach for it anymore. Begging your pardon, sir. But I have rather lot on my plate right now."

He left the room, headed straight for DC Primrose, sitting hunched over her desk. He felt the burning stare of Blakely at his back. With difficulty, he maintained composure, despite his pounding heart, the sweat on the palms of his hands.

"Given you asked me to do this a minute ago," said Primrose,

"I have very little, except photographs of each of the shooting victims, with corresponding names, and immediate family members. Which, in my humble opinion, is nothing short of remarkable. If not miraculous. Sir."

"Print them off, please."

"As we speak."

"The wonders of modern technology."

The baffled look returned to her face. "What's the connection?"

A guy came into the station this morning claiming to have had a dream about the killer, and I think there might be some credence to his story, so I'm using up valuable resource and police time following up this highly plausible lead. Ha-ha. No joke.

It sounded insane. Instead, McGuigan issued a curt response.

"Just a hunch."

He turned round – Blakely was on his way out, doubtless to plot McGuigan's fall from grace. So be it. He'd never really liked the job – another *ha-ha.* He loved the job. But if he were pushed out, then it had to be on his terms. And his terms were simple. That he sees the capture of *The Surgeon.*

He phoned Dawson, went to voicemail. Perhaps still interviewing witnesses. Someone attracted his attention.

"Sir. Doors were knocked on a small housing estate next to the hospital. Apparently you can drive through the estate to get to a side entrance, but it's used rarely. Someone thought they saw a car going to the hospital round about midnight, and leaving about a half hour later."

"Make?"

"A Mondeo. Blue. Perhaps an old model, he thought. He didn't catch the reg."

"Tell our witness he's failed the test. Next time a serial killer is in his vicinity, I expect the registration number."

"Very good, sir. I'll pass that along."

"Be sure you do."

He unwrapped the bubblegum he had taken from his pocket a second before being lassoed by Blakely, and put it in his mouth. The flavour was impossible to identify. Pure sugar, he decided. He let it rest on his tongue, allowing his tastebuds to absorb the sweet kick.

Bazooka gum. Stark used to have it when he was a kid, so he said, and the thought made McGuigan smile. Here he was, in his mid-fifties, still chewing it.

Blue Mondeo. Stark had said that as well. In his dream. The killer drove a blue Mondeo. A thought, lurking in the depths, was that Jonathan Stark was working alongside The Surgeon in some strange diabolical partnership. He dismissed the notion. The kid was no killer's accomplice. The kid was real.

"Sir."

Primrose handed him a sheaf of photocopies – photographs of each of the victims of Willow, those who were killed, those who survived. Below each, their name, date of birth, address and names of parents.

"Thank you."

He took them back to his office, sat at his desk, placed the bundle before him, and went through it. Fifteen people, who were unlucky to be in the building at the time. Pictures of each, taken at varying times, all within a year before the shootings. Most of them smiling. Fifteen killed by gunshot. For no other reason than a quirk in a guy's brain permitting such an atrocity. A twitch of a finger, a life gone. Easy and straightforward. That's what guns did, he reflected – they cheapened life, to the point that taking one was nothing special.

He came across two photos. The first was a young man, perhaps taken abroad, a playful grin, giving a thumbs up. He recognised this man. It was Jonathan Stark. He was one of the lucky ones. He read the brief summary – eight weeks in a coma, months of convalescing, and after that? A lifetime of night terrors. PTSD. Not that lucky, but better than dead. *Is this the origin of the dreams?* He put the photo to one side, continued. Number ten. A young woman. Twenty-three years old. Cynthia Lamont. Trainee solicitor. A picture of her presumably taken on her graduation day, and as such, decked out in all her graduation paraphernalia – black gown and a mortarboard cap. The same face as the newspaper clipping left by Karen Fleming's tenant.

Cynthia Lamont. He had a name. Beneath her name, her address, and beneath that, the names of her mother and father.

McGuigan looked up, stared at the far wall of his office, mind grappling with this new information.

A name leapt off the page.

A name he knew.

CHAPTER SIXTY-FIVE

Stark headed straight for the office. He screamed at every red light. He screamed at every green light when the car in front didn't move off quickly enough. He didn't wait at a pedestrian crossing. He gripped the steering wheel until his knuckles turned white. He got to the road adjacent to the offices of SJPS, bumped the car half onto the pavement. He sprinted in, through the main door. Whilst closed for the weekend, some staff still worked, chasing the buck, looking for overtime. But most stayed away. The atmosphere was less intense. Jeans and trainers were the order of the day. It was almost pleasant.

Stark, however, was not in a pleasant mood. He gave the sole receptionist a curt acknowledgement, headed straight to his office. He met Jenny in the waiting room, presumably on her way out. She looked somewhat pale and bleary eyed. A sure sign of late-night drinking. He suspected he looked just as awful. His appearance was way down the pecking order.

"I tried to contact you…" she started.

Stark had never been happier seeing someone. "I need help," he blurted. Clock was ticking. No time for inconsequentials. "I don't think I can do this on my own."

She arched an eyebrow. "And good morning to you too. What precisely is it that you can't do on your own? You've fucked something up?"

"Not quite. I need to check records, going back about five years. But I'm not sure if it's as simple as typing in a name, or if it requires special access."

Jenny seemed to consider. "You have aroused my interest. But then you're good at that. Expand, please."

Stark replied in a breathless rush.

"Let's get to the office. It's complicated. I'm glad you're here."

"I'm glad you're glad. I only came in to get my car keys. And here I am, assisting the new trainee in some nefarious scheme. You're leading me down a dark path, Jonathan."

Darker than you might think, he thought. He said nothing.

They passed through the disguised door, along the corridor, passing the basement entrance. As ever, it emanated a chill. Stark shivered. A place he had come to loath. The irony did not escape him – it could prove to be his sister's salvation. Still, a mountain to climb. He suppressed a surge of panic.

They got to their shared office. He faced her.

"I don't have much time," he said. "Apollo Letting. If I want to find out about contracts they've entered, with tenants, where do I go?"

She expressed bewilderment. "Apollo Letting? That's part of the residential arm of the practice. What are you looking for, Jonathan?"

"Okay." He got his thinking straight, which was difficult, given the circumstances. "About five years ago, Apollo had a contract with a woman called Karen Fleming. They effectively leased her home for four or five months. The basis of the deal was that they would find a tenant, collect rental, make sure everything was okay. Karen Fleming would have no idea who the tenant was. Only Apollo Letting, who would have entered into a separate sub-agreement with that tenant. On the face of it, Apollo is the tenant. The reality, they lease it on to a suitable candidate of their choosing. Therefore, somewhere, there will be a contract between Apollo and the tenant. Yes?"

She nodded, but the bewilderment didn't go away. "You want to trace a particular tenant."

"In one."

"You know the next question."

He blinked, wiped sweat from his eyes. He was scared, he was panicking, the alcohol from last night sat in his head like a stone. And his sister's life depended on his actions. He swept away any thoughts that she might already be dead. His priority now was to keep moving, and pray for a break.

"Jenny. I'm not drunk. I'm not lying. I'm not mad. But I'm terrified." He gave her a level stare. "This individual – this tenant – I believe, might be the serial killer we all know as The Surgeon." He swallowed, found the next words hard to articulate without a shake in his voice. "I believe he's kidnapped my sister."

He let it sink in for five seconds. She frowned, cocked her head, as if to say *What?*

"You don't need to believe me," he continued. "But believe the sincerity in my voice. I need to find this man. And this fucking firm holds the key. Will you help me?"

"Your sister?"

"Yes. Will you help me, Jenny?"

She responded with a decisive nod of her head. She sat by her computer, spoke as her fingers rattled on the keyboards.

"Lucky I was here. The property department enjoy their secrets. Each section of the firm is like a little fiefdom. We're supposed to be a team. But we're always competing. Past records are password protected. Five years ago? There will be a copy somewhere."

"You have this password?"

"I was working in property up until six months ago. The short answer – yes, I do."

The screen on the computer changed to a menu. She drew the mouse to a section headed "Archive", pressed. The screen changed again to further headings. She typed in 'Apollo' in the search box. Lists appeared – property addresses with the corresponding owner's names.

"There's hundreds," said Stark.

"It's a busy little side venture. Every time the rental comes in, the firm scoops up fifteen per cent. Easy money. You have a name?"

"I have the name of the owner. Karen Fleming."

"Should be enough." Again, the same routine, typing in the name in the search box. A copy of a document materialised. A duplicate of the paper version Stark had in his pocket. The lease between Karen Fleming and Apollo Letting.

"I need to find the tenant Apollo located."

"Sure. There'll be a sub-agreement." She clicked a link above the document. Another page appeared. Another contract.

Stark gazed at the screen.

Before him, a name.

Gabriel Lamont.

He swallowed, composed himself.

"Anything else?"

She slid the mouse, clicked on an attachment. Again, the screen changed. Now, copies of ID. A bank statement, a passport. The photo in the passport was grainy, but clear enough. The man he saw in his dreams. The man who stalked and murdered a young woman, by drugging her, tying her to a bed, and firing a metal prod through her neck. The Surgeon. His dream was true. The validation gave him little comfort.

"It's him," he said.

Jenny turned to him, looked at him blankly.

"The man who's taken your sister?"

"This man," he breathed, "Gabriel Lamont. He's The Surgeon."

A silence fell. The gravity of his statement felt like a weight was pressed in the room. Jenny responded, and not for the first time, expressed bewilderment.

"How do you know this?"

"If I told you, you really would think me as mad. But I promise I'll tell you. Can we get anything else? More on this guy?"

She twitched her shoulders in a gesture of doubt. "I'd be surprised. But I'll cross-reference his name, and see what comes up."

She typed it in – *Gabriel Lamont.*

A list came up. Addresses. Fifteen. Beside each address, a date, and beside each date, the constant name – *Gabriel Lamont.*

"Jesus," muttered Stark. He studied the screen. "He's had fifteen different addresses over the past five years. His first was Karen Fleming's house. No wonder the bastard can't be caught. He's a fucking nomad. And this firm enabled it to happen."

Jenny nodded. "Apollo Letting. In this particular case, it seems they didn't find tenants for vacant houses. The other way round…"

"…they found vacant houses for one specific tenant," finished Stark. "SJPS is connected." He leaned closer, studied the last address on the list.

"That date is recent. *Holm Farm Cottage, Eaglesham moors.* That's where he is. That's where I'll find him." He pressed his finger on the screen to the same set of letters beside each of the fifteen entries.

"What's that?"

Jenny squinted at the computer. "It's the initials of the particular lawyer dealing with the case." She paused, took a long breath. She spoke, a tremor in her voice –

"The same lawyer. I know who that is."

"Who?"

"I can hardly believe it." She looked at Stark, bewildered. "Lamont. It was her married name."

CHAPTER SIXTY-SIX

Stark's mobile buzzed. It was McGuigan.

"I checked the victims of the Willow killings. Everyone. Including the survivors, Jonathan." Silence followed, which conveyed more than any words. Then he spoke, quietly. "You never told me you'd got shot."

"I didn't tell you, because I didn't think it relevant," Stark replied. "It's *not* relevant."

"You worked together. You were there when Willow killed her."

"Now you know. But it was coincidence."

"I'm not entirely sure I believe in coincidences."

"Did you get her name?" asked Stark.

"Cynthia Lamont. A legal trainee. Gunshot to the head. She never stood a chance."

And yet I did, thought Stark.

"I have other information," continued McGuigan. "I have the name of her mother."

"It's Winnifred Marshall," said Stark. "Senior partner of SJPS, and head of property."

Another silence, indicating the affirmative. Stark spoke.

"I found information about Apollo. The tenant Mrs Fleming had in her house is called Gabriel Lamont. If you check, no doubt you'll find that Lamont was Winifred's married name. She got divorced eight years ago, and reverted back to her maiden name – Marshall." He regarded Jenny, who had supplied this information. No matter how discreet a person was, the past always seeped out, then seized upon, and served up in juicy morsels. The fact that Winnifred Marshall was divorced was common knowledge. Just another part of the rumour and gossip machine. Jenny knew. The entire office knew.

Stark imagined McGuigan's wise old head nodding as he absorbed this information.

"Brother, sister, mother," said McGuigan.

"Probably."

"We have a name, at last." McGuigan spoke in a hushed voice. "Gabriel Lamont. His sister was killed. He's been trying to... what? Resurrect her? Recreate her? I dare say he dresses his victims in the same way as his sister dressed that day. He's trying to turn back time, in his weird psychopathic way. And his mother..."

"Maybe she knew all the time. Or maybe she was trying simply to help her son find a home. I don't know, Chief Inspector. That's your job. I've got to get my sister, if I still have time."

Another silence, then – "What have you found, Jonathan?"

"You can't help."

Stark sensed the sudden urgency in McGuigan's voice.

"If you have an address, you need to give it to me. This man is dangerous. You've done well, up until now. But it stops. You let me take over. Give me the address, Jonathan."

"And then? An army of cops descend. What then? What about my sister? What will he do, confronted like that. How does a man like that react? Let me tell you. He kills. He kills the whole world, because he wants the whole world to burn. Like Archie Willow, who wanted nothing more than to bring down as much death as he could before the end." His voice took a harsh edge. "If we do it your way, my sister will die. Sure as fate. If I go, on my own, I reckon she has a chance."

McGuigan responded, his voice flat. "He'll kill you. Your sister will die. What will that achieve? Give me the damned address, Jonathan."

"Goodbye, Chief Inspector. Thanks for believing."

He hung up.

He faced Jenny. She was sitting at her computer, back stiff, face pinched and wan. He leant down, kissed her on the forehead.

"Thank you. Really."

"You're going to him. You're not telling the police."

"To save my sister. If I don't call you in two hours, ask for Chief Inspector Harry McGuigan. He's a good man. Tell him what we found. Give him the address."

Her eyes welled up. Her bottom lip trembled. She looked away. "You'll die," she said. "I don't want you to go."

"Promise me you won't call the police. Not right away. I need that time."

She nodded, said nothing.

"Thank you, Jenny."

He left the offices of SJPS, to his car, on his journey to the devil's lair.

CHAPTER SIXTY-SEVEN

McGuigan cursed, and showing some restraint, refrained from flinging his mobile against his office wall. It didn't stop him from pounding his fist on the office desk. He stood, marched into the main hub.

"Okay, people, we have a development!" The general noise reduced to a low buzz. McGuigan clenched his teeth in frustration. His patience was being tested. "Shut the fuck up. Please!" The noise stopped. He had their attention. He noted Kenny Dawson was in the room, presumably returned from the hospital.

"I have a name. Gabriel Lamont. A person of interest. Get me as much information as you can on that name. Anything at all. I don't care how insignificant. This is our new focus."

He looked about. Lots of puzzled expressions, but no one argued. He was in no mood to be crossed, and they knew it. He went over to Dawson.

"We're going on a visit."

He had an address for Winnifred Marshall. The search instigated in the offices of SJPS had allowed the police to get details of each member of staff, including the partners. Dawson called it up, logged it into the satnav.

22 Lillybank Oval, Bothwell. A plush village on the outskirts of Glasgow – where hundred-year-old houses jostled with sprawling new-builds. A haven for footballers and medical consultants. And lawyers.

Bothwell was thirteen miles from the station. The quickest route was via the motorway, and, with light traffic, could take less than fifteen minutes. The car was unmarked. McGuigan stuck a siren on the roof, and told Dawson to press his foot hard on the pedal.

"I want speed of light," he said. "Faster, if possible."

"And why are we doing this, sir?"

McGuigan's response was curt. "I'm trying to save lives." He would explain later. His mind whirled. He was functioning on adrenaline. He was anxious and unsure. Perhaps the whole theory was wrong. But it didn't sound wrong. Mother and son. Son killing young women to resurrect the memory of his murdered sister. Mother condoning and enabling her psychopathic son in his quest. And if the theory was right, and if Jonathan Stark had an address, what then? Stark was heading to his doom. He sat in silence, as the world rushed by. He was in no mood to explain, because what had happened in the last few hours was beyond explanation.

They arrived at Winnifred's house – a detached bungalow of red brick, enclosed by a low sandstone wall, upon which hung wicker baskets bright with flowers. In the driveway, a black BMW 3 Series.

"Looks like someone's home," remarked Dawson.

McGuigan said nothing. They got out. McGuigan rang the doorbell. The front door was solid wood, impossible to determine activity from the interior. He rang again. Nothing.

"Dead end," said Dawson.

"Really?"

McGuigan turned the handle, pushed. The door opened. "There's a surprise," he muttered.

Dawson's long solemn face suddenly blinked with startlement.

"Sir, we don't have a warrant."

"Very true, Kenny. You can see I'm concerned. Either you're coming, or you're staying."

The bemusement didn't leave Dawson's face, as he followed his boss into the house.

The hall was bright and spacious. Clean white walls. High ceiling. The floor oak hardwood. Impossible to mask the sound of footsteps. McGuigan wasn't trying, because he didn't care. Glass doors on either side. McGuigan went through into a large living room, stretching from the front of the house to the back. It was tidy and furnished to an almost clinical precision. On one wall, in a gilded silver frame, a large portrait of a young woman. The same woman killed by Archie Willow during his rampage of murder five years ago. Cynthia Lamont.

Sitting on a leather sofa, smoking, dressed in a simple black dress, was Winnifred Marshall. Dressed for mourning, thought McGuigan. On the coffee table before her was an open packet of cigarettes, a circular stone ashtray, an empty glass and an empty plastic bottle.

She regarded the two men, face pale as marble, devoid of expression.

McGuigan sat on a chair opposite. Dawson stood to one side.

"It's a hard habit to kick," he said.

Her mouth quirked into a sardonic smile. "I've smoked since I was sixteen. I have no intention of stopping now. Why should I stop something I enjoy, Chief Inspector."

He switched his attention to the picture on the wall.

"Your daughter?"

She took a deep draw, smoke streaming back out through her nostrils, coiling round her like serpents' tails.

She looked at the picture.

"It's not perfect. But we'll get there."

"We?"

"My daughter was murdered, Chief Inspector. When I had to identify her, half her face was missing. In a second, her life was taken, her beauty destroyed. Death and destruction. The two fundamental elements of evil, yes?"

He felt a small tingle of victory. The first part of the theory had proved correct. Mother, daughter. He was almost tempted to ask for a cigarette, such was the sudden intensity of his craving. He pushed it to one side.

"Perhaps," he said. He gave her a level stare. "There's insanity. A man can do a bad thing, which, to his mind, isn't bad at all, because his mind is unbalanced. Wouldn't you agree?" He paused, said, "Your son needs help."

Another deep drag. She tilted her head back, gave him a heavy-lidded stare. There, thought McGuigan, sits the real monster.

"*Bad?*" she replied. "What's *bad*? There are different versions of bad. My son isn't evil." She held his gaze. "Nor is he insane. He is... gifted. Gifted people are always shunned and misunderstood, in the beginning. But then their light shines through, and people, in time, start to understand. He is an angel, Chief Inspector."

"An angel?" he said softly. "Some might disagree. Where is your son now, Winnifred?"

She didn't respond.

He nodded, slowly. "It started with Bronson Chapel. Things began to tear at the seams when he saw your son leaving the house of Evelyn Stephens. But then, when we produced the photofit to the media, how you must have wondered. Did you think you were lucky, that we should get it so wrong? Did it give your son's great scheme the endorsement it needed? Perhaps he thought, truly, it was a task he was chosen to do. That maybe God, in his strange fashion, had spoken. Or maybe it got you more worried. That trouble loomed on the horizon."

"You don't know anything. You insult me with your inane chattering."

"The plot twisted again, when Bronson Chapel tried to blackmail Patricia Shawbridge. You told me yourself. She arranged a meeting with you and the other partners, Hutchison and Hill. She was in a fury at Bronson and what he had done. She told you he had a picture of a man on his phone that he claimed was The Surgeon. It looked like her son, for sure. But of course it wasn't. It could only be *your* son, if Bronson's claims were true. What then, Winnifred?"

"Leave now. Your presence offends me."

"Bronson had to be dealt with. Quickly. You knew he had a second home. You had a suspicion he would be there. His boat house. You had to act. You had to get his phone. So you took a gamble. You knew the address – a simple matter of checking with admin – and you issued the command. You arranged for your son to pay him a visit. Bronson was killed. Plus two others. That must have come as a shock for him. But, in his efficient way, he took care of matters. Five years of practice made him skilled at killing. And that should have been the end of it. But yet here we are, having our little chat."

"Here we are," she said. "It's over. I am in mourning. Can't you see? I wish to spend these last moments alone. Leave now. I'm tired."

McGuigan leaned forward, his voice low and urgent.

"There's more, isn't there."

She gave him a small sly smile. "You know nothing."

"Where is your son? We can save an innocent life. Tell us, please." His voice cracked. "Please!"

"This will be his greatest work," she said. "His final, wondrous coup de grâce. Why should I spoil his moment? Leave now.

Already I feel light-headed. The world begins to spin. I cannot tell whether this is real, or in my mind.

McGuigan stood, stretched over, picked up the empty bottle.

"What was in this?"

"Enough to make it permanent."

She stubbed the cigarette on the ashtray, seemed to shudder, sat back. Her eyes were distant, her mouth drooped. Her head lolled forward, as if she were drifting to sleep.

McGuigan seized her, shook her shoulders. "Where is your son!" Her head flopped from side to side, her body was limp. She gave a loose smiling response. Her voice was slurred.

"It doesn't matter now."

Her mouth frothed, her eyes rolled back, and she slipped into unconsciousness.

The ambulance arrived fifteen minutes later. McGuigan and Dawson watched on, as paramedics fought to resuscitate Winnifred Marshall. She had fallen into a coma, her vital signs weak, the chances of recovery slim. She was laid carefully on a stretcher, and carried into the ambulance. It sped off, all noise and lights.

During the process, neither McGuigan nor Dawson had spoken. McGuigan experienced mixed emotions. A roiling anger at his inadequacy, a deep dread for the young man Jonathan Stark, and his sister. So close! He needed an address. His need had not been answered. The conversation with Winnifred Marshall had served to heighten his fears. He knew with certainty that feeding the name Gabriel Lamont into the computer base would yield nothing. Such a man would live an invisible existence. And to get the information from the records of SJPS would require a warrant, and then a further trawl through their files. A long and complex affair.

Dawson faced his superior – "What happened in there?"

McGuigan looked up, into the sky. It was not yet afternoon. How so much can happen in a single morning, and yet nothing at all. The clouds had broken, allowing crisp shards of sunlight.

"You saw," he answered, his voice bleak. "She knew we were coming. She was prepared."

"Prepared?"

"Which brings us back to the riddle of Bronson Chapel, and the manner of his death."

"I don't understand, sir."

McGuigan gave a weary sigh.

"Three men were shot at the boat house. Two of them – Billy Watson and Frank Fitzsimmons – struggled to the end, judging by their final postures. Even at the last, they attempted to evade death. Fitzsimmons was in the kitchen, probably in an effort to escape. Watson was prostrate across the living-room floor, as if caught while leaping from the couch. They knew they were going to die, and survival instinct kicked in. Bronson however…"

"…was sitting in a chair, no sign of surprise, relaxed," finished Dawson. "He knew his killer."

"It's not over," muttered McGuigan. "There's another angle to this. A missing piece in the jigsaw."

"The man you mentioned at the station – Gabriel Lamont. He's the son of Winnifred Marshall? He's The Surgeon?"

McGuigan hunched himself in his coat. He felt cold. Probably through lack of sleep.

"Sister, brother, mother," he said softly to himself. "He's walking into a trap. And there's nothing I can do."

CHAPTER SIXTY-EIGHT

Stark placed his phone on the dashboard, and used the navigation to get to the address. Eaglesham moor was a large sweep of land, with little in it, save patches of dense woodland, a windfarm, and the occasional farmhouse.

His head pounded, his throat was dry. The effects of the whisky the previous evening. It occurred to him he was surely over the limit. A small worry in the scale of things.

He got to Eaglesham, on the periphery of the moors, to the village he knew so well, though he hadn't returned in years. Nothing had changed. The same row of shops. The park in the centre, running up a steep incline, where once a mill had thrived, now a scattering of stones hidden in the long grass. He drove past a quaint ivy-patterned hotel, to a crossroads, turned right, headed to the moors.

According to the map on his phone, he was to drive in a straight direction, using the main road for approximately eight miles. Then a turn-off, a further mile, at which stage, his destination would be reached.

The road was wide enough, just, for two cars. Each side was marked off as cycle lanes. Stark kept his speed as high as his car allowed, the chassis shuddering and rattling. The landscape was bare and bleak. Low hills, gorse and rock. In the far distance, the shimmer of lochs, green woodland, the horizon punctured by the stick silhouettes of white wind turbines, the great rotor blades making their ponderous revolutions.

He passed some cyclists. They gestured for him to slow down. He ignored them, kept the speed up. His mind was focused. He might be wrong. He might be heading to the wrong place. But it was all he had, and he clung to it, because if he didn't, he would drown in despair.

He reached the turn-off, went on to a narrow lane – more a track, than a road. The car lurched and bounced. He slowed. There was a real danger the suspension might cave.

He was close. Maybe a quarter of a mile. The land undulated. There was no sign of the house, though it could have been hidden behind a hill. He pulled onto the muddy grass verge, got out. He would walk from this point. No need to advertise his presence.

It was chilly here, in the open plains, where the wind was constant. He jogged forward, following the line of the road, senses heightened. He went round a curve, through a small cluster of bushes. There, at the bottom of a slight decline, a building – a white-walled cottage with a high-peaked slate roof, and a separate garage, sheltered by low conifers, presumably planted to create a break from the wind.

Parked at the garage, a blue Mondeo. He recognised it immediately. His stomach rose to his throat. He felt a strange combination of terror and euphoria. The address had proved to be correct. Only yards away dwelt the serial killer known worldwide as The Surgeon. Which meant his sister was there too. Alive, he hoped. Prayed.

In a low crouching run, he made his way to the side of the building, nerves sharpened to a point. Here, the wind lessened to barely a breeze. He pressed close to the stone. Next to him, a small window. On his tiptoes, with exquisite care, he edged closer, listening, straining for the slightest sound.

Silence.

He crouched low, and crab-like, he moved under and past the window. He straightened. He sidled further along, got to the front door, waited. With held breath, he remained motionless, consumed with indecision. Still, nothing. Now, a new sound – his racing heart.

He took a slow breath, tried to straighten his thoughts, calm his nerves. There was no other way. He reached over, gently turned the door handle, and pushed.

The door opened.

He pushed further. The door creaked. He stopped, stayed still. Now, time was measured in heartbeats. Three... four... five. He pushed again, with the tips of his fingers, inch by inch. Enough now for a gap to form. He crept through. He was in a hallway. It smelled damp. The wallpaper was old and faded, as was the carpet. Along one wall, on the floor, rows of polythene bags.

A noise from another room. He froze. A man's voice. It was soft and deep, almost melodic. He strained to listen, but the walls were thick.

He kept going, one step at a time, towards a door at the end, half-open. He reached it, slipped through, into a living room. It was poorly furnished. A worn two-seater couch, an armchair, the arms burst, its foamy innards bulging. Newspapers and magazines scattered on a threadbare carpet. At a window, a small, round dining table, upon which, cups and unwashed plates. The walls had the same faded wallpaper – some floral design, perhaps nice fifty years ago. In a corner, a portable three-bar electric heater. A small ancient television on a pile of books.

The voice of the man came again, a little clearer. On the chair was a heavy torch, maybe twelve inches long. Stark picked it up, its weight and solidity providing some reassurance. He grasped it in his right hand, ready.

At the far end, another door, ajar. He made his way towards it, quiet as a whisper, pushed gently. He went in. A kitchen. The same state of disrepair. Cracked lime-green linoleum, a standalone cooker, its silver handles rusted. A small fridge. Attached to the ceiling, an old-fashioned pulley, from which draped clothing.

There! On the worktop, something moved. His heart leapt to his mouth. A tabby cat. It stretched, and in a languid motion, leapt to the ground, and slinked back through to the living room Stark had just left.

Stark paused, blinked sweat from his eyes, calmed himself. He gripped the torch tighter, summoned his courage.

The door on the other side of the kitchen was closed. The man's voice was near, but low. Too low to make out clearly. The talking stopped. Now, silence, heavy and brooding. Stark stood, riveted. He heard the floor creak, the rustle of movement.

And then... a scream. It cut the air, a shrill sharp sound. Stark moved, without realising it. Instinct. He strode forward, barged open the door.

The scene he confronted was both vivid and surreal. On a bed, arms bent above her, hands tied to a rail, his sister, her face a contortion of terror and surprise. Hunched over the bed, wearing a black cowl, a man. In his hand, a strange-looking object, resembling a futuristic gun. It was poised by the side of her head. The man's face, white as death, was caught in a frozen moment, startled by Stark's entrance.

He stared at Stark. Stark stared back at the man in his dream. The Surgeon.

Mags screamed again. The man dropped the implement, drew a knife from his pocket, hurtled forward, swift and purposeful, uttering a wild screech. Stark stepped back, fended aside the rush, catching the other off-balance. The knife raked his arm, bringing sudden searing pain. He brought the torch down, landed a heavy blow to the man's shoulder. The man gasped, jerked back. Stark used the advantage, followed through, struck the man under the ear. The man staggered, then, teeth bared in snarling rage, launched himself again on Stark. Stark grappled him, the man's body all tense muscle and gristle. Stark tried to hack the larynx, missed. They fell to the floor. The man attempted to stab Stark's neck, but the angle was wrong, the movement awkward. The knife slipped from his grasp. Stark freed his arms, and using the hard rubber heft of the torch, dealt a sweeping blow to the head – once, twice. The man went limp, momentarily. Stark rolled on top, arched his back, and clutching the torch, raised his hands, struck down, a ferocious blow. The man sagged, went still. Stark struck again. And then a third time.

He got to his feet, heaving and gasping. He felt light-headed. The sleeve of his jacket was warm with blood. He focused. He heard a noise – his sister, shouting.

He bent down, got the fallen knife, tottered to the bed, cut Mags loose. She instantly embraced him, a tight squeezing hug.

"You came," she whispered.

"I have to look after my big sister."

She sobbed into his chest. He held her, stroking her hair, the back of her head.

"We've got to go," he said.

She nodded. The man on the floor groaned. His eyelids fluttered. They stepped over him, made their way into the kitchen.

And stopped.

A person stood at the opposite doorway to the living room, barring their way, pointing a pistol.

A person Stark knew.

CHAPTER SIXTY-NINE

"I'm sorry, Jonathan."

"What is this?" said Mags, voice hoarse and frightened.

"Good question," said Stark. "What exactly is this, Jenny?"

Jenny Flynn gave a small shrug. She was pointing the pistol at them in a two -handed grip, arms held straight. Her hands were shaking. Tears coursed down her face.

"It's a fucking mess, is what it is."

Stark said nothing. The cut on his arm was deeper than he had imagined. He was losing blood. He felt disorientated. Was he imagining this? It seemed unreal. Another of his vivid and disturbing dreams? He thought not. The blood was real. The fear was real.

"You shouldn't have come here," she said. "This wasn't supposed to happen."

Stark clasped his arm in an effort to staunch the wound. His head throbbed. He blinked, focused.

"Speak to me, Jenny."

"I didn't know he had taken your sister." Her voice shook with the slightest tremor. "That was never meant to happen."

"What was meant to happen? Indulge me, please."

"It's gone too far," she muttered. "The man who took you..." She gestured to Mags. "The man who tied you to a bed, who intended to kill you and sculpt your face into the semblance of another... he's my brother."

Stark could feel Mags tense.

"You knew what he was doing," she said.

"My name is Jenny Lamont. I had to change my name when I joined the firm. *She* wanted it that way, so as not to show favouritism. *She* didn't want anyone to know I was her daughter. It was our secret."

"Winnifred Marshall is your mother," said Stark. "What other secrets have you been hiding?"

She gave a crooked smile. "Cynthia was shot by Archie Willow. She was beautiful. She was... perfection. My brother tried to recreate her in all those women. He took pictures of his finished work, and I would paint their portraits. But none of them were good enough. He couldn't capture the essence of our sister's beauty. So he had to keep trying, and in doing so, kept failing, and it kept on and on."

"You're fucking insane," whispered Mags.

Jenny sighed. "When my brother saw you, he sent me your picture. You're the closest yet, Margaret. But I swear, I had no idea you were Jonathan's sister."

"And if she wasn't..." said Stark, "...that would be all right, yes? Another innocent, kidnapped, mutilated, murdered. All to satisfy some fucked-up mission your fucked-up family are on."

Jenny responded in a tired voice. "You don't understand. But it doesn't matter what you think. It's over. It was over, as soon as we discovered Bronson Chapel had a picture of my brother on his phone."

Stark found he was now leaning on Mags. The world seemed to waver. He clenched his teeth, concentrated on getting through each second.

"Bronson Chapel?"

"My mother contacted me as soon as she found out. The instruction was simple. We – Gabriel and I – drove up to his stupid little boat house in the woods. He let me in." She gave a sudden shrill laugh. "The puzzled look on his face when he saw me. He made me tea. So polite. I unlocked the front door. My brother entered, and shot him while we sipped Darjeeling. Not so polite." She took a long shaky breath. "But the killing didn't fucking stop," she whispered. "Two men arrived. That was unexpected. We let them in, and killed them too." She seemed to shiver. "So much blood."

"It has to stop," said Stark. He was weak, and growing weaker. A punctured artery, he suspected.

He staggered, his sister keeping him upright.

"He's bleeding out!" she shrieked. "He needs to get to a fucking hospital!"

Stark detected movement behind him. He turned. There, at the bedroom door, a ghastly wound to his head, face bright with blood, stood Jenny's brother. He swayed on his feet, one hand clutching the door handle. Dressed in his black cowl, he was a ghoul.

"Kill him," he rasped. "Kill him, Jenny. Look what he did to me. Kill the fucker!"

Stark turned back to Jenny.

"Please," he said, but his own voice sounded far away, as if it belonged to someone else, and the world was turning to mist and shadow, and things were melting to darkness.

"I'm sorry," whispered Jenny, and despite his fading consciousness, Stark sensed her despair.

The kitchen echoed with the sound of the pistol firing. Once, twice, three times. To Stark, it sounded like three explosions. The room became a sudden sparkle of blood. He heard his sister scream. He was aware of the floor rising up, meeting his face. His last image was of a raven, in flight, black against blue.

And then he let go, and everything became nothing.

CHAPTER SEVENTY

He opens the kitchen door. An eight-year-old boy. The noises woke him. He is scared. But his anxiety overcomes his fear. He knows something bad has happened. He has crept downstairs, on his toes, quiet as a breath. He saw the man leaving from his bedroom window, and wonders what it means. Nothing good, he thinks, and his dread is like a claw, squeezing his heart.

He opens the kitchen door...

Jonathan Stark awakened, to discover he hadn't died. Or if he had, then the "afterlife" experience seemed awfully similar to a bed in a hospital room, and an angel looked awfully similar to a hospital nurse.

"You're here, sleepyhead," she said, smiling, one eye on him, one eye on a chart on a wall. "Welcome back."

"Where am I?"

"The Queen Elizabeth."

His head was groggy. He tried to grasp the details, but it took effort. "How long?"

"Two days."

He tried to think. "Am I dead?"

She laughed, a light breezy sound, which was the most joyful noise he thought he had ever heard.

"I hope not," she replied. "But if you are, then God help us all."

He smiled back, and was glad he hadn't died. He drifted back into the darkness of his dreams. But then he remembered his sister, but was asleep before he could ask the question.

Detective Chief Inspector Harry McGuigan had been sitting on a rather comfortable chair in a corner of the hospital room. He had been there an hour. He had brought a book, to pass the time. But he had read only a page or two. His thoughts were elsewhere, as the recent events rolled and twisted in his mind. Try as he might, rational explanation eluded him. If that were the case, if the situation defied logic, what was left? This was the dilemma. One to which he had no answer. Perhaps there wasn't one. Perhaps it was another mystery, he thought. Like life itself. Perhaps that was the idea – that certain things had to remain a mystery, to remind us we were human.

Jonathan Stark stirred.

McGuigan got up, stood at the side of the bed. Stark's eyes opened.

"Welcome back," said McGuigan softly.

Stark blinked, took several seconds to respond as he adjusted his thoughts. Then he spoke.

"One thing I would like to say."

"Yes?" said McGuigan.

"The hospital food is not as bad as they say."

"That's reassuring."

Stark looked round. McGuigan handed him a plastic drinking vessel containing juice.

"It's vodka-free, I'm afraid," said McGuigan.

"That's a shame." Stark sipped from the little mouthpiece, handed it back.

McGuigan pulled up the chair, sat.

"Where do we start?" said Stark. He gave a wintry grin. "Do I need a lawyer, Chief Inspector?"

Dawson grinned back. "Bloody lawyers. The bane of my life. Where do we start? I think, rather, where do we end?"

"I can't remember much," said Stark. "Fragments. We were in his house. Jenny... had a gun. *He* – Gabriel... was at the bedroom door, shots were fired..." the memory left a bitter taste in his mouth, "...then blood. Lots."

"Not yours," said McGuigan. "At least not all of it. Nor your sister's. Jenny Flynn – or Lamont, whichever you prefer – shot her brother. The Surgeon is dead."

"And Jenny?"

McGuigan shook his head. "She turned the gun on herself."

Stark said nothing. His colleague at work, the woman who smoked and swore worse than anyone he knew, the woman he had made love to in his stupid broken little flat, was the sister and accomplice to a serial killer. It was too bizarre and heartbreaking to contemplate.

"When you went back to the office to find information on Apollo," said McGuigan, "it became clear to Jenny her world was unravelling. She telephoned her mother, presumably to warn her. To tell her it was at an end. Their great quest had failed. Winnifred knew I was coming. She was prepared. Never would she wish to go to prison. Nor her children. Such a notion was unimaginable. I suspect a pact was made. She swallowed a bottle of paracetamol. Jenny, rather than phone her brother to warn him you were coming, made the decision to go herself. To fulfil the promise. Kill her brother, kill herself. Mother, son, daughter. An unholy trinity."

Or was it love? wondered Stark. Did Jenny have any feelings for him? Did she kill her brother to save him? He would never know. Perhaps he was being naïve and vain. After all, he mused, in her own way, she was as guilty for the murders of all those young women as her brother.

"We went to her house," continued McGuigan. "It's quite something. She has a room converted into an art studio. Portraits were her thing. But portraits of only one person. Her dead sister. I counted ten. All of them slightly different. All of them unfinished."

"Mags would have been the eleventh," said Stark. "She said she painted. She was looking for perfection."

"Which doesn't exist, I have decided. Give me imperfection any day. Conclusion – The Surgeon is dead. We have balance and contentment in the world. For a while. And for that, I have to thank Jonathan Stark, and his affinity for dreaming strange dreams."

"Does it matter? Really? How we came to the end isn't as important as the end itself. As you said. The Surgeon is dead. The killing stops."

"The killing stops," echoed McGuigan. "Until it starts. I won't ask again. But I will continue going to church, and my wife will continue striving to make me a believer."

"And will she succeed?"

"She just might."

McGuigan shook Stark's hand. "Thank you, Jonathan. And I have a gift."

He put his hand in his pocket, pulled out a packet of Bazooka bubblegum, and placed it on the bedside cabinet.

"Good luck. I dare say we'll meet again."

CHAPTER SEVENTY-ONE

Later that morning, Mags came to visit. She saw him, and burst into tears. They embraced, as tight and close as when he untied her from a bed in a cottage in the Eaglesham moors.

"We made it," she said.

"Yes, we did. I reckon you owe me big style."

"I reckon I do."

"Free cappuccino for a year."

She laughed. "Deal. But you're still buying the pastries."

They talked, and didn't stop talking. But not once about what had happened. That would come later, he knew. When the need was real, and the nightmares came, and the trauma surfaced, and talking it through was the only antidote.

"It's over," she said.

But it wasn't over. He had lied to her from the beginning. He hadn't written to a million law firms looking for a job. He had only applied to one. To SJPS. And not to train as a lawyer.

To find the truth.

It wasn't over.

The worst, perhaps, was still to come.

CHAPTER SEVENTY-TWO

FULL CIRCLE

The fallout was far reaching, and possibly – probably – fatal for the firm of SJPS. It was now a matter of damage limitation. But the damage ran deep.

The death of The Surgeon had taken place a fortnight ago. The news was a nationwide sensation. It was like something from a true crime drama, perhaps a Netflix production, an unbelievable series of events, gripping the media and all those who watched, read or listened. The story unfolded, slice by juicy slice. First – the audacious attempt at blackmail by Bronson Chapel. Then, his murder at the boat house by the loch. And then The Surgeon, one of the worst serial killers to live and breathe on the British Isles, shot by his sister. And then another incredible layer – a family involved, a mother protecting her son, the son killing for his sister, to resurrect in his weird fashion his other sister, murdered by Archie Willow five years previously. The mother's suicide. Sister killing brother, then putting a bullet through her head. Sensational and gripping.

Lawyers, then more lawyers. The firm of SJPS in the middle. One of the senior partners, and the other – her daughter – an assistant, complicit in the murders of ten women. Using the firm's resources to protect their murderous activities.

The ship was sinking. Staff leapt off and swam for the life rafts, but the problem was, there were no life rafts. Having worked for SJPS was the kiss of death. Lawyers resigned, to begin the angst-ridden process of applying for new jobs. Clients chose to move their business elsewhere. The firm had been knifed and gutted. Police had swarmed on them like a cloud of locusts, examining everything and everyone, leaving nothing untouched. Boxes of files, computer hard drives, laptops, all were removed in a slow steady procession.

SJPS was toxic.

Stark had no intention of leaving. Not yet.

He went back to work two weeks after the shooting of Gabriel Lamont. His arm was stiff and still ached under the bandages. He would bear a six-inch scar for the rest of his days. A constant reminder of his tussle with a psychopath, he thought grimly.

Of the two receptionists, one had quit. The one remaining regarded him with fascination. Stark's face was now well-known. The man who rescued his sister from the clutches of The Surgeon. Stirring stuff. Stark had no desire to seek any limelight. It was his mission to forget and move on.

It was 9am. He made his way through the waiting room. There was no one there. He got himself a latte from the coffee machine. He got to the "sweat wing", made his way along the corridor. The place was quiet. Some of the offices were vacant. Those he saw gave him a nod, but little was said. The place held a gloom. He was reminded of a dying beast, wheezing out its last breath.

He did not go to his office. There was little point. It was not his intention to do any work. Even if it was, his computer would have been seized, and all his files, along with everyone else's, rendering the whole thing pointless.

Instead, he stopped at the door to the basement. *The dungeon.* As ever, it exuded a chill. He took a breath. The thought of once again entering this place brought dread to his heart. More than dread. Terror. He turned the handle, opened the door, switched the lights on, closed the door behind him, and went downstairs.

It remained as before. It seemed the police had taken little interest, if any, in this part of the building. Nothing had been touched. As before, the thick volume of recorded closures on the tabletop, containing lists of all the files sent for recording and ultimate destruction. The shelves upon shelves of boxes stood untouched, caught in time. The dust hadn't stirred. The whiff of dampness tinged the air. The same stillness and silence, as if it had always been thus, from beginning to end.

"I'm here!" shouted Stark. "Show me what you want."

Nothing stirred. The ground didn't shake. No voice rumbled from above. No eerie apparition floated past. Stark, if it weren't so crazy, would have laughed. But he wasn't laughing.

"Tell me what you want me to do!"

Silence.

He began his walk to where he had gone the two previous occasions, for no other reason than he had been there before – to the far end, to the chair, to the particular section earmarked for destruction.

The plastic boxes he had filled with old files were gone. Presumably uplifted and away. The two files he had placed to one side – Deborah Ferry and Marie Thomson – were still there.

But now there was a third.

He gazed at it. He considered his actions. He knew he had no choice. He picked it up, sat on the single chair, opened it. The first document he saw was a death certificate.

He read it, each line. Date of birth. Place of birth. Occupation. Occupation of father. Occupation of mother. He was fascinated.

He got to the section *Cause of Death.* The typed entry was as sinister as it was mysterious.

Missing. Presumed Dead.

He closed the file. There was no need to read further. He had asked, and it seemed he had been shown.

He placed the file back with the other two, and sat, staring at the corridor stretching before him. A corridor, one of maybe a hundred, the walls made of shelves, each wall eight shelves high, and on each shelf, boxes containing maybe fifty files. Thousands of boxes. Thousands of names. Thousands of lives – people who had lived and died, laughed and cried, experienced joy, suffered tragedy, the law firm of SJPS having touched them, in some manner. Each file, a fragment of a person's existence. Most now forgotten, to lie here, in this little capsule of time.

Not all forgotten, he thought. He stood and made his way back to the foot of the stairs.

A noise! He spun round. Perhaps. Perhaps not. Perhaps his imagination. He thought he knew the sound – the flap of wings?

He made his way up the stairs, turned the lights off, and closed the door.

Missing. Presumed Dead.

CHAPTER SEVENTY-THREE

The day drifted on. Stark went to his office, to discover his prediction was right. Both his computer and Jenny's computer were gone, along with all the files, all the paperwork. Hardly surprising. The desktops were empty. The only remaining items of any worth were the law books on the shelves.

The familiar figure of Des appeared at his door. His usual exuberance was gone. Now, a subdued solemnity. The eyes belonged to a man who had given up.

"The man of the moment," he said, without humour.

"That's all it is," replied Stark. "A moment. How you bearing up?"

His question was ignored. "Walter Hill is calling a meeting at twelve noon in the conference room. But we all know what it means. We're closing. After one hundred and fifty years, the doors are shutting. He's making the announcement today. Then we'll all go home." His voice took a harsh tone. "And then we wonder how the fuck we pay the mortgage, and pay the car lease, and feed the kids! You got an answer, Jonathan?"

Stark had no answer to give. He had never been rich enough to afford a mortgage, or a car lease, or anything, for that matter.

He had a brief memory of worrying about the price of a new suit for the job interview. Plus, he didn't have kids.

"I don't know..."

Des became indignant. "You brought trouble, Jonathan. You're bad luck. They don't bring a black cat on a boat. Well, sir, you're our fucking black cat!"

He left, slamming the door shut. Stark sat in silence, shocked at those sentiments. *Did people blame him?* Perhaps. Such was the human condition. Blame was easy, regardless of how irrational.

He got up. He had no intention of listening to Walter Hill's announcement. He took one last look around, left his office, and then left the building.

That night, he went to bed early. Sleep came surprisingly easy. He woke at 4.30 in the morning, alert, body trembling, bathed in sweat. He showered, changed into jeans, sweat top, trainers. He left his flat. He went downstairs to the ground floor. One of the owners liked to maintain the back common green, and kept a locker in the hall, containing gardening stuff, which was unlocked. Who, after all, would want to steal old picks and shovels? Who indeed, thought Stark, as he bundled the items into the back of his car.

The night was cold. The sky was clear, a black canvas, upon which, scattered, a thousand grains of light. He drove straight to the offices of SJPS.

He still had a key. He had no idea if the locks had been changed. If so, then he would resort to plan B, and break a window. The key turned, the main door opened, as did the inner door. The alarm beeped. He knew the code, switched it off, thankful it hadn't been altered.

He had his gym bag. It was open, and balanced on it, the pick and the shovel. He entered the basement, a shadow amongst shadow. He switched the lights on. No one would know. No one would see. There were no windows in the basement, for obvious reasons.

He went down the stairs, stopped, got his bearings. But he remembered. The details were clear in his mind. He headed to a far corner. The striplights flickered, the air was heavy, despite the chill. If the point was to frighten, then it was working. He reached the place. Here, one wall was bare, devoid of shelving or boxes. The wall was mottled bluish-black with mould, the colour of an old bruise.

He put the bag down. The floor was old, consisting of planks of wood, brown and springy.

Stark grasped the pick handle. His arm was still sore, but not enough to restrict his movement. He raised it up, brought it down, and began the process of breaking the timbers, to the earth below.

Time passed. How much, Stark couldn't tell. He was consumed in his work. The floorboards had been laid on a thin wooden sheeting, easy to penetrate. Below was rubble and random pieces of masonry, and then, below that, hard soil, which he broke up with the pick, and removed with the shovel.

He got down about four feet. He stopped, leaned back. He wiped the sweat from his eyes. He reached round, rummaged in his gym bag, got out a bottle of mineral water. He was parched. He glugged down half the contents, resumed his work.

He went down another foot, and then stopped again. Not because he was thirsty. He had found what he was looking for. He put the shovel to one side, bowed his head, and cried soft tears.

He made his way back to the foot of his stairs. He stopped. A figure he recognised stood, hunched and frail, leaning on the table.

"Hello, Jonathan," said Edward Stoddart. He was wearing his familiar dark suit, clean white shirt, dark tie. Incongruous for this place of dirt and death, thought Stark.

Stark approached.

"I was going to your office," continued Stoddart. "I saw the light under the door. What are you doing here?"

We're nearing the end, thought Stark. Not quite. Almost. Full circle.

"We've met before," he said. "Many years ago. Twenty, to be exact. You may not remember. I do, however."

Stoddart said nothing, his face sunken and drawn in the amber glow of the lights. *Like a cadaver,* thought Stark.

"You were leaving my back garden. I watched you from my bedroom window. You looked up. I saw your face. I will never forget it."

Still no response. *But his eyes,* thought Stark. *They gleam. Like pebbles in the fire.*

"That night," said Stark, "I went downstairs to the kitchen. I had been woken by shouting. I was scared. I tried not to make a sound. Just a little boy, afraid of the dark. I opened the kitchen door. I knew something had happened. But I didn't know what. I opened the door..."

Stoddart suddenly spoke, voice a dry rattle. "What did you see, Jonathan?"

Stark sighed. He felt hollow, drained of any emotion. Close now.

"What did I see? That's the irony to this whole saga. I saw nothing. Emptiness. A vacant space. Nobody was there. My mother had gone. That's the point. I never saw her again. My world had collapsed to nothing. I was abandoned in the night. Can you imagine how terrifying that would be for a child?"

Stoddart remained silent.

"I was taken into care, and then adopted. My new family loved me, and I loved them." He gave a small smile. "Especially Mags. We lived in Eaglesham. Then my parents died, and I got my law degree, and Mags got her medical degree. And life went on. But I always wondered."

He took a breath, as memories flooded back.

"Then Archie Willow, and everything changed again. And I lost my way. But I found it again. Do you know how?"

"Tell me."

"A quirk of fate? Possibly. Maybe something more. I was having a coffee in some cheap place on Great Western Road. I was sitting outside. It was the beginning of summer, last year. It was my day off. My arms were sore with heaving crates. I was watching people pass. And then I saw you. Walking by, without a care. I saw your face, and knew it was you. The same man who left my mother's house all those years ago. I followed you. You came to this building. The rest was easy. I established you worked here, that you were a senior partner. I know all about you. But I had to know more."

"And so you applied to join my firm," said Stoddart.

"Eventually. I thought, if I confronted you, you might give me an answer."

Stoddart sagged back, sat stiffly on the bottom steps.

"I'm tired, Jonathan. And I'm dying." He reached into his inside jacket pocket, and pulled out a sealed envelope.

"I wrote this for you, to try and make you understand." He blinked, rubbed his eyes.

Is he crying?

"I loved your mother. She loved me. But it was complicated. I was married. I couldn't leave my wife. Our affair had to be a secret. But matters were becoming more difficult. I promised your mother I would always look after her. Financially. Both she…." he looked up, fastened his gaze on Stark, "…and our son."

Stark's throat was dry. His heart thumped hard in his chest. He could think of nothing to say.

"You're my son, Jonathan."

A silence fell, save Stoddart's laboured breathing. He waved the letter weakly. "This was to be given to you when I died. But here we are." He coughed, took another wheezing breath, continued. "I have been watching you all these years. But there was nothing I could do. So much time had passed. I knew you had joined Willow's firm, and I was glad. When you were shot, I despaired. But you lived. And then, when you applied to join this firm, my heart soared. You would come here, and I could watch over you. And I thought, perhaps, if I told you the truth, you might come to love me. But I was scared. Scared you might reject me, after such a length of silence."

Stark stepped forward. "I would never reject you..."

Stoddart raised a hand. "But that night. I swear I don't know what happened to your mother. We argued, yes. She wanted me to leave my wife. I refused. I was scared. It was late. I said we would talk in the morning. I said I had to go back to the office, to clear up paperwork. But I didn't go there. I went home. I never saw her again. I swear, Jonathan, I have no idea what happened to your mother."

"But I do," answered Jonathan. The images of his dream reared up, horrifyingly clear. "Her body, or what's left of it, is buried here, in this room. In this basement. I know what she did that evening."

Stoddart stared at Stark, puzzled.

"She came here, to this building, because she thought that's where you were, because that's where you said you were going. And it was here she was murdered."

CHAPTER SEVENTY-FOUR

A silence fell. Then Stoddart spoke.

"How do you know this, Jonathan?"

"I'll use your words," replied Stark. "It's complicated."

A noise from the top of the stairs. The door opened. Stark, startled, looked up. Framed in the doorway, a silhouette.

"This is a cosy chat," came a voice. "Though not the cosiest of places, I think. You shouldn't be here, Edward. Not in your condition. The air will eat your lungs. And we know how shrivelled your lungs are. And Jonathan? What are you doing down here? There's no need. You can go home. The place is closed. Or hadn't you heard? Your services are no longer required."

The door closed. Now, the faint sound of footsteps on the metal stairs, as the figure climbed down towards them.

"Or perhaps you both like it down here." The figure was Walter Hill. Dressed casually. Jeans, Barbour jacket, climbing boots.

He was holding a rifle.

"What the hell is this!" said Stoddart.

"Don't fret. It doesn't matter anymore. The rifle is a Nosler

M21. She's a beauty, yes? Versatile and accurate. Such a thing should be kept under lock and key. But I like to hunt. Rephrase that – I *love* to hunt. This particular piece of equipment can knock the head off a stag from a hundred yards. Wouldn't have believed it had I not seen it with my own eyes. After my announcement yesterday that the firm was closing, I needed to blow off a little steam. You understand. I have some land up north, and so there I went. To partake in a little killing. I came back early this morning. And lo! Driving by the office but who should I see." He gestured at Stark with the muzzle of the rifle. "You skulked in, like a thief in the night. With a bag. What were you doing, I wondered? Nothing good, I thought. Something bad. Like a bad apple. Like a fucking cancer. I thought – you might be dangerous. After all, you seemed awful close to the serial killer, The Surgeon. Who knows what you're capable of. So I brought the rifle. And I waited. You were down here a long time, Jonathan. What were you up to, I wondered? And when Edward joined you, I waited at the door, and listened to your conversation, and decided then that this nonsense had to stop."

"With a rifle?" said Stark.

"The perfect conversation stopper," replied Hill.

"It was you," said Stark, voice hard and flat. "You killed my mother."

Hill took a long breath, sat on a middle stair, training the weapon on Stark.

"So long ago," he said. "Why rake up the past? She came that night. Straight up to Edward's office. I had no idea who she was." He focused on Stoddart. "You always kept your office locked. But I had a key. Imagine my surprise when the door opened, and there was someone I had never seen before, also with a key, able to get in. One of your dirty little secrets, Edward."

"You were in my office?" said Stoddart.

Hill sighed. "If you remember – and I know you do, Edward, because you remember everything – over twenty years back, we thought someone had been embezzling from the firm. Not a lot, but enough. That person was me. Just a little, every month. I wasn't a partner then, you understand. Living on an associate's wage. I had to keep the creditors away." He licked his lips. "I had to maintain the life I had become accustomed to. You understand? Of course you do. I knew you suspected a member of staff. I had to know if you suspected me. I had to check your records, because one thing I know about you, Edward, is that you like to keep records."

Both Stark and Stoddart remained silent.

"She found me at your desk. She asked me why I was there." He laughed, though it had a tinny undertone. "I asked the identical question. She said she would tell you she had seen me in your room, at your computer, looking through your personal files." He shook his head sadly. "And so…"

"And so you killed her," finished Stark. He wanted to end this. He wanted him to understand that he knew everything, that it was over. But more. He wanted to tell him the whole story. Because this story had a conclusion beyond the worst nightmare. "You stopped her from leaving. You grabbed her. She struggled and screamed…" His voice faltered. "The paperweight on the table. You used it." He saw the lump of quartz. He saw the blood. It never seemed to stop. "You struck her. Again and again. And then you carried her here, to this place, and you buried her in the darkest corner."

Hill regarded him curiously. "And how would you know such a thing?"

"You dug a hole, and you dropped her in." He floundered. The words weren't easy. The dream was vivid and clear in his mind. He felt her pain. Her terror.

He found the words. "But she wasn't dead," he said. "You buried her alive."

CHAPTER SEVENTY-FIVE

A silence fell. Hill stared at Stark, perfectly still, as if pondering this revelation.

He shook his head. "It doesn't matter," he said. "It's over."

Calmly, he pointed the rifle at Stoddart, and shot him in the chest. The impact knocked him from his feet. He fell back, colliding with the table, the index book spilling to the ground. He rolled, fell still, a ragged hole in his crisp white shirt.

Stark ran. Another shot rang out, the bullet puncturing a box above his head. He heard footsteps making their way to the bottom of the stairs.

"No point, Jonathan!"

Every point, thought Stark. He ran to the far side of the basement, to the chair where he had sat, beside the three files. Another bullet thwacked into the wall. He glimpsed a fleeting image – Hill striding down one of the aisles, towards him. Stark made his way up an adjacent aisle, slowly, quietly. He sensed movement. He stopped, held his breath. He squinted through a gap in the boxes. There, five feet from him, on the other side, he saw a Barbour jacket, a hand on a rifle, the profile of Hill's face.

Hill had stopped. They were next to each other, separated by a wall of paper, hard and heavy as concrete.

Suddenly, a sharp fluster of wings. A fleeting shadow, from nowhere.

A shot fired at the ceiling. Another, as the shadow flitted up and down, a whisper of movement, quick and sure. Stark took his chance. He heaved against the shelves. Something helped him. He felt a pressure, pushing with him. The column wobbled on its wooden legs, fell forward, slow and ponderous, each box a solid weight. It collapsed, Hill suddenly gone, disappearing under the deluge.

Stark waited. Silence resumed, save his own breathing and the beating of his heart. The aisle next to him no longer existed. Instead, a pile of boxes, contents spilled and scattered. Nothing stirred. Everything settled back to shadows and stillness.

Stark rushed back to the stairs. There, the broken bleeding body of Edward Stoddart. He groaned, his chest spasmed. He raised a hand. His fingers fluttered.

Stark crouched down, gently cradled his head on his lap. The ground was thick with blood.

Stoddart tried to speak.

"No," whispered Stark. "There's nothing to say. Time to rest."

A small sad smile formed on Stoddart's lips, he closed his eyes, and died in Stark's arms.

With great care, Stark rested Stoddart's head on the ground. Beside him, in the pool of blood, was the sealed envelope. Stark lifted it, opened it.

The letter was addressed to him. It was simple, and expressed the matter as eloquently as any letter could.

Two words.

I'm sorry.

Stark tucked the letter in his pocket, made his way back up the stairs. He had a last look back, turned the light off. The room was swallowed by darkness.

He closed the door.

The affair was over.

It was time to go home.

CLOSURE

"When I said we would meet again, I wasn't quite expecting it to be so soon."

"Sorry to have disappointed you, Chief Inspector," said Stark.

"Not at all. So what have we got? The body of your mother buried in the basement. A lawyer with a rifle and a broken neck. Another lawyer with a gunshot to the chest. And you. Quite a combination."

"Where do I start?"

McGuigan raised a halting hand.

"Let me guess. It's complicated?"

"You can read my mind."

"A talent I haven't yet mastered," said McGuigan. "I can only hope that after this, you don't go seeking any more trouble."

"Wouldn't dream of it, Chief Inspector."

THE END

ALSO BY KARL HILL

THE ADAM BLACK THRILLERS:

Unleashed

Violation

Venomous

Fury

Finale

STANDALONE

The Glass Box

A NOTE FROM THE PUBLISHER

Thank you for reading this book. If you enjoyed it please do consider leaving a review on Amazon to help others find it too.

We hate typos. All of our books have been rigorously edited and proofread, but sometimes mistakes do slip through. If you have spotted a typo, please do let us know and we can get it amended within hours.

info@bloodhoundbooks.com

Printed in Great Britain
by Amazon

31654630R00193